Murder by the Minster

Helen Cox is a Yorkshire-born novelist and poet. After completing her MA in creative writing at the University of York St John, Helen wrote for a range of magazines and websites as well as for TV and radio news. Helen has edited her own independent film magazine and penned three non-fiction books as well as two romance novels published by HarperCollins. She currently hosts The Poet-rygram podcast and works for City Lit, London. Helen's new series of cozy mysteries stars librarian-turned-sleuth Kitt Hartley, and is set in York.

Helen's Mastermind specialism would be *Grease 2* and to this day she adheres to the Pink Lady pledge. More information about Helen can be found on her website: helencoxbooks.com, or on Twitter: @Helenography.

HELEN COX

Murder by the Minster

Quercus

First published in Great Britain in 2019 by Quercus
This paperback edition published in 2019 by

Quercus Editions Ltd
Carmelite House
50 Victoria Embankment
London EC4Y 0DZ

An Hachette UK company

A CIP catalogue record for this book is available
from the British Library

PB ISBN 978 1 52940 220 9

10 9 8 7 6 5 4 3 2 1

Typeset by CC Book Production
Printed and bound in Great Britain by Clays Ltd, Elcograf S.p.A.

MIX
Paper from
responsible sources
FSC® C104740

For all the librarians

ONE

The corner of Kitt Hartley's mouth twitched. She closed her eyes, praying that when she opened them again Grace, her assistant, would be standing in front of her with the hot cup of Lady Grey she'd gone to fetch over fifteen minutes ago. Instead, when Kitt lifted her eyelids, she was still faced with the man in the forest green anorak. He still smelled like cabbage that had been on the boil too long, and his dark bushy eyebrows remained raised as he waited for an answer.

'Tess of the d'Urbervilles?' Kitt repeated the book title that had caused her lips to twitch.

'Aye, I can't find it. Our lecturer said it was a classic. Surely you've got a copy? This is supposed to be a library,' said Cabbage.

The librarian ran her fingers through the front of her long red hair. The gesture would seem natural enough to the student, while giving her the opportunity to tug on the copper strands, channelling her frustration. 'Yes, we have several copies, sir, on the fiction floor. You see, this is the Women's Studies section.' Kitt's stare flitted across to the large maroon sign at the top of the staircase that read, with excruciating clarity, 'Women's Studies'.

Countless times she had been forgiving about the fact that people entering a library didn't switch their grey matter to Reading Mode on the way in. With its towering oak book-shelves, stained-glass windows, and high ceilings painted with ornate murals, the Vale of York University Library could be an intimidating environment for newcomers. But, on this particular Monday morning, Kitt was still hungover from the weekend, and had a limited supply of patience. Especially pre-cuppa.

'Oh.' The man's almond eyes widened to walnut-size. He tilted his head back, as if he were taking in the details of his whereabouts for the first time. 'Well . . .' Cabbage said, 'I've only been studying here a week. Still orientating myself.'

'Of course,' Kitt said, forcing a smile so the man might feel less embarrassed over his failure to check what floor he was on before asking a question, 'it is a tricky place to find your way around at first, but you get used to it.' She smiled up at the mural on the patch of ceiling above her desk; it depicted Prometheus gifting humanity with the spark of fire. 'Give this place even half a chance and, before you know it, it will feel like a second home.'

'Mmm,' Cabbage said in the flattest of all possible tones. 'But I don't see why we need a Women's Studies section anyway . . .'

'Excuse me?' Kitt said, hoping she'd heard wrong, but knowing, by the heat flaring in her chest, she hadn't.

'Well, there's no Men's Studies section, is there?' he replied.

Kitt's mouth twitched again. If the man had merely rubbished her job she could have handled that; she had taken that kind of disservice on the chin for years. But comments like this came out of a dangerous sense of entitlement. Why did this man think he had the right to silence voices that weren't his?

With a storm brewing across her brow, Kitt mentally flicked through the dozen or so books she'd read on mindfulness. She recalled one particular chapter suggesting it helped to identify the physical feeling anger caused in your body. If you could alleviate that, the calm was supposed – by some sort of spiritual osmosis – to pass to your brain.

According to the textbooks, most people experienced anger as a perpetual clenching of the shoulders. In Kitt's case it was a searing sensation in her chest. There didn't seem much point in intellectualizing that feeling. If it were muscular, a person could take up Pilates. There was, however, no easy way to put out a bonfire blazing in your ribcage. By the letter of scientific law, deep breaths would add more oxygen to the flames.

'Actually,' Kitt said, 'we do have a whole floor almost completely devoted to Men's Studies. It's called the History section.'

The man's face scrunched in on itself as he digested Kitt's comment. 'That's very rude.'

Kitt put a hand on her hip. 'So is suggesting that stories different to your own aren't worth the paper they're written on.'

The man opened his mouth to say something else, but was interrupted by Grace's thick West Yorkshire accent – her vowels were almost as hard as her consonants.

'Lady Grey tea for the lady,' said Grace, as the soothing perfume of citrus floated up to Kitt's nose.

'Thank you.' Kitt accepted the mug and snuggled back into her pine-green office chair to which she'd added a plush purple cushion, embroidered with a peacock, to make it a more inviting place to sit. Cabbage glared at her. Avoiding his eye, she concentrated on smoothing the creases in her ankle-length navy skirt. This, alongside a white shirt, navy blazer and tan belt had, over the years, become her unofficial work uniform. Her wardrobe boasted several variations on this outfit, and little else.

Cabbage grunted, scowled at the two women, and walked away, muttering.

'What's up with him?' asked Grace, shaking her head hard enough to make her shoulder-length brown-black curls undulate.

'I think he's a bit put out that his early morning round of casual sexism didn't go to plan,' Kitt said, blowing on her beverage before taking the first sip. The balmy liquid slipped down her throat, extinguishing the flames stoked by her first customer of the day. But, as the fire burned down to embers, those familiar, doubtful moments amongst the ashes began. Perhaps she should have found another way to speak to that man . . .

'Oh dear,' said Grace. 'Can't imagine you're in the mood for that this morning. But I am a bit surprised you're still hungover from Friday night. You're usually quite good at handling booze.'

'Friday and Saturday night, thank you. Two nights on the trot,' Kitt protested. 'I blame Evie ... or Meg Ryan, I can't decide.'

'Meg Ryan?' said Grace. 'Somehow I can't imagine her down the Nag's Head with you and Evie on a Saturday night, pint in hand.'

'Me and Evie are good company. Meg Ryan would be lucky to have us,' said Kitt, smiling at the thought of her best friend, even if she was at least partly to blame for her hangover. Still, it seemed Evie wasn't feeling any spryer than she. Every Monday morning, Kitt received a message from Evie telling her just how much she wished she didn't have to go back into work. Every Monday, except today. Evie was something of a text addict, so if she couldn't face her phone screen she must be feeling it – sherry really was the fluid of the devil.

Glancing up, Kitt saw Grace executing her most sheepish gesture: tucking a curl behind her left ear before covering her mouth with her hand to hide a smirk.

'What?' asked Kitt.

'Nothing, what you said was amusing,' Grace said, with a dismissive wave. The turquoise sleeves of her long-line floral cardigan, which she had thrown on over a pair of blue jeans and a white shirt, dazzled against the tan of her skin, which had deepened in tone after her September trip to India to visit her maternal grandparents.

Kitt shook her head. Grace had studied Psychology at the

university for a year now, fitting library shifts around lectures to subsidize the commute she made from Leeds every day. But over the months of examining human behaviour, it seemed, she had not clocked how telling her own tics were. She had a neat, somewhat pointed face, with sharp cheekbones that emphasized even the slightest expression.

'That's not what you're smiling at. It's the mug again, isn't it? Are you ever going to get over that?'

'Never!' said Grace, watching Kitt sip again from the mug she'd bought her for her birthday back in April. It was neon yellow, with the words 'Kiss the Librarian' written across it in tall black lettering. 'That was the best day ever.'

'Grace . . .' Kitt tried, but it was too late. Her assistant had already snatched the maroon trilby resting on Kitt's desk. It had a black ribbon sewn just above the rim, and from autumn through to spring, Kitt was never seen without it. It also served as a useful prop for Grace's impromptu, and often unwelcome, skits.

Grace perched the hat on her head and held her hands six inches apart. 'A gift? For me? Oh, really, Grace, we haven't known each other long enough for that malarkey.'

Kitt smirked. 'I am nowhere near that posh.'

Ignoring her boss's protests, Grace continued to mime opening a box. 'Oh, how awfully delightful, a receptacle for my beverages . . . but do you think the wording is entirely work appropriate?'

'Give over, will you,' said Kitt, whipping her hat off Grace's head. 'You make me sound like Hyacinth Bucket on steroids.'

In any other part of the world, this kind of insubordination would have been interpreted as a sign of dislike. But born and bred in Middlesbrough, Kitt understood how interchangeable affection and mockery were in the county of Yorkshire. By this marker, Grace's gift to a woman who hadn't been on anything that resembled a date since the pair had crossed paths was a sign of undying admiration. For this reason, she had used the gift every day without fail.

And besides, even taking Grace's cheeky streak into account, Kitt understood she was lucky to have the luxury of an assistant. It pained Kitt to think about it, but she knew from her training days, and friends she had in other institutions, that public libraries all over the country were surviving only thanks to kind-hearted volunteers.

'When you're done laughing at my expense, could you please start on the returns pile?'

A smile lingered on Grace's thin lips as she pressed two fingers to the side of her head in a cheeky salute, and approached the first of the returned-book trolleys.

Swallowing a few more mouthfuls of tea, Kitt brought a hand to the side of her own head and gave the area a gentle rub. The older she got, the higher the price for having fun, especially when drink was involved. Hardy was right, Kitt thought, remembering the title of the fifth phase in *Tess of the d'Urbervilles*: 'The Woman Pays', indeed.

Looking out of the nearest window, Kitt began fiddling with a pendant she wore every day, etched with a quote from *Jane Eyre*. She sighed at the autumnal scene beyond. For all she had read, no verse or paragraph had ever romanticized death in quite the way an autumn day in the city of York could. The view was like a line Keats might have dreamed up but never got around to committing to the page. The rosehips and rowan berries blazed with a primal fire in the hedgerows. The river path was a trail of fallen conkers, pine cones and ivy leaves, and the dawn redwood trees glowed like embers against the sky. As if all this decaying beauty weren't enough, the university campus was close to the city centre and the Minster bells carried clear and true across the Ouse. A rousing sound, so often heard in the library's mock-Tudor building, which stood on the south bank of the river, on the periphery of Rowntree Park.

Suddenly, Kitt felt two sharp jabs on her right shoulder. This was an established code between herself and Grace. It meant it was time to look busy.

Looking up, Kitt saw her manager, Michelle, stalking towards her desk. Grace, with rabbit-like fear in her dark eyes, picked three more books than she could carry with any degree of comfort from the trolley and scurried off in the direction of the bookshelves.

Kitt sat up straighter and brought up the most complicated spreadsheet she could summon at speed on her computer screen. Michelle had a gorgon-strength judgemental stare that could transform even the gutsiest hearts to stone. Right now that stare was fixed on Kitt.

'Katherine?'

'Michelle,' Kitt said, trying not to cringe at the use of her Sunday name. 'Everything all right?'

'Not really.'

Kitt feigned surprise; nothing was ever all right in the world of Michelle. Her lips turned down at the corners without any effort on her part, and even her bobbed mouse-brown hair looked limp with displeasure.

No bounce. No volume. No sign of life.

'We've had a complaint,' said Michelle, cradling a lilac clipboard against her chest.

'Oh dear,' said Kitt, 'about what?'

'About you.'

'Me?'

So Cabbage had already filed his complaint? That was quick.

'A lady you served on Friday? Apparently, you, and I quote: "squashed her right to freedom of speech".'

'Oh, that,' Kitt said.

Kitt could hear one of Michelle's winter boots tapping against the library floor, which was tiled with a blue mosaic: a ceramic ocean that washed over all six levels of the building.

'She made a racist comment to another member of the library reading group.'

'She never mentioned saying anything out of turn to me,' said Michelle.

And you never thought to give me the benefit of the doubt, thought Kitt, after a decade of service. 'It wouldn't be in her interests to.'

Michelle folded her arms. 'You mustn't tolerate discriminatory remarks, but you must handle these situations politely.'

Kitt felt a strong urge to pass an ill-advised comment about doing her best to be nice to racists in future, but instead she let out a sigh heavy enough that Michelle would guess she had a few more things she'd like to say. 'I'll be as polite as I can,' Kitt said, which was the best promise she could make.

'Thank you,' Michelle said, though nothing in her face conveyed gratitude. 'So you know, I'm not in this afternoon. Hospital appointment.'

Michelle had suffered with stomach ulcers for as long as Kitt had worked with her.

'Hope it goes all right.'

''Ello, love,' a husky, familiar voice interjected.

Kitt turned to see Ruby Barnett hobbling towards the student enquiry desk. Ruby was a woman in her late eighties who frequented the library, though she had no connection whatsoever to the university. She suffered with arthritis, and as a consequence had to use walking sticks. She was panting from her ascent up two flights of stairs. There was a lift at her disposal, but she had always refused to use it for undisclosed reasons. This morning, however, she seemed to be more out of breath than usual. Which could only mean one thing: she'd had another psychic vision.

'We really must find a way of tightening security around here,' Michelle huffed in Ruby's direction.

Ruby curled her lip at Michelle's comment, but kept her eyes fixed on Kitt.

Michelle had never been Ruby's biggest fan, but six months ago the old woman had told Michelle she'd had a vision about her. In Ruby's imaginings, fuelled by the dubious dandelion wine she fermented in her bathtub, Michelle was going to be offered an opportunity to travel to South America and make an important discovery. As the weeks drifted on and the only travelling she'd done was a weekend away in Cleethorpes, Michelle's attitude towards Ruby had shifted from mild disdain to blatant irritation.

'I've seen it this time, Kitt. Something really important,' Ruby said, between huffs.

'Course you have,' said Michelle, her gorgon glare resurfacing.

'Why don't you sit down?' Kitt said, indicating the chair in front of the desk. Ruby's psychic predictions never came to anything, at least at no greater rate than the averages of probability, and did no real harm, but Kitt did worry about how excitable she got over them. Michelle probably wasn't in favour of Ruby making herself comfortable, but it seemed kind to at least offer her a chair while she collected herself.

'Not a second to waste, not a second to waste,' said Ruby, though she slumped down in the seat anyway. 'It's about your future. Your very near future.'

Kitt looked at the old lady. Her short hair was dyed a diverting shade of orange, and clashed with the over sized magenta raincoat she had on. There was no telling what was going on underneath that raincoat either. Once, in the middle of June, Ruby had walked into the library dressed as one of Santa's elves, and hadn't feel the need to explain her sartorial choice to anyone. Entertaining as all this was,

Kitt wasn't convinced she wanted to hear Ruby's version of her near future.

'If it's my near future, dear Ruby, then I'll know about it soon enough,' Kitt said, in the hope of calming the old woman down.

'No, no,' Ruby said, her green eyes bulging. 'I saw them.'

'Who?' Kitt asked.

'Police officers. Two. A man and a woman, they're looking for you.'

Kitt's head hopped back an inch. 'Police officers? I don't think . . .'

'Er, Kitt . . .' said Grace, who had just come back to pick up more books from the returns pile.

'What?' Kitt said, with a bit more snap in her tone than she intended.

'Look,' Grace replied.

Kitt followed the direction of Grace's wide-eyed stare to see two suited strangers, a man and a woman, walking towards them with an air of brisk authority.

TWO

'Excuse me, ladies,' said the male officer when he and his female counterpart reached the desk. His accent was local, but there were some unfamiliar edges to his words that Kitt couldn't quite place. He paused, and as his gaze sauntered around the group, Kitt noticed his eyes were the same blue as the ocean on a stormy day, much darker than her own, which were best likened to blue topaz. He looked at Michelle, Grace, and Ruby in turn, before his eyes landed, and remained, on Kitt. He then adjusted his posture to stand a little taller, produced an identification card from his inside pocket, and held it up so everyone present could see. 'I'm Detective Inspector Malcolm Halloran, and this is Detective Sergeant Charlotte Banks.' The detective indicated his colleague, who lowered her head in a single, stiff nod. 'We're looking for Katherine Hartley.'

Rising from her chair, the librarian frowned at Grace. She could feel Michelle's glare, but didn't dare look in her direction.

'Yes, that's me,' Kitt said. 'Is everything all right?' It was a silly question to ask, and she knew it. The police didn't come looking for you when everything was all right, and in a split second her mind was working faster than her mouth. 'Wait – are my family OK? It's not Mam or Dad, is it? Or . . . not Rebecca?'

Rebecca was Kitt's twin sister, a doctor who worked in a hospital up in Northumberland. The pair had always been close, but they'd never had the 'twin thing' where you're supposed to feel something somewhere in your body if the other is in danger or sick or dying.

'We're not here about your family,' said Halloran. His voice was deep but gentle, and he raised two firm-looking hands in the air to signal that Kitt should calm herself.

Placing her palm against her chest, Kitt closed her eyes for a moment.

'Sorry,' said Kitt. 'I'm not in the habit of receiving police visits.'

Halloran didn't quite smile, but pressed his lips together in acknowledgement. He looked again between Grace, Michelle, and Ruby's open-mouthed faces. 'Can we speak in private? It's a . . . rather sensitive situation.'

That sounded ominous.

As a keen reader, Kitt was adept at deciphering the world around her. The sky, the rivers, the ragged faces of the aged, stone buildings that comprised the city of York. And, of course, she read people. But by their presentation, neither Halloran nor Banks offered any clues as to why they might want to speak with a university librarian.

Even in her heeled boots Banks didn't reach shoulder-height

on Halloran. She did, however, have the deportment to make up for it. Tight-postured and stern-jawed with her dark hair pulled into a businesslike twist, Banks had probably had to prove herself as hardy as her male colleagues once too often, and wasn't difficult to decode.

Halloran's face, however, was not an easy read, perhaps because it was part-obscured by a dark beard trimmed close to the skin. Like his hair, the beard was speckled with grey. His blue eyes stared into Kitt's and her stomach tightened. For some reason she couldn't quite put her finger on, it was difficult to hold his gaze, so she lowered her eyes to examine the precise knot at the top of his dark grey tie, the crispness of the white shirt, and the strong, sharp lines of his suit.

Detective Inspector – that was how he had introduced himself. A senior officer.

That meant whatever he wanted to talk to Kitt about was probably more serious than he was letting on in front of the chorus line of library regulars.

'Excuse me, officers,' Michelle said, interrupting Kitt's analysis of these two unwelcome visitors. 'But I manage floors one to three here at the library, can you tell me what this is about?'

'I'm afraid it's a matter I can only speak with Ms Hartley about,' said Halloran.

Michelle's face wrinkled around the eyes, and she turned on Kitt. 'You better not be in any trouble here,' she said. 'The odd complaint about your sarcasm is one thing, but if you're in trouble with the police, that's cause for dismissal, you know. It won't matter . . .'

From Kitt's point of view, Michelle disappeared then and her voice trailed off to nothing. Inspector Halloran had taken it upon himself to stand between Kitt and her aggressor. She could now only see the back of his broad figure. She could, however, imagine the look of bewilderment on Michelle's face as she heard the inspector say: 'That's quite enough. We're here to speak to Ms Hartley and nothing more. Now if you don't mind, we need to go about our business.'

'Yes, of course,' said Michelle, her voice smaller than Kitt had ever heard it. For all her huffing and puffing, Michelle never quite knew what to do when people stood up to her, which Kitt was just about to have done herself before the inspector stepped in.

Halloran turned back to Kitt. 'So, is there a quiet room somewhere, Ms Hartley?'

'Er, yes, somewhere private,' said Kitt, meeting Halloran's eyes again for a moment. 'Grace, you don't mind just looking after the desk for me, do you?'

'No, don't mind at all,' Grace said, her tone a touch too casual given the intrigue of the predicament. Kitt was well-versed in the curious nature of her assistant. The second Michelle was out of sight she'd spend at least some of her time at the desk strategizing methods of getting close enough to the second-floor office to overhear what her boss and the police were talking about.

'Told you, didn't I?' said Ruby, with a sly grin on her lips. 'Ruby got it right this time. Saw it all coming.'

'Yes,' Kitt said, while Banks, who still hadn't opened her mouth, raised an eyebrow at the old lady. 'You predicted a visit from the police a whole thirty seconds ahead of time, a stunning demonstration of your prophetic abilities. There's absolutely no way you could've heard them asking for me at reception on their way in, is there?'

Dipping her head, Ruby started fiddling with the toggles on her raincoat. 'No . . .'

Kitt gave Ruby a grudging smile. As she did so, she sensed Halloran staring at her. He really was rather intense, but, Kitt reasoned, that was probably a CV-essential for a detective inspector. 'Follow me, please,' she said to the officers.

'One of your mature students?' Halloran asked, speeding up his own step to keep in time with the librarian, who only knew how to stand still or stride with purpose. There was no in-between.

Kitt glanced at the inspector out of the corner of her eye. So he really wasn't going to give her any clue as to why he was here until they were locked away in a private room together? That was an incentive to quicken her pace if ever there was one.

'Ruby? No,' Kitt said, and, despite the potential seriousness of a police visit, let out an unexpected chuckle, a sure sign her hangover was lifting. Smashing news considering one needed a clear head to talk to the police about a 'sensitive situation'. 'The university is an open campus. Ruby's our unofficial psychic-in-residence.'

'Ruby? Not Ruby Barnett?' asked Halloran.

'Er, yes. I think that is her surname,' Kitt said.

'Ms Barnett has rung the station with predictions about missing persons cases a couple of times,' Halloran explained.

'I hope she hasn't caused any trouble,' said Kitt, resting a hand on the pewter handle of the office door. 'She does get pretty over-excited when she thinks she's onto something. If I'd known she might waste police time with her predictions, I'd have been firmer . . .'

'You always get a series of calls on missing persons cases. People having a "feeling" about this or that. Some of them even pan out as viable leads,' Halloran said, and then lowered his eyes to the ground. They seemed, all of a sudden, to be weighed down by a single thought too heavy to speak out loud.

'What about Ruby's suggestions?' Kitt asked.

Halloran looked back up, examining Kitt's face. 'Sorry, I can't discuss individual cases in detail, Ms Hartley.'

'You terrible tease,' Kitt said, raising an eyebrow at Banks in an attempt to include her in the moment, but the officer's face registered no expression at all. There was something bothersome about the fact that Banks had remained so reticent. It was another clue, besides the seniority of Halloran, that whatever business brought the pair here was serious.

Clearing her throat, Kitt pushed open the door to the second-floor office and gestured to Banks, who strode in without a word.

Kitt looked again at Halloran, who stood opposite her in the doorway. 'I could have handled my boss back there myself, you know, you didn't need to step in,' she said, already unsure why she'd bothered making such a point of it.

'I've no doubt, but time is against us, and I thought the authority of the badge might offer a swifter resolution.'

The pair stared at each other.

'Ahem.' Banks cleared her throat, breaking the silence and prompting Kitt to wave Halloran into what was without question the most higgledy-piggledy office in the Vale of York University Library.

Possibly in the entire city.

It wasn't the fault of the staff on that floor, the room was just an odd shape in comparison to those built on the other storeys, as though the builders had made some discrepancies in their measurements and tried to cover them up by creating an office with the most unusual combination of nooks and alcoves Kitt had ever seen. Still, at least it smelled homely, thanks to the almost constant brewing of fragrant fruit teas.

'Do take a seat,' Kitt said, pointing towards two shabby-looking floral armchairs. 'Can I offer you a drink?'

'No, thank you, Ms Hartley,' said the inspector. 'As I mentioned, time is not on our side, and I think it's you who should take a seat. What we have to say might be hard to hear.'

Kitt sank slowly into the nearest armchair. A silence filled the room, so thick that Kitt found it difficult to breathe, and the strange turn this Monday morning had taken hit her hard. There was no distracting chitchat about aspiring elderly psychics now. Halloran closed the door after himself. She was trapped, alone, in a room with two police officers, with no idea what they were about to say.

THREE

'Given the urgency of the issue, I'm going to cut to the chase,' said Halloran while Banks took a notebook and pen out of her pocket. She stood there in silence, poised to write.

'Understood,' Kitt said, wishing that whatever it was, the inspector would just be out with it.

Halloran stared at Kitt. Something tightened in her chest as he did so. He went to open his mouth, then closed it again.

'Now this ... this is a very serious business, and we'll expect your full cooperation without question throughout.'

'All right,' Kitt said, trying not to let her body visibly sag at the anticlimax. The inspector's version of cutting to the chase differed wildly from her own.

'Can you tell us how you know Owen Hall?' asked Halloran.

Kitt lowered her brow. 'Evie's ex-boyfriend?'

He was the reason the police were knocking on Kitt's door?

'So you know him?' Halloran pushed.

'I . . . well, Evie's the best friend I have,' Kitt said, wondering what Owen could have done to make the police take an interest in him. 'But I don't know Owen very well as a person, if that's what you're asking.'

'They were together some time, from what we understand,' said Halloran.

'Almost two years,' Kitt said with a grimace. Two years of watching Evie being underappreciated hadn't been Kitt's idea of fun.

'And in that time, you didn't get to know him well?' Halloran asked.

'When Owen and Evie were together he'd scuttle upstairs to his Xbox within about five minutes if I ever paid them a visit,' Kitt explained. 'I only spoke to him when we were out with a bigger crowd, and even then we didn't have a lot to talk about. Think we once even resorted to talking about the curtains at the restaurant we were eating at.'

'But Evie must have spoken to you about him, if you're her friend?' said Halloran.

'It is possible to get her onto other subjects,' said Kitt. 'But not for long, especially since their break-up.'

'And what can you tell us about that break-up?' Halloran asked. Banks, who had been taking notes throughout this conversation, paused at this question and eyed the librarian with a ferocity that would have made a less strong-headed person shuffle in their seat.

'Why do you need to know about Evie's break-up?' said Kitt.

'It's best you just tell us what you know.' There was

a commanding note in Halloran's voice that invited compliance.

Kitt suppressed a sigh she was sure would come across as irritation. 'Over the past few weeks she's told me everything you'd want to know, and a lot you wouldn't.'

'Assume for now that every detail is important,' said Halloran.

'He broke up with her via Facebook Messenger while they were living together.' Kitt shook her head, remembering the awful phone call she'd had with Evie just after she'd received that message. 'What kind of person does that to somebody they're living with? Especially after two years, when the relationship could definitely be described as serious. Poor Evie had started buying bridal magazines.'

Kitt expected some kind of reaction from the officers. Sympathy. Outrage. Maybe even commiseration, but both officers stood straight and still and silent, their expressions level.

The librarian tilted her head as she tried to read the room. 'You already know all this, don't you?'

'Yes,' said Halloran. 'But we needed to know what you know.'

Kitt's eyes narrowed. 'Wait a minute, what's this about? Am I under suspicion for something?'

'Not as such,' said Halloran. 'But please, don't derail our inquiry with questions of your own. We need to be the ones asking the questions right now.'

'I've no desire to hinder you,' said Kitt, trying to keep the sting out of her voice despite the inspector's rudeness whilst thinking back to some of the articles she'd read on the council's website over the years, 'but the police force is a service funded by all tax-paying community members, and I am such an individual. I have agreed to speak with you and assist you, but it's only right I understand what these questions are in connection to.'

Halloran and Banks exchanged a look. Kitt wished for about the third time in the last minute that Banks would drop the silent act. She was helping them, after all; there was no reason to make this interaction more uncomfortable than it already was.

'All right, you're right,' said Halloran, running his index finger and thumb along his eyebrows before looking again at Kitt. 'But what I tell you isn't to leave this room. The press will get to hear about this in due course, but we need to make sure that information about this incident is carefully controlled.'

'I've no interest in becoming a YouTube sensation, I'll be discreet.'

Halloran crossed his arms over his chest. 'We're investigating a murder.'

'Murder?' Kitt froze. Murders were rare in York. If somebody died in the city it was more often than not as the result of a terrible accident – an inebriated student who had gone wandering by the river and fallen to their death. That was about the worst headline any local newspaper ever had to run. 'And Owen is . . . involved?'

'He was . . . the victim, I'm afraid,' Halloran said.

'What?' Kitt said, and her hand moved of its own accord to cover her mouth. 'Owen is . . . dead?'

Halloran nodded.

'But that's . . . ridiculous.'

'Ridiculous seems an odd choice of word,' Halloran said with a frown.

'Was it opportunistic? Was he mugged or something?'

'No, quite the contrary,' Halloran replied. 'All evidence points to premeditation.'

'Well, then I stick by my assessment of ridiculous,' said Kitt.

'And why is that?' asked Halloran.

'Look, I never thought Owen was good enough for Evie. While they were together he did nothing but take advantage of her good nature.' That familiar heat flared in her chest as she remembered what had happened when the pair had been due to vacate the flat they'd shared. Owen left Evie to do the final clean-up. Conveniently, things were 'mental at work' that week and, thanks to Owen's less-than-domestic leanings, Evie had spent two days alternating between disinfecting the room that had been his 'man cave', and ringing Kitt in tears. He might right now be scrubbing out the greasiest oven in hell just for that.

'What's your point, Ms Hartley?' Halloran pushed again.

'My point is that given half a chance he could be both spineless and undomesticated, but, well, who on earth would go to the trouble of killing a man like him . . . a man who sold luxury vitamin packages to the super-rich for a living? A man who spent his days in a business park on the outskirts of Leeds? He was just ordinary, as far as I know. Not into anything sinister.'

'So far, that's our understanding too,' said Halloran.

'Owen, dead,' Kitt said. She looked up to see both Halloran and Banks staring at her, and a question formed on her lips. 'How . . . how did he die?'

Halloran took a step towards where Kitt was sitting. 'The victim was found by his cleaner yesterday afternoon.'

Kitt resisted the urge to roll her eyes. Owen and Evie had separated six weeks ago, and Kitt wagered it had taken him less than two weeks to realize he wasn't going to make it alone without paying someone to do all the chores he had once left to her best friend.

'The medical examiner at the crime scene confirmed it was poison of some kind.'

'Poison.' For an instant, Kitt did not know what to say. 'Poison. People still do that?'

'Toxic substances are easier to access than knives and guns,' said Halloran.

Kitt took a deep breath in and out, trying to process the information. But then another thought occurred to her. 'Wait. Have you already spoken to Evie? About the murder, I mean.'

'Yes,' Halloran said.

'God, how is she?'

'She seems . . . distressed,' Halloran replied, before shooting a sideways glance at his partner.

Kitt stiffened in her seat and nodded with as much polite-ness as she could summon. She imagined that description was an understatement. If Evie's reaction to Owen leaving her while he was still alive was anything to go by, she was probably now going foetal in a dark corner somewhere, in dire need of a Malibu and Coke.

'Ms Hartley, I'm sorry to ask, but I have to,' said Halloran. 'Where were you on Saturday evening between the hours of ten and midnight?'

'Is— is that when Owen was murdered?' asked Kitt.

The inspector nodded.

'But, you said I wasn't under suspicion . . .' Kitt replied.

'*You're* not,' Banks said, looking up from the notes she had taken. The first words the officer had uttered since Kitt had come into contact with her were spoken in the coolest register, and in a Scottish accent.

The librarian looked into Banks's brown eyes, taking a moment to digest both the tone of her statement and the words themselves.

'Evie . . . you think Evie is responsible for this?' Kitt said, crinkling her nose up at the possibility. 'Why?'

'We have our reasons,' said Banks, her voice still prickly, almost threatening. Kitt didn't know what she had done to provoke this, but fought her natural instincts to push for an answer. Her whole life, Kitt had been a pusher. She'd pushed herself to excel in academia, to organize political demonstrations about important social issues, and to travel around the world with only herself for company. The thing Kitt was best at pushing, however, was her luck, and right now that didn't seem like the best course of action. Knowing her luck, she'd only get Evie into more trouble than she was in already.

'I'm surprised, is all,' said Kitt. 'I've known Evie for years, and we're very close. The idea that there would ever be a reason to suspect her of murder is . . .' ludicrous, Kitt thought, '. . . unthinkable,' she said.

'Well, she's got motive for a start,' said Halloran. 'And as you pointed out yourself, Ms Hartley, there's not a lot of that to go around. Mr Hall lived a very straightforward sort of life.'

'Well, yes, but . . .' Kitt began, cursing herself for having made the case against Evie worse without realizing.

'And that's just the start,' Banks snapped. 'Several aspects at the crime scene point to the involvement of Ms Bowes. You'd do well to cooperate and answer the inspector's question about your whereabouts without any further diversion.'

Kitt stared at Banks. It seemed that in the coin toss she imagined the two officers engaging in on the way into the library, Banks had been left with tails: bad cop. Why Banks thought speaking to Kitt in this manner was going to make her more cooperative, she couldn't say. But she was torn between trying not to aggravate the officers and shielding her friend from their accusations.

'I assure you, my aim is cooperation here,' Kitt protested. 'But you've got to expect some level of incredulity when you come to a person and accuse the most well-meaning individual they've ever met of murder.'

'No more stalling, Ms Hartley,' Banks said, her voice flat, but a little less stinging. 'Your whereabouts, on Saturday evening?'

'On Saturday . . . Evie and I were at my cottage on Ouse View Avenue.'

'House number?' said Banks, readying her pen again.

'Thirteen.'

'What time did Ms Bowes arrive?' asked Halloran.

'Around the eight o'clock mark. We watched a film.'

'What film?'

'*Sleepless in Seattle.*'

What a mistake that had been. Evie had protested that she was doing better after her recent disastrous break-up and even more disastrous post-break-up first date; that she could suffer the schmaltz. Kitt knew otherwise, but her best friend wouldn't have it, and, before they were even twenty minutes in, Evie was sobbing her heart out. Alcohol had been the speediest pain relief available. Kitt remembered opening a bottle of sherry after the fizz had run out, but everything after that was a bit of a blur.

'What time did Ms Bowes leave?' Halloran questioned her.

'She didn't,' said Kitt. 'Evie stayed over in my spare room.'

'What time did you go to bed?' asked Halloran.

'Well, we'd had quite a bit of sherry and time can work a bit differently under those circumstances, but I do remember looking at the clock on my bedside table just before I put the lamp out and it was quarter to twelve.'

Halloran looked over at Banks.

'So can I assume that this clears everything up?' asked Kitt, since the officers' expressions conveyed nothing to her. 'I mean, Evie was with me, so she couldn't have killed Owen.'

'That's assuming Ms Bowes doesn't have an accomplice,' said Banks.

Accomplice? Hearing Evie's name mentioned in the same sentence as that word was laughable, but Kitt didn't much feel like laughing. She wasn't going to pretend she could forgive Owen for the pain he'd caused her friend or drone on about all his good points as people always did when somebody died, but death by poisoning was not an ending she would wish on anyone.

'I know you think you've got reasons for suspecting her,' said Kitt, 'but Evie is not your murderer.'

Halloran crossed his arms, toned, presumably, from whatever physical training he did to ensure he could chase after criminals. His face looked darker than it had a moment ago, and the lines at the corners of his eyes had deepened. 'We don't always know people as well as we think we do.'

'I know my Evie,' Kitt said. 'Besides anything else, she's just getting over one of the most crippling break-ups of her life. She's currently eating handfuls of Haribo for breakfast. Surely we can agree that's not the behaviour of a criminal mastermind devising some intricate plot to poison an ex-lover.'

'That's a matter to be judged in a court of law,' said Banks, tucking her notebook away in her jacket pocket.

Halloran, seemingly reading the exasperation in Kitt's face, said, 'Thank you for what you've told us, Ms Hartley. Now, we'd better get back to the station.'

'All right,' said Kitt, rising from the armchair, 'but can you tell me where Evie is now?'

'At the station, of course,' said Banks.

'What?' Kitt heard her voice rise in volume as she spoke. 'Wait, you haven't locked Evie up, have you?'

'No,' said Halloran. 'She came in for questioning voluntarily, so there was no need for measures like that at this stage. But I am running a murder investigation here. Our job is to follow this trail wherever it leads until the murderer is brought to justice, and right now, all available clues are pointing at your best friend.'

FOUR

It had been more than two hours since Inspector Halloran and Sergeant Banks had left the library. In that time Kitt had helped a couple of students access the online journals, pacified both Michelle and Ruby with as little information about the police visit as she could get away with, and dealt with several crises involving the treacherous photocopier. None of these had proven to be long-term distractions from the fact that her best friend was at present the chief suspect in a murder investigation. The last text message she had received from Evie said the police had released her and she was on her way to the library, but waiting for her friend's face to appear at the top of the staircase was more suspense than Kitt could bear.

Consequently, she was doing what any curious soul might be doing under the circumstances: looking up a list of common poisons on the internet and trying to decide which was the most likely cause of Owen's death.

Prescribed medicines, or over the counter medicines, were at the top of the list. Kitt narrowed her eyes. As far as she knew, Owen wasn't taking any medication. This wasn't usually the kind of thing a person would know about their best friend's boyfriend, but discretion wasn't Evie's number one quality, so Kitt reasoned that if Owen had been on anything, she would have been apprised of the situation.

Next on the list was carbon monoxide. Kitt bit her lower lip and thought for a moment. The police didn't give any hints about how they had found the body, or any other clues. Surely they would recognize that kind of poisoning from the method involved? Still, a possibility, if the killer knew what they were doing, which, from the description of the crime, it would seem they did.

The librarian was just about to move on to a list of toxic cleaning products when a familiar voice cried out: 'Kitt!'

Evie's call carried over the whirr of the second-floor photocopier, the low gabble of study groups discussing concepts such as 'the androgynous mind' in the collaboration corner, and the strained groan of the ancient inkjet printer on Grace's desk.

The librarian turned in the direction of Evie's voice. She was walking towards the enquiry desk from the staircase, her turquoise patterned raincoat covering the cream canvas trousers and tunic she wore for her work as a massage therapist. Though the low slant of her shoulders betrayed Evie's sadness, her features were quite level. Kitt guessed she was trying to keep her pace and facial expression appropriate to the surroundings, aware that in a small city like York gossip about a half-hysterical woman causing a ruckus in a university library would soon spread. After a minute, however, the urge to be close to Kitt got the better of her, and she broke into a half-jog, her short peroxide curls bouncing as she closed the last few feet between them.

Kitt wrapped her arms around Evie, breathing in the scent of her perfume. It had top notes of almond and, on any ordinary day, left the librarian feeling a bit peckish, but not today. Being questioned about a murder was more than enough to put food out of Kitt's mind. Well, at least for an hour or two.

In the warmth of her friend's embrace, Kitt felt the sudden desire to cry. She managed to hold onto the tears, but only because she was well-practised at doing so.

'He's dead . . .' Evie wept into Kitt's shoulder, leaning her pixie-like body against that of her sturdier best friend. Resting her chin on Evie's head, Kitt could see several of the students looking in their direction, but she didn't care about that. Right then, she just wanted her friend to feel loved.

'I know, I know. I'm sorry. *Shhhh*,' Kitt soothed, stroking a hand over Evie's hair and squeezing her even tighter.

'They thought it was me,' Evie sobbed. 'That I—'

'I know,' Kitt said, before gripping Evie's arms and pushing her back a step so she could look at her as she spoke. 'But I know you didn't do it. I know you were too distraught over the adorable antics of Meg Ryan to commit murder that night.'

'Oh, don't make me laugh right now,' Evie said, managing to emit something between a giggle and a sob. 'That's not fair. This is awful.'

'Just telling it how it was,' Kitt continued to tease. 'And another thing, how have you kept your eyeliner flicks in place after all the crying you must have done?'

A small smile edged its way over Evie's lips. 'I'll teach you. After I figure out what the hell I'm going to do.'

'What need you do? The police let you go, didn't they?'

Evie looked over her shoulders to make sure nobody was listening in to their conversation. She lowered her voice to almost a whisper. 'I'm not out of the woods yet. They say they might want to speak to me again if new evidence comes to light. Kitt . . .' she paused, 'there were things . . . at the crime scene. They pointed to me.'

Kitt frowned. 'What things?' But then she held her hand up to stop Evie continuing. 'This is best discussed in private. Grace is in the office brewing us some tea for just that purpose. We'll talk more there.'

Evie looked as though she was going to cry again, but then something caught her eye over by the bookshelves. 'That man in the gender politics aisle is giving you a bit of a rum look.'

Anyone else might have remarked on Evie's use of outdated slang, but Kitt knew well enough that her friend's love of all things vintage extended even to words. This meant that occasionally a phrase popped out of her mouth that hadn't been used in casual conversation for a good fifty years.

Kitt glanced in the direction Evie was looking and saw the *Tess of the d'Urbervilles* fanatic she'd dealt with earlier loitering in the bookshelves nearest her desk, pretending to read a copy of *The Second Sex* by Simone de Beauvoir.

'Cabbage,' Kitt said.

'Cabbage?' Evie repeated.

'*Shhhh,*' said Kitt. Every ten seconds or so he looked over the top of the book in Kitt's direction. He was probably hanging around to try to annoy her after the comment she'd made this morning.

'What about cabbage?' said Evie.

'Never mind. I'll be with you in a minute, you know your way.'

Kitt watched her forlorn friend walk off towards the office, and then, turning to her desk, hunted out a pen and a spare piece of paper. On it, she wrote the well-worn, ingenious lie: 'Back in five'. No doubt Cabbage would be timing her absence from the help desk, but Kitt couldn't worry about that right now. She would send Grace along as soon as she could. The students would not be too long without a guiding hand, and besides, her best friend had been all but accused of murder. This was an emergency.

Walking towards the office and skirting to the left of the bookcases, Kitt traced her fingertips along the spines of the various volumes as she walked. She tried with all her might to think of a list of people who would have a plausible motive for wanting Owen dead. Besides Evie, that is. But Kitt couldn't think of anyone. He just wasn't a notable enough character to have a list of arch-nemeses. There was a possibility that Owen had been involved in something sinister, perhaps even criminal, and that had been his undoing, but neither Halloran nor Banks had made any suggestion of this. They'd leaped straight to the assumption that Evie was involved, that it had something to do with his personal life. Did that mean the police didn't have any other leads? Or had they just pounced on circumstantial evidence – the 'things' Evie had mentioned that somehow pointed to her?

By the time she reached the office door, Kitt was no closer to an answer. The door, painted in a dark, moss green and bordered with an architrave patterned with swans, stood ajar. Kitt was just about to push through it when she heard Evie's voice say: 'Did you say anything to Kitt about it?'

Kitt's hand rested on the pewter door handle, but she couldn't quite bring herself to announce her presence yet.

'No,' Grace responded. 'I do love to tease her, I know I've got her when she crinkles her nose up –'

Evie chuckled. 'She does do that.'

' – but it didn't seem right today,' said Grace. 'Not with what you're going through.'

'Yeah,' said Evie, a hollow note in her voice. 'But, do you really think Halloran was eyeing her up?'

'Definitely. I mean, as much as he could whilst still staying on task,' came Grace's response.

'Well, really,' Kitt muttered under her breath. She wished, given the fact that there was a murder investigation under way, Evie and Grace could find better things to talk about than some imaginary romance between herself and Inspector Halloran.

'How was Kitt with him?' asked Evie.

'She . . .' There was a pause. 'She did hold his eye when he talked to her. But I couldn't say she was moon-eyed or anything.'

Good job, thought Kitt. If you said that, I'd march right into the office and set you straight. Moon-eyed. The very idea.

Though it couldn't be denied that Inspector Halloran kept himself in shape, Kitt was no magpie when it came to her affections. It took more than a set of sparkling blue eyes to turn her head. She was the type to fall in love with souls, and, as a preference, those of fictional characters who remained perfect and untouchable on the other side of the page. Halloran seemed palatable enough and Kitt ventured he might even be dashing on occasion, but he was no Edward Rochester. A controversial choice of fictional mate, Kitt would concede. But she was uninterested in straight arrows void of any complication or nuance. No matter what her reading group thought of Rochester, they couldn't accuse him of being too straightforward.

'To be honest,' said Grace, interrupting Kitt's thoughts. 'I don't think she noticed. Maybe he isn't her type.'

'Nobody is,' Evie said.

'What do you mean?' asked Grace.

'Oh, nothing, it's all a bit sad.'

At her friend's words Kitt drew in a sharp breath, taking in the sweet scent of ageing books and dust, before leaning her back against the wall next to the doorway. She stared at the row of bulky directories shelved in front of her, all of their spines coloured warning-light red. If she had the strength to barge into the office now, this subject would be closed, but in a moment it was all far too late.

'Don't keep me in suspense,' Grace pushed. 'What do you mean, "sad"?'

There was a pause. Kitt's blue eyes flitted left and right as she wondered how her friend would respond.

'Well, the last bloke Kitt was with, he sort of disappeared,' Evie continued.

On the other side of the wall Kitt drew down the shutters of her eyelids, remembering.

'Disappeared? What, like a missing person?' said Grace.

'No, not exactly. One day, he just stopped communicating. Wouldn't return any of Kitt's messages. Or phone calls. When she went to visit him in the room he was renting in Manchester, he'd moved out.'

'Oh my God. When was this? Where'd he go?'

'Must be more than ten years ago now. She never found out where he went,' Evie said, her voice almost as small as Kitt had felt that day, when she had realized the man she loved was gone. 'Kitt said his flatmate didn't have a for-warding address. But he'd given proper notice. He'd known for four weeks that he wasn't going to be around.'

'Ugh,' said Grace. 'She got ghosted.'

'Ghosted?' said Evie.

'Yeah, when the person you're with just disappears. Like a ghost.'

Ghosted.

Kitt's mind turned the word over and over, like the ocean trying to smooth a rough pebble. A fitting word, she thought, for an experience that would haunt her for years to come. Fiddling with the pendant around her neck, she read the words, written by Charlotte Brontë, engraved across the gold. 'I am no bird, and no net ensnares me.'

Not even a safety net, Kitt thought.

'So that's why she never talks about boyfriends,' said Grace.

'There's been nothing serious in the time I've known her,' said Evie. 'But that's fine, I just want her to be happy.'

'She seems happy,' said Grace.

'You're right, actually,' said Evie. 'In spite of that temper of hers, Kitt's probably the happiest person I know.'

At this, Kitt's eyes sprang open. She willed the corners of her mouth to turn upwards. 'Courage, girl. Strength, metal,' Kitt said, reciting under her breath the words of encouragement her parents used whenever she or her sister, Rebecca, found themselves despairing over anything – from the death of an elderly relative to an unfortunate teenage wardrobe malfunction. Growing up in the eighties, the latter had happened more regularly than she would care to admit now.

Standing up straight, Kitt pushed her shoulders back and swung open the office door.

FIVE

Kitt's smile widened as she met the eyes of her two friends. The room was bathed in tinted afternoon sunlight streaming in through the only feature of undisputed beauty in the second-floor office: an ornate stained-glass window depicting a scene from Shakespeare's *Much Ado About Nothing*. There was a moment's silence.

'Kettle boiled yet?' said Kitt. Evie was sitting just to her right in one of the battered floral armchairs, while Grace was standing to her left at the dark wooden desk in the centre of the room.

'Just a second ago,' Grace said.

Kitt nodded at her assistant. 'I'll pour. You take a seat.'

The silence hung around while Kitt handed a teacup to each of her friends. She then pulled up a wooden chair next to Evie's.

'I'm afraid we can't get comfortable,' Kitt said to Grace. 'I left "Back in five" sign on the desk three minutes ago.'

'It's all right,' said Grace. 'I'll check on the desk in a few minutes. But at least let me hear a little bit . . .'

'Evie, are you up to talking about it?' asked Kitt.

'I think it will do me good,' Evie said, looking down into her tea. 'But I'll warn you I'm likely to cry again. It's been one shock after another this morning.'

'I know, love.' Kitt's brow dipped as she looked over at her friend, cradling the teacup as if it was the only warmth available to her in the world. 'Start at the beginning, and the moment you want to stop, stop.'

Evie moved her lips one over the other to moisten them as she looked between Kitt and Grace. 'The first I knew of it was when Halloran and Banks walked into the salon this morning,' she began, referring to Daisy Chain Beauty – she used the back room there for her massage appointments.

'What did they say?' asked Grace.

'They said I'd have to cancel my appointments because they needed to take me to the police station. Said they wanted to speak to me about a murder, and it was in my interests to cooperate. I said I'd be happy to help them in any way I could, but that I couldn't just cancel all my appointments – I need the money.' Every muscle in Evie's face slackened as she remembered what had happened next.

'That's when they told you,' Kitt said, 'who the victim was.'

Evie's voice wavered as she spoke. 'I just broke down. I wouldn't believe them to begin with.'

'I am so sorry,' Kitt said, leaning across and squeezing her friend's hand.

'I'm sorry too,' said Grace.

'I know, thanks,' Evie said. She was wincing with the pain

of retelling her ordeal, but continued. 'Anyway, Diane was on reception and said she'd cancel my appointments, and they drove me to the police station. They said they wanted to talk to me, but it wasn't just a chat. They cautioned me, you know how they do on the police shows.'

'You have the right to remain silent . . . ?' Kitt asked.

'Yeah. I saw cameras fixed near the ceiling. They recorded what I said. The word interrogation is a bit strong because the inspector was very calm all the way through, but they did question me,' said Evie.

'But why?' Grace asked. 'Because you're his ex-girlfriend?'

'No, it's not just that. For a start, there was no sign of forced entry. Which means—'

'Owen knew his killer,' Kitt finished. 'But that alone doesn't prove it was you. Owen knew lots of people. There's still not much reason to suspect you above anyone else.'

Evie glanced down at her teacup.

'What? What is it?' asked Kitt.

'The poison was slipped into some wine. The bottle was still in the kitchen when the police arrived. It was a bottle of Egly-Ouriet Brut,' said Evie.

'Oh no,' said Kitt.

'Is that not a very good wine?' asked Grace, looking between the two friends.

Kitt shook her head at her assistant. 'Owen impressed Evie by buying her a bottle of Egly-Ouriet on their first date.'

'Not that I know anything about wine,' said Evie, 'but I saw how much it cost and it wasn't cheap.'

'All right, I'll admit that doesn't look good. But how would the police know what wine Owen bought on your first date?' asked Grace.

'I'd posted on Facebook about it a couple of times because he bought a bottle on our anniversaries,' Evie explained. 'That's where gloating gets you.'

'Now, now,' said Kitt. 'Owen bought that wine for you. You've never bought any, have you?'

'Not on my wages,' said Evie.

'Then there are no financial records to prove you purchased the murder weapon,' Kitt said. 'A coincidence over a bottle of wine wouldn't be enough to convict you of anything anyway.'

Evie pressed her lips together and looked back at Kitt with wide, nervous eyes.

'There's more, isn't there?' asked Kitt.

'Owen was found . . .' Evie's mouth wobbled, but she recovered herself, 'they found him with a note pinned to his chest.'

'A note?' Kitt said. 'The police never mentioned that to me.'

'I imagine what I'm telling you is pretty much need-to-know only,' said Evie.

'What did the note say?' asked Grace.

'I don't know how else to say this . . .' said Evie.

'That's all right,' said Grace. 'Just take your time.'

'No,' Evie said. 'That's what the note said. "I don't know how else to say this."'

'Wait,' Kitt said, her breath quickening. 'Those words.

That was the opening sentence of the break-up message Owen sent to you.'

'Word for word.'

'Did it say anything else?' Kitt asked.

Evie shook her head. There was a pause before she continued. 'The police had searched through Owen's message history and found our break-up messages. We went back and forth on that thread for a few days, and the exchange doesn't show me in my best light. But it gets more macabre.'

'How do you mean?' said Kitt.

'The note, it was pinned to his chest,' said Evie.

'Yes, you already told us that,' said Kitt.

'It was . . . the killer pinned it to his chest by . . .' Evie trailed off, her mouth tried to make the right shapes, but no sound came out.

'What?' Kitt prompted, not sure if she really wanted to know given the look on her friend's face.

'Stabbing a fountain pen . . . through his heart. That's what was holding the note there. Through his heart . . .'

Kitt held her right hand to her chest, thinking.

'But that's just . . .' Grace began.

'Sick?' Kitt suggested.

'Yeah, and . . . weird . . . isn't it?' said Grace.

'I'm not sure weird really covers it,' said Kitt. 'Poisoning, stabbing through the heart . . . It's like *A Study in Scarlet*.'

Evie frowned at her friend. 'Is that librarian code for something?'

'No, it's Sherlock Holmes. One of the stories.'

'I don't remember that episode,' said Grace.

Kitt stared at her assistant. 'It's a book, Grace. You haven't read any Conan Doyle, then? Too busy watching all five *Paranormal Activity* films on a loop, no doubt.'

'Actually, there are six *Paranormal Activity* films, not including the unofficial spin-off—'

'Oh, good grief,' Kitt said, bringing a hand to her head.

'But no,' Grace continued. 'I was too busy reading the Byomkesh Bakshi stories, which I have been told surpass the Sherlock Holmes stories on several levels.'

Kitt's face broke into a smile. 'They are rather good. *The Invisible Triangle* was one of my favourites.'

'*Oi*,' said Evie, looking between Kitt and Grace. 'When you've quite finished your book club meeting, there's a human being in pain over here.'

'Sorry,' Kitt said.

'It's all right.' Evie sniffed. She paused then, and added, 'But in case it is somehow relevant, who was the murderer in that story?'

'There's a lot of back story in *A Study in Scarlet*, but essentially . . .'

'What?' asked Evie.

'The murders in that story were revenge killings, over a broken heart.'

'Oh,' said Evie. 'This really doesn't look good for me, does it?'

Kitt made a dismissive wave. 'Give over. You're innocent. There's no hard evidence, no DNA at the crime scene, or we wouldn't be sitting here right now.'

Evie nodded, but didn't say anything else. Grace took the opportunity to interject.

'So in *A Study in Scarlet*, someone is poisoned and stabbed through the heart? Like Owen was?'

'No, not exactly,' said Kitt. 'Two different people, and not with a fountain pen. So weird . . . You couldn't kill a person that way, I don't think. At least not easily. Halloran said that Owen was poisoned, which means the murderer must have stayed with the body afterwards to pin the note on him in this . . . this theatrical manner.'

'But would a fountain pen even cut through skin or tissue?' said Grace.

'Not without the use of great force. Or, I suppose you could stab the victim with something else first and then wedge the pen in there . . .'

Evie moaned and covered her ears.

'Sorry,' Kitt said, rubbing Evie's nearest arm. 'I don't mean to be callous, I'm just trying to understand it, I suppose.'

Evie tried to turn her lips up at the corners, but remained quite pale in the face. Perhaps, however, that was in part because since breaking up with Owen, she'd stopped indulging in those god-awful fake tans from the salon on Coney Street. All the staff there looked like they'd been Tangoed, which should have been enough to deter anyone from entrusting their skin to those people. Owen had let it slip on their second-ever date that he liked 'exotic-looking' women, and Evie, in her wisdom, had decided a fake tan was the closest she could get.

It had taken a few weeks, but she was at last starting to look more peachy than Jaffa.

'Did . . . did the police say what brand the fountain pen was?'

Evie stared at her friend. 'I know you love stationery, but do you really think that's the big question right now?'

Kitt sighed. 'If there's a brand, the police will be able to track down where the fountain pen came from. Not many people use fountain pens these days.'

Evie looked up to the ceiling, thinking. 'I think they said it was a Stanwyck fountain pen.'

'Well, I don't think that brand is even on sale any more in the shops. I certainly haven't seen them for years, so the killer must have gone to a specialist shop to find it. That's bound to narrow the police search for the culprit.'

Grace raised her hand in the air, like a schoolchild asking permission to speak.

'I'm not sure the hand-raise is totally necessary, Grace,' said Kitt.

'Sorry, just wanted to make sure you'd finished. In our criminal psychology unit, we were taught that the way a crime is committed tells you a lot about the ego of a person, particularly in murder cases.'

Kitt went quiet for a moment, digesting Grace's comment. 'Owen was poisoned. Which is a sort of sneaky method for killing a person, isn't it? It's not a death by brute force. And this thing with the fountain pen, it must have been done after the fact. It would take time. Which means the killer hung around to sort of orchestrate what the police would find when they got there.'

'You mean, to make the evidence point to Evie?' Grace asked.

'Yes,' said Kitt. 'But there's more to it than that. If they stayed at the scene to . . . well, to arrange things, that suggests calculation. Maybe even a lack of guilt over what they'd done.'

'I'm sorry,' said Evie. 'I think I was wrong. Talking about this is not helping.'

Kitt took Evie's hands in both of hers. 'No, *I'm* sorry,' she said. 'We don't have to talk about it. I just don't understand how the police could think you'd done such a thing.'

'Well, most people are killed by somebody who knows them,' said Grace.

'Yes,' Kitt said, glaring at her assistant. Evie had only just visibly recovered from Kitt's accidentally vivid assessment of how efficient a fountain pen might be at piercing the heart of her ex-boyfriend. 'Thank you for that comforting thought, but perhaps now would be a good time for you to check there's nobody waiting at the enquiry desk.'

'Oh . . . I— I didn't mean to sound insensitive,' Grace stuttered, standing up from her chair.

'I know, it's all right,' Evie said to Grace. 'Who knows what to say in situations like this?'

Grace pursed her lips and put her hand on Evie's shoulder for a moment before placing her teacup on the desk and leaving the room.

'I don't want you to worry about this,' Kitt said, looking at her friend.

'How can I not?' said Evie.

'Because,' Kitt said, 'the police need more than the fact you and Owen weren't on great terms to make an arrest for murder.'

'They have got more though,' Evie protested. 'The killer used the exact words of a break-up message Owen sent to me.'

'Yes, but anyone who knew about the message could have done that, couldn't they?' said Kitt.

'Yes, and Inspector Halloran did ask for a list of other people who knew about it, which I gave him.'

'Good. See? They can't cart you off to prison just like that. The police need evidence you were at the crime scene, and as you were with me that evening, we both know they're not going to find anything. There's a reason why the late, great crime novelist Sue Grafton started her alphabet series with *A is for Alibi*: it's one of the most important aspects of any criminal investigation, and you've got one.'

'You're right, and I never even went to his new place. I—' Evie was interrupted by her mobile phone. Due to her love of all things vintage, her ringtone was a recording of Shirley Bassey's 'Kiss Me, Honey Honey'. When Evie first downloaded that ringtone, the blare of the brass erupting out of nowhere used to make Kitt jump every time, but she'd since got used to it manifesting in her life without warning.

'Hello?' Evie answered the call. 'Oh, Heather. I'm sorry, I totally forgot. Today has been a nightmare, I can't even tell you.' There was a pause. 'Oh, they have? Yes, sorry about that, they asked for a list of people who knew about me and Owen breaking up.' Another pause. 'Shocking doesn't really cover it. Yes, all right, sorry again. All right, bye.'

Evie hung up.

'Completely forgot I booked myself in for a manicure this afternoon,' she said.

'Surely everyone at the salon must know you're unavailable to have your nails done today?' Kitt said.

'No, this is at another salon, on Bishy Road,' Evie explained. 'When I went on that date the other week, I didn't want everyone at work knowing about it. First one since Owen, and all that. So I booked in there instead. Heather, who owns the place, had a special offer on and the manicure was immaculate, so I decided to go back.'

'Makes sense,' said Kitt.

'But obviously today, with everything . . . I just forgot about the appointment.'

'Not surprising,' said Kitt. 'And I'm sure your clients won't notice if you skip a week.'

'Not exactly a top priority, to be honest. At least the police aren't wasting any time in running down the leads I gave them, I suppose.'

'Oh?' said Kitt.

'Heather was on the list of people I gave Halloran. I'd never met her before in my life, but had to put her on the list just because we got chatting about the break-up while she did my nails. God knows what she thought when the police walked through her door this morning.'

'I'm sure she was surprised,' said Kitt, 'as we all were.

But it's not like you can control how the police conduct the investigation. You just followed their instructions. Look, I checked, and there isn't anyone to cover me this afternoon. Are you going to be all right? You can stay in here if you just want to hide away from the world a little bit. Sit and read, or sleep?'

'I don't think I could do either just now. I'm going to go for a walk along the river.'

'Good salve for the soul,' said Kitt. 'Tea at mine?'

'Thanks Kitt,' Evie said, leaning across to give her friend a hug. 'Thank God, I can always rely on you.'

SIX

A loud thudding sounded at the front door of thirteen, Ouse View Avenue. Startled, Kitt sat upright in her bed, her heart thundering, her mouth dry.

She waited.

Had she really heard the noise, or was it just an echo from a nightmare? Nightmare was a bit strong, but she had been dreaming about the events surrounding Owen's murder. As dreams often are, it was something of a jumble. The last thing the librarian remembered was Inspector Halloran giving her his hard, blue stare whilst fastening handcuffs tightly around her wrists. For some reason, in the dream this hadn't seemed as alarming as she might have expected and, on waking, an unfamiliar flutter stirred in Kitt's stomach.

She sighed and shook her head. 'Freud would have had a field day with you.'

Kitt had hardly finished muttering to herself when the pounding against her weathered oak door started again, making her jump.

So she had been jolted awake by something more tangible than the vision of Halloran and his handcuffs. Kitt turned on the lamp that stood on her bedside table, pushing aside her journal and a copy of *A Murder Is Announced*, which she hadn't quite resisted checking out of the library before she finished her shift, to get at her wristwatch.

Two a.m.

She let out an involuntary moan.

But the person banging at her door didn't care that it was two a.m., which could only mean something serious had happened . . . again. Woe betide her late-night visitor if this wasn't an emergency.

Kitt swung her legs out of bed, crossed the short cold span of dark floorboards and pulled the curtain aside to look out of the window, into the street.

Squinting through the faint illumination provided by a lamp post a little further up the road, Kitt could make out a familiar hooded figure wearing a blue raincoat. A fox shrieked somewhere in the distance, startling both Kitt and the figure below. Then the figure looked up towards the window, and the outline of Evie's face became visible. Her hand made a little wave. Without thinking, Kitt waved back and then frowned. Evie had spent the best part of the evening here after tea. What on earth had brought her back to her best friend's doorway so quickly, and at such an ungodly hour?

Holding back another sigh, Kitt let the curtain fall back into its natural resting place and put on her silk dressing gown, patterned with white roses, before making her way downstairs. She knew her friend wouldn't wake her without good cause. Evie had experienced one or two of Kitt's hard stares over the years and, as far as she could tell, wouldn't do anything to invite one.

Her cat, Iago, gave her his yellow-eyed glare as she turned on the light in the living room.

'Not my choice to be up at this hour,' Kitt said to the cat. 'You often wake me at inconvenient hours. That's karma for you.'

Unmoved by his owner's words, Iago continued to glare, but Kitt didn't notice. She was too busy rattling the keys in the lock and then pulling hard on the handle to get the stiff old door to move inward. It never was cooperative once autumn set in.

Evie stood shivering on the other side of the threshold.

'Now then. Before you say anything, I'm sorry,' Evie said. 'I know you're not a morning person.'

'Not a two in the morning person, no. But come in,' Kitt said, stifling a yawn.

Evie stepped into the living room.

'Here,' said Kitt, closing the door and taking her friend's coat. 'Come and sit down and tell me what's going on. At this hour, I assume you weren't just passing.'

Kitt hung Evie's coat on a wooden peg next to the door and then joined her friend near the hearth.

'Mmm, it's so warm in here. It's bitter out there,' said Evie as she sank down into one of the two available armchairs, which were upholstered in a deep, pine green fabric. Kitt had picked it out because it reminded her of the colours of

Dalby Forest in the summer. Sunny thoughts weren't to be sniffed at on days like today – or yesterday, as it was now.

'I sat up and read for a bit after you went home,' said Kitt, deciding to keep the fact she'd chosen a murder mystery novel to herself lest it come across as a bit macabre. 'Only put the fire out a couple of hours ago. And I do have a lot of insulation.' Kitt nodded at the nearest bookshelf. The wall with the fireplace was in fact the only wall in the living room that wasn't lined with bookshelves, all of them heaving with paperbacks and hardbacks on every conceivable subject.

'Anyway. What's going on now? You all right?'

Evie shook her head. 'Where do I even begin?'

'That bad?' asked Kitt.

'Well, for starters, you remember I gave the police a list of people who knew about the break-up message Owen sent me?'

'Yes,' said Kitt, slowly. 'They don't suspect someone on that list, do they?' If Evie had told those people the finer details of Owen's break-up message, the likelihood was she trusted them. If Evie had trusted the wrong person, Kitt knew she would never forgive herself for what had happened after the fact.

'Beth Myers.' Evie's words were coupled with a shaky nod.

'Beth M— the lass who went out with Owen before you did?'

'That's the one,' said Evie. 'About an hour ago, I got woken up by a phone call from her mother. She was past herself. She'd been ringing around Beth's mates to find out if they were with her on the night of the murder. Said she gave the police an alibi that didn't check out, and they'd taken her in for further questioning. Her mum has been trying to find out who she was really with. Or why she would lie.'

'She couldn't have waited until a more reasonable hour to find that out?' said Kitt.

'Apparently not,' said Evie. 'She seemed to be basically going through Beth's entire list of contacts. Maybe her mum's a bit over protective?'

'Or a bit shocked to find her child caught up in a murder case,' said Kitt. 'Do you think Beth's capable of something like this?'

Evie crossed her arms and shrugged her shoulders. 'I admit, I don't know her that well. She was part of Owen's university crowd, you know, and we only saw each other when they all got together as a big group. But ... she's never shown any worrying signs ... at least her behaviour was never more worrying than everyone else's on a Saturday night. And she went out with Owen a long time ago now. They broke up a good six months before I met him, and he'd been on a couple of dates with other people between her and me. They always seemed on spectacular terms for two people who'd been in a relationship that didn't work out.'

'Possibly because he didn't break up with her via Facebook Messenger?' said Kitt, pursing her lips.

'Always helps,' said Evie. 'But in that sense the idea that she would kill him, especially in such a freaky way, doesn't add up. Not. At. All. When I asked Owen about their break-up, he said it was mutual.'

'So it was amicable,' said Kitt. 'She wasn't holding any grudge towards him.'

Evie stared at Kitt. 'Well, yeah, but you know what "mutual" really means most of the time if a lad's saying it?'

'Enlighten me.'

'If a lad says that, it usually means he was dumped.'

Despite the seriousness of the situation, Kitt chuckled. 'Oh, Evie, you can't possibly deduce that from someone telling you a break-up was mutual.'

'I can. One night, when we were out with his uni mates, I'd had a few drinks and curiosity got the better of me.'

Kitt took in a deep breath. 'Oh dear, what did you do?'

'Nothing too outrageous. Just followed Beth to the ladies and asked her about the break-up.'

'How did she take that question?'

'Well, she'd had a few drinks too, so was perhaps a bit more forthcoming than she might have been usually, but I was right. She broke up with him. Said she'd fallen in love with someone else. Though . . .'

'What?' asked Kitt.

'I've never seen her with another boyfriend, so that must have ended pretty quickly too,' said Evie.

'She's not had any other boyfriends?'

'Not in the two years I was with Owen,' said Evie, her eyes darting in Kitt's direction. 'But we can't chalk that up as suspicious behaviour. I only saw her every couple of months, and besides, there's a lot of that going about.'

'Fair point,' said Kitt, before raising both her eyebrows and staring into the blackness of the grate. Perhaps Beth had come to the same conclusion Kitt had, that intimacy was too dangerous a pastime.

'Besides anything else,' said Evie, 'Beth's a bit too ... prissy to be a murderer.'

'I don't think all murderers come complete with missing teeth and Z-shaped scars down their faces,' said Kitt.

'I know,' Evie said, mock-sneering in Kitt's direction. 'But Beth is super-fussy about her appearance. In all the times I've hung around with her, whether it was a night in with a film, or a night out on the tiles, she always looked just so. Immaculate manicures. Every hair in place, and I do mean always. The idea of her bloodying her perfectly-lotioned hands is madness.'

'Clearly the police don't think so,' said Kitt.

'The police thought I did it, six hours ago. Knowing my luck they'll come back with some theory that me and Beth were in it together.' Evie paused and looked at her friend. 'Unless ...'

Kitt narrowed her eyes. 'Unless what?'

'Well, on the way here I started thinking,' said Evie.

'That sentence always leads somewhere interesting,' Kitt teased.

'Better that than somewhere dull,' said Evie, and the smile Kitt had hoped to see on her friend's full, Marilyn Monroe-like lips made a brief appearance. 'What if we find out what Beth was really up to that night?'

Kitt's nose crinkled. 'How would clearing someone else's name help you? Wouldn't that just make you the prime suspect again?'

'I don't want to make my own situation worse,' said Evie, 'but the police seem to be making a proper mess of all this, and I don't want to see a friend suffer the same way I have. Besides, if I was guilty it'd make no sense for me to help Beth, the police will see that, and it might make them more open to the idea that I didn't commit murder last Saturday night.'

'Perhaps,' said Kitt, not wanting to seem dismissive about her friend's well-meaning but misguided plan. Evie had been through a lot in the last twenty-four hours, and self-preservation was not, the evidence indicated, at the top of her priority list. 'But how are you intending on finding out where Beth was? The police are working on this case full-time and, if Beth's mum is ringing around everyone, it doesn't sound as though they've had much luck in getting the truth out of their suspect.'

'We could try talking with her housemate,' said Evie. 'According to Beth's mum, Beth gave her housemate as her original alibi. Bet she has her suspicions about where Beth might have really been.'

'But wouldn't the police have already questioned the housemate?' Kitt countered. 'The likelihood is the housemate either doesn't know where Beth was, or is unwilling to tell the police the truth.'

'Maybe,' said Evie. 'But maybe the police didn't ask her the right questions. Maybe there have been some clues about where Beth really was, but her housemate hasn't pieced them together.'

The pair lapsed into a moment's silence.

Kitt knew that, despite the curiosity that had prompted her to look up a list of common poisons and devise various Christie-inspired theories before resting her head on the pillow that night, she must protect her friend from the consequences of an interfering, half-baked plan hatched at two in the morning.

'Look, even if I thought you might be able to get something out of the housemate that the police haven't, it's not a good idea for you to be connecting yourself with this investigation. You need to distance yourself. Otherwise your meddling might lead to the police being even more convinced that you and Beth are in on it together.'

'Well, about that, old chum,' said Evie, playing with the ends of the blonde curls that fell nearest her face.

Kitt recognized the slight sparkle in Evie's green eyes that so often spelled trouble. 'What?'

'You're right about the fact that it would probably be for the best if I didn't show up at Beth's house tomorrow, given that I'm a suspect in the case,' said Evie.

'Right . . .' said Kitt. 'So you're not going to interfere? I'm sorry, you're confusing me here.'

'The thing is,' said Evie, 'you're not a suspect, are you?'

Evie stared at Kitt as she digested what her friend meant by this question.

'No, no, no,' said Kitt, standing up. She paced along the navy carpet she'd had fitted in a vain attempt to mask the never-ending supply of black cat-hair tumbleweed. She was convinced that animal waited until just after she'd hoovered before shedding – one of the cat's many treacheries that had caused Kitt to christen him after a defector.

'Kitt, please. At least consider doing this for me. It's awful enough knowing Owen's . . . well, that he's gone. But the idea of them not catching the right person somehow makes it all even worse.'

'But when you come up with mad schemes like this, it always leads to trouble. Usually for me.'

Evie tilted her head to one side. 'This is a pretty niche situation. When have I ever come up with something like this?'

'The details differ, but the suffering's the same,' said Kitt.

'You're exaggerating.'

'Am I? Shall I remind you of that detox diet you begged me to join in with?'

'That was back in January, let it go,' said Evie.

'I will, once the horror of exclusively eating sesame seeds for four days solid has faded.' Kitt shook her head. They'd had to stop after four days because the sheer amount of seed oil they were digesting had caused raw, itchy rashes across their skin. The only thing to be thankful for was that the experience had obliterated Evie's appetite for fad diets for good.

'Kitt, come on.' Evie looked at her friend with wide, pleading eyes. 'This is a bit more serious than a post-Christmas crash diet. Beth might have been up to something she shouldn't have been, but she's not a murderer.'

'Evie,' Kitt said, her voice as gentle as she could make it, 'if she's not involved in this somehow, then why did she lie about where she was? You have to admit that her lack of alibi is a bit suspicious.'

Evie closed her eyes for a moment and took a deep breath before opening them again. 'I can't explain how I know that Beth's not to blame for this. I just do. I can't do anything to help her. But you can.'

Kitt didn't say anything. Instead, she ran her fingers through some of the knots in her long red hair and stared up at a gilt-framed painting that occupied the space above the mantelpiece. It depicted a border collie out on the moorland coaxing sheep into a pen.

'All I'm asking is that you go around to Beth's house first thing and ask a few questions. If the housemate doesn't know anything, I'll drop it. But we've got to at least try.'

Kitt put a hand to her head and looked at her friend. In truth, this wouldn't be Kitt's first foray into seeking justice. She had spent a couple of years travelling just before she met Evie, and there were some stories even her best friend had yet to hear. But those adventures had happened when she was in her early twenties and thus less aware of her own mortality, long before she had settled down to librarian life in the enchanting city of York.

'You know, Kitt,' Evie said. 'You know what nobody else knows. Why this is so important to me.'

At this, Kitt took in a sharp breath.

Three years ago Evie had entrusted Kitt with a secret about her past. She had almost shattered herself to pieces in the telling of it, and the pair had never referred to it since. The fact Evie had so much as hinted at that episode of her life told Kitt how important it was she acquiesce to her friend's request.

'All right,' said Kitt. 'I'll go on my way into work. But if Beth's housemate doesn't have any insight, can we please agree that we'll just let the police figure things out for themselves?'

'Agreed,' said Evie, with a sly smile that Kitt interpreted as a sign that her friend knew she'd stoked her curiosity. A curiosity that once ignited was all but impossible to put out.

SEVEN

Given what Evie had said about Beth's coiffed appearance, Kitt wagered the police's latest top suspect would rather be living somewhere a touch more glamorous than a shabby Victorian semi. Especially one situated at the wrong end of Holgate Road to be convenient for the city centre. With ever-spiralling rent prices, however, a room in a bygone terraced house slathered with flaking cream paint, not to mention the unmistakable mould problem in the front porch, was probably the best a young hotel receptionist could hope to afford.

After Evie's visit in the early hours, Kitt had been unable to get back to sleep. When writing in her journal brought her no peace, she had turned to the copy of *A Murder Is Announced* and read it through to the end, even though day had been breaking when she was done. In that story, the victim was a hotel receptionist with a shady background who had known too much about the killer. This had sparked Kitt's imagination, and she couldn't help but wonder if Beth was more involved with this unnerving incident than Evie realized. What if, for example, some secret had come out while Owen and Beth had been dating? A secret she didn't trust him to keep now that he'd found a new partner. A secret worth killing for . . .

Checking her watch once again to make sure she really did have time for all this palaver before going into work, Kitt took a deep breath and hopped up the few steps leading to the front door.

Delivering a firm knock, she tried to ignore the question that had been circling non-stop through her head ever since she'd left the cottage this morning: why had she let Evie talk her into this? Things like this happen, Kitt reminded herself, when you allow people a strong emotional hold on you. She was an expert at saying 'no' to almost anyone else, but not Evie.

There was a shuffling sound, and then a woman with her hair dyed in rainbow colours on just one side of her head came to the door. She frowned at Kitt, which was under-standable given it wasn't yet nine a.m. – far too early for unexpected visitors by all accounts.

Glancing over the woman's shoulder, though, Kitt could see she wasn't the first visitor to the house that morning. Down the hallway, two police officers were crossing between rooms, opening drawers and rummaging through various stacks of paper.

'Can I help?' the woman – who Kitt presumed to be Beth's housemate – said. She had a sharp note in her voice and was pulling on a green duffle coat.

'Gina?' said Kitt.

'Er, no,' said the housemate. 'You must have the wrong address. I'm a Georgette not a Gina.'

'Oh,' said Kitt, a small blush creeping into her cheeks. It was obvious this was the right address. The odds of the police having to search two houses on the same street in one morning were slim. Evie's less-than-spectacular listening skills were once again in evidence.

'Sorry, I think I may just have misremembered your name. I'm a friend of Beth's,' Kitt lied. It was only a little lie. She had met Beth and made small talk with her once or twice. They'd even, for reasons that were now a bit hazy, once had a rather in-depth conversation about the relationship between Johnny Cash and June Carter. According to Kitt's recollections, Beth had been an unexpected expert on the failed marriages the singers endured before finally meeting each other and settling down ... the random topics the intoxicated human brain can latch onto.

'She's, er,' the housemate looked down at her shoes, a pair of leopard-print Converse, and then back up at Kitt, 'not here right now.'

One of the officers, a woman with greying hair hacked short enough to create a silver frame around her face, came to the doorway. In her hands she held a small pile of items, likely belonging to Beth: a bunch of train tickets, returns to Leeds, and a stack of key cards from the White Horse Hotel, Beth's place of work.

That's odd, thought Kitt. Why would Beth need to take the key cards home with her? Kitt looked as closely as she could at the items in the officer's hands without drawing attention to herself, but the ink on the train tickets had faded, making it difficult to make out any of the finer details, while the keys cards were plain pieces of white plastic stamped with the White Horse Hotel logo and a serial number. Nothing notable there.

'Can I ask what your business is here, madam?' said the officer, interrupting Kitt's subtle scrutiny of any available artefact that might offer enough insight into Beth's movements to pacify Evie.

'Of course, I'm so sorry to be a distraction from your work,' Kitt said, biding time while her brain caught up with her tongue. 'I'm a friend of Beth's and heard what had happened. I was so concerned about the whole situation I couldn't help but come here to check in with her housemate, in case there is anything I could do . . .' Kitt tried to think if she'd ever read anything about the penalties for misleading the police when they were busy trying to solve a murder. Evie and her schemes . . .

The officer stared at Kitt for a moment, looking her up and down. Kitt widened her eyes, doing all she could to look innocent.

'I see,' said the officer. 'May I take your name?'

'Yes,' Kitt said, with a sinking feeling in her stomach. Now it was bound to get back to Halloran and Banks that she had been around to Beth's house the very morning after Evie had been questioned on suspicion of murder. That wasn't going to look good on her best friend, or Kitt probably.

'It's Kitt Hartley, Katherine if you want my Sunday name.'

She tried a forced little chuckle, partly because she wasn't used to lying, and partly in an attempt to keep things light. In response, the officer narrowed her eyes. She opened her mouth to say something else, but then her gaze drifted beyond Kitt to something going on behind her.

'Just what we need,' the officer said.

Kitt turned to see a small crowd approaching the property. At first Kitt couldn't work out who they were or why they might cause the officer any consternation, but on closer inspection she noticed one of the women in the party was carrying a camera. Just behind her, a young man pulled some sound equipment out of the back of a van parked up across the road. Not ten seconds passed before another car pulled up near the van, and two more men got out and headed straight towards Beth's doorstep.

'Reporters,' said Kitt, before turning to the doorway and looking at Georgette. 'Do you . . . do you have a back door or something?'

'Why?' asked Georgette, folding her arms.

'I . . . I'd really rather not be photographed or questioned by the media about this. It's just too horrible to talk about it all.' That was the truth, but Kitt also wanted to avoid her face appearing in any headline or story about the murder. She was Evie's alibi, the one thing standing between her friend and major suspicion. Above all, she had to remain credible in the eyes of the inspector.

'You can't come into the house while we're conducting a search,' said the officer, before her eyes once again riveted on the gathering gaggle of journalists approaching the doorway. Kitt recognized one of them as the presenter on the *Northward News* programme, which she occasionally caught on TV if she was back in time from her shift at the library. Chris something – she'd never paid that much attention to his surname. She'd been too distracted by how white and straight his teeth were. He had the teeth of a game show host, not a news reporter.

'All right, roll cameras,' Chris Something said, before pointing the microphone at Kitt. 'Are you related to the suspect in this case, madam?'

'No,' said Kitt. 'Anyway, I don't want to comment or talk to you.'

'Is that because you know something about the murders?' Chris pushed, squinting his hazel eyes and holding the microphone even closer to Kitt's mouth.

Kitt glared at him. 'Not at all. I just—' she broke off, distracted, as a camera flashed in her face.

'Didn't you hear the lady?' said the officer. 'She said no comment.'

A broad man with a belly poking out from his T-shirt, seemingly oblivious to the officer's words, held up a camera, while the woman next to him who was dressed in a neat khaki trouser suit thrust a dictaphone in Kitt's direction.

'Justine Krantz, *News on the Ouse*,' said the woman, before tucking her shiny black hair behind her ears. 'How do you know the suspect? Did she ever display worrying signs?'

'I'm not going to—' Kitt began, but she was again interrupted.

'Get in line, Justine. We were here first,' said Chris

Something before turning to the officer who was still frowning in the doorway. 'Investigating this case is in the public interest,' he said to her. 'Clear reporting on it might save lives.'

'Don't give me that,' said the officer. 'You're interested in ratings, not saving lives.'

Undeterred, Chris continued his questioning. 'Can the public be reassured that the killer has been caught, or is there a chance they are still at large?'

The officer set her jaw. 'Right, that's it, press conference is over. We've all made it clear we don't want to talk to you, and if you lot don't clear off, you'll find yourselves looking at harassment charges,' she said, holding her hand in front of the cameras.

Kitt turned to the officer then, and made her eyes as wide and pleading as she could. Truth be known, she could fend for herself, but the less footage the journalists had of her the better, and she needed to get inside the house.

The officer looked at Kitt's face and sighed. 'Ms Hartley, this way.'

Kitt obeyed the instruction, beyond relieved to be out of the spotlight. She stepped through the door just before the officer closed it on a groaning audience of columnists and commentators.

EIGHT

On entering the hallway, the scent of tropical fruit hit the librarian. Papaya, perhaps, and mango. It was some form of air freshener, likely designed to overpower the strong smell of damp that so often filtered through these old houses. Still, it was doing its job and, moreover, Beth and Georgette had done all they could to distract from the yellowing pop-corn ceiling and the fraying carpet, patterned with golden leaves. A vase of yellow dahlias stood on a small wooden table near the door and, further down the hall, an intricate wall hanging woven in felt and depicting the rolling purple wave of the Yorkshire moorland covered stale wallpaper.

The officer put the chain on the door and then stalked towards the rear of the property. Georgette followed, and Kitt trailed after her.

'You can leave through the back door to avoid that lot. Whatever you do, don't touch anything on your way through,' the officer said.

'I don't understand,' said Georgette. 'Why did they all show up at once like that?'

The trio entered the kitchen, which had windows long and tall enough to let in a great deal of the early morning autumnal light. A blessing, considering someone had thought to paint the room from floor to ceiling in a dark, dingy green.

'Someone who knows the suspect will have Tweeted about it,' said the officer. She dropped the train tickets and the key cards in her possession onto the kitchen table, next to several other items already in clear plastic bags. 'It wasn't you, was it?' she asked, eyeing Kitt.

'No, it was not,' said Kitt, trying not to let indignation sound out in her tone, and failing. 'I don't have time to be messing around on social media.'

'Good,' said the officer. 'Social media can be a right nuisance on cases like these. Lots of people spreading mis-information. It's—'

She was cut off by a loud crash in one of the neighbouring rooms. Slowly, she closed her eyes. 'Wilkinson,' she muttered, before opening her eyes again and marching off in the direction of the ruckus.

'What's going on through there?' said Kitt, craning her head out of the kitchen doorway.

'Apparently, they're doing an organized search of the house,' Georgette said, running a hand through the dark brown side of her hair. 'The guy doing the search looks a bit wet behind the ears, and judging by the noise levels he's pretty clumsy.'

That's all we need, thought Kitt. Why would they send someone so inexperienced to conduct a search on a case this serious? But then, all too quickly, she reached an answer: government cuts.

Pursing her lips, she turned back towards the kitchen table. Several items were bagged up: a faded old T-shirt emblazoned with the Coca Cola logo; several envelopes of varying colours, one or two, Kitt noted, postmarked from Leicester, but looking like standard letters from insurance providers or banks or similar companies; a pile of bank statements, and some other letters that looked more personal with the address handwritten on the front. Next to this odd assortment of artefacts sat the yet-to-be-bagged items the officer had put down a few moments before: the train tickets and the key cards from the hotel. The officer would no doubt be back at any moment to shoo Kitt out of the back door – there wasn't time to think about whether or not any of this shed light on where Beth really was on the night of the murder.

Quick as she could, Kitt pulled her phone out of her satchel and hit the camera function on the keypad.

'What're you doing?' Georgette hissed, looking between Kitt and the doorway. 'She said not to touch anything.'

The librarian's eyes widened. It had obviously been a bit rash to assume Georgette would approve of what she was up to.

'I'm not going to touch anything. But given what you told me about the teenager they've got on the case, it might be wise to take a couple of photos. Just in case something important is missed,' Kitt said, snapping as many close-up shots as she could of the envelopes, the key cards and the bank statements, before shoving her phone back in her satchel.

'Why do you care so much?' said Georgette, still being careful to keep her voice low.

Kitt raised an eyebrow. 'You don't mind if Beth is wrongly accused of murder?'

'Beth lied to the police about where she was when her ex-boyfriend was murdered. And she used me as a fake alibi.'

'Both questionable life choices, I agree, but do you really think Beth is a murderer?'

Georgette lowered her eyes further to the terracotta-tiled kitchen floor, but didn't say anything more.

'Look,' said Kitt, making one last attempt to get Georgette onside, 'as well as being friends with Beth, I'm also very good friends with Evie Bowes. Do you know her?'

Georgette squinted as though thinking hard, trying to place the name. 'Beth's mentioned her a couple of times. She went out with Owen after Beth . . . God, this must have hit her harder than anyone. Were they still together?'

'Quite recently broken up,' said Kitt. 'But I think, if anything, that's somehow made it all worse, and when Evie heard Beth had been accused of the murder, well, she was past herself. Any idea why Beth lied? I really want to put Evie's mind at rest.'

'Me?' said Georgette. 'I've already told the police everything.'

'I'm sure. It's just, the whole thing's a bit of a shock, and I was wondering if, on reflection, you had any idea about why Beth won't tell the police where she was that night.'

'No, but to be honest, Beth hasn't helped herself much in that regard,' Georgette said.

'How do you mean?' asked Kitt.

'Beth's a really private person. At least, that's the way she's been for a long time now.'

'You mean, she wasn't always so keen to keep her business to herself?' Kitt said, thinking about her theory that Beth might have a secret that Owen knew too much about.

'No, well, not when she was with Owen. She used to tell me all sorts about that relationship. Much more than I'd like a lot of the time. But after they broke up . . .'

'What?'

'She sort of went in on herself, at least when it came to her love life. She's never discussed it since then. Whenever I asked she just changed the subject, so after a while I stopped asking . . .' Georgette's body stiffened. 'She was mad to end things with Owen anyway. He was besotted with her, but she broke it off like it was nothing, like he was nothing.'

Kitt blinked in surprise and stared at Georgette, who, on realizing she had perhaps said more than she meant to, picked up a satchel off one of the kitchen chairs and threw in her keys and phone, which had been resting on a nearby counter.

'I've got to get to work,' she said.

Kitt was just about to ask another question when there was a shuffling sound at the door, swiftly followed by the words: 'What are you still doing here?'

'I, er, I wasn't sure if it'd be safe to leave yet. Do you think the reporters will be gone?' Kitt was doing her best to look helpless and confused. It was an expression so alien to her face she had almost forgotten how.

Eyeing Kitt, the officer strode to the back door, pulled it open, and looked both ways.

'You can walk along down the path here to the end of the row; any stragglers still hanging about will probably still be gawking at the front door.'

'Thank you, officer,' Kitt said, keeping her tone as carefree and breezy as she could. 'So sorry if I caused any trouble.'

The officer didn't respond, but watched on as Kitt stepped over the threshold. 'Coming, Georgette?' Kitt asked.

'Er—' Georgette looked between Kitt and the officer. 'No ... Just remembered ... I've forgotten something upstairs.'

'All right then,' said the officer, closing the door without even a second's delay, never mind a polite goodbye. Kitt could still see Georgette's face, bordered in the glass squares cut into the top of the door frame. As she stared into the woman's grey-green eyes, her breath quickened, but she had to act casual. The officer was also watching her through the window, so acting natural was a priority. Turning to her left and walking down the garden path indicated by the officer, Kitt felt her stomach tighten. Was Georgette lagging behind to tell the officer about the photographs she had taken? Or the things they had discussed? Kitt had a terrible feeling she had just made Evie's situation a whole lot worse.

NINE

'Grace, what is it?' Kitt said, without even looking up from the spreadsheet beaming out of her computer screen.

'What? Nothing.' Slowly, Grace turned to face her boss and cleared her throat, her brown eyes flinching as Kitt looked into them and caught them in a lie.

Kitt crossed her arms over her chest, and continued to stare at her assistant. Her morning had been far from productive. She'd exchanged tens of text messages with Evie about her visit to Beth's house. Her mother, Marjorie, had been on the phone twice already, unnerved that her daughter was walking around a city in which a murderer was on the loose. She'd received a voicemail from her sister, Rebecca, on a similar theme, and as if that wasn't enough to slow the process of cataloguing the department's latest book delivery, Grace was in a very distracting mood. More so than usual.

'You haven't got a lot to say for yourself this morning,' Kitt pushed.

'I asked you about the murder case,' said Grace.

'And just as well,' said Kitt. 'That article you read about it online this morning was absolute fabrication. But for the last half hour you've been hovering next to my desk and scuttling back and forth between the bookshelves without any discernible purpose.'

'Just 'cause you can't see it doesn't mean I don't have a purpose,' Grace said with a shrug.

Kitt tilted her head questioningly and raised both her eyebrows. 'Quiet, fidgety, *and* defensive?' Kitt said. 'Now I know something's up.'

'I'm not sure if I should say,' came Grace's wavering response.

Kitt leaned back in her chair and crossed her legs beneath the folds of her navy skirt. 'For you, of all people, to be coy about it, it must be something worth talking about. You may as well be out with it. You can't spend the rest of your life tiptoeing around whatever it is.'

Grace leaned against the side of her desk, which stood just a foot away from Kitt's. 'Please, don't be mad at me,' she said.

Kitt gave a dismissive wave. 'When, in all the time you've worked with me, have I ever been mad at you?'

'Well . . . you weren't best pleased the day I impersonated you over the phone to Michelle,' said Grace, her dark eyes sparkling.

'That wasn't anger . . .' Kitt said with a smile, 'it was frustration that after four months of working at my side you couldn't do a better impression of me than that. It hasn't improved either.'

Grace smiled in return. But then her eyes sank into the blue mosaic tiling at her feet. 'I just . . . I don't want to upset you.'

'Please. I'm a Boro lass. I've got a heart made of Teesside steel.'

'Well,' Grace said, flicking a strand of dark wavy hair out of her face, 'I don't want to be the Margaret Thatcher of your heart.'

Kitt chuckled. 'No mention of that particular prime minister in my presence, please. I'm not above starting a swear jar in her name.'

Grace laughed along, but then cut herself off short and fell silent again.

'I shouldn't worry about upsetting me,' Kitt said in her gentlest tone. She had just one or two bigger issues going on than whatever mischief Grace had been up to this time, but the last thing she wanted was for her assistant to feel she couldn't talk to her.

'All right.' Grace took a deep breath. 'Just please know, I did this out of goodness.'

'Did . . . what?' asked Kitt.

'Yesterday, Evie told me about a guy you once knew who sort of . . . disappeared.'

So that was her assistant's struggle. She felt guilty for talking behind Kitt's back.

'Evie told you about Theo?' said Kitt, with a thin-lipped smile.

'Yes,' Grace replied. 'About Theo, and how he disappeared.'

'And why would I be mad at you about that?' asked Kitt.

Grace pushed her fingers together in an awkward steeple. 'It's not so much what Evie told me, but what I did with the information.'

'What you . . . What do you mean?' said Kitt, sitting up straighter in her chair.

At the expression on Kitt's face, Grace looked at the floor once more and began breathing in that overwrought style actors do on TV when their character is experiencing a moment of crisis. Each breath made a whistling noise as it was pushed out between her teeth. 'Well, Evie didn't tell me anything much about Theo to begin with. But after she mentioned him, and what happened, I couldn't get it out of my head.'

'OK . . . Grace, what have you done?'

Grace's eyes dredged themselves from the blue of the ceramic tiles so they could look at Kitt straight on. 'If you could find Theo – if you could talk to him, and maybe get an explanation for what he did, would you want to?'

'Why do you ask?' Kitt said, her voice now sharpened by the rough edge of suspicion.

'I— I emailed Evie and asked for his name and, you know . . .'

'What?' asked Kitt, and, when Grace stammered, yet again repeated, 'What, what?'

'Tracked him down last night after work. On Facebook.'

Kitt sat still and quiet. Her eyes bulging as a wasp's nest of disturbing possibilities swarmed in her mind.

'Wh— what did you say to him?' asked Kitt, taking her turn to stammer.

'Nothing. Oh no, I haven't made contact. I just found him. In case you wanted to find him. In case you wanted the truth, about why he acted that way. It's just, something similar happened to one of my friends about a year ago now, and she's still struggling to . . . let it go.'

'You just looked him up on Facebook?'

'Yes.'

'Nothing else?'

'No.'

'Well then, don't you think all this posturing is a bit OTT? It's not like you invited him to York for a reconciliatory dinner date.' Kitt paused then, eyeing her assistant. 'You didn't, did you?'

'No, no, no. Of course not. It's just . . . it seemed like a good idea when I did it, but then afterwards the more I thought about it, I thought you'd say it wasn't my place.'

'When have you ever worried about what is and isn't your place around me?'

'I— I just thought you might want . . . closure.'

'Grace, I'm a librarian.'

'I know that . . . librarians don't like closure?'

Kitt rolled her eyes up at Prometheus, who looked down on them both from the ceiling.

'No. I mean, essentially, I'm a researcher by trade. If I'd wanted to find Theo, I mean, really wanted to find him, I could have. Facebook's been around longer than you can remember. I have no desire to see Theo again.'

And, Kitt admitted to herself, it was so much easier to

pretend he didn't exist. That he wasn't out there, some-where, living his life without her.

'You're not even a little bit curious?' said Grace, sidling closer to Kitt's desk.

'No.'

'He's aged badly.'

'Really?' Kitt said, her response so quick it fell almost on top of Grace's.

'I mean, I don't know what he used to look like when you knew him back in the day—'

'Back in the . . . I realize that you imagine my youth to have been captured entirely in sepia photographs, but thirty-five isn't that old, you know?'

'I know, sorry,' said Grace. 'But I can't believe for a second that his current hairline is the same as the one on the man you knew. Doesn't look as though the ageing process has been kind.'

'Well . . .' Kitt pondered. The logical thing was to just let this subject drop, but curiosity had always been her mis-tress, and this instance was no exception. 'Maybe you could send me his profile link. Just in case I change my mind.'

Grace nodded and made to move back to her chair. Kitt caught her hand as she did so and squeezed it. 'I'm not mad at you. Just so you know, I'm not even mad at him any more.' As those last words left her mouth, Kitt wondered how true they were. Or whether they just seemed like the mature thing to say. At her age she was supposed to be beyond anger, wasn't she? By now she was supposed to be in control.

Grace squeezed Kitt's hand in return. 'Good. But if you want, I can be angry at him for you.'

Kitt chuckled at this and shooed Grace back to her desk with her spare hand before turning back to her computer screen.

Not a minute later, an email from Grace popped up in Kitt's inbox. The subject line was a name that belonged in a past life.

Theodore Dent.

The last time she had seen his name, it was written in her own handwriting on a letter she was posting to his last known address. The hateful things she had written in that letter . . . She felt a smouldering in her chest just thinking about it.

The link to his Facebook profile sat in the white box below. Kitt hovered the cursor over the incomprehensible string of letters, punctuation marks and numbers that looked to be in as much of a mess as she had been all those years ago when she realized there would be no goodbye between herself and the only man she'd ever loved with all her heart. The muscles in her shoulders braced for the impact of a simple click of the mouse.

For a man who once didn't want to be found, Theo wasn't one for privacy settings. All of his pictures and comments were there on full view for anyone who might want to find them.

Kitt clicked on Theo's profile picture and it enlarged on the screen. He was standing shoulder-to-shoulder next to a brunette with a galaxy of freckles clustering in small her face. The pair were in a restaurant. They were smiling, but something about the smiles seemed strained, perhaps even forced. Or maybe that was just what Kitt wanted to see.

One thing was not up for interpretation. Grace had been right about time not being kind to Theo. His hairline meandered backwards to the apex of his skull and, to hide the fact that it was receding, he had cut his brown hair very close to the head. Still, his eyes hadn't altered. They were the same brown as decaying autumn leaves. Fitting, Kitt thought, for a man whose seasons could shift so abruptly.

Kitt's eyes drifted down Theo's profile page to his location and job title. He had become a specialist in Anglo-Saxon history for the Airedale Museum, and he lived in Leeds. Her untouchable dream of a man had been working a thirty-minute train ride away all this time. Kitt winced at the sting of that thought. The people of Leeds and York were back and forth for day trips all the time. They could have crossed paths in the street or in the pub – at the York Christmas market buying gifts for loved ones. The possibility, and the fact it still existed, left Kitt feeling quite sick.

The next thing her eyes focused on was his relationship status. 'It's complicated,' it read, and the librarian couldn't help but issue a wry smile at that. After all these years, Theo still hadn't managed to commit to anyone or anything. From an outside perspective Kitt supposed that many might think the same was true of her. But in truth, she had committed to something else: herself and the truth of her own heart.

She wasn't willing to pretend or settle for somebody convenient because that might be easier for everyone around her to accept. She had vowed never again to trade her whole heart for half of somebody else's, and it was an oath she intended to keep.

Kitt looked again at Theo's profile picture. She wasn't imagining it. There was no depth to that smile, it was all surface. It was a stranger to the smile he used to give her when she kissed him without warning, or when he found one of the love notes she'd hidden in his trouser pocket. Together, they had tasted true love. Kitt was sure of it. The question was, why had Theo thrown that away?

The phone on Kitt's desk trilled.

Sucking in a sharp breath, she pushed hard on the escape key. Theo's face disappeared.

'Grace, can you get that?' Kitt said, glaring at the phone. 'I can't bear having to reassure my mother, for the third time this morning, that I haven't been murdered yet.'

With a smile, Grace picked up the receiver. 'Vale of York University Library, Women's Studies, Grace Edwards spea— oh, hi Evie. Yes, she's here.'

Grace handed the phone over to Kitt, but instead of going to sit back at her own desk, she perched on the edge of Kitt's.

'Evie?' Kitt said into the receiver.

'Sorry I couldn't talk sooner. I had to go back to work today and do all the appointments I couldn't do yesterday,' said Evie.

'No need to apologize,' said Kitt. 'What did you think of my texts about the visit to Beth's place?'

'Georgette doesn't seem to have been much help. You really think she's going to tell the police you took those pictures?'

'I don't know,' said Kitt. 'The way she was going on she almost sounded like she had a thing for Owen herself.'

'Who knew he was such a ladies' man?' said Evie with a glum note in her voice.

'Not I,' said Kitt, and then, deciding it was prudent to move the conversation on, added, 'did you get a chance to look at the photos I took too?'

'Yeah, it looks as though they were mostly compiling bits and pieces from around the time Beth and Owen were together. The train tickets and what-have-you. Owen lived in Leeds when they were going out, and Owen complained more than once that Beth kept hold of one of his T-shirts. I'm guessing it's the one in that bag.'

'So nothing stood out as odd to you?' said Kitt, testing half a theory that had been building at the back of her mind.

'No, not really. Although . . . I don't know why she would have key cards from the hotel at home.'

'Oh?' said Kitt, trying not to give away anything in her tone.

'Yeah. I heard Beth mention once or twice that her boss at the hotel was a real stickler. She made out like he was always on her back about something.' Evie paused at the other end of the line. 'Maybe she's started stealing key cards just to spite him?'

'Maybe,' said Kitt. 'But it seems a weird way to get back at your boss.'

'That's true, she's mostly about staying out of his way, but why else would she have the key cards at home?'

'Maybe she picked them up by accident? Easily done if you're tired at the end of the day, and you pick them up with your keys and wallet and all that,' mused Kitt.

'Maybe,' said Evie. 'But then, why keep them? Wouldn't you return them or throw them out if you didn't want your boss to know?'

'All right, hold on,' said Kitt. 'Grace, give me three good reasons why a receptionist might take home hotel key cards?'

Grace frowned, thinking. 'She ... wants to invite her friends around to one of the rooms for a Sing Star marathon on Saturday night? Or there's something about a room she doesn't want anyone else to find out about – like maybe she broke something ...'

'Right ... that's two.'

'Well, which hotel is it?' asked Grace.

'The White Horse Hotel.'

'I don't know, she likes horses, and the key cards have horses on them?'

'Did you hear all that?' Kitt said down the phone.

'Yes,' Evie said with a giggle.

'Nothing particularly plausible to work with,' said Kitt, as Grace's face sagged in her peripheral vision. 'But anyway, the police have the key cards bagged up as evidence now. I'm sure they'll be asking Beth about them.'

'Maybe ... but how long will it take them to prioritize that particular piece of evidence?'

'You think I should pass this not-to-be-missed information to Halloran and Banks direct?'

'Do you want to talk to Halloran and Banks right now?

Given they might be aware of the fact you were meddling with their crime scene?' said Evie.

'Not ... particularly. All right, well, what are you suggesting? An anonymous phone call?'

'I'm suggesting that the White Horse Hotel is just a short cab ride out of town.'

'Oh, Evie,' said Kitt. 'Really, I ...'

'Come on, it's not like this is the first time you have done a little snooping around.'

Kitt's mouth tightened. 'If you are referring to the Seaton Carew incident, I told you, that was between us.'

'What's a Seaton Carew?' Grace asked with a frown, but Kitt just held her hand up to signal she was concentrating on the call.

'All right, all right. But what I'm asking you to do is nothing like the Georgette scenario,' said Evie. 'The guy she works with on the desk is a good friend of hers. Eli. Just find out if there's an explanation for her taking the cards home. That's all. If so, well then, we really haven't got anything and we'll have to leave it to the police.'

'It sounds a lot like playing with fire to me.'

'I know, but I can't sit back and do nothing. Every second the police are focusing on Beth, the real killer is getting further away.'

'Yes, but ...'

'Howay, Kitt. Hotels and a murder mystery. It's just like an Agatha Christie story. Aren't you a little bit intrigued?'

Kitt paused. Hotels were a murder mystery trademark and on more than one occasion in those books, just like in

A Murder is Announced, the hotel staff were linked with the murder.

'At Bertram's Hotel.'

'What's that now?' asked Evie.

'A Miss Marple novel. The people at the hotel are all part of a criminal gang. Maybe something criminal *is* going on at the hotel. If Beth's involved somehow, that might be why she lied to the police. Revealing her true whereabouts would reveal her criminality.'

'Mmm,' said Evie. 'I mean, that's one theory.'

Kitt tutted. 'Well, anything is better than her having murdered Owen, isn't it?'

'So you'll go?' Evie said.

'I'll go,' said Kitt. 'But if this brings us no closer to finding out where Beth was on the night of the murder, you might have to start facing up to the fact that Beth may be somehow involved.'

Kitt heard a sigh at the end of the line. 'I know. But please, just give me the peace of mind that the police aren't sniffing down the wrong hedgerow.'

Kitt nodded, even though Evie couldn't see her. 'That much I can grant you.'

'Thank you,' Evie said in the small voice she used whenever she knew she was asking for more than Kitt was willing to give.

'Talk soon.'

Kitt hung up the phone and caught Grace's wide and expectant eyes.

'Are we going on an adventure?' she asked.

TEN

Kitt and Grace hopped out of the taxi and stared up at the White Horse Hotel. Named after a limestone figure that the Victorians had cut into the hillside near Kilburn some twenty miles away, the building was a prim cuboid built in greying stone that stood on the outskirts of town on the A19. Long slender windows ran all along the east-facing front wall, designed to beckon in the sun at dawn and perhaps convince visitors that there was some warmth and light to be had in the north of England after all.

Striding across the gravelled car park, Kitt noted the silver lettering hanging above the doorway alongside the outline of a horse wrought in some kind of light metal – most likely tin. It was early evening, dusk was looming, and a couple of other taxis had pulled up outside the entrance. They had come to collect people dressed in sharp office wear, probably on their way to business dinners in the city – or on their way back to London.

'I looked up Seaton Carew. It's a village near Middlesbrough,' said Grace as the pair began walking towards the hotel entrance. When Kitt didn't respond she added, 'What happened there?'

'Nothing of interest,' Kitt replied, though she could see by the way her assistant was eyeing her that she wasn't convinced by that answer.

'All right, then how are we going to handle this?' asked Grace.

'*We* aren't going to handle this at all,' said Kitt, holding onto her trilby as a sudden gust of wind threatened to carry it off. 'I'm going to be doing the talking.'

'So glad I tagged along,' said Grace, kicking at a stray piece of gravel.

'I told you not to,' said Kitt.

'And I told you, nothing ever happens around here. I'm not missing this. At least I get to watch, I suppose,' said Grace.

'Isn't that why Netflix was invented?' asked Kitt.

'I prefer my drama live-action,' Grace said, throwing a couple of mock punches in the air as she walked.

Kitt stopped just before the threshold and turned square upon her assistant. 'Are you quite all right?'

'Yes,' said Grace, lowering her arms from the defensive position, leaving herself wide open to her invisible opponent. 'It's just . . . it's exciting.'

'Let's agree to disagree on that,' said Kitt. 'You're going to have to compose yourself if you want to come inside. This is serious.'

The sparkle in Grace's brown eyes dulled and she stood up straighter.

'Better,' said Kitt, before pushing through the heavy doorway trimmed in silver. The second she stepped inside she was hit by an immediate waft of Eau de Hotel: that strange mixture of bread toasting and ultra-strong air freshener that filters through the reception area of every boarding house and lodging in the Western hemisphere. In the case of the White Horse Hotel, lemon seemed to be their preferred synthesized fragrance, causing Kitt to mark, with some regret, that she hadn't had time for a cup of Lady Grey since lunchtime.

Kitt's eyes focused on a man standing behind a large desk built in mahogany. Two small brass uplighter lamps positioned at either side of him cast a sickly yellow light across his face.

'May I help you, madam?' asked the man. He had few wrinkles around his eyes, but his hairline betrayed his age. He had a large, pale forehead, smooth except for a small, brown hair island set further forward from the rest of the crop, a feature that betrayed his vanity. He would look much better if he just shaved that off, Kitt thought, rather than attempting to deceive the casual onlooker into believing he was younger than his years.

'Yes, hello. Is Eli on shift at all?' asked Kitt, stepping closer to the desk.

The man's smile disappeared at once. 'Eli is busy. He doesn't have time for visits from friends while he's at work.'

'Oh no, you misunderstand,' said Kitt, deciding, given his manner, that this must be the disgruntled manager Evie had mentioned. 'We're trying to be of help with the . . . sensitive situation you're dealing with at the moment.'

'Sensitive situation? I've no idea what you're talking about.' The manager's tone sounded convincing enough, but his gaze shifted upward to the glass chandelier hanging above.

'I see,' said Kitt, raising her voice half a decibel. 'So you haven't heard that your receptionist has been arrested for murder?'

'*Sssssshhhhh! Shhhhh!*' said the manager, slamming his hands down on the desk. His eyes darted to the guests passing in and out of the building.

'So you do know,' said Kitt.

'How could I fail to?' said the manager. 'If I hadn't received a phone call from Beth's mother notifying me of her arrest, I'd have heard about it on the news.'

'Well, we're here to try to help, you know,' said Kitt.

'And why would you bother to do that?' asked the manager, swiping a stray piece of cotton from the left sleeve of his black suit. He was wearing a black tie too, and to Kitt's mind looked a lot more like a funeral director than the manager of a small hotel on the outskirts of York.

'Well,' Kitt looked at the manager's name tag, 'Mr Buckhurst, the second we heard about Beth being taken in by the police we knew straight away there'd been some mistake.'

'I wish I shared your confidence,' said Buckhurst, curling his lip at Kitt.

Kitt's inner bonfire ignited in an instant. More than anything, she wanted to glare at this less-than-compassionate individual, but she had to keep him onside.

Time for a different tack.

'Oh, I see,' said Kitt. 'Grace, I suppose we'd best go straight to the papers and warn them.'

Grace's face looked utterly vacant, but the intensity of Kitt's eyes was enough to signal that she should play along. 'Oh . . . yes . . . we should warn them.'

'Warn them? About what?' asked Buckhurst.

Kitt resisted the urge to flash a smug smile at him. 'That the recruitment procedure is so lax at the White Horse Hotel that they employ murderers. Nothing personal. I just can't stand by in good conscience and let people stay at a place where they might not make it out alive.'

'Now, now, now, madam. I think you misunderstood,' Buckhurst blustered. 'The White Horse Hotel would of course never employ somebody of that background, even accidentally; we're very thorough.'

'In which case,' said Kitt, 'you won't mind helping us trying to find out where Beth really was on the night of the murder. If you only employ the best people, I'm sure you wouldn't want to see one of them wrongly accused of such a terrible crime.'

'I don't see how I can be of any help,' said Buckhurst, crossing his arms.

'You could start by finding out who last used the key cards with these serial numbers.' Kitt pushed a piece of paper across the reception desk while at the same time feeling pretty smart for taking close-up photographs of the key cards whilst she'd had the opportunity at Beth's house. Numbers weren't really her strong point, and the odds of her remembering whole strings of them, even when investigating something as serious as a murder, were slim.

'Key cards from this hotel?' asked Buckhurst.

'Yes, we found them at Beth's house,' Kitt explained. 'It seemed odd that she took them home and we thought they might be a clue to her true whereabouts on the night of the murder.'

'No wonder we're always losing key cards,' Buckhurst muttered. He tilted his head back so his nose stuck further into the air than necessary. 'I can't tell you who last checked into these rooms. It's a breach of customer confidentiality.'

'Have it your way,' said Kitt, turning to Grace. 'I can see the headlines now: *Killer Hotel*.'

Grace giggled. 'Oh, that's definitely one the *Sun* would run. What about *White Horse Head in Your Bed*?'

'*York's Own Bates Motel*,' said Kitt.

'Motel? Motel? I. Think. Not. This, madam, is a boutique hotel. A *boutique* hotel,' said Buckhurst.

Kitt stared hard at the man, not quite believing it was the word 'motel' that had most offended him about the game she and Grace had just been playing, but one had to take whatever advantage was afforded.

'Not once the press understands what kind of place you're running here,' she said.

Buckhurst sighed and picked up the slip of paper lying on the reception desk. 'Fine.'

The manager looked over both of his shoulders, before tapping the keyboard in front of him.

'Julian Rampling,' Buckhurst said. 'That's the first one.'

'Check the others too, please,' said Kitt.

More tapping on the keyboard.

'Julian Rampling,' Buckhurst said, and then, 'Julian Rampling again. This key card was given out on Saturday night.'

'The night of the murder,' said Kitt. 'But Beth wasn't at work on Saturday night?'

'No, it wasn't her shift. It was Eli's shift,' said Buckhurst, picking up the telephone and dialling a four-digit extension.

'Eli?' said Buckhurst. 'Get down to reception at once.'

Buckhurst's tone was more kindling to Kitt's inner bonfire. She hated managers who disrespected their employees. Perhaps she let her own assistant have a little bit too much rope, but at least Grace looked forward to coming in to work in the mornings.

A moment of quiet passed. Kitt looked at Grace and then back at Buckhurst.

'Do you know who Julian Rampling is?' asked Kitt.

'So difficult when one is a busy manager to get to know all guests by name,' said Buckhurst and then added, 'but he's stayed here a few times so I might know him by sight. Ah, Eli . . .'

Kitt turned to see a young man walking down a staircase just off to her left. His pace was slow and his head hung low, but then it was unlikely that any of Buckhurst's employees were ever in a hurry to have a conversation with him.

Eli stood in front of the desk looking first at Grace, then at Kitt, and at last at Buckhurst. 'Can I help?'

'Does the name Julian Rampling mean anything to you?' asked Buckhurst.

'He's a regular guest,' said Eli. 'Insurance broker from Leicester.'

Leicester. The letters Kitt had seen at Beth's house, they were postmarked Leicester.

'Anything else you want to tell me about him?' said Buckhurst, staring down his nose at Eli. 'Anything relating to Beth?'

Eli's mouth twitched, but he said nothing and shook his head. He again looked around the group of people, the smooth olive skin of his forehead now creasing. Kitt was beginning to suspect the truth that was weighing on him, but couldn't reveal her suspicion in front of Buckhurst. If she was wrong, it could cost Beth her job.

'In any event, I'm going to pass his name to the police,' said Buckhurst.

Eli's brown eyes widened.

'If you think that's wise,' said Grace, raising both her eyebrows. Kitt looked at her assistant. Was Grace thinking the same things she was?

'Wise? Let me see,' said Buckhurst, sneering at Grace. 'These key cards were all in the possession of a murder suspect, and were all last used by the same person – most likely her accomplice.'

'Or,' said Kitt, 'there is a more innocent explanation and you could save your hotel a lot of negative publicity by giving this man a call and settling the whole matter quietly.'

'It can be settled quietly without me doing that,' said Buckhurst.

'I wouldn't count on it,' said Kitt. 'The media were at Beth's home address this morning.'

'Yes, we have received one or two calls about the matter, but have refused to comment.'

'That's enough for the press today, writing a smug "the owner declined to comment" line in their articles,' said Kitt. 'But if the police hold onto Beth another day, the reporters will be baying for answers. I'm guessing her place of work will be their first stop.'

Buckhurst glared at Kitt, but she glared back just as hard until the hotel manager at last rubbed his hand up and down his face a couple of times and picked up the telephone. He looked at his computer screen as he dialled, and then rapped his fingertips on the desk.

There was a slight click to be heard from the receiver as the call was picked up.

Buckhurst's frown got deeper. 'No, this is not Beth,' he almost shouted.

Tutting, Kitt snatched the phone off Buckhurst. They weren't going to get any information out of Julian Rampling if Buckhurst was in charge of the questioning.

'Hello,' Kitt said into the phone, 'sorry about that.'

'I— is this the White Horse Hotel?' asked the man on the other end.

'It is,' said Kitt. 'Are you Julian Rampling?'

'Thought I recognized the number. Yes, I am,' he said. 'I'm confused as to why I'm receiving this call, however.'

'You're receiving this call, Mr Rampling, because Beth,

who it seems you know, is currently sitting in police custody. She's been arrested on suspicion of murder,' said Kitt.

'M— murder?' Julian stuttered. 'Is that a joke?'

'I'm afraid not,' said Kitt.

'But that's ridiculous, Beth's not a murderer. Who is this?
Is this the police?'

'My name is Kitt Hartley, I'm ... an acquaintance of
Beth's. I agree with you that from all I know about her,
Beth doesn't seem the murdering type.'

'So why is she in police custody?'

'She knew the deceased, who was murdered on Saturday
night.'

'Saturday night,' Julian repeated.

'Beth gave a false alibi, which is why she is at this moment
facing the prospect of a murder trial. Amongst her posses-
sions were some hotel key cards.' As Kitt said these words
she realized her suspicions must be correct. It was the only
logical explanation. 'All of the keys were last used by you,
the most recent on Saturday night, so we thought it was
worth giving you a call.'

There was a pause at the other end of the line. 'She ...
was with me,' Julian said in the smallest of voices.

'I see,' said Kitt, and, even though she had guessed the
answer, she still had to ask, 'but why would Beth lie about
that?'

Another pause at the end of the line. 'Because I'm married.'

Kitt nodded, and then remembered she wasn't face-to-
face with Julian. 'I thought that might be the case,' she said.

'What should I do?' Julian asked.

Kitt wasn't sure if he was really asking her or thinking out loud, but answered anyway.

'Call York Police Station and ask for DI Halloran. You tell him that you can vouch for Beth's whereabouts on Saturday night.'

'Yeah . . .' said Julian. 'I guess that's the right thing to do.'

'Yes, it is,' said Kitt, sensing some hesitation on the other end of the line. 'If you're concerned about your wife finding out, you should know the police have done all they can to keep this incident under wraps from the press so far. I can't see them releasing your name or anything of that sort.'

'Good . . . that's good,' Julian said with a vague note in his voice that suggested shock. 'This really isn't a joke?'

'No,' said Kitt.

'How do I know you're telling the truth about Beth?'

'I would suggest you ring her mother, but explaining how you know Beth might prove a bit tricky,' said Kitt. 'Look, check the online news channels. You'll see there's been a murder in York. A man called Owen Hall. Did Beth ever mention him to you?'

'Her ex,' said Julian. 'Oh God . . .'

'You understand now why the police might be looking at her, especially without an alibi?'

'Yes, I still can't believe . . .'

'I know. It's been quite a shock at this end of the wire too. But you must call the police and let them know Beth was with you.'

'Yes,' said Julian. 'I suppose I'd better.'

'I'll end this call so you can get through to the police

station, OK?' Kitt said, in the gentlest voice she had at her disposal.

'OK,' said Julian. 'Bye.'

Kitt replaced the receiver and looked between Buckhurst and Grace. Kitt's end of the conversation had been enough for them both to glean what had been going on. Buckhurst who, running a hotel, must be used to turning a blind eye to this kind of rendezvous, was nodding to himself, while Grace shook her head in much the manner one would expect from a youthful idealist. Glancing at Eli, Kitt guessed he might have been the one person Beth had confided in about her tryst. His face was hardly a portrait of surprise.

The librarian herself kept perfectly still. Inside, however, all she could do was hope that Julian cared enough about Beth to call the police station, that his desire to protect Beth outweighed his desire to protect himself.

ELEVEN

Striding up Bishopthorpe Road, past Frankie and Johnny's Cookshop and Forever Young Beauty, Kitt's eyes fixed on Sure Bet, a bookmakers that stood just three doors down from Retro Rags – the vintage shop where she was supposed to be meeting Evie. The librarian looked at her watch. She still had a few minutes before her friend would miss her. Time enough to make a couple of enquiries that might help her answer the question she'd spent all of the night before contemplating, as she tossed and turned in bed: if neither Beth nor Evie had killed Owen Hall, who had?

It wasn't her job to find that out, she knew that. But if the text messages she'd had from Evie over the past twenty-four hours were anything to go by, her best friend was getting more anxious by the minute to uncover who was really behind this terrible act. And, if Kitt were really honest with herself, she was just too curious a person to let a question like this slide. Even though that curiosity had got her into trouble once or twice in the past, it was an impulse she had never quite managed to quash.

Pushing through the door of the betting shop, Kitt immediately cursed her curiosity as she was hit with a fog of sweat, cigarette ash, and the smell banknotes get when they've been passed between greasy, filthy hands for generations. But then, she reminded herself, vintage clothes shops didn't smell a whole lot better. The electric blue carpet, patterned with orange geometric shapes, felt soft, almost spongy underfoot. Kitt didn't want to know what kind of liquids this carpet had absorbed over the years – she preferred to hope the place was just suffering from a bad case of damp.

A teller sitting in a little booth in the corner raised his head, peering at her through small round spectacles perched on the very tip of his nose. 'Can I help you, madam?'

As casually as she could, Kitt surveyed the two other people in the room. A man with a long bushy beard and a tummy that hung over the waistline of his jeans was filling in a betting slip. The other man was thin, almost spindly, and had the narrow facial features of a whippet. He was staring at a horse race beaming from one of the big screens that hung on the wall. From this quick assessment, Kitt gathered she perhaps wasn't the most likely customer for this establishment, which unfortunately meant she was conspicuous.

'No, just having a look around,' Kitt said with a smile, but then, remembering this wasn't a second-hand bookshop, added, 'I've never made a bet before, so I'm just getting the lie of the land.'

The teller looked Kitt up and down from her trilby hat

to her suede ankle boots and nodded before returning his attentions to his smartphone.

Sauntering over to the blue plastic stand at the centre of the room, strewn with biros and betting slips, Kitt looked again at the man with the bushy beard. His gaze moved back and forth between a magazine and his betting slip as he filled in the appropriate boxes.

'Excuse me,' Kitt said. The man lifted his head and looked at Kitt, but didn't speak. Kitt smiled in a way that she hoped might make her seem a little bit vacant. 'I've never placed a bet before. Any advice for a beginner?'

'I'm not sharing my luck with you.'

'Oh.' Kitt let all of the muscles in her face droop. 'Thing is, I sort of need the money. Was hoping for a big win.'

The man's mouth tightened and, looking at him again, Kitt realized his eyebrows were so bushy she didn't know where they ended and where his hairline began. 'I'm not sharing my luck with you,' he repeated. But this time there was a hint of agitation to his tone.

'All right, I understand,' Kitt said with a slow, sombre nod, 'but, do you know where I could borrow some money then? Off the books, as it were.'

The man frowned at her. 'You mean, like a loan shark?'

'If that's what you call them, yes,' Kitt said, doing all she could to act the innocent.

The man shook his head. 'I won't tell you a thing about gambling, but I'll tell you this: you don't want to get caught up with that lot.'

'Why not?' Kitt asked, widening her eyes further.

'Let's just say, some people who borrow from that type and can't make payments often aren't seen again.'

Kitt drew a hand to her mouth in mock shock. The man pressed his lips together, seemingly satisfied his message had got through. Kitt offered the man a brief smile of thanks, and then, without another word, walked back to the door. On her way out she felt a tap on her arm and turned.

'Couldn't help overhearing,' said Whippet Man, slouching in his turquoise tracksuit. His blond hair was slicked back with far too much hair gel.

Kitt raised her eyebrows, and waited.

The man glanced over his shoulder to be sure the other punter was once again engrossed in his betting slip. 'I might know someone who can lend you some money. But he only comes in here on Mondays.'

'That's very useful,' said Kitt. 'If I don't make alternative arrangements before then, I'll come back on Monday.'

The man winked and clicked his lips at her in a way that made her pray that another lead – any other lead – would open up on the murder investigation between then and Monday.

Smiling at the man, she exited the shop, relieved to feel the fresh October air in her lungs.

Less than a minute later, Kitt stepped over the threshold of Retro Rags to see Evie balancing an elaborate turban woven of gold and fuchsia fabric on her head. The red costume jewel positioned at the front had two midnight blue feathers sticking out behind it.

Evie turned on hearing the little bell above the door chime. 'Now then. Where've you been?' she asked.

'Er, human traffic,' Kitt lied, turning to close the door behind her so Evie wouldn't see her face as she did so. She would be hard pushed to lie if Evie pressed her, but there was no point volunteering information when right now she had nothing more than a theory. 'Tourists on a go-slow everywhere.'

'What do you think?' Evie said, once Kitt had turned to face her again.

'For tonight?'

Evie nodded her head in a manner that made the turban jiggle back and forth.

'It's . . . maybe a bit much,' said Kitt, although she conceded to herself in private that this was likely to be the most sensible item her best friend had tried on since she'd got here.

Kitt had spent many a lunch break in this shop watching Evie try on garments her own grandmother would have thought the height of fashion, and left to her own devices she would always pick the most eccentric garment to try on first.

Evie turned back to the long thin mirror propped against the wall, and giggled at her reflection.

'I'm surprised you even feel up to going to this thing,' Kitt said, referring to the Belle's Ball, an annual networking event for local beauty industry specialists. In truth the word 'ball' was something of a misnomer as it was really just a glorified business dinner. Evie had dragged Kitt along to this gathering every year for the eight years of their friendship, but this time she had presumed the murder of an ex-boyfriend might get in the way.

'You mean, you thought you might get out of talking about the best rain-resistant mascaras all night with a bunch of people you don't know?' Evie said, smirking at Kitt through the mirror.

Kitt raised her hands in the air, palms to the Artex ceiling. 'It's just been a tough week, that's all, for everyone involved.'

'And it's only Wednesday,' said Evie. 'I can't pretend it'd be my first choice of entertainments this week, but I can't cry off this thing. I get most of my massage referrals from people who've met me there.'

Kitt pursed her lips. 'I know, I know, you're right.'

'Besides, I'd take just about any distraction from thinking about the funeral on Friday.' Every muscle in her face dropped an inch.

'You've decided you will go then?' said Kitt.

'Yeah,' said Evie. 'I think so – can you get the time off to come with me?'

'I'm sure I can swing that.'

'Michelle will understand?'

'No, but Michelle's disapproval hasn't stopped me taking time off for emergencies over the last decade.'

Evie turned to Kitt and raised an eyebrow. 'If you call queuing outside a second-hand bookshop to take advantage of their sale on first editions an "emergency".'

'Yes, I do,' said Kitt, smiling at her friend before picking a tea dress patterned with oranges and lemons off the nearest rail. 'How about this?'

'Oooh ...' Evie snatched the dress out of Kitt's hands, peeled it off the hanger and began to pull it on over the top of her cream canvas workwear. Not a manoeuvre the average person would be able to accomplish with any grace. Evie, however, had spent enough hours in vintage shops without proper changing rooms to have developed a patented technique.

She turned full circle in front of the mirror, surveying herself as she did so. 'Spiffy.'

'It'd go nice with your mustard cardigan,' said Kitt.

'Good call,' said Evie.

Kitt diverted her eyes then to a small pile of books sitting on a nearby table. She lifted each in turn as she looked at them, and said, 'So . . . is this a private enough place to talk about your conversation with Beth?'

Kitt had tried to find out all the particulars from her friend the moment she had called to invite her to an emergency lunchtime shopping spree to find the perfect garment to wear to the Belle's Ball, but Evie had been standing on Skeldergate Bridge at the time and, knowing how small-town gossip could spread, was keen to be somewhere other than a main thoroughfare before explaining all about Beth's release from the police station late the previous night.

Evie looked over her shoulders, scanning the shop. The pair were the only customers at present, and the shop assistant was perched on a stool, safely engrossed in the latest issue of *Vintage Life* magazine.

Evie beckoned Kitt nearer and lowered her voice. 'She was in a right state when I called her, so I didn't speak for long, but she was grateful for what we did.'

'I'm glad,' said Kitt, putting the books she had been

fidgeting with back down on the table before taking a step closer to where her friend was standing, 'and did you find out if Georgette had relayed anything to the police? About the photographs I took?'

'Beth said she'd ask Georgette what that was about. I got a text message back saying Georgette had come close to telling the police, but decided not to in the end. Apparently she was a bit jealous of Owen and Beth's relationship.'

'I rather got that feeling,' said Kitt. 'So, she wanted to be with Owen?'

Evie shook her head. 'I didn't get that impression from the message. It seemed more that Georgette was jealous of the kind of relationship they had – or the kind of devotion Owen showed to Beth while they were going out, and thought Beth was stupid for throwing that away.'

Evie's eyes dropped to the floor. Kitt watched her friend work out the painful truth she had already pieced together for herself. Owen had never been that passionate during his relationship with Evie. At least not once the initial thrill of the chase had worn off. Owen had been on the odd date between ending things with Beth and picking up with Evie, but nothing that could be called serious. The more Kitt understood about the kind of relationship Owen had had with Beth, the clearer it became that Evie had been Owen's rebound girl.

'I assume Beth's family were relieved to have her free again?' said Kitt, changing the topic of conversation.

'Her mother went off the deep end about the affair. Beth was joking, but she made out that police custody was actually more welcoming than the reception she received from her parents when she was released.'

'Probably the last thing she needed just then,' said Kitt.

Evie shrugged. 'I do understand why her parents went for it. It's not the kind of hope you have for your only daughter – for them to spend their life as a mistress.'

Kitt leaned her head to one side. 'From what you say, Beth isn't the kind to maliciously hurt anybody.'

'She said she fell hard for the guy, which I suppose must be true for her to even consider something like that,' said Evie.

'People do odd things for love,' Kitt said. 'She kept the key cards as mementos?'

'We didn't get around to that level of detail, but I assume so,' said Evie, and then, at once, her eyes shimmered with mischief. 'She did mention that the police weren't exactly rejoicing at the prospect of releasing her.'

'Yes, well. Our interference got Beth out of trouble, but it's put the police back to square one. It's not a complete surprise they wouldn't be thrilled about that,' said Kitt.

'Yep,' said Evie. 'Beth said Halloran was especially mono-syllabic when he came to let her go.'

Kitt's eyes, which had been fixed on a fraying patch of teal carpet, flitted up to Evie. 'Why do you single out Halloran especially? Given how Banks behaved when the pair were questioning me, I'm sure she's equally put out.'

'I'm just reporting back what I heard,' Evie said, smiling much harder than Kitt thought appropriate, given the topic of conversation.

'What's that smirk for?' asked Kitt, hearing the sharp edge in her tone.

'Nothing, you just seem a little bit too keen to dismiss Halloran's feelings.'

'Halloran is a professional, Evie. I mean, it's not his first day on the job. Dead ends in an investigation are not unfamiliar obstacles to him, I'm sure.'

'Still,' said Evie, 'I wouldn't like to be in his position. A high-profile murder case with no solid suspect.'

'You want to volunteer for that position?' said Kitt. 'I'm sure he'd be glad to have you.'

'One trip to the police station was enough for me. But . . .'

'What?' asked Kitt.

'I am rooting for him and Banks to solve the case. They're my only hope of seeing Owen's killer caught.'

Kitt looked at her friend then. If she was going to let her in on the fact she hadn't quite finished investigating this case for herself, now was the time. Somehow, however, that didn't seem like a good idea. The whole situation was complicated enough without raising Evie's hopes that she might be able to swoop in and save the day. Given the way Detective Sergeant Banks had conducted herself in the library, Kitt couldn't deny it would give her a certain level of satisfaction to crack the case before they did. For now, though, it was safer to convince Evie that the police had things well in hand.

'I presumed you weren't betting against them.' Kitt stepped closer to her friend and put an arm around her. 'They've not had much luck so far, but don't forget there's the forensics to come back yet. That'll open something up, I'm sure.'

Kitt's mobile buzzed in her pocket. She sighed and picked up the phone. A familiar and infectious giggle sounded out as Kitt put the phone to her ear.

'Grace? Is that you?'

'Y-y-yes . . .' Grace managed, before breaking again into another giggling fit.

Kitt closed her eyes and shook her head. 'Will you please stop giggling long enough to tell me a) what can't wait thirty minutes for me to get back to the library, and b) what is so funny?'

'H-have you seen the news?'

'What news?'

'Well, I'm looking at a video on Twitter – I think it's from the local lunchtime news.'

'I ask again, what news?' Kitt said, holding back a tut, but only just.

'It's about the murder. There's a clip of you refusing to comment. You look so cross.'

This comment sent Grace into further hysterics.

Evie tilted her head at Kitt.

'I'm so pleased you're enjoying the clip of me on the news, Grace,' Kitt said, while Evie covered her mouth and tried not to smile, 'but I don't think that me saying "no comment" really falls into the "news" category.'

'They're doing a piece on how evasive the police are being over answering questions about the incident. Since you're stood next to a police officer in the shot, they're insinuating even local residents are part of the conspiracy.'

'Oh well, that's typical,' said Kitt. 'They even manage to twist no news into news.'

'It's so funny,' said Grace. 'You should watch it.'

'No, thank you,' said Kitt. 'Is that all you called for?'

'Yes – oh, and to let you know Ruby dropped by and said she will read the Tarot cards for you if you want to find the murderer before the police do.'

'Thanks,' Kitt said, her tone flat enough for Grace to understand that was never going to happen. 'I'll see you in half an hour.'

Kitt looked over at Evie to see the smile had fallen from her face. She had taken the tea dress off and was staring with intensity at a single spot on the floor, which, as far as Kitt could see, had nothing remarkable about it.

'What's wrong?' asked Kitt, half-expecting Evie to break into tears by the look on her face.

Evie moved her lips one over the other, moistening them before speaking. 'Something . . . something just occurred to me . . . that I didn't think of before.'

'What?' asked Kitt.

Evie's eyes widened as she looked up at Kitt. 'I think I know who the murderer is.'

TWELVE

The Belle's Ball was held each year at an old Tudor hall, just a stone's throw from the Minster. Each year Kitt pulled her green silk evening gown with the sweetheart neckline out of the back of the cupboard for the occasion, and each year the conversation about cosmetics drooped to levels so inane, Kitt contemplated falling on one of the antique swords locked away in the glass cabinets hanging on the walls. Even an excruciating trip to A&E would be less painful than the irrelevancies oozing from the surrounding flock of over-painted lips.

Kitt sighed down at the crustless leek and feta quiche on the plate in front of her. It had been served with a 'side salad' that comprised three leaves of baby gem lettuce. Kitt had forgotten about the portion sizes at this event, or perhaps, she had, as with all other years, tried to convince herself that they were not as small as she remembered. But they were. Everyone in the room was 'watching their waist', a dull pastime that Kitt had given up on long ago. Life was so short and cruel, why deny yourself good food?

Kitt glanced at the others seated around the circular table alongside herself and Evie. Diane, who owned Daisy Chain Beauty – the salon where Evie worked – was leading the discussion on a new brand of hair wax they were buying in. Her partner, Keith, was sitting next to her with a sorrowful look in his watery grey eyes. Apparently he was finding the conversation at this event just as dull as Kitt. They were in a minority, however, as Deniz, the salon's chief stylist, his boyfriend Scott, and a trainee stylist called Jazz, were hanging off Diane's every word. And from what Kitt could hear in the background, the other fifty or so attendees, seated around similar tables, were relishing conversations along similar lines.

Unable to listen to one more word about how the levels of magnesium ascorbyl phosphate in this new product line would keep the hair looking healthier for longer, Kitt's mind drifted to the epiphany – of sorts – Evie had shared with her earlier that day. The realization that there was someone she had omitted from the list of people she gave to the police. Mr Ritchie Turner, the guy from a dating site that Evie had met with the week before Owen's murder, should also have been added to the list of people who knew the details of Evie's break-up with Owen. Kitt couldn't deny it seemed more than coincidental that this person had entered Evie's life right before her ex-boyfriend was murdered.

'With a bit of luck, whoever's responsible for that murder will have moved onto another town by now,' said Diane, jerking Kitt out of her thoughts.

It seemed the topic of conversation had moved on. Hardly

surprising, given the murderer who had struck four nights ago was still at large and, according to the news outlets local and national, the police still didn't have any suspects.

'Does that make it any better?' Evie asked, her glum face in contrast to the sunny tea dress Kitt had picked out for her. Evie pushed a piece of lettuce around her plate with her fork in a manner so sullen, Kitt wished they had kept the conversation on lighter issues, like the best methods of ensuring lipstick stayed on all night.

'I know it's not much,' said Diane, bringing a large glass of red wine to her lilac lips, 'but we've got to take whatever comfort we can get in times like these.'

'I don't think they will have moved on,' said Jazz, who was wearing one of the most dazzling dresses Kitt had ever seen. Jazz's black skin was draped in gold fabric from shoulder to toe, and the garment had sequins sewn in around the neckline. It flashed so brightly under the light cascading from the candelabra at the centre of the table, it was almost difficult for Kitt to look directly at her.

'Oh, here we go,' said Deniz, rubbing a hand over his designer stubble. 'Jazz, you're so macabre. Have you seen her Kindle wish-list?'

'Funnily enough I've been a bit busy running a salon to make time for that,' said Diane. 'Should I have?'

'It's an eye-opener.' Deniz opened his eyes wider for effect as he spoke. 'Every book is either the latest crime novel guaranteed to leave you with nightmares for months, or it's a book about serial killers.'

Jazz's left eye twitched. 'No, it's not.'

'I tell a lie, *The Notebook* is on there too,' said Deniz.

'I love that book,' Scott said.

Kitt wanted to give her tuppence worth on *The Notebook* and how there were much better books out there if romance was what you were in the market for. She also wondered about the other books on Jazz's wish-list, and if they were any good. But Jazz's tantalizing theory about why the killer had yet to leave the town was still to be discussed. Though Kitt knew her best friend wouldn't appreciate her continuing this line of conversation, if she wanted to make sure Evie was really off the suspect list for good she had to pounce on every piece of information that might lead her to the real killer.

'Why do you think the murderer is still in town, Jazz?' asked Kitt.

'Well,' Jazz glanced at Evie, 'Evie told us that the murder had been premeditated and elaborate.'

'So?' said Deniz.

'So, people who plan an elaborate killing like that often take pleasure in sticking around to watch what happens next,' said Jazz. 'Don't want to go into too much detail at the dinner table, but the kind of person who'd do that sort of thing would want to stick around and check out the carnage.'

'Seems like everyone in town's got a theory about this murderer,' said Keith, pouring himself another glass of blood-red wine, the same colour as the silk shirt he was wearing. Following Keith's comment, some other people at the table started to chip in with their own theories.

'Are you OK?' Kitt murmured in Evie's direction.

'Not really,' said Evie. 'If I'd known my ex-boyfriend's murder was going to be dissected over dinner, I probably wouldn't have come.'

'I'm sorry,' said Kitt, wishing she had managed to find another way to talk to Jazz and spare her friend. 'You know Yorkshire folk. Turning things over and over with their friends is the only way we really have of dealing with anything.'

Evie nodded. 'I know. But if everyone in town has got a theory, I don't see how it can hurt to let Halloran and Banks in on mine.'

'I told you,' said Kitt. 'I'm not stopping you from doing that.'

'But you don't think it's a good idea,' said Evie.

Kitt tilted her head at Evie. 'I didn't say that either; I said it's important not to get hysterical and throw around accusations. Passing his name onto the police is one thing, especially given he came into your life on the eve of this catastrophe. But you can't provide a clear motive, so it's unwise to make solid allegations. Especially given there is no physical evidence that we know of. That kind of detail will play a key part in catching the suspect.'

Evie folded her arms and stared at her friend. A small smile appeared on her lips. 'You've been reading up on murderers, haven't you?'

Kitt sat up straighter in her chair. 'No, of course not. I haven't got time to sit around looking at books about murder.'

'I don't believe you,' said Evie. 'I think you're secretly in research mode.'

Kitt sighed. 'I may have accidentally stumbled across one or two volumes about profiling criminals when I was clearing a bookshelf in the library today, but I hardly think that constitutes research.'

Evie shook her head at her friend. 'You'll take any excuse to read a new book.'

'Be that as it may, what I said stands,' said Kitt. 'Ritchie's a local bartender with zero connection to Owen as far as we know. He doesn't have a motive.'

Evie shrugged. 'Ashes to Ashes is one of those goth, metal clubs. Maybe he's into something dark?'

'You frequent vintage clothes shops, but you don't send all messages by carrier pigeon,' Kitt said, grinning at the idea.

'Maybe that is a bit stereotypical, but stereotypes exist for a reason, you know?'

'Yes, to belittle people.'

'All right, you've made your point.' Evie took a sip of her wine. 'Anyway, I don't really need to rely on stereotypes. I know why Ritchie did it.'

'I'm listening,' said Kitt.

'I hadn't eaten much when I went on that date, and got rather drunk really quickly, and told Ritchie ... well, everything.'

'Yes, you said you harped on about your break-up with Owen all night and it was clear there wouldn't be a date two, but what's that got to do with Ritchie's motive?' asked Kitt.

'That is his motive,' said Evie.

'What?'

'I didn't just harp on about the break-up. I told him my entire relationship history from start to finish. I even told him about the towels.'

Kitt raised both eyebrows. Whilst they were together, Evie subtly tried to convey to Owen that she looked good in bridal colours by buying a set of luxury white bathroom towels and parading around the flat in them every chance she got. She was convinced that if she came out of the shower wrapped in white every day, it was going to lead to a proposal.

'You must have been drunk,' said Kitt.

'I prefer the term "squiffy",' said Evie.

'And you think that the ordeal of listening to your relationship history provoked his killer instinct?'

'You don't think listening to me wailing about a break-up for three hours is enough to drive someone to murder?' said Evie.

Kitt forked slightly more quiche into her mouth than was polite, while trying to think up a diplomatic answer to that question. If her friend wasn't so desperate about what had happened, she'd have joked that if that was the motive, Kitt herself would be the chief suspect. She hadn't been tallying the number of hours she had spent listening to Evie's ongoing break-up monologue, that wouldn't be the action of a good friend, but what she did know was that it totalled more than the length of a dinner.

'But the police believe that the killer is known to Owen,' Kitt said, once she had finally swallowed her quiche. 'There was no sign of a break-in. Ritchie and Owen didn't know each other, and your theory about his motives is, at best, dubious.'

'I don't know for sure they didn't know each other,' said Evie. 'York is quite a small place when it comes down to it. And what about the way I met Ritchie? He's my first online dating experience. A total stranger. Everyone else I've been out with, I've connected with through a friend or workmate.'

'His presence on a dating website doesn't automatically make him suspicious,' said Kitt. 'After all, you were using the website too – LoveMatch, wasn't it?'

'Yeah, I guess it's just a frightening idea. I didn't know him at all, but through my own stupid fault he knows everything about the break-up. He could use the information against me, if he wanted.'

'Hi Evie,' said a velvety voice so rich and cloying it was almost smothering to the ear.

Evie turned her head towards a lady with sea-green eyes that caught the light in a way that was almost hypnotic. 'Heather, hi. Kitt, this is Heather, the woman who's been doing such a good job of my nails lately.'

'Pleasure to meet you,' said Kitt, admiring the way in which the woman's ash-blonde hair fell in rivulets over the scarlet dress she was wearing.

'You too,' said Heather, before turning back to Evie. 'I really just came over to check in with you. I'm surprised to even see you here after all that's happened.'

'It was a stupid decision. Which seems to be the one thing in life that I am good at,' said Evie.

'Hey, that's my best friend you're talking about,' Kitt said.

'Best friends,' Heather said, smiling between Evie and Kitt. 'I'm pleased to hear there's somebody looking out for you, especially at this difficult time.'

'In that respect, I am lucky,' said Evie.

Heather rubbed her arms as though she felt cold all of a sudden. 'You know, me and my boyfriend don't live far from Fulford, and we'd been out in that area the night the murder took place. It could have been us.'

'Well, it wasn't,' Evie said, lowering her eyes to the table. No doubt thinking about who *had* been murdered.

'What about you?' Heather gave Evie a sideways glance.

'What about me?' asked Evie.

'Were you . . . anywhere nearby where it happened?'

Heather wasn't looking at Kitt, but Kitt was scowling at her anyway. How could she ask Evie something like that? She was basically asking for her alibi. As if Evie hadn't been through enough without suspicion from her friends.

'No, I was staying at Kitt's house on the other side of town,' Evie said, her voice faint. No doubt she was worrying about what the rest of the people at the table thought. If they suspected she had a hand in Owen's death, despite her protests.

'So glad you weren't anywhere nearby,' said Heather, her tone even more sugary than before, perhaps to over-compensate for her blatant suspicion of Evie. 'I just wish I could catch them for you.'

'Me too,' said Evie. 'Whoever's responsible, I just wish—'

'Oh my God,' said Jazz, her voice striking a hard note of

fear as she pressed five talon-like fingernails against her cheek. 'Aren't they the coppers who were in the salon the other morning?' Deniz and Scott looked in the same direction as Jazz, and let go of each other's hands.

Heather also started and took a step backwards. 'Yes, they visited me too. That's them,' she said.

Looking to her left, Kitt saw DI Halloran striding towards them. His jaw was tight. His eyes were a cold, steel blue, just as they had been in her dream the other night. DS Banks stalked silently behind him.

On reaching the table, Halloran looked first at Evie and then at Kitt.

'Wha—' Kitt began, but Halloran cut her off.

'Evelyn Bowes. Katherine Hartley,' he said, before producing a pair of handcuffs. 'You are under arrest for the murder of Owen Hall.'

THIRTEEN

Kitt frowned at Evie, but her friend sat still and unresponsive. The librarian looked around the table of gawking faces. More people on other tables were starting to turn in their direction. Whispers passed from person to person, and all this was kindling to Kitt's fire. She couldn't lose her temper, however. It would look suspicious, and that wasn't going to serve either of them well just now.

Swallowing back her anger, Kitt rose slowly from her seat and stood face-to-face with Halloran. Even in heels she was no match for his height, but she glared at him all the same. The inspector didn't falter, but held her eye.

'*We* are under arrest?' Kitt said. Despite the sting in her tone, she kept her voice low.

'That's what I said,' Halloran replied.

'On what grounds?' said Kitt.

Halloran paused, probably assessing whether he should answer this question with an audience looking on. Some part of him must have understood, however, that Kitt and Evie were at a gathering amongst friends and colleagues.

Arresting them without any explanation may cause more trouble for him. 'We have forensic evidence that points to Ms Bowes's involvement in the murder, and given that you're her alibi, you're under arrest as an accessory.'

Kitt blinked hard. 'I don't believe it. A mistake has been made.'

Kitt waited for someone else at their table to chime in and agree with her. She glanced over at Diane, who had employed Evie for the last five years. Diane's eyes slowly dropped to the table, and she began fidgeting with her knife. Everyone else followed suit and refused to meet Kitt's eye.

Looked like it was Kitt and Evie against the world, then.

'What you do or do not believe is unimportant,' said Banks, the consonants sounding hard in her Scottish accent. 'You have the right to remain silent,' she continued, beginning to read Kitt and Evie their rights. The whole way through Banks's speech, Kitt kept her eyes on Halloran, her lips scrunching tighter in disgust with every sentence. Everyone in the room was looking over at their party now. Banks's penetrating voice was the only sound reverberating off the sandstone walls, the wooden beams that lined the ceiling, and the steel plates of the suit of armour standing in the corner of the room.

'Are handcuffs really necessary?' Kitt asked, glancing at the pair in Halloran's hands.

He paused, looking Kitt up and down from head to toe, making some unspoken calculation. He shook his head and tucked the cuffs away in his jacket pocket.

Kitt turned to her friend, who still hadn't spoken. 'Evie,' she said, tapping her on the shoulder.

Evie started, as though she'd just come out of a trance. 'I didn't do it. I didn't do this.'

'I know, neither of us did,' Kitt said. 'But we need to go with the officers now and sort this out. OK?'

Evie made the smallest of nods to confirm she'd heard Kitt's words.

'Now, put your coat on. It's not evening-dress weather out there,' Kitt said, leading by example and pulling her crimson winter coat over her green dress. Evie watched Kitt for a moment and then put her arms through the sleeves of her blue waterproof.

'Banks?' said Halloran.

'Sir?'

'Transport Ms Bowes back to the station in your car.'

'Sir,' said Banks, who planted her hand with unexpected gentleness on Evie's shoulder and led her out of the hall.

'This way, Ms Hartley,' said Halloran, as he waved towards the door.

Kitt began to walk in the direction Halloran had indicated. The inspector walked close enough behind her that she could almost feel his breath on the nape of her neck. His left hand pressed softly against the small of her back, guiding her forward as the assembly of Yorkshire-based beauty therapists began to mutter amongst themselves.

Kitt quickened her step. It was better not to hear what the local gossip mill was going to make of this incident. It would be quiet at this time of night in the Minster area.

Some cool night air and natural peace – rather than the oppressive silence of a social gathering gone wrong – would help her clear her head.

Outside, Halloran directed Kitt to his car and opened the rear door. Without looking at the inspector, she stepped inside and slipped onto the back seat. She expected the door to slam behind her, but the thud never came. Halloran was holding the door open for some reason. She glanced up to him frowning down at her. Perhaps he had something to say, but he wasn't being forthright about it, and Kitt had no particular desire to talk to him just then so she turned to catch hold of her seat belt, fastened it, and looked straight ahead until he at last closed the door.

The car had an earthy, mossy smell about it that reminded Kitt of the fresh air that drifted over the moorlands on a dewy spring morning. She had previously caught teases of this scent from Halloran himself, but in his car the effect was cumulative. Its potency somehow made it seem more masculine, and, against her will, Kitt breathed the scent in deeply.

Looking out of the window on the opposite side of the car, Kitt saw Banks drive past. Evie was in the back seat, her head pressed against the glass, no expression at all registering on her face.

Halloran slid into the driver's seat and looked at her through the rear-view mirror. Kitt narrowed her eyes, shook her head, and looked away.

There was a pause before Halloran started the ignition, checked his blind spot and eased the car out of the space on Goodramgate.

'So you're aware, we're going to be searching your property this evening, along with Ms Bowes's house,' said Halloran.

Kitt didn't look at the inspector, but said to a passing kebab shop, 'No need to feed the cat, I fed him before I came out tonight.'

'When we get to the station you'll be taken to the custody suite.'

Kitt caught Halloran's eye in the rear-view mirror and scowled. 'What a polite way to describe a police cell. Have you ever thought of being an estate agent? They're very good at descriptions like that. Although they do over-use the adjective "stunning".'

Halloran was concentrating on the road, but Kitt noticed his jaw tighten.

'It's standard procedure. You'll be searched too. And your fingerprints will be taken, and a photograph.'

'At least I'm wearing a nice dress for my first mugshot, I suppose.' Kitt folded her arms and looked out of the window.

'Just thought you should know what to expect,' said Halloran. His tone was a low, quiet warning that Kitt took unexpected pleasure in ignoring.

'Why? Did you draw the "good cop" straw again?'

'You're not helping yourself with that attitude, you know,' Halloran growled.

'How would you like me to respond to being arrested?' Kitt said. 'With a smile on my face? That's how the world thinks women should respond to everything.'

'That's not what I'm saying.'

'Then what are you trying to say?' asked Kitt.

'That I'm just doing my job, and that maybe you should have a bit of respect for that rather than looking at me like I'm the devil incarnate.'

Kitt's face slackened for a moment, but then she remembered Evie's blank expression in the back of Banks's car. Her inner bonfire was alight in an instant. Why did they have to make a scene like that in front of everyone? They had both been nothing but cooperative. Couldn't they have spared her and Evie the humiliation? 'I wouldn't think a seasoned police inspector would much care what a dirty criminal like me made of him.'

Halloran gripped the steering wheel tighter as he took a right towards Fulford. 'We have to follow the evidence where it leads. That's what an investigation is.'

Blindly, thought Kitt. But even in her petulance she thought better of saying that out loud.

'So if you've done that, your conscience is clear, isn't it? You don't need me to validate your actions.'

'I didn't say that I did,' Halloran said.

'You're leading me in conversational circles,' said Kitt. 'And in the meantime, the real killer is getting further away.'

Halloran shook his head. 'We have the killer in custody. Or at the very least the person most likely to be responsible for the killing.'

Kitt looked out of the window again.

'You're not even willing to consider the idea that your friend, the most likely suspect, is responsible for this crime?'

'No,' said Kitt, 'Evie would never take a life. She holds life more precious than vintage Chanel shoes, and for her that's really saying something.'

'Why does she feel that way?' said Halloran.

Kitt paused. There was an answer to that question, but Kitt feared giving it. 'It's a fairly natural philosophy, don't you think?'

'It has nothing to do with the overdose then?' said Halloran.

Kitt started and, without warning, her eyes filled with tears. Despite her surprise, she refused to let them fall. Crying would only make things worse. Being weak wasn't an option right now. She had to be strong for Evie.

'You know about that?'

It was a few years back now, that Evie had made her confession to Kitt. The pair had never discussed it again. The whole episode was Evie's greatest shame: when she was younger and her mum and dad were going through a divorce, she had tried to end her life by swallowing what was left of the family bottle of paracetamol.

'For serious crimes, we can get access to a suspect's medical file,' Halloran explained.

'She was fourteen, and didn't much understand the magnitude of what she was doing,' said Kitt.

'She wasn't in her right mind, and she did something unthinkable,' said Halloran.

'Exactly,' said Kitt.

'And I suppose that could never happen again?' Halloran said.

Kitt's breath caught in the back of her throat. Were the

police really going to hold Evie's most shameful moment over her head at this time of emotional distress? Could something Evie had done when she was fourteen really be factored into a murder case twenty years later? Kitt sat in silence for the rest of the journey, wondering what would become of her best friend, and of herself.

FOURTEEN

Kitt was awoken from her unscheduled nap by a firm tap on the shoulder. Halloran's eyes stared into hers. Her first instinct, thinking she was dreaming again, was to smile, but in a moment she remembered where she was. She had been curled up on a blue floor mat, one that resembled the kind used in PE classes at school. It was the only place to perch in the 'custody suite' she'd been assigned to at York Police Station. On entering, Kitt had been determined to stand out of pure cussedness, but that had lasted about ten minutes before she had slumped down on the sole soft surface and balled her body into a position that was comfortable enough to rest in.

'What time is it?' said Kitt.

Crouched down next to the mat Kitt had been sleeping on, Halloran looked at his watch and then back down at Kitt. 'Nearly two.'

'In the morning?'

'Yes,' Halloran said, before standing and offering Kitt his hand.

The librarian gave his hand her sternest stare. If she had dared to she would have narrowed her eyes for effect, but instead she sat upright and leaned on the wall for support as she manoeuvred into a standing position. On her way up, she noticed that her green evening dress was not designed for lying down in – at least not without revealing more cleavage than was proper.

Kitt adjusted the silk neckline into a more modest arrangement. A bit over-dressed for prison, she thought, but that was hardly her fault. If being arrested for murder had seemed in the realms of possibility, she would have worn her slacks.

She looked up to see Halloran slowly lower his outstretched hand. He inclined his head towards the door. 'This way, Ms Hartley.'

The corridor, though far too bright for Kitt's weary eyes, was much warmer than the custody suite had been. She was aware that her bare arms were covered in goosebumps and began rubbing them.

Halloran watched Kitt's movements, but didn't speak. Instead he waved a hand down the corridor and, just as he had before, placed his hand in the small of Kitt's back to guide her. She noticed her breath quicken when he did so, but reasoned this reaction away as nervousness. She was locked up in a police station for a crime she hadn't committed: of course her breathing was erratic.

In less than a minute, Halloran stopped outside a grey door and swung it open.

'Take a seat,' Halloran commanded.

Kitt took three steps into what she assumed was the interrogation room and sat down in a plastic chair next to a small rectangular table. She heard the door close behind her. Halloran's heavy footsteps echoed down the corridor lino. She was alone in a stark box room with grey walls that matched its grey door, and the atmosphere in the room for that matter.

Glaring at the large mirror set into the wall, Kitt wondered if it was two-way, like the mirrors in all the bestselling thrillers – did North Yorkshire Police have that kind of budget? Her understanding of police procedure was pretty much limited to the vintage mystery novels she had devoured growing up, and she had a feeling that things may have changed a bit since the days of Poirot and Nancy Drew.

Rubbing the end of her nose, she tried to ignore the stale scent hanging in the windowless room. It was reminiscent of festering, mouldy bread. Probably the consequence of one too many vending machine sandwiches being served in here after late-night interrogations. Even that unpalatable smell, however, was a welcome diversion from Kitt's thoughts about the state Evie must be in right now. Had Evie already been interrogated, or were they saving that to see what Kitt said first? Before Kitt had time to dissect the inspector's most likely interrogation tactics, the door swung open with a creak. The librarian turned in her seat to see Halloran striding into the room. Banks followed a pace behind him.

Halloran was carrying a mustard case file and a blue blanket. He paused to place the blanket over Kitt's shoulders.

'Thank you,' Kitt said, pulling the blanket close around her shoulders.

Halloran leaned over to a recording machine sitting on the table. He pushed the appropriate button and then looked back at Kitt. 'Have you been informed of your rights?'

'I have,' Kitt said.

Without another word, the two officers pulled out a grey plastic chair apiece, scraping the metal legs across the balding, beige carpet, before sitting in synchrony. Banks glared at Kitt across the desk, her lips pinched together. Halloran's expression was just as indecipherable as it had been when he had first appeared in the library, but his jaw was clenching in a manner that conveyed a certain sternness.

Kitt looked from one to the other. She opened her mouth to speak, but before she even finished her first word, Halloran produced a photograph from the case file and held it in the air. He then placed it on the table, pressed two fingers down on the image, and pushed it towards Kitt until it was sitting between her hands. With a frown, Kitt let her eyes drop from the blue depths of Halloran's to the photograph.

A pale, vacant-eyed Owen lay outstretched on what looked like laminate flooring. His arms were crossed over his body, and something was sticking out of his chest. A Stanwyck fountain pen? Kitt didn't want to look close enough to be sure.

She closed her eyes for a moment and then shook her head. 'Did you have to show me this?'

'Given that you're at least in part responsible for it, it seemed only fair,' said Banks.

Kitt pressed her lips together and stared into the negative space between the two officers.

'Aren't you going to deny it?' said Banks.

'That would be to credit the assertion with a degree of intelligence,' Kitt said, glancing first at Banks and then at Halloran.

'When in a police station, Ms Hartley, it is wise to deny murder if you're accused of it,' said Halloran. 'Assuming you think yourself innocent. Otherwise, we'll take your confession down now.'

'Fine,' said Kitt. 'I deny playing any part in the murder of Owen Hall.'

There was a pause.

'Ever been out to the Owl and Star on Fossgate, Ms Hartley?' asked Halloran.

'Once or twice. I live towards Clifton, so I'm more likely to stop off in the Exhibition at Bootham than anywhere else.'

'Interesting,' said Halloran. 'A witness placed a woman matching your description in that bar last Saturday night, with Owen. It was the last time he was seen alive.'

Kitt frowned. 'Exactly how did the woman fit my description?'

'Early thirties, red hair. Would you like me to show you a mirror?' said Banks.

'I wasn't aware that I was the only person fitting that description in the York area,' said Kitt.

'That's true,' said Banks. 'Let's not forget you have a twin sister. Perhaps she's doing your dirty work.'

'My sister has dyed her hair raven black for years,' said Kitt.

'Then that circles us back to you. Given you're the only redhead we know of with motive,' said Halloran.

'And what motive is that?'

'Well, must have been hard, seeing your best friend go through that kind of humiliation. Being ditched over Facebook, after nearly two years of commitment,' said Halloran.

'I won't deny that,' Kitt said, with a wave of her hand. 'But it only confirmed that he didn't deserve her. She put so much into their relationship, and he never seemed that grateful for any of it.'

'And for that, Owen deserved to be taught a lesson,' said Banks.

'No,' Kitt said. 'For that, Owen didn't deserve Evie's affections.'

Banks looked across at her partner, who produced another item from his file. A thin plastic bag containing a sheet of cream writing paper, spattered with crimson. Halloran pushed the bag over to Kitt. By the matte finish, Kitt could tell the page was of expensive stock, the kind you would have to buy from a stationery specialist. There was a note written across the paper in thick ink, which read: *I don't know how else to say this . . .*

'So this is the note Evie mentioned? The one at the murder scene.'

'That's right,' Halloran said. He was examining Kitt's face now. 'We didn't find any stationery like this when we searched your house, but what about if we searched your place of work, would we find writing paper like this?'

'Well, I do have a weakness for good stationery, by-product of being a librarian, but I don't recognize this brand.'

The officers stared at her.

'This is madness,' said Kitt. 'Evie and I were with each other at the time of the murder, which means we both have an alibi.'

'A very convenient alibi,' Banks said, folding her arms on the desk.

'Convenient?'

'The night Evie's ex-boyfriend is murdered, the two of you just happen to be having a night in together, with no other witnesses to prove your whereabouts,' said Banks.

'Why would we need another witness? Neither of us have any kind of criminal track record.'

'But you did have the means to kill Owen Hall,' said Halloran.

'What?' said Kitt.

'The toxicology report came back from the wine Owen ingested. He was served a deadly cocktail of toluene and hydrogen peroxide.'

'Peroxide, like bleach?' said Kitt, putting a hand around her throat, imagining.

'That's right,' said Halloran. 'Toluene is used in nail polish remover.'

'But who would voluntarily swallow those things?' said Kitt. 'You'd know straight away if you were handed a glass of wine with bleach in it.'

'Owen's bloodwork contained high quantities of diazepam.'

Kitt's heart started to beat faster and a frown crossed her face. Evie had a current prescription to diazepam.

'What is it, Ms Hartley?' Halloran said, his tone knowing. 'Can I take it from your expression that you know your friend has access to that particular substance?'

Recovering herself, Kitt glared at the inspector. 'You try leaning over massage clients all day. It makes Evie's back ache something terrible. The doctor prescribed the diazepam for the muscle spasms.'

'That's the story she's told you. But Evie didn't just have access to the drug used to sedate the victim, she had access to both of the chemicals used to poison him too, through her job at the salon,' said Banks.

'Evie had the means, she has motive, and she had opportunity,' said Halloran. 'She wouldn't need to break into Owen's home to attack him. She could just swing by, unannounced, and he'd open the door to her. Just as he opened the door to his killer.'

Kitt sighed and put her head in her hands. This was a nightmare. Kitt couldn't argue with the officers that all signs pointed to Evie, who seemed, as far as they were concerned, to have had some help from a mystery redhead. But it wasn't true. She wasn't going mad. She and Evie had spent last Saturday night at her cottage. They were innocent, no matter what the evidence suggested.

Kitt raised her head again and looked at the two officers. 'I suppose you have some hard forensic evidence to back up that theory, inspector?'

'We've just outlined the toxicology report . . .' Halloran began, but Kitt, losing patience, cut him off.

'I'm not talking about that. I'm talking about hard evidence. Evie's fingerprints. Her DNA on the wine glass. You have that?'

Halloran's jaw clenched even tighter than it had before.

'Perhaps we are giving Evie too much credit.' There was that growl again. 'Perhaps she's just a convenient scapegoat, for you.'

'So now I'm the killer? Not Evie? Seems a bit indecisive.'

'Oh, she's involved,' said Halloran, 'but perhaps she's just your pawn?'

'Don't you specialize in Women's Studies in your role as a librarian, Ms Hartley?' asked Banks.

'What? Yes. Why?'

'You must have an acute sense of the struggles women go through. It's not unbelievable that when your friend was treated in this way you decided to take matters into your own hands,' said Banks.

'Or maybe this isn't about Evie at all. Maybe it's about Theo,' said Halloran.

Kitt's head jolted in Halloran's direction. All oxygen left her lungs, and she could feel the pained expression painting itself across her face. 'How do you know about Theo?'

'We found a notebook in your handbag.'

'You read my journal?' Kitt crossed her arms loosely over her chest.

'Yes,' Halloran said.

'I can't believe you did that; reading my diary is like

seeing me naked,' said Kitt, thinking about all the things she had written in there that she thought nobody would ever see. Notes of anger about Michelle's reluctance to stand up for any good cause, in-depth descriptions of how she had felt for Theo, and how she'd felt after he had left, and, most excruciating of all, detailed sexual fantasies that, being perpetually single, she had explored in the private pages of her diary rather than in the flesh.

Halloran stared hard at her. 'Within the realm of the law, I'll do whatever I have to do to be able to tell Owen's mother that we've caught the person or people who killed her son.'

Kitt saw a flinch flutter over Halloran's face as he said this.

She hadn't thought about that. About the fact Halloran and Banks would have had to inform Owen's mother that her son was no longer alive. In her defence, she had been preoccupied with how all this was affecting Evie. Kitt looked at the lines around Halloran's eyes and wondered if there was a mark for every time he had knocked on a door to deliver the worst possible news. If so, he had done this more times than anyone would want to.

'Do you have a partner of your own, Ms Hartley?' asked Banks.

'No,' Kitt said, blinking a few more times than was natural.

'How long have you been single?' said Halloran.

Kitt placed a hand to her temple. 'How is this relevant?'

'Answer the question,' Halloran said, in a quiet, dangerous tone.

'About . . . ten years now,' Kitt said. It'd been a long time since she'd had to outright confess that fact, and her head suddenly felt very heavy, desperate to tilt downwards. Still, she fought to keep her chin level and refused to let her eye contact with the officers waver.

'Ten years?' Halloran repeated. It was lightning quick, but Kitt still caught it – his eyes darting down her upper torso before snapping back to her face. 'So, nobody since Theo?'

'Nothing serious. But, last I checked, it's not a crime to be single.'

'But you have been single for a very long time,' said Banks, placing emphasis on the word 'very'. 'Why is that?'

Kitt's stomach muscles clenched. 'I really don't see how this is relevant to a murder case.'

'When interviewing a suspect, we have to explore any unusual behaviour in our line of questioning,' said Halloran.

Kitt bristled. 'And being single falls into the category of unusual?'

'Not for one year, or two, but for ten years, that's the kind of behaviour that might indicate a loner, an outsider, someone with a great deal of resentment towards the social world they're not a part of.'

Kitt nodded. 'I see. So by your assessment I am both in collusion with my best friend, and a loner. What a complicated life you imagine I lead.'

The inspector offered Kitt nothing more than a hard stare in return. Realizing he was not going to retract his question, Kitt sighed and added, 'There is nothing suspicious about being single. Perhaps that could be put on police record somewhere. I haven't met a partner who I've felt was worth all the hassle of a relationship. I'm not the kind of woman who'll settle for just anyone who comes along.'

'All that time, and nobody has turned your head?' asked Halloran.

'No,' Kitt almost whispered.

'You've got to understand how this looks,' said Halloran. 'Your best friend gets her heart trampled on. You've held onto all this anger over what happened to Theo.'

'I'm not angry,' Kitt interrupted, wishing Halloran would stop saying that name.

'Your diary tells a different story,' said Halloran. 'It's a portrait of a woman who is angry about the way she was treated. A woman who might take matters into her own hands.'

Kitt's eyes filled with tears in spite of herself – the idea that Halloran or anyone else would see her that way was too much. 'If you read my diary from cover to cover and came up with such a reductive opinion of me, then I'm sorry for you,' she said.

Halloran's eyes flickered. It wasn't quite a wince, but it wasn't far off.

Determined to press her advantage, Kitt continued: 'The only time I've taken matters into my own hands lately is when you wrongly arrested Beth Myers. I imagine Mr Rampling mentioned my involvement?'

Halloran cleared his throat. 'Yes.'

'Why would I help you discount another suspect if I were the murderer? Or if my best friend were the murderer?'

'To try and throw us off the scent. I've dealt with my fair

share of people who've been led astray by friends with criminal intentions and murderous manipulators in my time on this job. The only question is, which one of these two people are you?' said Halloran, the tightness around his mouth showing again.

'You have no hard evidence I was involved,' said Kitt. 'Look, I've come in quietly, I've answered your questions, I've explained my whereabouts, and you don't have any forensic detail to tie me to this murder. If you're going to hold me any longer, I'm going to have to insist on having a solicitor present.'

Halloran and Banks looked at each other in silence and then back at Kitt.

FIFTEEN

The doors of York Police Station swooshed open and Kitt turned to see Inspector Halloran striding towards her. Arms bared to the night-time chill, Kitt rose from her perch on the concrete steps and held out her hand for her satchel. Overcome with the desire for fresh air the moment the officers had granted her release, Kitt had requested to wait outside while her personal effects were recovered.

'Thank you,' Kitt said to Halloran as he held her coat while she put her arms through the sleeves. For all his growling and snapping, he could be a gentleman when the situation called for it. She buttoned her coat in silence, arranged her navy scarf around her neck, and placed her trilby on her head. When she at last looked up, she realized Halloran had been studying her every move.

'You really won't consider releasing Evie?' Kitt said. She hadn't been allowed to visit her friend, and Kitt could only imagine what kind of state she had worked herself into by this point.

'We can't release her,' Halloran said, his tone much gentler than it had been in the interrogation room.

'But you're releasing me . . .'

'A decision that can be reversed if there's something you want to tell me,' said Halloran.

'That's not what I meant,' said Kitt, with a sharp note in her voice. 'I have the same alibi she does.'

'Yes, but you didn't have direct access to the murder weapon. Your friend did. You may not be her accomplice, but someone else may have been. Just because she didn't administer the poison herself doesn't mean she wasn't behind the killing.'

'I know she wasn't.' Kitt kept her voice steady. 'What about financial trouble? I wondered if that could be a factor.' The librarian thought back to what the man in the betting shop had said about the people who borrow from loan sharks who are never seen again. She had wondered if Owen might have been one of them – it was what had driven her to investigate that avenue.

'Nothing in Owen's financial records indicate anything suspicious,' said Halloran.

Kitt breathed a small sigh of relief that she wouldn't have to go back to Sure Bet and meet Whippet Man's contact, but in the same moment realized that without that theory Evie looked guiltier than ever.

'Evie's not your murderer,' Kitt said. 'Why can't you see that?'

Halloran took a step closer to Kitt, until he was standing just a pace away, and looked deep into her eyes.

'You really need to start considering the fact that your friend could be lying to you. People aren't always who we want them to be. Or who we think they are.' The inspector's brow lowered. 'Given that Owen was last seen alive with a red-haired woman, she may even be going so far as trying to frame you.'

It wasn't comfortable to hold his gaze, but Kitt pushed herself to anyway. 'You really have a low opinion of people, don't you? Aren't police officers supposed to believe in the tenet of innocent until proven guilty?'

'In a court of law, yes. But a detective can't afford to think that way. Not without paying a heavy price.'

Halloran's features had hardened, and Kitt couldn't help but wonder if the price Halloran had paid was his faith in people. Kitt lowered her eyes at the realization that she related to that feeling all too well. Would she wind up like Halloran one day? Unable to see the good even in a soul as well-meaning as Evie?

She decided to have one more go at convincing him. 'I'm sure that more often than not the culprit in these cases is the most obvious person, but in this case, I can vouch for the fact that it's not. Won't you at least consider the idea that the killer is someone you haven't thought of?'

'It is a consideration,' said Halloran. 'But I have to warn you it's highly unlikely, especially given the amount of evidence that points to Evie.'

'But sometimes the evidence must point in the wrong direction. What about *The Moonstone*, *And Then There Were None*, *The Long Goodbye*?'

'What are those, books?'

'Please tell me you've at least read some Raymond Chandler in your time?' Kitt huffed. 'Surely that's required reading for a police inspector?'

'I don't remember being issued with a reading list,' Halloran said, a small smile just about visible behind his beard. 'Do I need to have the talk with you about the difference between fiction and reality?'

Kitt sighed; people were always so dismissive about how much truth there was in fiction, but writers had to get their ideas from somewhere. 'All right then, *High Dive*, *In Cold Blood*, er . . . *The Long Drop* . . .'

Halloran shook his head at Kitt. 'What are you doing now?'

'Listing books based on real-life murders.'

'You know, not all the answers are found in books,' he said, lowering the pitch and volume of his voice. 'Some answers are found through experience . . . through the senses. Through seeing, and tasting, and touching . . .'

Kitt swallowed hard. There was something distracting, perhaps even enthralling about Halloran's voice in that register. Was he doing this on purpose? Diverting her from her task of making a case for Evie's innocence? If so, he was doing a better job of it than Kitt would like to admit.

Remembering the importance of putting sisters before misters, she cleared her throat.

'Doesn't the fact that Evie would know all of this evidence would point to her give you pause? Why would anyone go to the lengths of orchestrating a murder this intricate only to make all of the clues point to them?'

Halloran took in a deep breath. 'There's a certain inno-cence about you, Ms Hartley, that's somewhat endearing, and I wish I didn't have to be the one to shatter it.'

Innocence? If Halloran still thought her to be the innocent-minded type, he couldn't have read her diary that closely.

'Some people rely on the evidence pointing at them as a get-out,' Halloran continued. 'They make exactly the excuse you just did. Explaining how stupid they'd have to be to leave clues that point to them. Deep down they're just playing a sick game, watching the police struggle to solve the puzzle from close quarters.'

Kitt shook her head. Helplessness was her least favourite state of being. How could it be that there was nothing she could do to better her friend's situation? No matter what she said to Halloran, he wasn't going to change his mind, at least not unless she could present him with another plau-sible suspect.

It was this thought that summoned an idea in Kitt's mind, the kind of idea that only seems like a solid prospect at three a.m. after very little sleep.

Kitt glanced at her watch. 3.10 a.m. Ashes to Ashes was, she believed, open until around the five o'clock mark. There was still time.

'I understand your dilemma,' Kitt said with a meek smile. 'I— I have to go.'

'Home?'

Kitt nodded. 'I've got to be at work in six hours.'

'I can drive you,' said Halloran.

'No, I'll walk.'

'It's safer if I drive you.'

'I'll be perfectly safe,' said Kitt. 'I don't need to worry at all, do I? You've caught the real murderer.'

Halloran sighed and folded his arms over his chest as Kitt turned and walked as quickly as her feet would carry her towards the city centre.

SIXTEEN

Kitt peered into the murky blankness of Mad Alice Lane. It was one of the city's many winding snickelways and named after the legendary Alice Smith who was hanged at York Castle in 1825 for, as the name implied, being two bob short of a pound. A fact Kitt recalled learning many years ago on a school trip to York from her home town of Middlesbrough. Back then, her twelve-year-old brain imagined madness as a sort of malevolent sprite that sneaked up and caught a person unawares, making off with their soul without any prior warning. Although the unsettling atmosphere of the snickelway – which reeked of nicotine and sour drains – had no doubt played its part in her nightmarish childhood vision, it occurred to her that perhaps the assessment she had made in her tender years wasn't that far off the mark. Moreover, she couldn't help wondering if her soul was the latest to be claimed.

Certainly, forty-eight hours ago the idea of hanging around the city's alleyways after dark in a bid to question a would-be murderer based on some whim Evie had wouldn't have struck Kitt as an even remotely sane prospect. But then again, neither would the idea that a person might take the time to off Evie's ex-boyfriend, especially in the uncanny, melodramatic manner in which it had happened. Kitt had kissed sanity goodbye the moment those police officers had walked into the library three mornings ago, and the only way of returning the universe to its rightful order was to find out who had really killed Owen.

Somewhere down this snickelway she would find Ashes to Ashes, the nightclub where Ritchie Turner worked. The winding passages off the main tourist tracks through the city wouldn't ordinarily give Kitt pause, even in the dark. The library was open late to accommodate the odd working schedules of university students, and she quite often found herself walking home along the lonely river long after nightfall.

After all she had been through overnight, however, she couldn't stop thinking about the fact that whoever the murderer was, they must have some kind of connection with her life. If the culprit knew all the details of Evie's break-up, it was a sensible deduction that they knew the identity of her best friend too. With the revelation of the red-haired woman last seen with Owen, it seems they were counting on the fact that alongside Evie, Kitt would be under suspicion from the police when the body was found.

Despite her unease, the librarian stepped forward into the darkness, wishing she could shake the image of Owen lying vacant-eyed in that photograph Halloran had pressed her to look at. Why did she have to think of a thing like that at a moment like this when there was not so much as a dim streetlight to comfort her? Even the *clip-clack* of Kitt's black court shoes echoing along the alley sent a shiver right through her, the sound scratching its fingernails down to the end of every nerve.

Walking further into the alley, Kitt stroked the faux fur cuffs of her crimson winter coat. The gentle textures soothed her and served to steady her breathing.

At least, until she heard it.

A shuffling sound, not ten paces behind her. Not sure enough to be footsteps. It was a much slyer sound. The noise shoes make when they're trying not to be heard; a soft scuffing against paving.

Kitt's shoulders stiffened, but she didn't turn or stop walking. She kept her pace unaltered as though she hadn't noticed anything. The nightclub couldn't be too far down here. It was unlikely that whoever was behind her knew where she was going. If she could just make it as far as the club she could duck inside before they had a chance to stop her. Whatever happened next, at least there would be witnesses. She could call for a taxi if she didn't think it was safe to go back outside. But it was probably nothing, just some drunk, or maybe a homeless person seeking shelter. It might not even be a person at all. That kind of sound could be made by a piece of stray litter being blown across the ground, Kitt told herself.

But her heart knew better.

Somebody was following her. She could now see the red neon sign for Ritchie's club blazing out of the blackness.

Against her will, Kitt's stride quickened. Safety was in sight. Or at least temporary safety, given she was on her way to talk to a murder suspect.

Speeding up, however, had been a mistake. Whoever was following her had speeded up too.

Perhaps they did know her destination after all. But how?

Abandoning all hope of seeming casual, Kitt scurried towards the club's heavy black door and, without looking back, bolted inside.

The thumping of her own heart was at once drowned out by the thundering beat of music Kitt could only categorize under the banner of heavy metal. The club itself turned out to be little more than a blacked-out room with strobe lighting. Through the flickering white flashes, Kitt noticed that large red skulls had been stencilled onto the walls, but other than that, it was pretty bare. A makeshift sign Sellotaped to the wall proclaimed the £8 entry fee. The 'ticket booth' consisted of a lad with a thick crop of green hair that almost touched his shoulders, sitting on an upturned beer crate.

The young man held out his hand and Kitt riffled through her handbag, pulling out her purse so she could pay the eight pounds. As she did so, the man pressed a black stamp onto the back of her hand. When he removed it the word 'Sinner' was revealed in thick black ink. Kitt raised an eyebrow at the unwanted brand, but thanked the heavens Grace wasn't here to witness this moment – she'd never hear the end of it.

Kitt turned towards the dance floor to see gangs of sweaty

twenty-somethings leaping up and down in time to the rhythm – or as close to that as they could get given the rau-cous nature of the music – heedless of the unwashed smell emanating from every surface, or the minimalist décor.

Evie had said Ritchie worked at the bar, which stood at the other side of the room. Kitt began her passage across the dance floor, her journey punctuated by looks of narrow-eyed confusion and pointing fingers. She reasoned that this was because she was the only person not wearing a faded T-shirt declaring allegiance to her favourite metal band, or perhaps because Kitt insisted on walking, as she always did, with a sure, authoritative march. Her shoulders were pushed back and her eyes were fixed straight in the direction of travel. Given that most of the patrons had already drunk enough to have difficulty standing, let alone walking, she didn't exactly fit in.

On reaching the bar, which was just a length of plywood flooded with a river of stale lager, a barmaid with bob-length cherry red hair came over to serve.

'What can I get you?' she asked, tugging on a studded leather collar around her neck that looked a touch too tight for comfort.

'Actually, I was hoping to talk to Ritchie. Is he on shift tonight?' said Kitt.

The barmaid's eyebrows, black as Whitby jet, sank into a slight frown and she looked Kitt up and down before replying: 'Yeah, he's just at the end of the bar over there; he's off to do a glass collection in a minute so I'd catch him quick.' With that, the barmaid strutted partway down the bar in her fitted black satin dress and fishnet stockings to serve another customer.

The second Kitt looked at the man she assumed to be Ritchie, she could see why Evie had agreed to go on a date with him. Evie was a sucker for any potential suitor who had height on their side, and she also had a weakness for men with brown hair. Ritchie ticked both of these boxes and was dressed in a sharp black shirt and a pair of black jeans. His fingernails were painted with black nail polish and, given that Evie grew up in the quaint market town of Thirsk, about twenty minutes outside the city, Kitt imagined her friend had thought that a rather edgy, alluring feature. The only obvious problem with him was his shoes, which were white, pointy leather affairs with tassels at the ends of the laces. Kitt wondered where anyone would even go to purchase shoes like that post-1978. Perhaps he had picked them up in one of the vintage shops along Gillygate, mistakenly believing he could bring that look back. His crimes against style aside, he didn't look like a murderer. But what did a murderer look like, anyway? According to Halloran, Kitt herself fitted the description.

She walked towards Ritchie and tapped him on the shoulder. 'Mr Turner?'

Turning from the stack of glasses he had been pushing over the bar, he looked hard at the stranger in front of him. 'Yeah.'

Kitt raised her voice to make sure she was being heard over the music. 'My name is Katherine Hartley. I'm here to speak with you about Evie Bowes.'

Ritchie's frown deepened. 'That bird off LoveMatch?'

'Bird?' said Kitt, at once regretting the harsh note in her voice. That was hardly likely to put Ritchie in the mood for a friendly chat regarding his whereabouts last Saturday night. She was over-tired and not thinking clearly. She needed to get her head straight on her shoulders if she was going to be of any use to Evie.

'If you're here because she's after a second date, you can forget it,' Ritchie said.

'That's not—' Kitt began, but Ritchie cut her off.

'I was proper gutted about that. A date with a blonde masseuse.'

Kitt bit hard on her tongue. Evie hated the term masseuse. She thought it made her sound cheap, and Kitt agreed that it did have unsavoury connotations. 'Massage therapist' was the preferred term, but having just objected to his use of 'bird' she couldn't very well start interjecting again. She needed Ritchie to feel at ease.

'I couldn't believe she was single,' he continued, 'but when we got to the restaurant she cried on and off for two hours solid. Said one of the waiters reminded her of her ex, and that was it. I wound up getting her bloody life story. Still, at least she paid for her half of the bill, I suppose.'

'She always pays her way, our Evie,' said Kitt, doing all she could to ignore the heat building in her chest. Sure, listening to Evie wailing over an ex wouldn't be fun when you were supposed to be on a date with her, but those were the actions of a distraught human being, and anyone paying even half as much attention as they should could tell Evie was a woman with a good heart within ten minutes of meeting her. A little compassion wouldn't have gone amiss.

'Anyway,' Ritchie said, seeming to remember himself, 'I'm at work so I can't really talk. What do you want?'

'I won't keep you long,' said Kitt. 'It's just that something rather terrible has happened. It's quite distressing, and if I can help it, I'd like to spare you the details.' Kitt looked into Ritchie's brown eyes, trying to make contact with his sensitive side. She wanted to believe he had one. 'It would help me a great deal if you could remember where you were on Saturday evening.'

Ritchie took a step back and folded his arms. He looked at Kitt sidelong. 'What you want to know that for?'

'Thing is,' Kitt began, 'there's been a murder.'

'A murder,' Ritchie said, taking a moment to digest the information. 'In York?'

'Yes,' Kitt said. 'Didn't you hear about it on the news?'

Ritchie shook his head. 'Don't read the news much. I sleep the days and spend my nights in here.'

'Of course, working nights must be a killer,' said Kitt, and at once widened her eyes at her own phraseology. It almost sounded like an accusation, though Ritchie hadn't seemed to take it as such.

Kitt studied his face for any hint of expression. Any tick or giveaway. He was denying knowledge of the murder. That was a piece of information to note; if she was careful about what she said he might give himself away by knowing too much. She tried to remember exactly what she had read about the murder in the early evening paper. What information could be considered common knowledge, and what details only the killer might know. But it had been difficult to focus on those details, because, although they hadn't named Evie, it did mention that the victim's ex-girlfriend had been questioned by police. Evie had been devastated, and all this had happened just hours before she was officially arrested for murder. Kitt seethed at the injustice: whoever was framing Evie deserved locking up, and more.

Ritchie stared harder at Kitt. 'Are you the police or something?'

'No, I'm not the police,' said Kitt.

'Who are you then?'

'I'm ... well, I'm a librarian,' Kitt said.

'A librarian?' Ritchie echoed with a scoff. 'Yeah, you look the type. But then,' he added, leaning in so his face was only a couple of inches away from Kitt's, 'they do say it's always the quiet ones.'

Kitt held Ritchie's eye, not permitting the muscles in her face to so much as twitch. 'I never said I was a quiet librarian, Mr Turner. I simply stated my job title.'

'Well, I don't know what business you've got asking me questions, but whatever's going on, it's got nothing to do with me and I haven't got time for this.' Ritchie was about to walk away when Kitt put her hand on his arm. He was being awkward and, though that wasn't a crime, it was making him look more suspicious by the minute.

'The ex-boyfriend Evie told you about ... he's the one who's dead,' said Kitt. Ritchie didn't speak or move or even flinch. He just stared at Kitt and waited for her next sentence.

'Several clues at the crime scene suggest the culprit knew all the intimate details of Evie's break-up. The number of people on that list is short, and anyone on it is automatically a police suspect, including you. If you have no reason not to answer my question about your whereabouts, please tell me where you were on Saturday. If you refuse, I'm going to waste no more time before passing my concerns about you onto the police.'

Ritchie turned and squared up to Kitt, his stare dark and intense. 'And what concerns do you have exactly? Given that this is the first time you've ever met me.'

'My chief concern is that three days after you learned all of the intimate details of my friend's break-up, her ex was found dead with a note pinned to his chest quoting his break-up message to Evie, word for word,' said Kitt.

Ritchie swallowed hard enough and paused long enough to raise Kitt's hopes that he might cooperate.

'Ritchie, I could do with a hand if you're finished talking to your friend,' another bartender called over. Kitt glanced over to see who it was who had interrupted at a rather pivotal moment and saw it was a stout, blocky young man with dark grey eyes and a closely shaven haircut that made the angles of his face seem severe. He had fewer lines at the corners of his eyes than Ritchie, so was probably a little bit younger. As his eyes shifted from Ritchie to Kitt, she noticed a sort of emptiness in them that left her feeling as one does while walking home on a bitter winter's night, when your muscles lock in the chill. Looking at him, Kitt made a mental note not to suggest a work night out to Ashes to

Ashes. She wasn't convinced she was tough enough to survive a whole evening in company like his.

'I can't get into this, I'm busy,' Ritchie said, drawing the librarian's gaze back to him.

'But—'

'Look,' Ritchie said, grabbing both of Kitt's arms tighter than she remembered anyone doing in her life, and shaking her.

'I suggest you let the lady go,' a man's voice said somewhere off to the left, just loud enough to be heard over the music. It was a voice Kitt recognized.

Slowly releasing his grip on Kitt, Ritchie turned to see Halloran standing just a foot away. He produced his badge from the inside pocket of his dark grey coat.

'Ritchie Turner, I presume?' said Halloran. 'I'd like to ask you a few questions.'

Ritchie frowned between Kitt and Halloran for a second before turning and making a run for it, presumably towards a back door. But Halloran was after him like a shot and he didn't get more than ten paces. Within moments Halloran had Ritchie's hands clasped behind his back, walked him back to the bar, and pushed his head down on the surface as he handcuffed him.

Kitt's widened eyes met the moody blue of Halloran's. He glared at her for just long enough to let her know he was deeply displeased, before turning away to concentrate on keeping a struggling Ritchie in check. Kitt didn't need Ruby's professed psychic abilities to foresee a return visit to the custody suite in her near future, and at that thought the librarian bit down hard on her lower lip.

SEVENTEEN

Halloran paced the musty-smelling carpet, which was beige and patterned with dark green diamonds. 'You better start talking, fast.'

It had been some minutes now since a uniformed constable had shunted a handcuffed Turner off to the police station, where, it was understood, Banks would question him, and no doubt Evie, further. The inspector had wasted no time in escorting Kitt into the Ashes to Ashes back office to ask a few questions of his own. The room was panelled in dark hardwood, and Kitt wouldn't have liked to have guessed how long it had been since the place had been given a decent wipe down. The bulbs on the black beaded chandelier hanging overhead were so covered in grime they were doing little to illuminate the situation, and a sickening mist of stale nicotine hung all around.

'I'm sorry, I . . .' Kitt began, but then sighed and lowered her head. She couldn't think straight, not right now.

'You can start by explaining why you ran straight to the next suspect on our list the second you were released from police custody.' Halloran's eyes were fierce and unblinking.

Kitt opened her mouth to speak again and then paused. The scuffling sound in the alley. Halloran interjecting at just the moment Ritchie grabbed hold of her . . . 'Wait, did— did you follow me here from the station?'

Halloran tilted his head. 'You're a suspect in a murder case. Of course I followed you.'

Not being a trained officer herself, Kitt had no idea if this was as normal as Halloran was implying, but one thing was clear: the inspector was going to take every possible advantage and opportunity to solve the case. It was a thought that should have comforted Kitt and yet somehow there was a disconcerting element to it. Something about him seemed more obsessive than professional.

She watched Halloran as he continued his protest march, causing small dust plumes to mushroom out of the carpet. In fact, dust was a major theme in the Ashes to Ashes office. One felt that, with another round of brainstorming, the owners could have come up with a far more appropriate name for their establishment.

'So, letting me go, that wasn't because you believed I was innocent,' said Kitt, her heart sinking. 'It was just an opportunity to follow me.'

Halloran stared at her. 'I hoped you'd go straight home, like you said you would.'

'Wish I had,' said Kitt, raising her eyebrows. 'That way, I'd still believe I'd got through to you. That you were coming around to the idea Evie and I weren't responsible for Owen's murder.'

'You haven't answered my question, about why you came here and tipped off a potential suspect,' said Halloran.

Kitt closed her eyes, resting them for just a moment. 'My best friend was rotting in a police cell for a crime she had nothing to do with. My best friend. I couldn't let that kind of thing happen on my watch.'

'If you had your suspicions about Turner, why didn't you say something about him when you were being questioned?' Halloran said, folding his arms across his chest.

'I assumed Evie would have mentioned him as a potential suspect: she's been talking about it for the last day or so,' said Kitt.

'Evie did mention him. Why didn't you?'

Kitt put a hand on her hip. 'Because I've had a little experience over the last few days of what happens when a person is falsely accused. I wasn't about to go and put someone else in that same boat without being sure there was something to it.'

'It's not your job to decide that, it's mine,' said Halloran.

'I acted in good conscience. I'm sorry if you don't agree with that.' Kitt's voice had risen in volume. Halloran's expression grew sterner, and she checked herself. 'Besides anything else, I didn't want to waste any more police time.'

'It's not your place to decide what is and isn't a waste of time on my investigation.' He took a step closer to Kitt.

Kitt ran a hand through the front of her hair and sighed.

'Look,' said Halloran. 'You saw Ritchie's reaction when he saw me.'

'At the very least, he's got something to hide,' said Kitt.

'And that something could have something to do with Owen's death,' said Halloran. 'And Evie.'

Kitt frowned. 'So now you think they're in on it together?'

'Unlike you, I have to be open to the possibility.'

Kitt looked at the lines creasing the skin at the corner of Halloran's eyes. 'That may be, but he only met Evie last week.'

'So?'

'So, that doesn't seem long to plot a murder . . . not that I would know anything about that,' Kitt said, raising her hands in mock surrender.

Halloran cleared his throat. 'You seem to mean well, Ms Hartley, but you're going to have to promise me you're not going to take matters into your own hands again. What you did was dangerous.'

'I can't make you that promise. Not so long as Evie's a suspect in this case. She's my best friend. She's one of the few people on this planet who's ever got close to understanding me . . .' Kitt's eyes widened. That was a slip. She would never usually convey something that personal to somebody she didn't know. 'Never mind. You get where I'm coming from.'

'Kitt,' said Halloran. It was the first time the inspector had called her by her first name, and the sound raised the hairs on her arms. 'Keep this up and there's a chance I'll have to arrest you.'

'Wouldn't be the first time.'

'I mean it. Perverting the course of justice in this kind of case is taken seriously.'

'I understand,' said Kitt. 'You do what you've got to do. I'll do what I've got to do, for my friend, and to keep things square with my own conscience.'

'Kitt . . .'

Halloran took another half-step towards her and looked as though he was about to say something else when his jacket pocket began to vibrate. The inspector sighed, walked a couple of paces in the direction of the door, and pulled out his mobile.

'Halloran,' he said into the receiver. 'What—?' Halloran swallowed hard and a shadow that had nothing to do with the dim lighting fell over his face. 'When?' he asked, his eyes flitting over at Kitt. 'All right. I'll be right there.'

Halloran shoved the phone back in his pocket and was silent. It was one of those hard silences one knows not to break. The inspector's breathing deepened as he looked once more at her.

'Does the name Adam Kaminski mean anything to you?' His voice was quiet, dangerous.

'Adam . . .' Kitt frowned.

'Don't play games with me, do you know him?' Halloran half barked.

'Of the two of us, I am not the one playing games here,' said Kitt, that feeling of uncertainty about the inspector rising to the surface again. The feeling that he wasn't completely in control.

'Do you know him?' Halloran shouted.

'No!' Kitt shouted back. 'I've never heard of him. Why?'

Halloran ran both hands through his dark hair and tugged. His whole posture had stiffened. 'He's just been found near the old chocolate factory, murdered.'

'I . . .' Kitt brought a hand up to the collar on her winter coat and stroked the soft material. 'I'm so sorry to hear that. Does this mean . . . ?'

Halloran strode back towards Kitt. 'Have you been near there tonight?'

'You know where I've been tonight, in police custody.'

'Earlier today then?'

'I have a job, Inspector Halloran. I was at the library.'

Halloran stared down at Kitt, his face only a few inches from hers. 'Don't be surprised if I come knocking on your door again. I'm not going to stop until I catch whoever's responsible for this.'

The inspector shook his head before stalking out of the office, leaving an open-mouthed Kitt wondering what on earth she should do next for the best.

Pulling her phone from her satchel, she began writing a text message to her sister, Rebecca.

Becca, have you ever treated any patients who have been deliberately poisoned? What kind of circumstances does it usually happen under? Please keep this convo between us. Mam doesn't need to know.

Then she wrote another message to Grace.

Good morning. There's been another murder. When you wake up, please use your incredible cyberstalking skills to find out all you can about a man called Adam Kaminski. Lives in York. Tell nobody.

EIGHTEEN

Kitt was pretending to read the latest budget report for her department on her computer screen. In truth, she was flicking between that and the local news website – *News on the Ouse* – scanning the article about last night's murder for the third time.

This time the police had not been able to control information about the killing. The insomniac dog walker who had found the body at the old chocolate factory in the early hours of the morning, not a mile from where Kitt was now sitting, had called 999 first, but his subsequent calls seem to have been to every known media outlet in the county. When interviewed, he had spared not one gory detail about the scene he had stumbled upon, which seemed just as macabre as that of the first murder, if not more so. Just like Owen, Adam Kaminski had been found with his arms crossed over his body and a fountain pen lodged in his chest. The make wasn't listed, and Kitt wondered if it was the same as the one used in the first murder. If it was, surely that was a lead for the police? The number of people bulk buying Stanwyck fountain pens these days must be small.

Kitt was just rereading the part about the note pinned to the victim's chest, which was composed of the sickening words, 'Eat your heart out', when a large rock landed on her desk with a thud. Kitt stared at the alien object, then looked up to see Ruby grinning down at her.

'There you go, love,' she said, as though that sentence alone was explanation enough for why she'd thrown a filthy-looking hunk of stone onto her work station.

Crossing her arms, Kitt sat back in her chair. She'd had nowhere near enough sleep last night, what with being arrested and all. There was a good chance she had nodded off. That said, would her eyes still be stinging from weariness in a dream? Would her bones ache from lying on the unforgiving concrete of the police custody suite? Even in nightmares, one usually has the luxury of blotting out such physical complaints. The odds were she was perfectly awake and experiencing yet another of Ruby's surreal moments.

'What's this?' asked Kitt.

'A gift,' Ruby said, her eyes shining as she *hmmph*ed down in the chair near Kitt's desk. 'Found it on't moors yesterday, and thought of you.'

'You ... shouldn't have,' Kitt said, dusting away some dry soil that had crumbled off her 'gift'. She looked over at Grace, who was sitting at the next desk over. For once, she wasn't taking the opportunity to giggle about the latest weird incident to befall her boss. Instead, her gaze was fixed on her screen. Kitt had never seen her assistant so focused. Hunting down details about the latest murder victim, it seemed, was all-engrossing. Given the similarities between the two murders, Kitt had instructed Grace to start with ex-girlfriends. A break-up had inspired the grisly elements of Owen's death. It was the most obvious starting point for tracking down useful information about the last breaths of Adam Kaminski. Kitt couldn't get the similarities between real-life events and *A Study in Scarlet* out of her mind. The first murder revolved so heavily around the end of a relationship, she was sure a broken heart had its part to play in this mess.

'I know you're having a difficult time of it at the moment,' said Ruby, re-establishing Kitt's attention. 'Best friend locked away for murder and that. A certain police officer getting you into a twist.'

Kitt felt a heat building in her cheeks and glared at Ruby. 'Halloran does not get me in a twist.'

'I was talking about that Banks lass,' said Ruby, cocking her head in a manner that was far too innocent to be the least bit believable. 'You said she barely spoke when she came in on Monday, and was spiteful when she did.'

Kitt nodded, but in truth Halloran's accusatory behaviour had been far more distressing than the silent treatment Banks favoured. 'How do you know Evie's been arrested? Has that made the news already?'

'Don't know about official outlets, but news 'as passed to the 59.'

Kitt raised an eyebrow. 'The 59?'

'Aye, the bus I take into town. Anything you can't learn on the 59 isn't worth knowing.'

'Duly noted,' said Kitt. 'And the solution to my problems is . . . a rock?'

'Not just any rock. A magic rock.'

'A magic rock.'

'Well, all rocks are magic, really.'

'Yes, well, I don't mean to seem ungrateful, but I'm not sure this rock is going to help me much.'

Ruby shuffled in her seat and knocked the side of Kitt's desk with one of her walking sticks.

'Think you know everything because you've read a few books, do you?'

Kitt pressed her lips together. This was the second time in twelve hours she'd been berated for her bookishness. Since when did reading books make you seem *less* knowledgeable?

'No, I—'

'There's a whole universe outside books, you know,' said Ruby.

'Yes, I'm well aware—'

'Put the rock in your coat pocket and keep it there.'

'What?'

'Put it in your coat pocket.'

'It's a bit heavy for that, isn't it?'

'No, just the right size. Ruby knows. Go on.'

Sighing, Kitt picked up the rock and shoved it into the deep pocket of her coat, which was hanging on the back of her office chair.

'Now, whenever you feel overwhelmed by a situation, if you feel out of your depth or even in danger, put your hand in your pocket and hold onto that rock. It's part of the earth that holds you up. It'll steady you, no matter what's going on.'

Kitt smiled at the old woman. Ruby's rationale seemed nonsensical, but her heart was kind. The librarian's smile disintegrated, however, when a familiar figure caught her eye. Standing just beyond Ruby, in the feminist history aisle, was Cabbage. Kitt had seen him hovering about more than once in the last couple of days, even though, as far as she understood from their first and only exchange, he had no business in the Women's Studies section. Realizing he had drawn Kitt's attention, the man held a copy of *The Second Sex* by Simone de Beauvoir up a little higher, so it covered his face. Such odd behaviour. What on earth was he up to?

'A-ha,' said Grace.

Kitt turned towards her assistant.

'Had a breakthrough, love? Working on something important?' asked Ruby.

'Er . . .' Grace looked at Kitt.

The librarian gave an almost undetectable shake of her head.

'Just a eureka moment with an Excel spreadsheet, nothing to write home about,' said Grace, before turning back to her computer and tapping hard and fast on her keyboard.

A moment later, an email popped up in Kitt's inbox with the subject line: AK.

Adam Kaminski. Good on Grace for thinking to write in code. Kitt had no idea how often or even if IT checked their email content, but she didn't need Michelle finding out that they were carrying out a secret murder investigation during office hours. Kitt was about to open the email when she heard a somewhat-familiar voice say, 'Katherine Hartley?'

Kitt looked up. It was Justine Krantz – the reporter who'd been shoving a dictaphone in her face just a few days ago. The reporter who had posted that footage of Kitt standing on Beth's doorstep to every known social media outlet.

'You can't film in here, Ms Krantz,' said Kitt, glaring at the man standing to her right with a video camera perched on his shoulder.

'It's an open campus, isn't it?' Justine said. 'Roll cameras.'

'Excuse me.' Kitt rose to her feet. 'Did you not hear what I just said?'

'We have it on good authority you and a Ms Evelyn Bowes were arrested at a social function last night, is that right, Ms Hartley?'

'Good authority from whom?' asked Kitt.

'I can't reveal my sources,' said Justine.

'Probably because they're not reputable,' said Kitt.

Justine sighed. 'I'll tell you this. It's a person Ms Bowes knows professionally.'

That wasn't too surprising. Anyone at the Belle's Ball could have spoken to the press. Given the way Evie's co-workers had behaved when the pair were arrested, Kitt couldn't rule out that it was one of them. She narrowed her eyes at the reporter. 'I'm going to give you three seconds to stop filming. Otherwise I'm calling security.'

'Dodging our questions for a second time,' Justine said, looking to camera briefly before turning back to Kitt. 'What are you hiding, Ms Hartley? Are you trying to protect your best friend from the truth coming out?'

'I've got nothing to say,' said Kitt.

Without hesitation, Krantz fired another question at Kitt. 'Can you at least tell us if you know the second victim – Adam Kaminski?'

'I knew an Adam once,' said Ruby. 'He wasn't a Kaminski though. He was a Fawcett. Do you know the Fawcetts?'

Justine frowned at Ruby, shaking her head at the distraction.

'Grace, run down to reception and tell security we have a situation on the second floor, will you?' Kitt smiled across at her assistant as though she were unfazed and in control.

At once, Grace started heading in the direction of the staircase, but before she'd gone even a few paces, the worst possible person rounded the corner.

'What is going on in here?' asked Michelle, her grey eyes flitting from the camera operator, to Justine, and then to Kitt.

'We're calling security,' said Kitt.

The camera turned on Michelle, and she put both hands on her hips, glaring down the lens.

'How do you know Ms Hartley?' Justine asked.

'I am the manager of floors one to three at this institution,' said Michelle. 'I'm telling you now to switch that camera off and leave the premises quietly.'

'Were you aware that Ms Hartley was arrested for murder last night?' Justine asked, with a knowing smile.

Michelle's jaw tightened. 'Well, given that she's out and

about now, there can't have been much to that, can there? Now stop filming and leave, before security have to escort you.'

Ruby let out a cackle. 'That's you told.'

Justine sighed and tapped the man holding the camera on the shoulder. 'Stop rolling,' she said, looking between Michelle, Ruby, Grace and Kitt. 'We'll leave, but I'm not going to stop searching for the truth on this story. Lives are at risk.'

'Will you even know the truth when you hear it?' said Kitt. She knew it was unwise to elongate this interaction, but she couldn't help herself. The whole situation was a nightmare, and an invasive press visit was the last thing she needed.

'You know, you should be on my side,' Justine said. 'The police can't be trusted on matters like this. They're creating a false sense of security, and it's not healthy. Ninety-nine per cent of all crimes committed are withheld from the media. Ask yourself why that is.'

With that, Justine signalled again to the man holding the camera, and he turned towards the second-floor staircase, following 'the talent' towards the exit.

Kitt wiped a palm across her forehead and sighed.

'Michelle,' she began. 'I can't thank you enough for sticking up for me there.' Kitt was more surprised than grateful about this, but tried not to let it show. She couldn't remember a time when Michelle had actually fought her corner on something.

'That wasn't for you,' said Michelle. 'I had to get rid of

that lot as soon as possible, and now they're gone, I think you'd better go home.'

Kitt stared at Michelle. 'Are you suspending me?'

'I don't know,' said Michelle. 'I don't know what we'll do with you as we've never had an employee get themselves into this position before. But I know one thing, the board of deans will not let anyone bring this institution into disrepute.'

'But I haven't done anything wrong,' Kitt said, her eyes watering at the idea of being dismissed from the library. It had been her whole life for ten years.

'We can't have the media traipsing in and out to talk to you,' said Michelle. 'It's disruptive. Go home. I'll speak to the management team about the situation, and see what's to be done.'

Swallowing hard, Kitt began throwing the essentials into her satchel. She could feel Grace and Ruby looking at her, but didn't dare meet their eyes in case she broke down. Cabbage was probably looking at her too, and the rest of the students using the second-floor facilities, but she didn't have the strength to face any of them and so kept her head down.

She glanced at her computer screen and remembered the email Grace had sent to her. It read:

The last girlfriend Adam Kaminski had was an actress called Zoe Gray. They broke up eight months ago, which is why she was so difficult to track down. She's currently playing Lina Lamont in the Majestic's production of Singin' in the Rain.

Even as she was scanning the message, Kitt knew how she would have to use her unscheduled afternoon off. She didn't know Zoe Gray. As far as Kitt was aware, neither did Evie, so the odds of her being Owen's murderer were slim, but she was the next link in the chain to her best friend's redemption. If Zoe knew something, anything, about how Adam or Owen died, Kitt would know about it before the day was done.

NINETEEN

'Can I help you, madam?' said the receptionist at the Majestic Theatre. Her uniform comprised a white shirt matched with a magenta pencil skirt. Her black hair was cut very short in a pixie crop, and there was a sparkle in her eyes that suggested youth and optimism. After a restless night and being kicked out of her place of work, Kitt wasn't in an optimistic space, but had to take advantage of the receptionist's desire to please if this plan was going to work.

'Oh, I do hope so,' said Kitt, putting on an over-friendly smile and flashing her staff ID card. 'I'm from the Vale of York University. I'm due to interview Zoe Gray for a research paper I'm working on before the matinee begins.'

'Oh – Ms Gray is expecting you?' said the receptionist. She seemed to be competing with Kitt over who could smile the hardest and widest. Certainly, she had the perkiest cheekbones the librarian had ever seen.

'Yes,' Kitt lied. 'She's very excited about the interview. She said I should just ask to be shown to her dressing room.'

'How thrilling,' said the receptionist. 'Just walk straight

through the fire exit doors at the end there. Take two left turns, and then a right, and then another left. Walk up three steps, then down five steps. You'll see a door right in front of you. Don't go in there, that's the laundry area. Instead, look to your left and you'll see Ms Gray's dressing room.'

Though a frown was bubbling under the surface, Kitt managed to keep her expression level. It was important to keep things jolly to avoid planting any doubt or negativity in the receptionist's mind. Or anything else that might lead to questions. The fledgling frown wasn't threatening just because the directions to Zoe Gray's dressing room were rather on the long-winded side. What was more concerning was how easily Kitt was being permitted into the backstage area. Had these people not heard there was a murderer on the loose? It was amazing how far a staff ID card and an authoritative posture could get you in life.

Kitt smiled at the receptionist, giving thanks for her help, and strode towards the fire exit doors. It was at once evident that the librarian had entered a staff area as back here there was no sign of the lavish red carpet that adorned the floors in the foyer. The lighting was dim too, in a way that cast her shadow rather spookily on the opposite wall.

Kitt's stomach clenched as she navigated the bare brick corridors and tried not to think about how quiet it was back here. How isolated. She distracted herself by totting up how many lies and half-truths she'd dispensed in the last week, concerning herself with the question of whether she was accidentally becoming a mistress of deception.

Earlier this week, she had lied about her connection to

Beth Myers. Today, she'd lied to the theatre receptionist about interviewing Zoe Gray, and, since this whole nightmare had begun, she had lied to herself about how much the threat of losing her best friend was getting to her. She had to put a brave face on it in front of Evie, but now that she wasn't here to see her crumbling, Kitt wondered what on earth she would do if she couldn't find some information that would clear Evie's name. Iago and her books were company enough, but nobody could replace her quirky, cheeky and rather sweet best friend.

That wasn't the only thing she was deceiving herself about either. There was also the question of Halloran. The discomfort she felt around him, and the way she had to divert herself from thinking things she shouldn't about him.

Reluctant to dwell too long on that last point, Kitt's thoughts turned to the text messages she had received back from Rebecca on the topic of poisoning. She had explained that deliberate poisoning was very rare. Thanks to the popularity of TV murder mysteries, most people understood that poisons were now much more traceable and identifiable than they had been a hundred years ago when women were using them to off husbands they would rather not put up with. But poison was still, she said, more likely to be used by a woman. It was a murder method that didn't require physical force. Kitt couldn't say yet whether Adam Kaminksi had suffered precisely the same fate as Owen, even if the manner in which he was found made it quite likely. Even if the murders weren't identical in every respect, however, the fact that the killer had drugged Owen with diazepam before ending his life suggested they were more manipulative than muscular.

Within a couple of minutes, Kitt located a door that had a laminated A4 sheet stuck to it. The text on the paper simply read: 'Zoe Gray'.

Taking a deep breath and straightening her posture, Kitt knocked on the door.

'Whoever you are, I'm preparing to go onstage and I do not wish to be disturbed,' came a muffled voice from the other side.

'Ms Gray, please open the door . . . I'm here about Adam Kaminski.'

There was a pause. A shuffling sound. And then a low swoosh as the heavy door was pulled open just enough to reveal a single brown eye, dusted in silver eyeshadow, which glittered like stars against black skin.

'Who are you? What about Adam?' said the voice on the other side, questions accompanied by the slow batting of a neat row of fake eyelashes.

Kitt's face drained of colour. She hadn't counted on this. She had assumed everyone would have seen the news this morning. Her eyes widened as she realized she was going to have to break the news about Adam's death to someone who had known him and cared for him. So this was how Halloran felt whenever this task fell to him . . .

'My name is Kitt Hartley, I work locally at the university. I need to come in to tell you why I'm here,' said Kitt, swallowing hard. 'It's bad news, I'm afraid.'

The actress swung the door wide open, revealing the fact

that she was wearing only a silk dressing gown the colour of whipped cream. The garment looked far too big on her, but Kitt thought that was probably because, like a lot of the actresses Kitt saw on TV, Zoe Gray could do with a decent home-cooked meal or two. 'Whatever that idiot has got himself into now, that's his problem.'

'Ms Gray—' Kitt tried, knowing Zoe would soon regret those words.

'No.' The actress held up her hand, palm flat. 'I'm sorry. But I have excommunicated that man from my life.'

'That's—' Kitt tried again.

'Do you know what it's like to be made a fool of? To be completely humiliated by the person who told you they loved you?'

Kitt looked down at the bare wooden floorboards just over the threshold of Zoe's dressing room.

'Yes,' she whispered, but the actress didn't hear her.

'To have all of the people who call themselves your friends sniggering about you behind your back for months afterwards?'

Kitt looked at the woman before her. A frown, deep as a fault line, cut through her forehead, and her lips were pulled thin in anger.

'He treated you poorly, then?' asked Kitt.

'You've got that right. I only went out with him in the first place because I felt sorry for him,' she said, her mouth twitching at the corners. Because she was lying, Kitt guessed. 'Six months of my life I gave him. You wouldn't believe the promises that fell out of his mouth.'

'But he didn't keep them,' said Kitt, taking a deep breath, trying to focus on Zoe's words rather than the image of Theo's face, half-bathed in the early light of dawn. Half-asleep and whispering the word 'always'. Why was it that the most unwelcome thoughts always came in the least convenient moments? Right now she had to focus on Ms Gray and *her* catastrophic love affair.

'No . . .' For the first time since opening the dressing-room door, Zoe Gray's expression betrayed something other than general irritation. Her eyes filled with tears and she shook her head.

'Zoe, listen,' said Kitt. 'There's something I need to tell you.'

'What?'

'Adam . . .' Kitt's lips clamped together, unwilling to release the next sentence, but she steeled herself and pushed the words out anyway. 'He's dead.'

'Dead?' the actress echoed, and then, pressing her right hand to her temple in a fashion only a lady who had spent time on the stage could, added, 'God, no.'

'I'm sorry to be the one to tell you,' said Kitt.

'I— I need to sit down,' Ms Gray said, shaking her head.

The actress left the door open. Taking this as an invitation, Kitt followed her into the dressing room. It was a small nook of a room. There was space enough for the two of them, but no more. To her left, Kitt noticed a costume hanging on the door of a carved mahogany wardrobe: a dress sewn from neckline to hem with silver sequins paired with a white fur tippet. Perfect for the role of Lina Lamont. Along the back wall were a row of mannequin heads housing a variety of wigs. One made of platinum blonde curls. One of long red hair. One of silky ebony waves.

'How did it happen?' asked Ms Gray, as she slumped into a chair in front of a dressing table filled with uncountable pots of powders and potions.

'You heard about the murder that happened in the city last weekend?' Kitt said.

Zoe nodded.

'It looks as though he was murdered by the same person. He was found by a dog walker at the old chocolate factory late last night,' Kitt said.

'God,' Zoe repeated. Her eyes wandered towards the dressing table. 'Do you mind if I . . .' she said, pointing at a large bottle of gin and a small tumbler standing to the right of the mirror.

'I'd never stand in the way of a woman and her gin,' said Kitt.

Zoe's hands shook as she poured the gin neat into the tumbler. 'And you're sure – you're sure it's a murder, not some terrible accident?'

'There is, I'm sorry to say, no doubt of the fact given the nature of the crime scene,' said Kitt.

'Are you the police or a reporter or something?' Zoe asked.

'No. Like I said, I work at the university. I'm . . . investigating this privately. You see, my best friend Evie, she was an ex-girlfriend of the man who was murdered last weekend. Perhaps you heard about that?'

Zoe nodded. 'On the news.'

'Up until now the police have been under the impression my friend was the culprit and have had her in custody for the last day or so. But the way in which Adam was found suggested he had been killed in the same manner as her ex-boyfriend was, so—'

'If last night's murder was committed by the same person and she was in custody when it happened . . .' Zoe began to reason.

'I know, that should be enough to have her released, but the police are obsessed with the idea that she might have an accomplice, so I'm not sure it's enough,' said Kitt.

'Do you think that's true? Do you think she murdered Adam?' said Zoe, her shoulders tightening.

'No,' said Kitt. 'Evie would never hurt anyone.'

'How can you be so sure?'

Kitt pursed her lips. Why was everyone so quick to point the finger before they had any real facts? Kitt cleared her throat, trying to control her temper, reminding herself how overprotective she could be when it came to her best friend. 'I've known Evie many years. She wouldn't hurt anyone, and the police have no evidence that says she did.'

The actress was about to say something else, but Kitt cut her off, keen to regain control of this conversation.

'There's something else you should be more worried about,' said the librarian.

Zoe looked at Kitt sidelong. 'What?'

'Despite no physical proof, the police were quick to decide that Owen's ex-girlfriend was the killer. The same could happen to you.'

Zoe's eyes widened for a split second and then narrowed. 'If there was no physical proof, there must have been something else that pointed to your friend.'

'Yes,' said Kitt. 'There were things at the crime scene that related to Owen and Evie's break-up. The murder was ... odd, and, as I say, so was Adam's. He was found at the chocolate factory. A fountain pen was ... lodged in his chest, with a note that said "Eat your heart out". Does any of this mean anything to you?'

Zoe's hand shook even harder than before as she took a large gulp of gin. 'Oh God,' she whimpered. 'They're going to get me. They're going to come after me.' She pulled a black holdall bag from under her dressing table and began throwing pots of creams and potions into it at a frantic rate.

'Zoe, stop,' said Kitt, placing a hand on the bag. 'What's going on?'

Tears started to stream down the actress's cheeks and she slumped back into the chair. 'I can't bear to talk about it.'

'You'd better tell me what's going on here.'

The actress swiped tears from her cheeks with both hands and looked up at Kitt. Kitt wondered whether she was staring into the eyes of a murderer.

TWENTY

'It all changed so quickly, between me and Adam.' Zoe seemed to slip into a sort of trance as she spoke. 'For a long time everything was perfect to the point that on our first Valentine's Day together, he brought up the topic of marriage. Told me he couldn't imagine a life without me. Wanted to know if I felt the same . . .'

'Did you?' asked Kitt.

'Yes. It had been a whirlwind romance. The kind of love you read about in books and plays. So, of course, I was swept along with the idea that it would last for the rest of my life.'

Kitt had felt that once. So long ago now, but she remembered the urgency of it and how delicious it was to surrender to the idea you'd found what everyone else was looking for.

'What happened next?'

'I got a bit ahead of myself. I told all my friends what he'd said. They bought a bottle of champagne to celebrate the engagement. Between us girls, we almost had the wedding planned out.'

'You must have been so happy,' said Kitt.

'I was.' Zoe's smile was tight and bitter. 'But then two days later Adam turned up on my doorstep. Said he'd had a change of heart and that instead of thinking about an engagement we should break up instead.'

Kitt took a deep breath. 'He got scared?'

'He wouldn't say, but probably.'

'I'm sorry.'

'So am I.'

Kitt stared at the actress. What exactly was she sorry for? The end of the relationship? The shattered dreams? Or something else? Something that had spurred her to start packing a getaway bag the moment Kitt described the murder scene.

'Zoe.' Kitt made her voice as gentle as she could. What was coming next couldn't sound in any way judgemental if she wanted to keep Zoe onside. 'How upset were you over this?'

'I was a wreck,' she said.

'Were you angry?'

'Yes.'

'Did you want revenge?'

Zoe hesitated before giving her answer. 'Yes.'

A cold feeling crept over the librarian, as though a winter gust was blowing somewhere inside, under a doorway that didn't quite fit in its frame. 'Zoe, did you kill Adam?'

Zoe's eyes, which had glazed over, seemed to focus again. She frowned.

'What? No!'

'OK, OK,' said Kitt, raising her hands.

'I was here last night,' said Zoe.

'All night?' said Kitt, and then, when she saw Zoe's eyes narrow, added, 'I'm just asking what the police will ask. According to the news, Adam's body wasn't found until half past three, but the murder is believed to have happened around midnight. Do you have an alibi for that time?'

Zoe rose from her chair and squared up to Kitt. 'Yes, I do. I was with the cast, having after-show drinks at the bar. The bartender saw us all, and the cast members can vouch for me.'

'I believe you,' said Kitt, 'I do. It's just you said you wanted revenge.'

'I did,' Zoe said. 'But I didn't kill Adam, I would never have . . .' She trailed off. 'I wouldn't hurt him. Even after what he did to me. Even though he never properly explained himself.'

'Then what's all this panic about?'

The actress folded her arms loosely across her chest and started stroking the sleeves of her dressing gown. 'On Valentine's Day, right before we broke up, Adam gave me a gift. It was a large chocolate heart, and it was inscribed with a quote from *Antony and Cleopatra*.'

'Which quote?' asked Kitt, and then shook her head. Her bookish instincts were always looking for an opportunity to surface, but that was hardly the most pressing detail right now.

'"Eternity was in our lips and eyes." He used it as a way of opening up the conversation about our engagement. It seems a bit cheesy in retrospect, but at the time it felt really romantic. Cute. Even a bit whimsical. I was touched that he'd put the thought into creating a gift that meant something just to us two,' Ms Gray said. 'You see, *Antony and Cleopatra* was the play he first saw me in. The first time he noticed me. We started dating soon after.'

A tragedy: how appropriate, given how things turned out. Kitt wanted to pass comment on the symmetry, but decided that would be insensitive. Besides, she needed to bring the focus back to Zoe's break-up with Adam.

'So he gave you this gift, the chocolate heart,' said Kitt.

'Yes, then two days after that he turned up on my doorstep and broke up with me. Who does a thing like that?'

Kitt offered a flimsy smile. She could think of one other person who had done something like that, and he had suffered the same fate as Adam. She had been right about heartbreak being something of a theme here. 'So, what did you do when he broke up with you?'

Zoe looked down at her feet. 'Moped for a while. But then I got angry, really angry. So I sent him a return gift. Another chocolate heart.'

'I would say that's at the tame end of the revenge spectrum,' said Kitt, her nose crinkling.

'Well, the chocolate, it was . . .'

'What?'

'Designed for dogs.'

'Dogs?'

'Yeah, well, he'd behaved like one. Worse than a dog actually. Dogs are loyal. I saw the chocolate heart in a pet shop window – you know, one of those pet pampering shops for pets that live better lives than their owners?'

'I know the sort,' Kitt said with a small smile.

'I bought it, iced it with a message, and posted it to Adam.'

'What message?' asked Kitt, fearing she already knew the answer.

Zoe exhaled a long, slow breath. '"Eat your heart out." I was trying to bait him into eating the chocolate.'

'The same words that were on the note at the crime scene,' said Kitt.

'I don't understand it,' Zoe said, shaking her head.

Kitt put her hands on Zoe's arms. An over-familiar move, but Zoe had to understand how important her honesty was right now.

'Who else did you tell about this?'

'There are a lot of people who know we were talking about an engagement and then split up soon after. But when it comes to the most intimate details, it's a short list. I was mortified.' Zoe broke away from Kitt's hold and crossed her arms. 'When something like that happens to you it's not the kind of thing you go spreading around.'

Unless you're Evie, Kitt thought. She waited all of ten minutes before posting to her timeline about Owen's message. Why she would want anyone to know about that kind of life event was beyond Kitt, but people posted all kinds of things to Facebook. Misguided political manifestos. Videos of their shenanigans after one too many beers. The images from their ultrasound scans. Kitt loved her friends, but didn't need to see pictures of their wombs. That wasn't her preferred way of knowing them inside and out.

'What about Adam?' asked Kitt. 'Did he tell anyone?'

'I don't think so. I was so embarrassed. I told him if he ever told anyone what he'd done . . .'

'What?' said Kitt.

'I said I'd kill him. It was a figure of speech. I wasn't actually going to do it.'

Zoe picked up the tumbler of gin she'd poured earlier and knocked back the last of it without wincing.

'What a mess,' said Kitt, thinking. Two men murdered. Two men who had broken up with their girlfriends in less-than-ideal circumstances. That couldn't be coincidence.

Zoe started chewing on her thumbnail. 'What are the police going to think?'

'Your best bet is to go straight to them with what you know,' said Kitt. 'Explain you heard about the details of Adam's murder, and you realized it was connected to your break-up.'

'Yes,' said Zoe, a slight sparkle returning to her eyes. 'That's a good idea. Go forward with the information. That'll reflect well on me. Maybe even one or two of the papers will want to do an interview with me about how bereft I am.'

'Oh, you can count on that,' said Kitt, thinking back to an hour ago when she'd have done anything to get rid of Justine Krantz before Michelle had discovered she was in the building.

'Well, it'll have to wait until after the matinee. I have to get ready to go onstage.'

'You're still going to go through with the performance?' said Kitt, taking in a sharp breath. They may have broken up eight months ago, but Zoe had said she had loved Adam. If somebody Kitt loved had been murdered, she would without a doubt be calling in sick to work.

'Today's our last day of the show,' said Zoe, in a tone that indicated that should be justification enough.

'But—'

'I'm not giving my last shows to the understudy. She can't do a proper American accent.'

'All right,' said Kitt. 'I suppose I'd better get going and leave you to it. But here,' Kitt removed a notebook and pen from her satchel and began scribbling down her name and number, 'if you can think of anything else that might help with the case, please call me. Even if it's a detail that seems too small to bother the police with.'

Kitt handed the paper to Zoe. She looked at it, and then up at Kitt. 'All right.'

'Oh, and, er, it's probably best not to mention our conversation to the police when you speak to them,' said Kitt, in as casual a tone as she could.

'Why not?'

'To be clear, I'm not suggesting you lie to the police. That would just make everything worse, but with Evie under suspicion, we don't want them thinking that you two have any connection to each other – because you don't, right?'

'What was her name?'

'Evie Bowes.'

'No, never heard of her.'

'And if the police find out I've been here they might think you're the accomplice, or jump to some conclusion that further derails the investigation. My hope is to unravel the truth, not make it more difficult for the police – or anyone else – to find it.'

Zoe stared at Kitt for a moment. 'All right, I'll keep it to myself.'

'Thank you, goodbye now,' said Kitt, opening the door and stepping back into the corridor.

It was cooler out there. Quiet. She closed the dressing-room door and began walking in the direction of the exit, wondering whether Zoe's story held up. She did seem distraught about the untimely end of her ex-boyfriend, but she was an actress. A woman paid to make you believe whatever she wanted you to believe.

Footsteps echoed further down the corridor, loud enough to make Kitt jump. Two people were heading this way, soon to discover her in an area of the theatre she had no right being in. They were talking, and as she listened she realized one of the voices – the man – had a familiar depth to it.

Halloran. He was here. With Banks, by the sound of it.

Kitt scurried back along the corridor towards Zoe's dressing room. She had to find some nook to hide in. The officers could not find her here. Kitt opened the door adjacent to Zoe's, the laundry area. Hopping inside, she pulled the door closed and waited, holding her breath. She could hear the officers approaching.

'My gut tells me neither of them did it,' said Banks.

'Ritchie went on a date with her the week before, and only has an alibi for the first murder. Evie and Ritchie could be in it together.'

Kitt wanted to fling open the laundry-room door and tell

them how wrong they were. Instead, she cursed her heart for beating so loudly. From the sound of their voices, the officers were standing just a few paces on the other side of the door.

'She . . . I don't know . . .' Banks said.

'What?'

'I just don't think Evie is our killer.'

There was a pause.

'She's a pretty girl,' said Halloran. His voice had a teasing tone to it that Kitt wouldn't have expected.

Another pause.

'Sir . . . that's not why I think she's innocent. Anyway, it's irrelevant how pretty I think she is. I'm not her . . . type.'

There was a hollow note to Banks's voice that almost made Kitt feel sorry for her. Almost.

'Evie Bowes is where all the evidence is pointing. We can't afford to rely on our gut instincts. Not this time. There's too much at stake.'

'What about you, sir? Are you holding up all right?' asked Banks.

'I'm fine.' Halloran's response came too quickly to sound anything other than defensive.

'It's just that—'

'I know, we're looking at a serial case.'

'Just wanted to make sure, can't be easy after—'

'I said I was fine.'

Standing still and silent behind the laundry door, Kitt wondered what they were talking about, but before Banks could say anything else, a hard knock rang out.

'Ms Gray, I'm Detective Inspector Malcolm Halloran, this is Detective Sergeant Charlotte Banks, can we come in?'

Kitt listened as Zoe invited the officers in and her dressing-room door thudded shut. It looked like Zoe wasn't going to make it onto the stage for her final performances after all.

TWENTY-ONE

A roaring breeze shook the yew trees planted in small clusters around the edges of Fulford Cemetery. The vicar scattered soil over the coffin as it was lowered into the earth, while Kitt put an arm around Evie and squeezed. The poor thing had kept her peace all the way through the service, but the finality of this moment got the better of her and she sobbed, covering her face with a tissue.

DI Halloran stood on the other side of the grave next to Owen's family, his arms straight by his side as though he was standing to attention, but with his head bowed just a touch out of respect. Not for the first time since Halloran had arrived at the funeral, he stared first at Evie and then at Kitt, no doubt still looking for signs of suspicion, even in this sacred space.

Kitt watched Owen's mother shake with grief as she looked on her son's coffin for the last time. Her cries were so violent her bobbed, grey hair whipped about with the force of them. Halloran extended his arm, placing his hand on the woman's shoulder. She grabbed at his hand and continued to weep.

Kitt's eyes filled with tears as she looked back into Halloran's. His eyes were teary too. He would probably have to go through this again with Adam Kaminski's mother. Kitt found herself wondering how many funerals Halloran had attended, and if some were harder than others for him.

'Let's not hang around,' Evie whimpered. 'I can't bear this any longer.'

'Come on,' said Kitt, linking her arm through her friend's. 'You need some rest.'

Evie had been released from the station four hours before, after the police had interviewed Zoe Gray the previous afternoon and at last decided there was likely some bigger plot at play. Given that Evie now had an alibi for the first and second murder, her solicitor had argued for her release. Despite Kitt's best efforts to help Evie recover from her ordeal in police custody, however, with her skin pale next to her black shift dress and cardigan, she looked more ghost than human being.

The pair turned away from the grave and began walking in the direction of the black iron gates that stood at the entrance of the burial grounds.

'Should I be happy the police let me go?' asked Evie, her voice hollow.

'I think not being charged with murder is generally to be chalked up as a good thing,' Kitt said. Given that Evie had no discernible links with the second murder, Halloran had had no choice but to let her go, even though Kitt knew from his parting words at Ashes to Ashes early the previous morning that neither of them were necessarily off the suspect list yet.

'Then why do I still feel like I'm locked away? Or that I should be.'

At her friend's words Kitt found herself swallowing back more tears. 'You feel that way because you're a good person. You . . .' Kitt trailed off and her eyes narrowed as she looked towards the entrance of the cemetery.

Evie followed her friend's gaze and the pair stared at a broad, dark figure standing by the ornate gates. Whoever it was, they were wearing a long, black hooded cape. The hood kept the stranger's face in shadow. The only distinguishable detail, the detail that had caught Kitt's attention, was the strands of red hair that hung about their shoulders. The length of the hair suggested that the person in the hood was likely female, but the breadth of the figure was more typical of a man.

Halloran had mentioned a woman with red hair during his interrogation. That somewhere in York there was a woman with red hair, like Kitt's, who was the last person to see Owen alive.

Kitt took three more steps towards the gate. Still the figure's face was shrouded in shadow, but she got a closer look at the hair. The colour didn't look natural. It looked dyed or . . . like the colour of a red wig. Like the colour of the wig Kitt had seen just yesterday . . . in Zoe Gray's dressing room.

'Hey!' Kitt shouted, without thinking.

Startled by Kitt's call, the figure lowered their head even further, looked off to the left, and then scurried off to the right.

'Zoe!' Kitt called, even though the figure in front of her

was far too portly to be the waif of an actress she'd been talking to the day before.

The figure stopped at this, turning briefly towards Kitt, before vanishing into the autumnal mist.

Kitt sped towards the gate and, once out of the cemetery, looked as far down the road as she could, but there was no sign of the mysterious figure. How could they disappear from such a long residential street? Perhaps they had hopped over one of the hedges and charted a path across the neighbouring gardens.

'What was that about?' asked Evie, out of breath from catching Kitt up.

'Did you see that?'

'I saw . . . something.' Halloran's voice came from behind them.

Kitt turned towards the officer and sighed. 'Something' wasn't enough to clear Evie's name for good. 'You saw them? That person?' Kitt said.

'I was a little way behind you. So didn't get as close a look. But I saw them, in a black cloak.'

'They had red hair,' said Kitt. 'You know, like the woman you said was seen with Owen the last time he was alive.'

Without another word Halloran whipped his phone out of his pocket and dialled.

Kitt and Evie frowned at each other.

'Banks? Listen, we need to set up a search perimeter at Fulford Cemetery.'

Halloran paused for a moment.

'Yes, let's start with a two-mile radius. The suspect has red hair and was last seen wearing a long black cloak . . . Yes, I know. Weird. All right. Thank you.'

Halloran hung up the phone and looked at Kitt and Evie.

'Did that person look familiar to you?'

'You mean, are we friends with anyone who runs around in a big black hooded cloak?' Kitt asked. Halloran gave Kitt the hardest of stares. The librarian crossed her arms. 'No, they didn't look familiar to me. Evie?'

Evie shook her head. 'They might just have been dressed in black for the funeral.'

'Then why run?' said Kitt. 'And the red hair . . . isn't it too much of a coincidence? I saw a wig just the same colour as that yesterday.'

'Where?' asked Halloran.

Kitt's body stiffened. Why couldn't she shut her mouth?

'Where?' Halloran repeated in a dark, quiet tone that made it clear he wouldn't appreciate repeating himself again.

'Zoe Gray's dressing room,' said Kitt.

Halloran stared at her, with a curious half-smile she didn't much care for.

'Excuse me,' said a woman's voice off to Kitt's left. She turned to see Justine Krantz poised with a notebook and pen. Kitt had been so caught up in the revelation of the hooded figure, she hadn't heard Justine's car pull up. Had one of Evie's work colleagues given her another tip-off, or had she actually used her research skills to uncover the location of the funeral?

'I'm—'

'I know what you are,' said Kitt, 'a vulture.'

Justine's eyes narrowed. 'I'm just trying to get the truth to the people who need it.'

'Pick another time,' said Halloran, a deep frown cutting into his brow. 'The family needs time to grieve in peace.'

Kitt looked at Evie, and the pair started walking towards the bus stop across the road. Though Evie had a 1968 Morris Minor sitting in her garage, she had been in no fit state to drive this morning.

Despite Halloran's warning, Justine followed them. 'Come on now, don't you want justice for Owen?'

Without warning, Evie turned on the reporter and pointed a finger at Justine's chin.

'Don't you say his name. You didn't even know him. You don't care about him. You just care about your story.'

Justine started and took a step backwards. Kitt had never seen her friend's face contort like that before. Her features suddenly became thin and sharp. But then, in an instant, that same face crumpled in on itself, and she pushed her head into Kitt's shoulder, crying.

'I suggest you leave us alone. You've surely met your daily harassment quota?' said Kitt.

Justine didn't say any more. She stalked back towards the gate and looked as though she was going to ask something of Halloran, but he ignored her and walked over to Kitt and Evie.

'How long to the next bus?' he asked.

Kitt looked at her watch and then at the timetable hanging on the concrete post next to them. 'Just twenty minutes.'

'I'll drive you,' said Halloran.

'No, thank you, we—'

'I think Evie's been through enough for one day without having to hope York buses are running to timetable, don't you?' said Halloran.

Kitt bristled. So Halloran had finally understood that her friendship with Evie could be exploited. She had hoped it might take him a little longer.

'Don't you need to stay here and search for the hooded figure in our midst?'

'No, Banks is sorting that. I need to get back to the station. We've got two murders to solve now.'

The librarian looked into the wide, green eyes of her friend, so weary and full of distress.

'I can have you back to Acomb in less than ten minutes,' said Halloran.

Sighing, she waved Evie towards Halloran's car, which she knew would be saturated with his overwhelming, earthy scent. Halloran opened the back door for her and, without looking at him directly, she held her breath and slid inside.

TWENTY-TWO

Halloran pulled his car up outside Evie's house and put the handbrake on. Unbuckling his seat belt, the inspector exited the vehicle and opened the back door for Kitt and Evie. Halloran offered his hand to help Kitt out, just as he had done back in the police custody suite.

Kitt looked at the hand, and then up at Halloran.

She didn't want to take it. It was an unnecessary gesture. She was quite capable of getting out of the back of a car by herself. But he had just given them a lift. And had let her best friend out of custody. And had just been to a funeral where he was comforting an old woman over the loss of her son. You can't refuse a kindness from someone who hits all three of those criteria in the space of six hours. Kitt was fairly sure there was a law about that somewhere.

Slowly, she placed her hand in Halloran's. On contact, Kitt's pulse quickened and, as Halloran tightened his grip, her heart rate only escalated further. The inspector kept his eyes locked with Kitt's as he pulled her out of the car and, as if that weren't enough, he held onto her hand a moment longer than she felt he by any right needed to.

'Give us a hand,' said Evie's voice from the back of the car. Clearing her throat and straightening her posture, Kitt reached back to her friend and tugged her out of the vehicle.

'Thanks for the lift,' said Kitt. 'I can take things from here.'

'Actually,' Halloran said, 'if you don't mind, I'd like to come inside. There are a couple of things I'd like to talk to you about.'

Kitt's lips pressed hard against each other. So Halloran hadn't escorted them home out of the goodness of his heart. She wished she was surprised, but also wished there wasn't always an ulterior motive.

'You need Evie's blessing, not mine. It's her house,' said Kitt, hoping her friend would sense from her tone that she would much rather it was just her and Evie for the rest of the afternoon. They still had so much to catch up on. She still hadn't told her about what Banks had said about her backstage at the Majestic Theatre, but, on reflection, Kitt wasn't sure if it was really her place to tell Evie that Banks might be taking a shine to her anyway.

'Are you going to arrest me again?' asked Evie.

'It's not my plan,' said Halloran.

'All right, I'm too tired to argue about it. Come in.'

The trio walked towards Evie's door. It was a narrow house on the end of a terrace that was deceptive about its size. Looking at the modest frontage, with a slim garage attached, you wouldn't think it stretched as far back as it did. The rooms had been built in a sort of procession: a small hallway headed up the parade, with the living room, kitchen, bathroom, and a small patio following on behind.

Once over the threshold, Evie steered Kitt and Halloran straight into the living room where she dropped down onto her favourite piece of furniture – a mahogany chaise longue upholstered in green velvet. It was one of the many charity shop bargains with which she'd furnished the room. Most people with a love for vintage would style their rooms in a particular era, but Evie had never had the budget to be that fussy and thus her house was a strange collage of furniture from the late 1800s through to the 1970s. It was probably a little bit unsettling to Halloran's untrained eye, but Kitt had got used to it. To her, it just felt cosy.

Evie looked at her friend and it seemed to Kitt as though she was going to have to take the lead in this conversation.

'So what can we do for you, officer?' asked Kitt. She decided to remain standing. She didn't want to give Halloran any cue that it was OK for him to take a seat or make himself too comfortable.

'I wanted to apprise you of a few things,' the inspector said. 'It's clear from the two crime scenes on this case that whoever killed Owen also killed Adam.'

'Yes, isn't that a given?' asked Kitt.

'No, not in cases like these. You can sometimes get copycat crimes. Or the original killer can pay someone off to commit a crime that looks similar to theirs so they can secure an alibi for that crime, making it more difficult to prosecute.'

'Oh,' said Kitt. 'But you're sure that in this case it's the same killer?'

'As sure as we can be without any DNA evidence,' said Halloran. 'In the case of a copycat there are usually subtle differences to how everything's arranged.'

'But not in this case?'

Halloran shook his head. 'The arms were crossed over the body, just like they were with . . .' Halloran glanced at Evie for a moment. Perhaps after seeing the way Evie responded to Justine Krantz when she mentioned the O-word he was thinking twice about what he said in front of her. Or maybe he was just being sensitive. 'Like they were with the first victim. It looks as though the same chemicals were used to sedate and poison him, and precisely the same pen and notepaper were used as those at the first crime scene. It's the same handwriting on the note too. We didn't release specific details to the press, so anyone wanting to forge the crime would have difficulty replicating it.'

'What about Ritchie?' Evie asked, still with her eyes closed. 'Kitt said he ran away from you.'

'Initially we thought we were onto something there. He didn't have an alibi for the second murder, which happened between ten and midnight, before he started work. He claims he was in bed before his shift – not very convincing. But he did have an alibi for the first murder and, with no phone records or financials linking him to either of the victims, we had to cut him loose.'

'Then why did he run?' asked Kitt. 'He must have something to hide.'

Halloran cleared his throat. 'Mr Turner was in possession of some recreational substances that he shouldn't have been. That's why he ran.'

'So the only person left on the suspect list is someone in a black hooded cloak and red wig?' said Evie, her eyes opening.

'Whoever they are, it's likely they're at least involved,' said Halloran. 'People who commit crimes like this often get a sick satisfaction from watching the aftermath. The funeral of their victims can often draw them out.'

'But why wear a costume? It only makes you more conspicuous,' said Kitt.

'A black cloak isn't that conspicuous at a funeral,' said Halloran.

'Not if you're a character in *The Woman in Black*,' said Kitt. 'It's a bit 1910.'

'Odds are, as we've suspected all along, that the killer is known to the victims and their friends, but the disguise suggests they're not very close to them.'

'Yes,' said Kitt. 'If they were close to them they could just show up. No one would suspect anything.'

'So the likelihood is we're dealing with somebody on the periphery. Somebody who watches closely but doesn't really engage.'

'You two are freaking me out,' said Evie, moving her shoulders as though there was an insect scuttling along them that she was trying to shake off.

'I'm sorry,' said Halloran. 'I know the idea of being watched isn't a comforting one.'

Kitt narrowed her eyes. 'Hang on a minute, why are you telling us all this? Before, you would barely tell us anything. You're being very open all of a sudden.'

For the first time since Kitt had crossed paths with Halloran he smiled a real smile. 'I have a proposition for you.'

'Not interested,' Kitt said.

'We haven't even heard what it is yet,' said Evie.

'Don't need to,' said Kitt. 'If it's got anything to do with these murders we don't want to be involved. This could be entrapment for all you know.'

By the smirk on his face, Halloran was clearly entertained by this idea. 'I assure you, I'm a good enough detective that I don't have to resort to entrapment.'

'Then be out with it, but I doubt we're interested,' said Kitt, hoping that her act was convincing enough to mask her curiosity, whilst deep down suspecting that it wasn't.

'The murders started with you two. I mean, someone you knew was hit first.'

'So . . .' Evie said, her voice wavering. After two nights spent in police custody she was probably more than a little bit wary of saying something that might land her back there.

'So, I don't know how yet, but I think you two are the key to this case, and because of that it makes sense for the police to keep you close at hand.'

'You mean . . .' Evie's eyes widened.

'I mean, I think you might be able to help us out, so we can prevent another murder.'

'You think the killer is going to strike again?' asked Evie.

'In cases like this, the culprits don't usually stop,' Halloran said. 'Until they're caught.'

'And . . . you're asking for our help?' said Kitt, crinkling her nose.

'Despite being arrested, I have to admit that you've been quite helpful – at least in ruling out suspects. It would have taken Julian Rampling much longer to come out of the woodwork without your involvement, and Ritchie Turner for that matter.'

'But I only looked into those people because you suspected Evie,' said Kitt, while wondering to herself if inquisitiveness would have got the better of her anyway. 'I'm not trained to investigate a murder.'

'I'm not asking you to take the lead, I'm just asking you to pass on any information or ideas you have.'

'We've been doing that anyway,' said Kitt.

'Have you?' said Halloran. 'I don't remember receiving a phone call in advance from you about Julian Rampling. Or Ritchie Turner, or Zoe Gray.'

Kitt shook her head. Halloran already knew that she had tried to be careful about implicating innocent people. 'You never gave me your number,' she said drily.

Halloran took a step towards Kitt, put a hand in his jacket pocket, and produced a card. 'Let me rectify that.'

Kitt paused before reaching out and taking the card. The name 'Detective Inspector Malcom A. Halloran' was printed across it in a bold serif font, and on the reverse were his contact details, including the aforementioned phone number.

'Trust me, if I'd known you were that eager to have it, I'd have given it to you sooner.'

Out of nowhere, Evie giggled. 'Said the actress to the bishop.'

Kitt sighed in her friend's direction and then looked back at Halloran. It was her understanding that detectives were not supposed to try it on with suspects. She couldn't decide if Halloran's line was a sign she was no longer under suspicion, or if that was one rule he didn't care to follow. 'Trust me, if I'd been that eager to have it, I'd have asked for it before now.'

'Now you're doing it on purpose,' said Evie. 'It's no fun when you make innuendo that easy.'

'I see you're getting your strength back,' said Kitt.

'Not really, just comforted at the thought of you working on the case,' said Evie.

'I haven't agreed to do that,' said Kitt. 'I'm not convinced it's a good idea.'

If this murder spree really was being orchestrated by the kind of sick individual Halloran was suggesting, maybe all that had come so far was just the warm-up. What if some new piece of information was planted to further incriminate her and Evie? The police might argue that they had manipu- lated their way onto the case, putting themselves in a better position to stay one step ahead. Or worse, maybe this was just a manipulation on Halloran's part, to keep them close and monitor their behaviour. Surely it was best to keep their distance until the true culprit was behind bars?

'Oh no, come on,' said Evie. 'I'll feel so much better if I know you're helping.'

Kitt lifted her palm to her forehead. 'Evie . . .'

'The quicker the case is solved the better, right?' said Evie.

Kitt crossed her arms. 'Right . . .'

'So, what harm could it do to pass on information, or do a little digging if anyone in our circle starts acting suspiciously? You've sort of already been doing that anyway.'

'I— I'll think about it,' said Kitt, and then she jumped as the opening chords of 'Kiss Me, Honey Honey' blared out. Evie rooted around in her coat pocket for a minute and pulled out her phone.

'Hi Mum,' she said, scraping herself off the chaise longue and pointing towards the door to indicate she would take the call elsewhere.

Kitt waited for the door to close and listened for the sound of Evie's footsteps on the stairs before turning on Halloran.

'Why did you have to bring that up in front of Evie? She's very vulnerable at the moment. Your suggestion only got her over-excited.'

'I don't see why you wouldn't want to help,' said Halloran.

'Because I don't trust you,' Kitt blurted out.

Halloran tried to correct a wince. 'I suppose arresting a person can have that effect.'

'And their best friend,' added Kitt.

'That too,' said Halloran. 'But I was only doing my job. Work with me, and you'll learn that on the whole I am considered a trustworthy person.'

Kitt stared at Halloran before raising an eyebrow. 'On the whole.'

Halloran was fighting a smile and, in spite of herself, Kitt was too.

'I can't take full credit for the leads we've had so far,' said Kitt. 'My assistant Grace has rather worrying cyberstalking skills and has been helping me find information on certain persons of interest.'

'Like Zoe Gray?' said Halloran.

'Yes,' said Kitt. 'You didn't seem surprised earlier. When I told you I'd been to see her.'

Halloran started walking towards the door. 'I already knew you'd talked to her.'

'She told you?' said Kitt, following after the inspector. So much for Zoe keeping that to herself.

'No,' Halloran said, flashing a small smile. On anyone else, Kitt would have described the smile as cheeky, but up until this moment she wouldn't have thought that was a quality Halloran possessed. Without saying any more, he opened the front door and stepped back out into the biting October air.

'Then how?' Kitt pushed. If someone was onto her private investigation or was passing information on about her to the police she wanted to know.

Stepping down the two steps that led up to Evie's front door, Halloran turned to face Kitt. With the inspector on lower ground, for once Kitt was able to stand eye-to-eye with him.

He leaned a little closer and lowered his voice. 'Do you really want to know?'

'I didn't ask for my health.'

Halloran stared straight into Kitt's eyes. 'I could smell you.'

'I beg your pardon?'

His smile broadened then. 'Your perfume. It's got a citrus scent about it, like ripe grapefruit. It was hanging in the air of Zoe's dressing room.'

Kitt frowned. Her stomach was turning over at the idea that Halloran could recognize her that way, but she wasn't going to give him the satisfaction of believing this was in any way romantic, or, God help her, sexy.

'A sure sign that I should cut down on how much I'm wearing.' Kitt blushed. If Evie was still listening in she would have a field day with that sentence. 'Perfume, I mean . . .'.

'That's what I thought you meant,' said Halloran, before breaking out in a grin. Kitt wished she could think of a way of knocking it off his face.

'Are you always this animal?' she tried.

He stared at her. 'Only when the situation calls for it.'

Before Kitt could say anything else, Halloran turned on his heel and walked off towards his car. Kitt watched after him for a moment and then quickly closed the door. Just in case he happened to look back and catch her smirking.

TWENTY-THREE

The next day, just as morning lapsed into afternoon, Kitt stormed up the spiral staircase to the second floor of the library. Her stomach turned over and over to the point that she thought she was going to be sick. At the top of the steps she clung to the banister rail for a second, steadying herself before striding over to the student enquiry desk where Grace was sitting.

Her assistant wouldn't usually be working a Saturday. There was a skeletal staff rota at the weekend, but Kitt had texted Grace asking her to come in especially today, and right now she was more grateful than she could have imagined that she had been available at short notice.

Kitt opened her mouth to explain she needed her assistant's help. To explain to her what had happened, but the words were stuck in the back of her throat.

'Grace . . .' she managed in a wavering voice.

Grace, who had been staring at her computer with a big smile on her face, looked up at this and at once her smile faded.

'What's wrong? Oh God, has there been another murder?'

Kitt shook her head and held up her mobile phone with a trembling hand.

Grace leaned forward to get a closer look at the screen, and then her eyes widened.

'A friend request, from Theo?' she said. 'Is that all? You scared the life out of me there. I thought it was serious.'

'This is serious.'

Grace tilted her head at her boss.

'Oh, all right, not murder serious. But don't the trials of the living still count?'

Kitt tried to steady her breathing. She knew she was being over-dramatic. She wouldn't be over-dramatic about anything else. She had even taken being arrested for murder on the chin, but when it came to Theo she wasn't known for her level-headedness.

'Did you send him a message?'

'I've made no contact at all,' said Kitt. 'All I did was look at his profile the other day, probably for less than a minute. On the way here, this notification popped up on my phone.'

'Uh-oh,' said Grace, tucking a dark curl behind her left ear.

Kitt crossed her arms and looked at her assistant. 'What do you mean "uh-oh"?'

'There are two possible scenarios.'

Kitt remained silent, waiting.

'Either, it's complete coincidence and after ten years of not communicating he has decided to get in touch on the same week you happened to look at his profile.'

'Or . . .'

'Or, well. There is this app you can get on your phone. That tells you when someone has looked at your Facebook profile.'

'What?'

'Yeah, it's not good form, but some people do install it. It's a Facestalker's worst nightmare.'

Kitt threw her phone down on the desk, slumped down into the nearest seat, and put her head in her hands. 'If I'd known that app existed, I wouldn't have risked clicking on his profile.'

'Sorry,' said Grace. 'I sort of forgot. Nobody uses it. Or, at least, nobody I know. Most of us are happy living in blissful ignorance about who has and hasn't clicked on our profiles.'

'It's not your fault,' said Kitt. It was her own fault for letting curiosity get the better of her after all these years of trying to put distance between herself and Theo. After a decade of throwing herself into work. After every promise she had made to herself that she wouldn't give him her time and energy, she had caved at the first opportunity. 'What do I do now?' she asked.

Grace stood up and walked around the desk to put her arm around Kitt. 'Depends on what you want. If you want to get back in touch with him, accept the request.'

'And if I don't?'

'Just ignore it.'

'Ignore it . . .' It seemed such a cold thing to do, but then so was disappearing without a word to your girlfriend of twelve months.

'If you respond in any way, he'll see it as an invitation to start a conversation.'

'Even if it's just to say I don't want to talk to him?'

'You know guys aren't always brilliant at accepting that we mean what we say.'

'No. They can be a bit hazy on that when it suits them.'

'If you ignore it, he'll get that you don't want to talk to him.'

Kitt nodded. Ignoring it was probably for the best. She had enough going on now without reopening old wounds.

'It's good to see you,' said Grace, with a smile.

'Yes, I don't know how you managed without me for a whole two days.' Kitt returned her smile.

'Grace, Kitt,' said a deep, familiar voice.

Grace's eyes flared wide and Kitt swivelled in her chair to see Halloran and Banks standing just behind her. How much of this conversation had they overheard?

'Oh, you're here already,' said Kitt, while Grace, as casually as she could, walked back to her seat behind the desk.

'We're actually a little bit late,' said Halloran. 'You did say twelve, didn't you?'

'Yes, yes, I did,' said Kitt.

The previous afternoon Kitt had called Michelle to explain that there'd been a misunderstanding and that she was now assisting the police in their investigation as opposed to being a prime suspect. Michelle had in turn informed her that as no charges had been brought and due to Kitt's record of service, the management team had decided to welcome her back to work starting with a few hours early Saturday afternoon, and that was when Kitt had had an idea . . .

Halloran looked from Kitt to Grace.

'Everything OK?'

'Fine,' Kitt said, a little too fast, and then added, 'it's just been a long week.'

Halloran pressed his lips together, a frown forming on his brow.

Kitt leaned forward in her chair so she could look beyond Halloran's broad figure. 'Hello DS Banks, thanks for coming.'

Banks didn't respond. Halloran turned to her, his look stern enough to dredge a 'Hello' out of his partner.

Apparently Banks wasn't as enthusiastic about joining forces with civilians as her superior.

'I— I have the presentation ready,' said Grace, in an attempt to cut through the awkward silence. Kitt smiled at the eagerness of her assistant. She could see Grace was doing all she could to temper her excitement, but it was obvious to anyone who knew her that giving this presentation was a big deal for her. Not least because she was wearing her smart black trousers and a mauve silk blouse that made her look that little bit more professional than her usual boho style. 'I've made a new discovery that might even help you get to the bottom of this.'

'Wonderful. Let's hear it,' said Halloran. 'No time to waste.'

'This way,' said Grace, leading the officers to the computer room.

Kitt followed, and Halloran made a point of holding the door open for her. Kitt started to smile but, remembering Theo's friend request, corrected her expression. She didn't want or need any male attention. There were more important things to focus on right now.

The computer room, for reasons Kitt could never understand, smelled strongly of plasticine. This inexplicable scent was fused with that of overheating metal. For this reason, Kitt spent as little time as possible in here. She pulled out a chair sitting at one of the computers and signalled for Halloran and Banks to do the same, while Grace was busy firing up the projector and pushing her USB into the main PC.

The agreed plan was that Kitt and Grace would share all information they'd gathered so far on persons of interest in the murders. Halloran would share whatever information he could without being disciplined for compromising an ongoing investigation, and between them they would try to look at any overlapping links or patterns. As Kitt had spent the previous day first at the funeral and second comforting a very over-tired Evie, she'd had to leave Grace to prepare the agreed presentation unsupervised, which meant there was no telling what they were about to witness.

A PowerPoint flickered up on the screen. Owen's name stood in a bold font at the top of the slide. Underneath it was a picture of Brad Pitt. Sighing, Kitt covered her face with her hands.

'So this is a rundown of the suspects so far, starting with the first victim, Owen Hall,' said Grace.

'What's with the picture of Brad?' asked Kitt.

'I wanted to enhance the presentation with images, and I didn't have time to scroll social media profiles looking for photographs of everyone involved, so I've had to make some . . . substitutions.'

'Sir . . . if Percival finds out about this . . .' Banks began, her tone weary.

'Detective Chief Superintendent Percival said to do whatever it took to bring these people to justice,' Halloran said. 'Just give it a chance.'

'We haven't got time for this,' she argued.

'Rushing in hasn't done us any favours either,' said Halloran. 'Let's take a step back. Humour a new perspective.'

Banks said no more, but Kitt watched as she sighed and pulled out her notebook and pen.

Grace, impressively unruffled by the interruption, flicked to the next slide. Angelina Jolie's face hopped into view, accompanied by a text box with Evie's name in it. 'The wine, the sedatives, the chemicals used to poison the victim, and the wording of the note left behind by the killer at the first crime scene pointed to Evelyn Bowes.'

Kitt prayed Grace was going to keep this segment brief. She had only just convinced Halloran that Evie was innocent . . . or she thought she had. At any rate, Banks thought Evie was innocent, and that had to count for something.

'Evie provided the police with a list of people who knew about the break-up, and one person's alibi didn't check out.' Cue the next slide, a photograph of Jennifer Aniston. The name Beth Myers beamed above it. 'Beth lied to the police about where she was on the night of the murder. We talked to Beth's housemate Georgette, and her manager Mr Buckhurst at the White Horse Hotel, and uncovered the fact that Beth had spent the evening with a married man named Julian Rampling. Beth's housemate, however, acted a little weird around Kitt.'

'Weird how?' asked Halloran.

'She didn't seem to want to help Beth,' Kitt explained. 'She seemed jealous of her relationship with Owen.'

'She had feelings for him?' Halloran said.

'Apparently not. Evie spoke to Beth when she was released, and it seemed she was just jealous of the kind of relationship they had.'

Halloran looked at Banks and then back at Kitt.

'Sounds a bit flimsy. We'll make a note of that. Georgette was at home alone the night Owen was murdered. She didn't have an alibi.'

Grace flicked to the next slide. 'With Beth discounted, suspicion was placed once more on Evie and her best friend.'

Kitt's jaw dropped. The visual aid for this particular part of the presentation was a candid photograph that looked as though it had been taken on Grace's iPhone. In it, Kitt was sitting in the second-floor office, eating a forkful of her home-made ginger cake.

'Grace . . .' said Kitt, as she caught Halloran looking at her out of the corner of his eye, rubbing a hand over the lower part of his face to conceal a smile. 'Didn't you have any other photograph besides this one?'

Grace put a hand on her hip. 'I only found out this was happening this morning, I had to use whatever materials I had to hand.'

Kitt opened her mouth to ask why of all the pictures Grace had taken of her boss without permission, this was the only one she had to hand, but decided she didn't want the answer.

'Nothing wrong with that picture,' said Halloran.

Kitt frowned at him; if there was one thing she couldn't stand it was platitudes.

Halloran stared back at her and leaned just a fraction in her direction. 'Appetites shouldn't be denied.'

'Except the appetite for murder,' said Banks.

'Yes, except that one,' said Halloran.

'Or an appetite for violent crime, or theft.'

'Yes, all right, Banks, you've made your point.'

Kitt wanted to smile at how Banks had undercut Halloran's obvious flirting, but she was concerned he might read it as her taking pleasure in his advances, so she hid her amusement and looked back at the screen.

Halloran waved at Grace. 'Please, continue.'

Grace nodded at the inspector. 'A person matching Kitt's description was the last person seen with Owen while he was alive. They were seen in a bar – I forget which one Kitt said.'

'The Owl and Star, on Fossgate,' said Halloran. 'Adam's financials show he was there on the night he was murdered too. Only an hour or so before he was found at the old chocolate factory.'

'So the killer takes all their victims to the same bar?' said Kitt.

'Or meets them there,' said Banks, making her first cooperative contribution to the discussion.

'This is strictly off the record, and not to be shared with

anyone else, but we've already questioned the bar staff,' said Halloran. 'They don't remember seeing Adam or a woman with red hair, but I'll probably try going there undercover tomorrow night and monitor the behaviour of the redheads in the room, maybe even chat to a couple of them. See what shakes out.'

Kitt swallowed hard and tried to keep her face straight. She allowed herself to glance at him, just long enough for her eyes to follow the hard line of his jaw in profile. He was, Kitt conceded, an attractive man. She was sure he would have no difficulty using his charms to get information.

'Is sitting in a bar on a Sunday night really the best way to solve a murder?' she asked.

'Perk of being the DI,' said Banks. 'He gets to go to the pub for a swally while I'm doing the real work, running down phone records and searching through lists of local businesses that stock fountain pens.'

Grace frowned and mouthed the word 'swally?' at Kitt.

Kitt, by way of explanation, mimed bringing a glass to her lips and swallowing.

Once Grace gave a nod of understanding, Kitt smiled over at Banks.

She didn't smile back.

'I've paid my dues,' said Halloran. 'Besides, these murders happened less than a week apart. If there's going to be another one, it's going to be soon. I've got to check it out from every possible angle, and the bar is the first link we've found between the two victims.'

'It might be the first, but it's not the only one,' said Grace.

She had a smug little smile on her face that Kitt wasn't sure she had seen before.

'You've found something else?' said Halloran, excitement rippling through his voice.

Grace flicked to the next slide. A promotional photograph of Zoe Gray filled the screen.

'Elements of the second murder scene pointed to Zoe's break-up with Adam,' said Grace.

'Yes, we spoke to her,' said Halloran, his excitement fading. 'The similarity of the MO suggested not that Zoe was the killer, but that it's someone who knows Evie, Zoe, Owen and Adam – or at least two of them.'

'MO?' said Grace.

'Modus operandi,' said Kitt.

'The victims were killed by the same method,' Banks clarified.

'Oh, right. Got it,' said Grace. 'Well, there is someone Evie and Zoe have in common. Someone who has already been taken in by the police for questioning.'

'Who?' asked Kitt.

Grace tapped the keyboard and brought up her final slide.

Kitt squinted at the screen and then back at Grace. 'Colin Farrell?'

Grace looked up at the slide. 'Oh, I was in a hurry, so I forgot to label this one, sorry. It's Ritchie Turner.'

Halloran's eyes narrowed. 'He knows Zoe as well as Evie? How did we miss this?'

'It wasn't a straightforward trail.' Grace was looking far too pleased with herself for Kitt's liking, but she let her assistant have her moment. She had earned it, it seemed. 'According to Evie's Facebook profile, she's signed up to that dating website, LoveMatch, and that's where she met Ritchie.'

'Yes, she mentioned that in interview,' said Banks, her voice striking what Kitt thought was a heavier note than usual. Was it because she had no faith in Grace's investigative skills? Or was it the reminder that Evie probably wasn't going to fall into her arms any time soon? If it was the latter, Kitt sympathized. Unrequited love, or even loving someone who didn't love you as much as you loved them, was the worst.

'How is this connected with Zoe Gray?' asked Kitt, trying to refocus.

Grace raised her dark eyebrows. 'I had to set up my own LoveMatch profile to look at Ritchie's whole dating history. Alongside Evie, and quite a few other women, one of his love connections is Zoe Gray.'

'Love connection?' said Halloran.

'It's a website designed to help people find love, so to stop people misusing the site there's a display on each profile page of who else they're seeing, or have seen in the past.'

'How do you misuse a dating website?' asked Kitt.

All eyes in the room fixed on the librarian. In them she read a mixture of pity, incredulity, and amusement.

'You use it to cheat,' said Grace. 'To date multiple people or . . . you know.'

'What?' asked Kitt.

'To . . . ghost someone.'

Kitt didn't say anything. She just waved in a manner that suggested they should continue the conversation.

'So you think Zoe Gray and Ritchie Turner dated after she broke up with Adam?' said Halloran.

'According to the date on the love connection they dated about four months ago,' Grace explained.

'But if Ritchie Turner is our killer and he's using this site to find his victims, wouldn't he have murdered Adam four months ago?' asked Kitt. 'He didn't waste any time in killing Owen. Why would he wait so long to strike against Adam?'

Halloran rubbed the back of his hand against his beard. Kitt watched him and found herself wondering what it felt like to do that. He looked at her, and her eyes darted back to the screen, to the close-up of Colin Farrell sitting in a green sports car.

'Given the level of premeditation, odds are the murderer was thinking about this for some time. Fantasizing about it,' said Halloran.

'Maybe something finally happened to tip him over the edge, or maybe he just couldn't resist any more,' said Banks. 'And if that's true, anyone on Turner's love connection list could be related to the next possible victim.'

Halloran nodded. 'We're going to need that list of people. And we need to get Turner back in the interrogation room.'

'I'll arrange for him to be picked up,' said Banks, standing and taking her phone out of her jacket pocket. She exited the room to make the call.

'There's something else,' said Kitt. 'I'm not sure if it

means anything, but Justine Krantz said that someone Evie worked with tipped her off with information on the case.'

'Did she say who?' said Halloran.

'She wouldn't say, but it was somebody at the Belle's Ball, and if they are in the beauty industry, they would have access to the same chemicals Evie does.'

'We'll put some pressure on Ms Krantz to reveal her source. If she's as keen on the public interest as she pretends to be, she won't mind assisting us in that particular line of enquiry.' Halloran paused and looked at Kitt. 'It might be a good idea if you watch Ritchie's interrogation.'

'Watch? No, I don't think that's a good idea. I didn't entirely endear myself to Turner on our first meeting.'

'He won't know you're there. We'll put you behind the mirror. If he gives us a story about Evie, you might be able to corroborate or discredit it on the spot.'

'When will it be?' asked Kitt. 'I said I'd go back to Evie's, make sure she's all right.'

Halloran paused. 'It will be at the earliest possible moment we can get our hands on Mr Turner.'

Kitt pursed her lips, thinking.

'Consider this,' Halloran said. 'Maybe the best way to serve your friend right now is to be somewhere other than at her side.'

Kitt took a deep breath. What Halloran said made sense, and she had agreed to help the investigation in any way she could. 'All right,' she said. 'Count me in.'

TWENTY-FOUR

Kitt was doing her best not to inhale the fusty smell that saturated the dim cubicle she had been standing in for the last ten minutes. Nobody could have smoked in there for years, at least not legally, and yet that old, bitter tang of nicotine remained. The only other person standing alongside her was PC Wilkinson, the fledgling constable who had been responsible for searching Beth's house the morning Kitt had paid a visit. His pasty skin and wide eyes left him so young-looking Kitt half suspected he was not a police constable at all, just a local lad playing fancy dress. Halloween was on the near horizon after all.

The pair stood in front of a large pane of glass. Beyond it Halloran and Banks sat opposite Ritchie Turner, who was slumped in his chair with his arms crossed around his chest. The suspect had been picked up at home just after four o'clock and was dressed in a much more relaxed fashion than he had been the night Kitt had tried to question him at Ashes to Ashes. Clothed in a pair of faded jeans and a long-sleeved khaki T-shirt, Ritchie's casual attire was in sharp contrast to the look on his face. A shallow pool of sweat had formed along his hairline, and his dark brown eyes glared at each of the officers in turn. Waiting it out, forcing them to make the first move.

Halloran pressed the record button on the machine sitting on the table. Ritchie narrowed his eyes at the inspector and continued his silence.

'We've been speaking to an acquaintance of yours, Mr Turner,' Halloran said, the sound of his voice warped by the glass between him and Kitt. Even in profile the stern intensity of the inspector's stare was enough to make her shuffle on the spot, shuffle into another space that was somewhere between discomfort and excitement.

'Really? Who's that?' Ritchie said, almost sneering.

'A Ms Zoe Gray,' said Banks, her lips snapping out every word.

'Zoe?' Ritchie repeated, his glare morphing into a frown. 'What about Zoe? What's going on with her?'

'Her ex-boyfriend has been murdered,' said Halloran.

Ritchie's head jumped back an inch. 'Wait . . . what, like that Evie bird?'

'Bird, indeed,' Kitt said behind the glass, tutting to herself and thinking that perhaps those white pointed shoes she saw him wearing at Ashes to Ashes were actually a good fit for him. Both his footwear and his attitudes to women belonged in the seventies.

For his part, Wilkinson shook his head at Ritchie through the glass.

'Do you know the only person Evie and Zoe have in common?' asked Halloran.

Ritchie didn't respond with words, but Kitt noticed his eyes narrowing.

'It's you, Mr Turner,' said Banks, interlocking her fingers and placing them on the wooden table between her and Turner.

'I'm sick of this,' Ritchie said, pressing his index finger hard onto the table. 'Being dragged into police questioning twice in three days when I've done nothing wrong—'

'Nothing?' said Banks. 'I suppose that substance we found on your person the other night was oregano, was it?'

Ritchie scowled. 'There must be someone else who's crossed paths with both of them. York is a small place, you know. Not a very big pool to fish in.'

Halloran and Banks looked at each other a moment, before turning back to Ritchie.

'If you had an alibi, that might help you,' said Banks. There was a sly note in her voice.

'I do have an alibi.'

'For the first murder, yes, you were at work. But not for the second murder.'

Ritchie's scowl returned. 'I told you, I was in bed. You saw me at work in the early hours of the morning, isn't that good enough?'

'Not when the murder was committed between ten and twelve, and you didn't start your shift until one a.m.'

'I was asleep.'

'Alone?'

'Yes. You must have been on late shifts in your line of work. You sleep as much as you can before the shift starts. I was in bed until twelve fifteen that night, before I got up and went into work. Like I said.'

'But nobody else can verify your whereabouts?' asked Halloran. 'Another girlfriend, perhaps?'

Ritchie paused and swallowed. 'No. My flatmate is up in Scotland visiting family.'

'So in other words, you don't have an alibi for the murder that took place on Wednesday night,' Banks said, her eyes scanning the suspect's face, up and down.

'Well, no. But I've got an alibi for the other murder. So it can't be me going around killing people off, can it?'

'Maybe, if someone's in on it with you. Certainly, the crimes have been carried out in a manner that would indicate a lot of careful planning. Likely between more than one person,' said Halloran.

'But this is all . . . what do you call it?' said Ritchie, waving a hand at the officers. As Turner made this gesture, Kitt focused in on his hand and remembered something, a detail that hadn't struck her as so important that night at Ashes to Ashes, but now seemed to carry more weight.

'Is there any way of communicating with them?' Kitt asked Wilkinson.

He shook his head. 'It's not a good idea to interrupt Halloran in the middle of an interrogation.'

'This is all what, Mr Turner?' asked Halloran.

Turner paused, trying to find his words. Banks and Halloran, stared at the suspect, letting the weight of the silence bear down on him. Seizing the moment, Kitt opened her satchel, plucked out her mobile, and sent Halloran a text message. Looking at him, she saw a momentary dip in his brow as the message arrived. He wouldn't have a ringtone on in an interrogation. But perhaps he had it on vibrate, in case of urgent messages. Halloran didn't move. Kitt re-sent the message. 'I need to talk to you, now,' it read. Again, except for the dip in his brow, Halloran didn't move.

'Are you texting the inspector?' Wilkinson asked, a waver of disbelief in his voice.

'I need to talk to him,' said Kitt, hitting send again, and this time, Halloran's head travelled in the direction of the glass.

'Excuse me a moment,' he said.

'Inspector Halloran has exited the room,' Banks said for the benefit of the interview recording. There was a pause, presumably while Halloran retrieved his phone from his pocket and checked his messages. A second later, the door swung open.

'This better be bloody important,' Halloran almost growled at Kitt. 'I'm interrogating a murder suspect, for God's sake.'

Kitt cleared her throat, determined to keep her cool. 'I know that.'

'Then what is it?'

'Ritchie, he wears nail polish.'

'You called me in here for that?' said Halloran.

Kitt sighed. 'Toluene. Didn't you say it was used in nail polish remover?'

Halloran paused for a moment. He looked at Turner

through the glass. 'He's not wearing any today, but when we talked to him at Ashes to Ashes . . .'

'He was wearing black nail polish,' Kitt finished. 'The figure we saw outside the funeral, it was definitely a man by the shape of them. I couldn't see his nails, he was too far away, but he was wearing a black cloak. He could have been wearing black nail polish too.'

'It's certainly another thread that ties him to this case,' said Halloran, and then, looking straight at Kitt, added, 'thank you.'

She smiled as he closed the door to the partition. A moment later he reappeared on the other side of the glass.

'Inspector Halloran has returned to the room. Mr Turner has been telling me that he thinks this is all speculation, sir,' Banks said.

'Is that so?' said Halloran.

'Yeah,' said Ritchie. 'The second murder took place at the old chocolate factory, right? Well, you don't have any evidence that I was hanging around there last Wednesday.'

'How can you be so sure?' asked Banks.

'Because I wasn't there.'

'But perhaps your accomplice was,' said Halloran, and then he looked down at Ritchie's hands. 'Weren't you wearing nail polish last time we spoke, Mr Turner?'

Banks sat up straighter in her seat at this question. Ritchie, narrowing his eyes to make it clear he sensed a trap, didn't answer.

'Based on your connection with these two murders we've already put a request in to search your premises, Mr Turner,' said Banks. 'There's no point hiding something like that from us. If you wear nail polish, we'll find the evidence at your home.'

'I might have been wearing it last time we talked,' said Ritchie. 'I often wear it at the club. It's part of the culture of the place. Don't see what that's got to do with the murders.'

'Only that we have found a chemical at both crime scenes that is used most regularly in nail polish remover,' said Halloran.

'Millions of people wear nail polish. Men and women,' said Ritchie.

'Yes, but those millions aren't romantically connected to both Evie Bowes and Zoe Gray,' said Halloran. 'There's far too much going on here for this to be coincidence, Mr Turner, that much I do know, and it's only a matter of time until the rest of the truth unravels. If you've something to tell us, now is the time.'

'I'm not saying anything else without a lawyer present,' said Turner.

'As Banks mentioned,' said Halloran, 'we have grounds enough to search your property, and we will. You'll get a lawyer; you can either provide us with the details of yours—'

'Do I look like I've got a lawyer?' said Ritchie, seemingly forgetting that just moments ago he'd said he was going to keep schtum.

'Or a solicitor can be called on your behalf,' Banks said, finishing where Halloran had been interrupted.

'But until we get the results of that search, you will be staying put,' said Halloran, standing up from his chair.

'Well, how long is this going to take?' Ritchie snarled. 'I've got a life, you know?'

'Yes. And two people have just lost theirs,' said Halloran. Ritchie's eyes dropped down to the table in front of him.

'You won't find anything,' said Ritchie, through gritted teeth.

'That doesn't mean you're not somehow involved,' said Halloran.

'I'm not. You're holding an innocent man, unnecessarily.'

'We're going to have to agree to disagree on how necessary this is, Mr Turner,' said Banks, standing by her partner's side. 'Two people are dead. You are connected to both of them. We can hold you for up to ninety-six hours and, if necessary, that's exactly what we're going to do.'

Ritchie rested both elbows on the table and put his head in his hands.

'That won't do you any good, Mr Turner. You'll have to come with us now,' said Halloran.

'Interview terminated at 17.07 p.m.,' Banks said before cutting off the recording.

Slowly, Ritchie obeyed Halloran's instruction. Kitt watched with a hard throbbing in her chest as they hand-cuffed Ritchie and led him out of the door, presumably to the same cells with which she and Evie were now well-acquainted. As she watched him exit the interview room, a cold chill came over her as she realized she could be looking at a killer.

TWENTY-FIVE

The heels of Kitt's suede boots clicked against the cobbles as she approached the Shambles, an area that served as an open-air slaughterhouse during medieval times, when the gutters had run red with pigs' blood. Now it was a quaint shopping street just off Kings Square, lined with wooden-beamed Tudor buildings. The architecture along the Shambles wasn't exactly built to modern specifications, and the irregular jutting of the upper storeys made it feel very much as though the buildings were leaning over you as you walked along the narrow lane. On summer days, it was a relief to hide out in the shadows. But on a crisp October morning like today a bit more light and warmth wouldn't have gone amiss, especially given the circumstances that had brought Kitt to this area of town so early on a Sunday.

About halfway down the street, just beyond Roly's fudge shop, Kitt could see Banks standing to attention next to the yellow crime-scene tape, fluorescent even in the faint morning light. As Kitt approached she had to wonder: how did that woman have the energy to make her body that angular this early in the morning?

'Hi DS Banks,' said Kitt, unable to stifle a yawn due to the fact she was carrying a coffee cup in each hand. 'Is DI Halloran inside?'

'Yes,' said Banks, eyeing the coffees.

'May I go through?' asked Kitt.

Banks sighed. 'Halloran said you could.' She lifted the tape so Kitt could bow underneath, but the librarian noticed the officer scrunching her lips up as she did so. 'I'll be in shortly, I'm just waiting for a PC to get here and relieve me.'

'Would you like a coffee while you wait?' Kitt asked, once on the other side of the cordon line. 'It's not exactly tropical out here.'

Banks narrowed her eyes as though the offer of a coffee was some kind of cruel prank. 'I assumed those were for you and Halloran.'

'They weren't for anyone in particular,' Kitt lied. Banks had hardly done anything to inspire Kitt to buy her a cup of coffee, but it probably wasn't wise to miss an opportunity to get on her good side. 'It's just so early, I thought I'd grab a couple of coffees on the way, in case people needed a pick-me-up.'

'Oh . . .' said Banks, looking from Kitt to the coffee cups. Kitt could see the officer's dilemma. In an ideal world, Kitt wouldn't be tagging along with this investigation, but as Banks looked at the coffees, the warm gleam of the two cups reflected in her eyes. At least, Kitt convinced herself that the officer's eyes looked browner than usual.

'Oh, all right,' Banks said, choosing instantaneous comfort on a cold morning over feeling a bit superior.

Kitt handed her the coffee she had originally intended for herself, and smiled. Banks took a sip and closed her eyes, the heat of the drink immediately spreading to her cheeks. Fending off, if only for a few moments, the chill in the October air.

'Oh, I meant to ask,' Banks said, just as Kitt was about to go and find Halloran, 'how is Evie? Owen Hall was buried on Friday, wasn't he?'

Kitt noticed that Banks was doing all she could to keep her tone casual. To pretend she had just remembered that Owen's funeral had been on Friday, even though she herself had witnessed Halloran call Banks from the cemetery gate. Still, there was no point in being cruel about the crush Banks had developed on Evie, especially when she had just scored Brownie points with a free coffee.

'Thanks for remembering,' said Kitt. 'It was hard for her.'

Banks shook her head. 'I can imagine. Wish there was something I ... uh, I mean I wish there was something we could do for her, but unfortunately that's not the way justice works.'

Kitt paused, wondering what to say. From the way Banks was speaking it was obvious she thought of Evie as much more than just a 'pretty girl', as Halloran had phrased it. But in Kitt's limited experience of the sergeant she was also all about professionalism. There was no talking to be done about this issue head-on, best just to keep things polite.

'I think the funeral gave her some degree of closure. I

HELEN COX | 240

met with her for a drink last night, and she seemed a bit brighter.'

'A drink?' Banks squeezed her lips together. 'I'm sure that made her feel better.'

Kitt looked at the officer, trying to read her expression. There seemed to be something sorrowful about her eyes. Was she just feeling bad on Evie's behalf? Or, given her acknowledgement that she found Evie attractive back at the theatre, was something else going on?

'It seemed to,' Kitt said. 'Perhaps after the burial she has a chance of moving on.'

'Aye, hard as the funeral was, she did right to go. Saying a proper goodbye to a person is always important.'

'Yes,' said Kitt, trying to ignore the stabbing in her heart. 'You're right, goodbyes are very important.' Shame Theo never gave me the opportunity, Kitt thought.

'Anyway . . .' she said.

Banks returned to her angular pose and nodded.

Turning away from the officer, Kitt looked up at the hand-painted sign for Très Parisienne. The swirling typography was written in the colours of the French flag, and the capital 'A' in Parisienne had been designed to make it look like the Eiffel Tower. According to Halloran's monosyllabic text message at some ungodly time this morning, a man had been found dead on the back doorstep of what must be one of the most visited restaurants in the city.

Stepping over the threshold, Kitt was greeted by rows of small tables draped in white cotton tablecloths. A small arrangement of flowers sat on each of them in varying shades of pink and red, and the silverware was sparkling even though the ambient lighting was quite subtle. Kitt had never dined here herself, but seemed to remember that Owen had brought Evie here one Valentine's Day. It was the closest thing to a trip to Paris Evie was ever going to get with him.

Further back in the restaurant, near the kitchen, Kitt could see Halloran's broad figure leaning over a young girl who was sitting in a chair, drinking a glass of water and sobbing her heart out. She wore a black fitted dress with a white apron over the top of it. No doubt she was one of the waitresses, and given the tears streaming from her bottle-green eyes, she was also the person who had found the body.

Kitt set the coffee she'd brought for Halloran on the nearest table and summoned the softest tone she had at her disposal. 'Hi there.'

Halloran turned to Kitt, notebook and pen in hand. The lines near his eyes seemed to be cut deeper today. 'Deon, this is Ms Hartley.'

''Ow do you do,' said Deon with a musical French lilt to her voice. Though her tone was curdled with sorrow, Kitt knew the instant she heard it that a thousand men had fallen in love with that voice.

'I'm so sorry this has happened,' said Kitt.

'Thank you, you are most kind,' Deon said, trying to smile, but failing and bursting into tears again. 'I 'ave never seen a dead body before.'

'It is a great shock the first time,' Halloran soothed. 'Somehow, it never looks quite how you expect it to look.'

Kitt examined Halloran's face again. How many dead bodies had he seen? She didn't want to calculate that figure. Something about the idea of Halloran having to look at all that cruelty and horror roused an emptiness inside her.

Deon reached for a glass of water from the table next to her and took a sip. ''E was slumped up against the back door. At first I thought 'e was sleeping. That 'e was just a vagrant using the shelter of the alley to stay warm now the weather 'as turned. I was going to offer 'im some leftover croissants I 'ad from yesterday's breakfast. But when I touched 'is shoulder . . .' She scrunched her eyes tightly shut, as though that gesture could somehow erase the memory of what she had seen. 'Well, you can see, I didn't move 'im. I just dialled 999.'

'Which was the right thing to do,' said Halloran. 'And get yourself inside quickly. You never know how long somebody who commits a crime like this is going to hang around.'

Deon's face looked even whiter than it had a moment before. 'You mean, 'e could 'ave been in the alleyway? The killer?'

'Unlikely, but you can never be too careful,' Halloran replied. 'If you don't mind, Deon, I'm going to give you a moment, as I have a few issues to discuss with Ms Hartley.'

Deon offered a weak smile and took another sip of her water.

Halloran placed a gentle hand on Kitt's shoulder. 'Follow me,' he said.

Kitt looked at Halloran's hand and then followed him as he headed out into the kitchen.

She was quite taken aback by how narrow the kitchen was, especially given the popularity of the restaurant. It wasn't so bad lengthways. There was enough space for an industrial oven, two sinks, and a dishwasher. Not to mention a couple of worktops for chopping ingredients and lining up plates to be delivered to the tables. Widthways however, it was a touch too narrow to stand face-to-face with anyone without invading their personal space. Kitt and Halloran tried it for a moment. In this position, Kitt could almost feel his breath on her skin and it was at once clear to her that this set-up was not going to make it easy to concentrate on the details of the latest victim. She sidled back towards the doorway, leaning against a cupboard next to one of the sinks.

'Tim Diallo,' said Halloran. 'That name mean anything to you?'

'Tim Diallo,' Kitt repeated. 'No, sorry, it doesn't. Third victim?'

Halloran put away his notebook, pulled out his phone, and swiped across the screen. 'This . . . it's not a pretty picture, but it will save you from having to look at the body in the flesh, as it were.'

Kitt offered a polite nod. She didn't have the heart to tell the inspector that she had had the misfortune of seeing a dead body in the flesh once before. Still, she braced herself before looking at Halloran's phone. On the screen was an image of a thin, bespectacled man with black hair cut very close to his head. His green-grey eyes were opened wide, but there was no life in them. His arms had been crossed over his body like the other victims, and there was a patch of blood around his chest.

Kitt cleared her throat. 'I don't recognize him, but it looks like the same MO, right?'

Halloran nodded. 'Diallo was poisoned. All signs point to the same chemicals used for the first two murders, but we haven't confirmed that yet. He had a note pinned to his chest, with a fountain pen just like the first two victims.'

'What did the note say this time?'

'"We'll always have Paris."'

Kitt frowned and took a deep breath. 'So, we've narrowed our suspects down to Humphrey Bogart fans with a sick sense of humour.'

Halloran's jaw tightened. 'And someone who wears nail polish, let's not forget that oh-so-important fact.'

'What about the fountain pens? Are they all the same brand?'

'This hasn't been released to the press, so you need to keep it quiet, but the killer is using Stanwyck fountain pens. It's a defunct brand, so it's only possible to get hold of them second-hand. We've been running down leads in local stockists and online stockists. We've interviewed everyone who lives in the district and has bought more than one of them, but the list is short and so far no one has any connection to this case.'

Kitt stared at the inspector. Unlike Banks, he wasn't standing straight and tall. His head had a noticeable bow to it and some dark circles under his eyes told the story of a sleepless night. Perhaps several. Though Kitt didn't have dark circles of her own, she felt them. Had it really been only a week since this nightmare had begun?

'I know this is a stupid question,' she said, 'but are you all right?'

'I don't have any choice but to be,' said Halloran.

'That's not true,' said Kitt, taking a step towards the inspector. 'At least, not when it comes to me. I'm not an official police employee. I'm not going to feed anything back to your superiors.'

'I appreciate the concern,' said Halloran, his eyes wandering across the kitchen surfaces until they met with hers, 'truth is, I don't have time to wallow. The first two killings happened four days apart. The gap between the second and the third was just three days.'

'He . . . might be escalating,' Kitt said.

'Seems to be. I need to stay active. Pursue every lead.'

Instinct took over then. Kitt put her hand on the inspector's shoulder and squeezed. 'Don't lose hope. We'll work this out, we will,' she said.

He looked down at her from his six-foot-something vantage point and put his hand on top of hers.

For a moment, all Kitt could focus on was the pressure, the pleasing weight and the warmth of his skin. His hands were large and firm and strong . . .

'So,' Kitt continued, withdrawing her hand. 'Given the nature of the other murders, the links to their past relationships, we're assuming that this guy did something excruciatingly cruel to an ex-girlfriend during a mini-break in Paris?'

'Something like that,' said Halloran. 'As soon as a PC gets here to relieve Banks, she'll be off trying to locate his latest ex-girlfriend. You'd think I'd get more resources on a case like this, but not a chance. It's clear by now that it's unlikely the ex-girlfriend will be the killer. But there might be another clue somewhere in her statement.'

'And I take it you still have Turner in custody?'

'Don't even say it,' said Halloran. 'Yes, the crime was committed while he was in custody, which makes pinning any of this on him even harder.'

'Still going with the accomplice theory?'

'The more elaborate this thing gets, the less likely it is that the killer is acting solo.'

Kitt paused. 'And if you really think about it, if there is an accomplice, this was the perfect time for them to commit another murder. It proves his innocence, or near as damn it.'

'We might be able to use that line of argument. But it's still circumstantial, and we're running out of time to hold him,' Halloran admitted. 'The tests came back from his house, we found nail polish remover, but not in large quantities, and no peroxide or diazepam. We're still waiting on the forensics from his locker at work though.'

'And what about this crime scene? There weren't any clues left behind? Forensic or otherwise?' said Kitt. 'At some point whoever is doing this has to have made a mistake and missed something.'

'Well, the paper the note was written on was the same as the other murders. We might find something in that, but it's thin. There is one other glimmer of hope though,' said Halloran.

'Hope? You mean I was dishing out sympathy for no good reason?' Kitt said with a faint smile. Halloran had the same gleam in his eyes she had noticed back on Evie's doorstep on Friday.

Kitt swallowed hard, wondering. What was going on in that mind of his? And then, yet again, she checked herself. Curiosity like that only caused trouble. She had taken Grace's advice and ignored Theo's friend request, so at least that was the end of that. But she couldn't risk developing an attachment to the inspector when there was so much at stake. If this case, and her general experience, had taught Kitt anything, it was that romantic entanglements rarely led anywhere good.

'There's a camera in that alleyway and the strong likelihood of CCTV footage.'

'You might have mentioned that earlier,' said Kitt.

'Sorry. Tired.'

Kitt raised both eyebrows. 'You think the killer is on tape?'

'Not by accident.'

'What do you mean?'

'They've been so careful up until now. No traces of forensic evidence. Few clues. It's out of character.'

'Mmm. Patrick Bateman.'

Halloran frowned at her. *'American Psycho?'*

Kitt's smile broadened. She wagered a police detective might have read that book, or at least seen the film, which, much to Grace's amusement when they had discussed it, scared Kitt more than she'd expected. It wasn't the blood or the gore. It was the idea that someone who seemed so charming could in fact be the end of you. Who wouldn't think it was a good idea to go home with Christian Bale? He scrubbed up well enough.

'Patrick Bateman was playing a sort of game, to see what he could get away with. See how close he could get to being caught.'

'It's part of the thrill.'

'This is good news,' said Kitt.

'How?'

'It means they're going to go a step too far at some point. It means we're going to catch them.'

'I was always going to catch them,' said Halloran. 'The problem with cases like this is, it isn't about catching them. It's about catching them before they kill anyone else.'

'I could text Evie that name, Tim Diallo, and ask if she knows him. Maybe there's a link there?'

Halloran lowered his eyes. 'That makes sense. I'm going to the Owl and Star tonight.'

Kitt nodded. 'You know, there must be a way the killer is finding out about all these break-ups. Maybe they're over-hearing them in the Owl and Star – people do talk about that kind of thing down the pub.'

'It's more likely that the killer is directly connected to the victims in some way, but definitely something to consider. And given the rate of escalation, the odds are strong the killer will show their face there tonight.'

'Most things that concern Yorkshire people are settled down the pub, don't see why a murder case should be any different,' said Kitt.

'You should join me,' said Halloran, meeting Kitt's eyes again.

'What?'

'It will look more natural if I'm not sitting alone, but I don't have the resources to take another officer.'

'Oh . . . I see. W-well . . .'

'What do you say? Want to come along and help me look less conspicuous?'

Kitt searched for an excuse. But the truth was she didn't want to make one.

Instead, she narrowed her eyes at the inspector and put her hand on her hip. 'I'll do my best, but I'm not a miracle worker.'

Halloran smiled.

TWENTY-SIX

'Walls?' said Evie.

Kitt looked askance at Evie. 'Sorry, what?'

'Do you want to walk the walls?' Evie pointed up at the iron gateway, complete with the county's white rose emblem, which led up to the Roman city walls at Victoria Bar.

'Howay then, less tourist traffic up there than there is in the streets at this time of day.'

On their way to lunch on the other side of town, the pair hopped up the stone staircase and at once their hair was caught in the gusts of wind ripping through the battlements at the top. Kitt held onto her trilby for a moment until they moved to a less exposed portion of wall. From their new vantage point, it was possible to look out over the rooftops of the red-bricked suburbia below. A weak sun cowered behind the gauze of grey cloud, making the buildings look duller in colour than they might have on a clearer day. But there was still some serenity to be had, looking down at the world like that. A reminder of how good a shift in point of view could be for the soul.

'Have you asked Zoe if she knows Tim Diallo?' asked Evie, while Kitt tried to ignore the outline of the old chocolate factory, looming in the distance over the cul-de-sacs and cottages. She instead turned her gaze towards the Minster. From almost anywhere in the city centre, it was possible to get a glimpse of those thirteenth-century gothic spires that seemed to cut through any amount of fog.

'The police are dealing with that bit, I just had to check in with you,' Kitt replied, squinting into the middle distance in case it was possible she could pick out the sails of Holgate Windmill through the haze. It was, just about. The sight of that old mill, restored to working order by loving local residents, usually brought a smile to her face. But she hadn't been so quick to smile over the last week, and she wasn't the only one. Even in somewhere like London or Manchester, this killer would still have left their mark, but in a place the size of York this kind of tragedy had cast a shadow over the whole community, its ugliness lurking in all the nooks and corners that were once thought safe.

Evie sighed. 'I wish I did have some nugget of information to unravel this whole case. To stop everyone thinking I am a murderer, and to stop any more people dying. When will it end?'

'I don't know,' said Kitt, patting her friend on the shoulder. 'And not everyone thinks you're the killer. I don't, and neither does Grace, or Banks.' Kitt wished she could have added Halloran to that list, but she still wasn't sure about that.

'Banks thinks I'm innocent?'

'That's what I heard her say,' said Kitt. As the conversation had been overheard it didn't seem right to reveal the context, but she felt it important for her friend to know there was hope.

'Well, that's something at least. Maybe she knows what it's like to have a boyfriend break up with you the way Owen did me, maybe she sympathizes.'

'It would be a girlfriend in her case, from what I understand, but maybe she does know what it's like to go through a bad break-up. Whatever her reasoning, she doesn't believe you're guilty.'

Evie offered a frail smile and went quiet for a moment. She stepped aside so that a young couple could pass on a narrow part of the path. Kitt did the same and watched the lovers squeeze by, secretly hoping the young man didn't take it upon himself to break up with the young woman in some cowardly way. Right now such a move could prove very bad for his health indeed.

With the couple out of their way, Kitt and Evie started walking again.

'Sorry about not being able to give you a lead on Diallo,' said Evie.

'It's all right, it's just eliminating lines of enquiry at this stage. I already texted Halloran, so he can rule that out.'

Evie swung her head around at this and a knowing smile came over her full lips, which she'd painted deep red. 'Been texting the inspector a lot, have you?'

'About the case, a bit,' said Kitt, trying to keep her tone casual.

'Just about the case?'

'That's what I said.'

'You haven't talked about anything else?'

'No,' Kitt said, a bit too quickly. 'Well, a bit about how the case is affecting him, but that still technically counts as the case.'

'So he's opening up to you? Letting you in on what he's thinking?'

'A bit.'

Evie giggled to herself.

'Whatever just ran through your mind,' Kitt said, 'don't say it.'

'There must be some big perks to dating a detective.'

'Evie, stop teasing.'

'I'm not teasing. I'm just talking generally about the pluses of having a man of the law on your arm. No more parking tickets.'

'I doubt that's true.'

'You'd get the inside scoop on all the most dramatic happenings about town.'

'According to Ruby I could achieve that by taking the 59 bus.'

'Not the same,' Evie said. 'Besides, it's never a terrible thing to date someone who owns a pair of handcuffs.'

Kitt sighed at her friend. 'The only thing I'm in the market for right now is a gag.'

'Oooh,' Evie said with another giggle. 'Kinky.'

'With the right person, I'm sure,' said Kitt, determined not to give Evie the satisfaction of rising to this. Or give her friend any indication about the thoughts racing through her mind just now. They were centred on Halloran's large, strong hands. A feature that would probably give him little use for handcuffs in an intimate situation . . .

'Do you know if the killer was caught on CCTV, like Halloran thought? Or which Belle's Ball attendee might be leaking information to the press?' said Evie, seemingly understanding that she wasn't going to draw Kitt any further on the topic of Halloran.

'Haven't heard back on either of those things yet. Hopefully, I'll find out tonight.'

'What's happening tonight?' Evie asked, raising her eyebrows.

So, she had just pretended to drop the subject.

'I'm meeting Halloran at the Owl and Star for some undercover work. And before you say something you consider clever, yes, that was undercover work, not work under the covers.'

Evie chuckled. 'So you say . . . So the third victim was picked up there too?'

'It was on the police agenda even before the third killing, but Halloran texted to say the financials suggested he'd been there last night, yes.'

'Just the two of you, tonight?'

'I don't know.'

'Bet you a hundred pounds it is.'

'Halloran has got enough on his plate, don't you think, without concocting excuses to get me alone.'

'When you're that busy you have to be efficient. Do you really think the killer is going to show there, tonight?'

'Halloran says the murderer is escalating. That they'll try to kill someone else soon, so it could very well happen.'

'I'd love to be there when you get him,' said Evie. 'I'm going out for a few drinks with Jazz and Heather tonight.'

'Do you really think it's a good idea to be going out at the moment? With people being picked off by an unknown killer?'

'Not people,' said Evie, 'men.'

'Oh yes, that's true,' said Kitt. 'For once it's relatively safe to be a woman out after dark.'

'Maybe we should swing around to the Owl and Star when we're finished at The Maltings?'

'Much as I'd love to see you, that's probably not a good idea.' Kitt put her hand on her friend's arm. 'If the killer is there, your presence might tip them off or make them alter their plan in some way, and we need to draw them out.'

'Hmm. Good thinking. Though it could be an excuse just to keep Halloran to yourself . . .'

'Would you cool your heels on that? Nothing is going on between me and Halloran.'

'Not yet,' Evie said, 'but undercover work is sexy, everyone knows that.'

'Not the way I do it.'

'We'll see, old chum . . .'

TWENTY-SEVEN

Walking into the Owl and Star, Kitt's eyes searched the early evening cocktail crowds for a familiar face. It took her a minute or so to find one. Not because she didn't recognize the face, but because she was looking for a man in a smart, dark suit, and the man she thought she recognized was wearing a tight, white V-necked T-shirt and faded blue jeans. On noticing Kitt he waved over at her. The man looked strikingly like Inspector Halloran and, at the same time, nothing like him at all.

With a frown on her face, Kitt continued over to the corner where he was sitting. He stood as she reached the table.

'Thanks for coming,' he said. 'Can I get you a drink?'

'Just something soft, thanks, a lemonade,' Kitt said, placing her trilby down on the table and hanging her satchel on the arm of the nearest chair.

'You sure? Just because I'm on duty doesn't mean you have to miss out on any fun,' Halloran said with a smile.

'Just the lemonade, thank you, Ins—' but Kitt cut off

there as Halloran shook his head in a sharp movement. Of course, there was no point in Halloran wearing plain clothes if she was going to announce him to the room as a police inspector.

'Malcolm,' Kitt corrected herself.

'Actually, it's Mal,' said Halloran.

'Mal,' Kitt repeated, enjoying the way her tongue rolled its way around the 'el' sound, whilst ensuring none of this enjoyment played out on her face.

Kitt took off her coat and sat down, which was Halloran's cue to go to the bar. It had been a while since Kitt had been to the Owl and Star, perhaps even a couple of years, but it still pulled in the crowds on a Sunday. With its polished floorboards, wood-panelled bar, and rugged brickwork around the fireplace, there was no disputing the cosiness of the place. It was the perfect venue for forgetting you had to get up and go to work in the morning.

Kitt smiled to herself, but, as she watched Halloran ordering from the bartender and paying for the lemonade, her smile faded. As he reached over the bar to pay, she noticed the short sleeves of his T-shirt bordered a tattoo on his left arm. It looked like some kind of lettering, but only the base of the letters were visible, so she couldn't make out the word. Nonetheless, she smiled again, and her lips tingled at the thought of kissing along that tattoo. She was an avid reader, she told herself – it was only natural she'd be attracted to ink.

She sat up straighter in her seat, trying to shake the strange stirring she felt. But it didn't shift. Her breath deepened as she took in how tall and broad he looked, even in casual clothes. No matter how much she had tried to deceive herself since they had first crossed paths, she couldn't deny it now. She wanted him, and that was the most frightening thought she had had that week – a week in which she'd been arrested for murder.

Halloran turned back to bring the drinks over and she snapped her head away so he might not guess she had been studying him.

'There you go,' said Halloran, setting down Kitt's drink before sitting back in his seat. He was close enough that his legs pressed against Kitt's under the table. It was possible to move an inch in the opposite direction so that just a bit of space was made between them, but Kitt stayed where she was. It was a small table, and Halloran had long legs, so she had an excuse if anything was said about her quietly enjoying the warmth of him.

'Seen anyone who might fit the killer's description?' he asked, his voice more businesslike than it had been before.

'Give me a chance, I've just sat down,' said Kitt, glossing over the fact she had been far too busy watching him to be paying attention to the rest of the room.

'Well, we caught them on CCTV,' said Halloran.

'The killer? You've seen their face?'

'Not exactly, but there has been a bit of a twist. Do you want to see?' Halloran pulled his mobile out of the pocket of his jeans.

'You made a copy?'

'I did, and just so we're clear, I'm not supposed to, and if anyone asks you haven't seen this.'

'Noted. You know, most people have cute cat videos on their phones.'

'It's sweet that you think that's what most people have saved. When you're a DI you really get to see the darkest corners of people's lives.'

'I guess, since I was a suspect earlier in the week, that applies to me too.'

Halloran smiled. 'Nothing I saw unsettled me. Quite the opposite . . .'

'It . . . settled you?'

Halloran chuckled. 'I see we're feeling literal tonight. It intrigued me.'

Unsure quite how to respond to that in a way that wouldn't get her into trouble, Kitt let her gaze drift from Halloran to his phone.

He tapped the screen and the footage jumped to life.

Given the fact it had been taken down a side alley, the footage was shadowy, but Kitt could make out a figure with long red hair. At first they seemed to be attacking Tim Diallo. It took Kitt a while to realize that the redhead wasn't attacking Diallo, but kissing him. The fact that Diallo could barely stand was making the exchange seem more confrontational than it really was. So the killer had used diazepam on this victim too. A few moments later, the redhead handed Diallo a bottle of wine, the one that had been found on him at the murder scene. Smiling, he held the bottle to his lips and drank. The redhead held the base of the bottle up so he took in more of the liquid than he might from an ordinary sip. He flailed, trying to struggle, but the killer held the bottle and Diallo's head in place. A moment later Diallo staggered backwards against the wall, clutching his throat and convulsing.

Kitt smothered a gasp with her hand.

Halloran reached out and stroked her arm. 'You all right?'

Kitt didn't respond in words. Instead, she kept her eyes fixed to the screen.

After less than a minute, Diallo stopped moving. The killer bent forward and placed the wine bottle in his hands. Straddling the victim, the killer drew their arm back low, and then plunged it upwards in a stabbing motion. It was impossible to see exactly what had taken place, but Kitt assumed the killer had just pierced Diallo's heart.

There was some shuffling about then. The killer had their back to the camera, so it was impossible to see what they were doing, but if she had to guess, Kitt would say they were crossing the arms over the body and securing the note on the victim's chest with a fountain pen.

Slowly, the killer stood, drew up their hood, and turned to face the camera, their head lowered just enough that the hood covered their face. They stretched out their arms in a swift dramatic fashion and bowed. They held the pose for a few seconds before stalking off down the alleyway.

Kitt sat rigid in her seat. 'Oh my God. That's ... that's beyond creepy. Are you trying to give me nightmares, showing me this?'

'Is that your way of saying you don't feel safe being alone tonight?'

Kitt crossed her arms and gave Halloran a withering look. 'Such an altruistic thought, but I'll brave it.'

Halloran didn't say anything else, but continued to stare at her.

Kitt stirred the straw in her lemonade, making the ice jingle. She wouldn't normally fiddle like this, but she would take any distraction right now. 'I believe you said there was a twist?'

'Yeah, the killer is definitely a man.'

'How can you tell?'

'Well, if you look at the dimensions of the person in the video they do look a bit broad for the female frame – at least going by averages.'

'Some of us are sturdier than others, you know?'

Halloran held his hands up. 'And there's nothing wrong with that, but Diallo was gay, so that person kissing him is most likely to be a man.'

'Are you sure?'

'Sure as we can be, why?'

Kitt shrugged. 'Maybe nothing. It's just my sister Rebecca, she's a doctor. I asked her about poison cases. She said it was more common for women to use poison.'

'It's possible that it's a man and woman working together,' said Halloran, resting his hands on the table, not far from where Kitt was resting hers.

'So you think the guy in the video is wearing a wig?'

'Yeah. According to Diallo's ex-boyfriend, they both dabbled in cross-dressing now and again.'

'Did you ask Zoe Gray about the wig I saw in her dressing room? Or if she knew Tim Diallo?'

'Yeah. The wig doesn't belong to her, it's the property of the theatre. Although she had access to it, she had no access to the chemicals or the sedative, and she has alibis for all three murders. She doesn't know Diallo either.'

'So Zoe's out. What about Tim's ex-boyfriend?'

'Francis,' said Halloran. 'Banks tracked him down. He's an old boyfriend from about six months ago. He'd caught Diallo texting someone else while they were away for a weekend in Paris, at the top of the Eiffel Tower.'

'How romantic,' Kitt said in the flattest of all possible tones.

'Isn't it? Similar problems when it comes to marking him as a suspect though. He had no access to the chemicals. No links to Owen or Adam, yet. I mean, we're still digging.'

Kitt wondered if he was also still digging when it came to Evie, but knew that conversation would only lead to an argument. She moved her hands, which had been sitting happily within reach of Halloran's, closer to her body.

'So the first two victims were heterosexual and the third homosexual? Is that the twist you were talking about?'

Halloran nodded. 'Sometimes you see this in serial killer cases – the killer changes something small in their MO. Trying to break up the pattern and reduce the chances of getting caught. There is one other lead that's come out of this however.'

'One that will crack the case?'

'Maybe. According to Diallo's financials he has been to Ashes to Ashes a couple of times in the last month.'

'Which links him back to Turner.'

'Yes, but Turner was in custody when the third murder was committed, and we're still waiting for those bloody forensics to come back on his work locker. It's taken so long we've had to release him. You'd think with a case of this scale, toxicology would be pushed through as a priority, but it's a slow process.'

'Isn't the fact that Diallo went to Ashes to Ashes enough to bring him back in?'

Halloran shook his head. 'We need hard evidence to make a conviction. But I can't shake the idea that he is involved somehow. That he knows something. It's rare that you're led back to the same suspect three times without cause.'

'What I can't get my head around with him is motive,' said Kitt. 'I think it's clear that the culprit, or culprits, are driven by some kind of heartbreak-related vendetta.'

Halloran's eyes gleamed. 'I had no idea you were an expert criminal profiler.'

'Do you need to be? In every instance, the victim has been a person who has committed some cruelty against an ex-partner. The killer, or killers, have an obsession.'

'I can't argue with that, but Turner's relationships have all been short-lived, nothing dramatic or odd, and we can't immediately assume this is revenge for some personal slight. Some people will take any excuse for vigilante-like behaviour. Some people just have superiority complexes.'

Kitt smiled at the inspector. 'All I'm saying is, I know from what Evie's been through that these things are just desperately painful for those on the receiving end.'

'I know.' Halloran lowered his eyes, staring into his cola.

'Francis told Banks he was still recovering. Said Tim was the first man he'd ever fallen in love with.'

Kitt's body stiffened. 'It is difficult to get over that first heartbreak,' she said, and then tried to think of a way to change the subject. 'What about Justine Krantz? Did she give up her source?'

'With a little bit of pressure, yes. Banks said she named her source as Jasmine Brewster.'

'Jasm— Jazz? Who works at Evie's salon? Evie's out with her right now.'

'I don't think there's cause for alarm,' said Halloran.

'Really? Because she has access to the same chemicals as Evie . . .'

'She also has alibis, for all three murders.'

Kitt sighed. 'Well then, why would she go blabbing to the press?'

'She told Banks that Krantz had ambushed her.'

'That's not difficult to believe.'

'But apparently Diane Phelps, who owns the salon, had also told the staff that it would look better if they were open with the media.'

'Really?' Kitt frowned. 'Why?'

'She thought it would look bad on the salon if they didn't comment, and they wanted it known they were cooperating with the police.'

'I suppose that's understandable,' said Kitt, while noticing that her mobile was buzzing. Seeing it was Evie calling, she gave Halloran an apologetic look and answered.

'Hello?'

'Kitt!' Evie half-screamed down the phone.

'Evie?' Kitt raised her voice so her friend could hear.

'He's after us, he's chasing after us. Heather got stabbed.'

'What— where are you?' Kitt said.

'We've made it to the Wonky Donkey.'

'Stay there. We're on our way.'

TWENTY-EIGHT

Kitt barged through the door of the Wonky Donkey, or, to give the pub its official name, The Three-Legged Mare, on High Petergate with Halloran a step behind. The pub was quiet at this time on a Sunday, and it took Kitt mere seconds to scan the room and find Evie, Jazz, and Heather sitting around a circular wooden table. Evie and Jazz were wrapped up in their winter coats, but Heather had taken hers off and was clutching a white cloth to her forearm. The cloth was spotted with red.

The group was too engrossed in Heather's injury to notice Kitt had arrived, and so the librarian strode towards them, calling out her friend's name as she did so.

Evie jumped up at once and scurried over for a hug.

'Are you all right? What happened?' asked Kitt, putting an arm around her friend's shoulder and walking her back to the table.

'We saw the killer,' said Jazz, unhooking her green duffel coat.

'You saw his face?' said Halloran.

Jazz shook her head. 'Some of it. The lower part. Just from the nose downwards really. He was wearing a . . . like a cloak with a hood, and a wig, by the look of things. A red one.'

Halloran's shoulders tensed.

'It was the same person we saw outside the cemetery gates at Owen's funeral, or someone dressed just like them,' said Evie.

'He followed us down Mad Alice Lane as we were making our way here for one last drink,' Jazz explained.

'Mad Alice Lane,' Kitt repeated, and looked at Halloran. 'Where Ashes to Ashes is situated.'

'Turner,' Halloran growled.

'Heather tried to confront him,' said Jazz.

'That was a very dangerous thing to do,' Halloran said.

'I know it was stupid,' Heather said. 'I thought three against one would be good odds. Thought I'd take the chance to find out who the killer was and save us all this trouble. But he was carrying a knife.'

'That cut looks nasty.'

'It's not as bad as it looks, I don't think, but I'm not a doctor.'

'When he cut Heather like that, we made a run for it,' said Evie. 'It was clear he wasn't messing around.'

'You did the right thing,' said Halloran. 'Excuse me, I need to put in a call about this.'

As the inspector walked away, Kitt turned back towards the table. A chill came over her as she looked around the small circle of friends. 'This can't have happened by accident.'

Evie cocked her head. 'How do you mean?'

'I mean, the killer must have known where you'd be tonight. It's too much of a coincidence.'

Evie swallowed hard. 'So, you think the killer is ... actively stalking us?'

'Stalking is time-consuming. The odds are they are focusing their energies on one individual,' Kitt said, unable to make direct eye contact with her friend.

There was a pause while Evie considered this. 'Me? You think they're stalking me?'

'That would make sense, my sweet,' said Heather. 'The killings started with someone connected to you.'

'But stalking me has to be the most boring job in the universe,' Evie said.

'Maybe whoever it is gets off on watching people get massages?' said Jazz.

'Suppose that wouldn't be any less weird than the rest of it,' said Evie.

'Maybe the police should put some kind of security detail on you,' said Kitt.

Evie frowned. 'That's going a bit over the top, isn't it?'

'It might help them catch the killer. They might notice who it is, lurking in the background. Besides, you can't take any chances with stalker stuff, that story doesn't go well. Have you ever read *Never Let You Go*?'

'No,' Evie said, 'and I'm getting the impression it might not be the most comforting read right now.'

'Perhaps not,' said Kitt. 'But that story was totally different to yours. Unless you have an abusive ex-husband who has just escaped from prison you forgot to mention?'

A wry smile formed on Evie's lips that suggested she had sussed Kitt's plan to tease her into feeling better about being stalked by a murderer. 'I think that might have come up by now.'

'Just checking, these trifles can slip our mind.'

'Right,' said Halloran, returning to the circle. 'Every copper in the city is looking for this guy, and for Ritchie. If he's still out there and is going to commit a crime tonight, we've got a good chance of catching him. Anything else to report here?'

'Kitt was just breaking the news that this incident probably means the killer is stalking me,' said Evie. 'She wants to know if I can get police protection.'

'We don't have the resources to have someone on guard 24/7, but I could move you to a safe location where you could stay until we catch them,' said Halloran.

'You mean . . . go into hiding?' Evie said, wrapping her arms around herself.

Halloran nodded. 'Just until we catch the murderers.'

'No, I don't think so.'

'Evie,' said Jazz. 'At least think about it. I've read a lot of true crime in my time. You don't know what these people are capable of.'

'I don't want to hide. Even if I'm scared, I don't want to give the killer the satisfaction of thinking they've won.'

A broad smile stretched across Heather's lips. 'That's very brave.'

'It is,' said Halloran. 'But if you insist on staying in plain view, you at least need to be vigilant.'

'In what way?'

'Like we said about the incident at the funeral, whoever it was couldn't show up in person as they'd be recognized as out of place. Whoever it is, you know them, but not well. You're going to need to watch the people around you, carefully. Look for any suspicious behaviour.'

Evie looked slowly from Heather to Jazz and then to Kitt as though one of them might be the killer. Kitt sighed and shook her head. Her friend had been through enough without having to suspect the people who were supposed to care for her had a hand in this.

'We'd better get you to A&E,' Halloran said to Heather.

'Oh, no. I don't think we need to. The bleeding has pretty much stopped and the NHS is stretched as it is.'

'You should still have someone take a look at it.'

'Honestly, it's fine. It's not deep, it was just a shock.'

'Well, if you're sure?'

'I'm sure, I'm more concerned about how we're all getting home safely,' said Heather. 'Shall we share a taxi?'

'No need,' said Halloran. 'My car's just around the corner, I'll drop you all where you need to be. Just in case the killer puts in another appearance.'

Kitt was about to say that there was hardly any need for the inspector to go out of his way when it was unlikely the killer would risk returning tonight, and there were taxis available just around the corner at Bootham Bar, but before she could get a word out the whole table had thanked Halloran and told him how relieved they were to have a police escort.

'Don't look so glum, Ms Hartley,' Halloran said. 'I know you were hoping it would just be the two of us this evening, but I'll let you ride up front.'

Kitt scowled at Halloran and then, as she heard Evie gig-gling, immediately regretted rising to the bait.

'I'm sorry, inspector,' she said, trying to recover some dignity. 'The stress of this case has clearly left you quite delusional. Nobody in this room fancies you half as much as you fancy yourself.'

More giggling from the table, this time Heather and Jazz pitched in.

Halloran took a step closer to Kitt. 'You underestimate how much I fancy myself if you think that's a cutting remark. If anyone in this room likes me half as much as I like myself I'm still chalking that up as a win.'

In spite of the dramatic turn the evening had taken, Kitt couldn't help but chuckle at this. Arrogance itself was an abhorrent quality, but mocking your own narcissism turned out to be somewhat charming. Kitt noticed a gleam in Halloran's eyes as she laughed, which made laughing all the more worthwhile.

'Oh, do give over,' she said, straightening her face. 'We've got damsels in distress to get safely home.'

'I hadn't forgotten,' said Halloran, before gesturing for the ladies at the table to follow him. Kitt, still determined not to show any enthusiasm at the prospect of being driven home by Halloran, followed on last. She wondered whether the inspector would insist she took the front passenger seat when they got to his car. Whether she would have an excuse for sitting by his side, thigh-by-thigh, his hand on the gear stick, begging to be covered with hers.

TWENTY-NINE

Halloran pulled up outside Kitt's cottage and put the hand-brake on. The detective looked over at the librarian, and she tried to put out of her mind the funny look Evie had given her when they had dropped her off ten minutes ago. It was most peculiar. At a guess, Evie was trying to insinuate by expression alone that Halloran was going to make a move on her. Kitt had shaken her head at her friend and waved her into her house. The last thing she needed was more taunting about Halloran, particularly now that she was starting to admit to herself that she was attracted to him, which was really just miserable news.

When she first broke up with Theo she thought she was going to have to put in a lot of hard work into not being attracted to people. Over the years, however, she had come to realize how much it took for a person to turn her head. Something about Halloran was different . . .

His blue eyes glimmered in the yellow light cast by a nearby lamp post. The white T-shirt he was wearing – in October as though the cold meant nothing to him – fitted tight against his toned chest. Lower down it clung to a small paunch, which wasn't visible when he was standing. Kitt imagined running her hand across it. Thought about how soft it would feel in contrast to his muscular arms clinching around her. Catching herself staring at him, she cleared her throat.

'It's getting late.'

Halloran ran his thumb and forefinger over his eyebrows. 'Yeah, sometimes I forget why I signed up for these late nights in the first place.'

'Why did you?' asked Kitt. If Evie's relationship radar was anything to go by, every extra minute Kitt stayed in the car the likelihood of Halloran making a move on her increased, but the question was out of her mouth before she could stop it.

Halloran chuckled. 'For all the wrong reasons.'

'I don't believe you.'

Halloran studied Kitt's face. 'There was a lot about my upbringing I couldn't control. I didn't much like that.'

'I don't think any of us do,' Kitt said.

'Being a copper, I knew it'd be a lot of responsibility, but I also knew if I climbed the ranks I'd get to control my own investigations.'

'Looks like you're exactly where you want to be.'

Halloran sighed and rested both hands on the steering wheel. 'Looks can be deceiving.'

The smile that had been on Kitt's lips faded. 'How do you mean?'

'I mean, there are costs to this life. There's a cost to everything.'

'Like what?' Kitt knew this was prying, but Halloran had started this line of conversation, so she didn't see why she shouldn't have her curiosity satisfied.

Halloran pressed his lips together, thinking. 'I had a wife.'

This piece of information sliced right through Kitt, and it was all she could do not to wince. Why did this surprise her? Did she really think a man who looked like Halloran was likely to have much experience of being single? Especially given his age. They hadn't discussed it outright, but given the smattering of grey in his dark hair, Kitt had guessed he was somewhere in his forties.

'And . . . the job took its toll on your relationship?'

'You could say that.' All of a sudden, Halloran's voice was weak to the point of breaking.

Kitt didn't dare say anything else. She stayed quiet and waited for him to change the subject.

But he didn't.

'My wife . . . was murdered. About five years ago.'

Involuntarily, Kitt rubbed the palm of her hand against her heart. She wanted to reach out to Halloran, to put her arms around him, but it wasn't appropriate to push herself on him when he was confiding in her. 'I don't know what to say,' she admitted. 'I can't imagine what that must have been like. I'm so very sorry.'

'Nobody's fault but mine.'

'I can't think that's true.'

'Feels it,' Halloran said, his words clipped. 'She died . . . because of a case I was working on. The guy who killed her, he was a suspect in a serial case, but I didn't get the evidence together in time to make an arrest before it was too late.'

'None of this makes it your fault that your wife is no longer with us,' said Kitt. 'The responsibility rests with the person who committed the act, you know that.'

'I know,' he said, 'but part of me doesn't believe it. I don't usually talk about it . . . but I wanted you to understand why I had to take you and Evie in as soon as the evidence pointed at your involvement.'

Kitt half smiled. 'I knew you were just doing your job.'

'Yeah, but you hated the way we did it.'

'Wish I could deny that. Not sure that anything you could say would make it OK that you read my journal.'

'Perhaps now you know more about my story, you understand why I had to do that.'

'Did you . . . really read it all?'

'It was my job to.'

'Even, you know, the sex stuff?'

'That's what I meant when I confirmed I'd read all of it.'

'I see. Well, if you think I'm sorry I wrote any of it, I'm not. Don't get me started on the injustice that women are simultaneously criticized for being prudes and for daring to enjoy sex.'

Halloran stared at her and his brow dipped. 'Let me say on record that I'm in no way criticizing anything I read in those pages, and could be considered a person in favour of women enjoying sex.'

Kitt was, at that moment, intensely grateful for how dark it was in the car as she could feel her cheeks burning. The temptation was to lower her head so she didn't have to look directly at Halloran, but pure cussedness made her hold his gaze. How had the conversation veered in this direction? She reminded herself of Theo's friend request, and consequently how easy it was for curiosity to lead somewhere dangerous and disorientating.

'It really is late now. I should say goodnight.'

'And how does a Middlesbrough lass say goodnight?'

Kitt unbuckled her seat belt, determined not to give the inspector even a moment to capitalize on the intimate conversation they'd shared. 'We say, "'night".'

Swinging open the car door, Kitt stepped out of the car and leaned into the footwell to pick up her handbag.

'Kitt,' Halloran said, putting a hand on her arm.

She raised both eyebrows at him in expectation, but didn't speak.

'When I read your journal, I learned how much Theo hurt you.'

Kitt's body drooped and she shook her head, not knowing what to say.

'If you want me to, I can make life difficult for him.'

'Of course I don't want you to . . . How, exactly?'

Halloran rubbed his beard, and Kitt was reminded again how much she wanted to do that herself. 'Once this case is over, I could become very interested in how vigilantly he pays his taxes.'

Kitt, unable to help herself, started to laugh and held her hands against her ribs. Halloran joined in for a minute, but then had to ask, 'Is it really that funny?'

'It's just the idea of punishing a person for bad relationship choices via tax evasion. Makes Theo sound like the Al Capone of broken hearts.'

Halloran started laughing again. He had a deep, loud laugh that filled the car. 'Well, my offer stands if you change your mind, but in all seriousness, I meant what I said about everything coming with a price. Even loving people. But most of us wouldn't give up the time we had with those people to escape the pain of losing them.'

Kitt tilted her head to the left in a sort of sideways nod. 'You're right, of course, which is very annoying.'

'I hope that one day you can share yourself as openly with another person as you do with your journal. You've got a lot to give.'

Kitt's eyes lowered. 'I don't know if I can.'

'If you don't know for sure that you can't, then there's hope,' said Halloran.

Smiling, Kitt gently closed the car door, began fishing in her handbag for her door keys and made for the entrance of her cottage, which, save for a less-than-welcoming feline, was dark and empty.

If she didn't want to be alone tonight, she knew all she had to do was turn and invite Halloran in. He had started the car engine, but was waiting, probably to see that she got inside OK. He knew, just as she did, what it was like to go back to an empty house, night after night. She could turn back to face him, flash him a knowing smile, and beckon him seductively with one finger the way a brave, carefree woman would in the books she read. If she had their courage, she would already know the weight of Halloran's body on top of hers, how tightly his hands could grip her wrists against the headboard, what kind of man he became when he was not bound by the badge or public duty. But Kitt was not a brave, carefree woman, at least not when it came to love, and she wasn't quite sure how to become one. She could only think to do the sensible thing: turn the key in the lock, switch on the living-room light, and close the door behind her without looking back at the handsome face that, if only she'd had the courage, could have been the face she woke up to in the morning.

THIRTY

'Right, that's it,' said Grace. 'I'm calling time on what must be the least eventful day in all of history.'

'Things have been a bit slow today,' said Kitt, trying not to let the note of disappointment sound in her voice. Kitt hadn't heard a word from Halloran since last night. She had half-expected, or half-hoped for, a message of some sort after what he had shared with her. She would even have settled for a photo of Al Capone popping up in her emails as a wry little joke. But it was eight p.m. and her inbox was still *sans* Scarface. It wasn't so surprising, Kitt told herself. The man was in the middle of solving a murder case. His priorities were rightly elsewhere. 'On the plus side, we haven't had any phone calls about dead bodies. For that at least we should be grateful.'

'Aye, you're right. That's not the kind of excitement I'm in the market for. Oh, ey up. Suppose we've still got Cabbage for entertainment.'

Kitt looked up from her computer screen for the first time in the last half hour and squinted over at the bookshelves where she could see that now-familiar forest-green anorak.

'For goodness' sake, which feminist tome is he hiding behind this time?'

'Looks like *The Beauty Myth.*'

'What is his game?' said Kitt, shaking her head. And then she paused. Various pieces of an incomplete jigsaw began to fall into place. 'Halloran said we had to be vigilant.' The words came out of her mouth almost on autopilot.

'Kitt? You all right?' said Grace.

Kitt looked at her assistant. 'Halloran said the killer was likely to be someone in our lives, but someone who was on the outskirts. He told us to be vigilant, to look out for anyone acting suspiciously.'

Grace frowned. 'Right . . .' Then she looked over at Cabbage and made the connection. 'You don't think . . . Cabbage?'

'The first time I encountered him was on the morning the police came to visit.'

'Aye, I remember. You were hungover. I haven't forgotten your rotten mood that day either.'

'Since then, he's been . . .'

'Lurking . . .' said Grace.

'That's how I'd describe it,' said Kitt. 'He's been watching us all along.'

'But he doesn't know Evie, does he?'

'Doesn't need to. Not if he followed her, and then that in turn led him to me.'

'Why would he follow her?'

'Dark minds don't need much of a reason. Ever read *Perfume?*'

Grace put a hand on her hip. 'Haven't quite prioritized

that one above all the other titles you've recommended in the past week.'

'In that, the killer stalks and murders his first victim just because he really likes the way she smells.'

'One reason not to shower every day,' said Grace. 'But Cabbage?'

'Only one way to find out if he's got something to hide,' said Kitt, rising from her office chair and smoothing the creases out of her navy skirt.

'What are you going to do?'

Kitt looked at her assistant, but didn't respond. She didn't really know the answer to that. Still, she strode over to where Cabbage was standing and tapped him on the shoulder. His brown eyes widened.

'Anything in particular you're looking for, sir?' asked Kitt. 'I think I explained to you that we don't have a copy of *Tess of the d'Urbervilles* in this section of the library.'

'I know that, I know, I – er.'

'My colleague and I couldn't help notice you've been hanging around this section quite a bit in the last week.'

Smart move, thought Kitt. Let it be known to him that it wasn't just her who was onto him, that other people had noticed his behaviour.

'Didn't know there was a law against reading books in a library,' said Cabbage.

'There isn't, but your behaviour has struck us as rather odd. You seem to divide your time between the books and watching us. Any explanation for that? It seems very peculiar.'

Cabbage shoved the Naomi Wolf volume back on the nearest shelf. 'I don't need to explain myself to you.'

He nudged Kitt's shoulder as he bustled his way past.

'Just you wait a minute,' said Kitt. If she was wrong she was sure to get the sack for this, but she couldn't take the chance of letting the killer get away. Or even an accomplice. 'I oversee this floor of the library and I insist on knowing if something underhand is happening here.'

'Underhand? Underhand?' Cabbage hopped around on the spot. ''Ere, what are you accusing me of?'

'Nothing,' Kitt said, determined to keep her voice calm. 'I'm simply waiting for you to explain why you've been watching me and my colleague for the past week. It's unsettling behaviour, and we will have to report it if you can't explain it.'

'I haven't been watching you,' said Cabbage.

'My colleague and I feel otherwise,' said Kitt.

Cabbage looked between Kitt and Grace before letting out a deep sigh.

'All right, I *have* been hanging around in your section of the library.'

'And watching us.'

'Not in the way you think.'

'What do we think?'

'I don't know, but there's nothing creepy about it.'

'That, we'll have to disagree on,' said Kitt.

'The only reason I kept looking at you is because I was trying to work up the courage to come over and apologize.'

Kitt crossed her arms. 'Apologize?'

'I thought about what you said. About voices that aren't my own.'

'You did?'

'Yeah. Decided to read a few of the books around here to see what you were talking about. Don't get me wrong, in the beginning I did it to prove I had a point. That there wasn't any need for a Women's Studies section. But . . .'

Kitt looked at Grace and then back at the man.

'From what I've read, I was wrong to be dismissive. I wanted to say sorry, but I was too embarrassed.'

Kitt frowned. The man seemed genuine, but was it really possible for him to make such a U-turn? She had to find a gap in the logic here. Cabbage had been behaving too suspiciously for the answer to be that simple.

'If you were so embarrassed, why did you keep coming here to read the books? You could have bought them and read them at home?' Kitt tried.

'They're bloody expensive them books, you know?'

'Academic works are always more expensive,' Kitt conceded. 'So, that's it?'

'That's it. I'm sorry. That's it.'

Kitt could not remember a time in all her experience as a librarian where a rude student had gone out of their way to reassess their attitude towards her. Fair enough, in this instance the man had hoped to corroborate his narrow-minded views, but when that turned out to be fruitless, he had educated himself further and had even tried to push himself to apologize. Few people would go to those lengths in the same circumstances. The best thing she could do now was to try and encourage him to open his mind further.

'Were you enjoying the Naomi Wolf?'

'It was . . . enlightening, you might say.'

Kitt picked up the book from where the man had shoved it just a minute before. 'Let me check this out for you, sir; do you have your library card?'

The man smiled and followed Kitt over to her desk.

'Pleased to meet you . . . Vincent Clarke,' Kitt said, reading the name off the library card when he handed it over. She scanned his card and then the barcode inside the book. 'My name is Kitt, this is Grace. If you have any questions you think we can help with, don't ever feel like you can't ask.'

Grace smiled at Vincent. He looked between the two women, his eyes shining. 'Thank you.'

'It's entirely my pleasure,' said Kitt.

With that, Vincent headed towards the spiral staircase, waving the book in the air as he went in what Kitt read as a gesture of thanks.

The second he was out of earshot Grace started giggling.

Kitt raised an eyebrow at her assistant and put a hand on her hip.

'That was hysterical.'

'I don't see why.'

'Are you kidding?' said Grace. In a split second, Grace had swiped Kitt's trilby off her desk and placed it on her own head. She stood a little straighter and stretched out her arm, pointing at a space to her left. 'You've been lurking here too long, you murderer!' Then, hopping into the space and looking back at where she had been standing just a second ago, she removed the hat and raised her arms in mock surrender. 'Sorry, missis, I just wanted to read feminist literature.' Hopping back into her previous position, she placed the hat on her head again and outstretched her arm once more, booming, 'Reading feminist literature, in the Women's Studies section? A likely story.'

'Grace!' Kitt said in a tone stern enough to stop her assistant's uninvited skit. 'That's not how it happened.'

'No, but that's how I'm going to tell it.'

'Isn't it time for you to be off?'

'Yeah, and as always I could rely on you to brighten up an otherwise dull day.'

'Be off, and get home safe,' said Kitt, while her assistant pulled on her coat and picked up her rucksack.

Grace pressed two fingers to the side of her head, dishing out her trademark cheeky salute, before putting her earbuds in and heading towards the stairs.

Once she was sure Grace had disappeared from view, Kitt pulled her phone out of her satchel. She wouldn't check it again until she got home, she told herself. But she would take a quick look now, just in case.

Still no messages in her inbox.

It was conspicuous. Not so much that she hadn't heard from Halloran, though she had heard from him every day since she had said 'yes' to helping him on the case. It was more the absence of text messages from Evie. She had been a bit hampered by being taken into police custody this week, but under ordinary circumstances, rarely did a morning or an afternoon pass without some update on the life and times of Evelyn Bowes. The fact she hadn't texted to find out what had happened between herself and Halloran after they'd dropped her off definitely fell into the 'out of character' category.

No word from the inspector. No word from Evie.

The last time she had noticed a break in Evie's text communication was the morning she had found out about Owen's murder. The morning Halloran and Banks first took her in for questioning. Exactly a week ago today. A heavy feeling settled in Kitt's stomach. Had the investigation uncovered more evidence that led back to Evie as she had feared it might? If so, would Halloran tell Kitt about it? What if he had been playing her all along? Using her to get information about Evie. He had shown a romantic interest in her, but what if that was just a pretence? There was no particular reason why a man like Halloran would look twice at Kitt. She wasn't bad-looking, but she could be cold, closed off. The more she thought about it, the less likely it seemed that his advances had been anything other than a play.

Last night, he had made a show of opening up to her. For all she knew, the sob story about his wife was a work of fiction designed to get her to lower her defences, and, if he had got the information he needed, if he had been able to take Evie into questioning again, that would explain the radio silence.

Narrowing her eyes, Kitt began searching her contacts for Halloran's name. She was just about to hit the dial button when she heard about the last thing she had ever expected to hear.

'Hello Kitt-Kat,' said a deep voice that Kitt couldn't quite bring herself to believe was part of her own reality. Her whole body tensed as she turned in the direction the voice had come from.

'Theo?'

THIRTY-ONE

It was just another dream, or another daydream, Kitt couldn't quite be sure which right now. But she was dreaming again, about all the things she would say to Theo if he were standing in front of her.

The mirage was dressed in a long, brown suede jacket and sandstone trousers. He was wearing glasses and had a leather satchel slung over his shoulder that was, if Kitt had to guess, full of books. Like her, he was a slave to the page. He took another step closer to the enquiry desk. Kitt blinked hard. Twice. The mirage didn't disappear.

Her eyes widened and she opened her mouth to speak, but no sound came out. That didn't seem right. In all of her other dreams some sharp, witty line tripped off her tongue. The kind of thing the vixen would say in a noir movie from the forties when the love of her life came crawling back after some cruel misdemeanour.

'Sorry to drop by unannounced,' Theo said, with those lips that Kitt knew to be so soft and kissable, 'and so late. I did come by earlier, but the staff at the front desk said you were working the later shift.'

Drop by? Is that what you call reappearing in a person's life after a ten-year absence? But Kitt still didn't say anything out loud. She couldn't. If she did, it would confirm he was really there.

'Well, say something, Kitt-Kat. I'll even take one of your trademark digs about what I'm wearing,' Theo pushed.

Kitt looked around the library. Nobody else was here at this late hour. If this was a hallucination, perhaps it wouldn't hurt to indulge it. Perhaps it would even be cathartic.

Slowly, Kitt rose from her seat. She swallowed hard and walked around to the front of the desk where the figment of Theo was standing. She looked up into his brown eyes, searching for words, but there weren't any words right now – they'd all been devoured by that inner fire that had never quite gone out.

Without warning, she raised her hand and delivered a sharp slap to his left cheek, only to hop backwards in surprise when her palm made contact with actual skin and bone.

'Oh good God!' Kitt cried, drawing a hand to her mouth and shaking her head.

Theo moaned, cowering for a second and then, on realizing another slap wasn't soon to follow, glared at Kitt and started to massage his face to relieve the sting.

'You're . . .' said Kitt. 'I didn't think you were . . . I didn't mean to do that, I . . .' Kitt trailed off. She had been about to say sorry, but could not push an apology past her teeth, not a sincere one at any rate.

The hardness about Theo's stare began to soften and a boyish smirk crossed his lips. 'If this is the effect surprise has on you, I'm glad I never threw you a birthday party without your knowing.'

A small part of Kitt wanted to join in with Theo's joke, to be easy with him again. But those familiar flames seared in her chest and, though tears threatened in her eyes, there wasn't enough water in them to put the fire out. He was trying to make this into a joke, just like he had done everything else when they were together. If Kitt was honest with herself that had been part of Theo's charm: how much he made her laugh. So many other couples they had known at the time were sullen. Say what you want about Kitt and Theo circa 2008, but they could never be accused of that.

Right now, however, Kitt didn't want Theo the clown. There was nothing funny about him showing up like this, and it was that truth that allowed Kitt to find her tongue again.

'What are *you* doing here?' There was no point pretending that she had any time for pleasantries. With everything that was going on with the murder case just now this was the last thing she needed.

'I wanted to see you. I mean, I wanted to see if you were OK.' He was looking at the ground, but slowly brought his dark eyes up to meet Kitt's.

'A strange thing to suddenly take an interest in after ten years,' Kitt said with an unmistakable dryness in her tone.

'Please,' Theo said, 'don't be like that. I saw this clip of you on the news, you know, about the murder, and then when I saw you had looked at my profile I thought you wanted to reach out but didn't feel like you could.'

Kitt shook her head. 'Well, you were wrong, I wasn't trying to reach out.'

'All right then, what were you doing?'

'I— I don't know. Checking you were still alive, I suppose,' said Kitt.

'Sorry to disappoint you on that score,' said Theo. Another smirk threatened at the corners of his mouth, but Kitt's glare stopped it in its tracks.

'Now that you've seen I'm OK, you can leave,' said Kitt.

'What? That's it?' said Theo.

'What were you expecting?' asked Kitt.

'I don't know, I . . .' Theo trailed off and ruffled his short brown hair. 'Thought we might get a drink, or something.'

'A drink?' Kitt said. 'Why? We're not friends or anything. We're strangers.'

'I know you don't really believe that,' said Theo.

Kitt crossed her arms, but didn't say anything.

'You know,' Theo said, taking a step closer to Kitt, 'I never stopped thinking about you.'

'Oh, please,' said Kitt. 'If that's true then why didn't you get in touch?'

'Because I didn't think you'd want to see me after . . .'

'You vanished without a trace?'

'Yeah,' said Theo. 'But I have thought about you, a lot, and I've regretted what happened. I really have.'

Kitt smiled. Theo no longer knew Kitt well enough to

notice, but it was a dangerous smile. 'I've thought about you a lot too.'

'You have?' said Theo.

'Oh yes, I've thought to myself, why would somebody do something like that? Especially to somebody who loved them. Why? Over and over again.'

Theo sighed. 'You're right, I owe you an explanation.'

'Owe me?' Kitt said, her voice rising in volume. 'This isn't about what you owe me. It's about what I deserve. I didn't deserve what you did.'

But for a long time, I thought I did, she thought. Theo had made her believe it. That she was . . .

'I know that, and I am sorry,' said Theo. 'The way I ended things was . . . unforgivable. But the truth is, I was young and an idiot and I just got scared. You know, you were pretty intense, Kitt, and at the time I just didn't know how to handle that. I've tried to forget about what happened with us for a decade. But when I saw you in that news clip, when I saw the woman you'd grown into, it hit me like a train. Nobody has ever loved me the way you did, and whether it's too late or not, I wanted you to know that I regret letting you go.'

Kitt thought about slapping Theo's face a second time. Not just because it would be satisfying, but because she couldn't quite believe what she was hearing. Six months, a year, hell, three years after Theo had vanished she would have given anything to hear him saying the things he was saying now. But on hearing them, one thought struck her like a knife to the gut: she didn't want to hear them any more. Whatever love she'd had in her heart for Theo was long gone. She hadn't shied away from relationships all this time because she still loved Theo, she had stayed single to protect herself, to make sure nobody could ever hurt her that way again.

Kitt looked straight at Theo and spoke in a low voice, the coolness of which surprised her. 'Do you have any idea what it did to me when you left like that?'

'Kitt-Kat . . .'

'Don't call me that. It's not my name,' Kitt said. A silence mushroomed between them. Kitt could see the pain in Theo's eyes and that cut her deeper than she'd like, but he had to understand that there were consequences for turning his back on people. 'Thank you for coming. Thank you for giving me the opportunity to say what I've wanted to say for ten years . . . goodbye, Theo.'

Kitt watched Theo's head lower, and then he raised it again. Finally, after a decade, he was able to look her in the eye and say what he should have said back then. 'Goodbye, Kitt. If you ever, well . . . I'm not far away if you ever need me.'

Kitt crossed her arms, holding in her breath and so much else. Theo began walking towards the staircase. Kitt's eyes followed after him and in doing so, she saw Halloran. They didn't speak, but he and Theo eyed each other as they passed. Kitt had no idea how long Halloran had been standing there, but seeing as their conversation was none of Halloran's business, she did her best to act as casual as possible.

'Inspector Halloran, what brings you to the library at this hour?' Kitt said as he walked towards her.

'I tried calling, but you weren't picking up,' said Halloran.

Kitt watched as Theo's head disappeared down the spiral staircase, knowing that was the last glimpse she would ever have of him.

'Kitt?' Halloran prompted.

'Oh, while I'm at work, my phone's on vibrate. But I'm done here now. Just packing up.' This wasn't true. Strictly speaking, Kitt was due to be in the building another half hour, but she needed to go home and scream into a pillow as a matter of urgency. She would make the extra time up tomorrow, when an ex-lover hadn't just walked back into her life again and tried to beg her back into his arms.

'Oh, well, I wanted to let you know we've had a major break on the case,' said Halloran. He was puffing his chest out and beaming in a way Kitt just didn't have the stomach for at present.

'Really,' Kitt said, trying to sound interested as she threw her notebook, pen and keys into her bag. She was, in fact, very interested, but the fire in her chest felt more like magma right now, and she was keen to get somewhere isolated before the inevitable eruption.

'Yes,' said Halloran, his tone flattening a little bit on seeing Kitt's distracted manner. 'In fact, I think we've caught our murderer.'

Kitt was pulling on her coat as those words left the detective's mouth, and she paused to look at him. She opened her mouth with the intention of making a sincere and helpful comment, but somehow that was not what came out. 'Who do we think it is today? If you still think it's me and you're here to arrest me again, I won't be best pleased.'

Halloran tilted his head. 'That's a bit unfair.' It wouldn't have taken a detective to see that there was something off about Kitt's manner. 'Are you all right?'

'I'm fine,' Kitt lied, grabbing her satchel and turning off her monitor. She could feel hot tears forming behind her eyes, but swallowed hard to hold them back. 'I'm sorry, I just want to get home.'

'I can drive you,' said Halloran.

'I'd prefer to walk, thank you.'

Kitt needed the cold night air in her lungs. She needed to clear her head and listen to the musical drift of the river. To her mind, it was the only thing right now that could extinguish the heat burning inside.

'You know I don't like you walking around late at night when there's a murderer on the loose,' said Halloran.

'But there isn't, is there? You've caught them,' said Kitt, scurrying down the steps, bookshelves scrolling by in her peripheral vision. Halloran hurried after her and the pair left the library through the tall oak doors at the front entrance.

'We've caught one of them, but remember we think they have an accomplice,' Halloran said. Kitt didn't answer.

'Don't you want to know who it is?' asked Halloran, striding to keep up with the librarian, who was walking with quick steps in the direction of Skeldergate Bridge.

'Yes, of course. I'm sorry, I just had to get out of there,' said Kitt, she pulled at the scarf around her neck so it hung a little looser.

She shouldn't have opened that Facebook link. She shouldn't have opened that door again. After how hard she'd worked to put Theo out of her mind, how could she have been so stupid as to undo it all with the click of a mouse?

'We found traces of diazepam and the chemicals used to poison Owen in Ritchie Turner's work locker,' said Halloran.

This statement caught Kitt's attention and she frowned over at Halloran. 'So it was him. But he had an alibi for the first killing.'

'Yes, he was at work,' said Halloran, 'and where did we find the evidence? At work. So the odds are somebody who works with him is in on it. We just have to crack Turner and find out who.'

'Oh,' Kitt said.

'Thought you'd be glad to hear we are on the brink of closing the case,' said Halloran, frowning at Kitt.

'I am, yes, of course I am.' Kitt paused, thinking. 'Has he confessed?'

'No, but in my experience the evidence doesn't lie and murder suspects do. For all they're worth once they've been caught,' said Halloran.

'Mmm,' said Kitt.

'Sorry, I'm not totally fluent in Librarian yet,' said Halloran. 'You'll have to translate that "mmm".'

Kitt wanted to smile, but her lips wouldn't work that way. 'It's just . . . do we know what Ritchie's motive is yet?'

'We're still working on that,' Halloran admitted. 'But he doesn't exactly seem very sensitive or respectful to the women in his life, so that might have something to do with it.'

'Yes, I suppose it could,' said Kitt. 'Wish he was the only man I knew who fits that description.'

THIRTY-TWO

Kitt's blue eyes followed the trail of the Ouse, across to the north bank where the city was illuminated against the night sky. The floodlit spires of York Minster gleamed gold in the blackness. They were almost at Skeldergate Bridge now and before long she would be curled up in bed with a book, far away from the world of murderers and ex-boyfriends. The librarian deepened her breathing, taking in and letting go of oxygen as slowly as she could.

'Are you sure you're all right?' asked Halloran.

'Yes,' Kitt said, but even she could hear how the word was hissed out through her teeth.

'You don't sound it,' said Halloran.

'So what?' Kitt shouted. Not at Halloran, but at the river, the stars, the cold night air that was already biting at her ears. 'So what if I'm not all right? Why do I have to be all right all the time?' These follow-up questions were directed at Halloran, who watched Kitt in silence. 'Since you apparently have to get to the truth of absolutely everything, no. I'm not all right.'

Halloran's face didn't even twitch, he just watched as Kitt continued.

'I mean, what the hell did he think was going to happen? Ten years it's been, ten years of wondering why he threw away what we had without any explanation, and since you read my journal with such intrusive interest, I would guess you know who I'm talking about.'

Halloran pressed his lips together before speaking. 'That was Theo.'

'Full marks, you were paying attention,' said Kitt, pressing a hand against her forehead. 'He walks into the library as though he's just come back from the corner shop and I'm never going to be able to not see him now, standing there. Whenever I look up from my computer or cross over to the bookshelves, I'll remember him standing in that spot. Spouting all those words that I know don't mean a bloody thing. I've heard them before. I wonder how many women have. How many have been told there isn't anyone else like them?'

'I don't know,' Halloran began, 'but in your case—'

'And you know what?' Kitt continued. 'People always talk about how forgiveness is something you give yourself, not the person who's wronged you. Look on any social media timeline and you'll find some unsolicited inspirational quote telling you that. But that's just a line, and it's as false as all the lines he dished out. He made me believe . . . he made me believe that I was unlovable, and I will never forgive him for that. Never, never—'

Halloran pressed his hands against Kitt's shoulders,

holding her steady. Her breathing was sharp and short after her outburst, and she glared at Halloran as though he were somehow responsible for it. The inspector didn't say anything, he just kept his blue-eyed gaze on her. Looking harder into his eyes, Kitt's breathing began, bit by bit, to plateau. Halloran's hands still gripped her shoulders and his face was fixed in what seemed like deep concentration. He was studying her. Their eyes remained locked for the longest minute Kitt could ever remember experiencing, and thousands of tiny thrills pushed up through the skin along her arms as Halloran slowly brought a hand up to her temple and ran his fingers through the length of her red hair.

A question danced in the logical part of Kitt's mind: What are you doing? But in posing that question to herself, she realized she already knew the answer and couldn't summon that query, or any other, to her lips.

Without breaking eye contact, Halloran took a gentle step forward, and another, nudging Kitt backwards, pushing her up against the dark stone wall of Skeldergate Bridge. Again, he paused, staring into her eyes, not speaking a word. Kitt had U-turned from panting in exasperation to barely daring to take in oxygen. Halloran began leaning forwards, his face drifting towards hers. She stood utterly still as he turned his head a fraction, pressed his right cheek against her left and gave it a small push, the way lions do their mates in the wild. Kitt closed her eyes the second she felt his skin against hers, listening to Halloran inhale the scent of her, and she did the same to him. That fresh burst of moorland after the rain overwhelmed her. She felt Halloran's breath then, the warmth of it tingling down the side of her face, and her own breathing deepened. She tilted her head back, just a little, exposing her neck and this, it seemed, was the only invitation Halloran needed.

Sliding his hands from Kitt's shoulders to embrace her, Halloran gripped the back of her coat and pulled her body closer into his. Gasping, she felt her arms wrapping around him in return. His scent was so deep, so earthy, so intoxicating, it blotted out thoughts of anything else. The next sensation was that of Halloran's lips and tongue and beard against her neck as he kissed her in a way that made her whole body arch towards his. The softest moan escaped Kitt's lips and in an instant it was swallowed up by the warmth of Halloran's mouth.

At first, Kitt only opened her mouth halfway, but Halloran's gentle tongue teasing over her lips was unexpectedly tempting, daring her to open up, and let the softness of her tongue touch his. When they met, Kitt heard what could only be described as a low growl echo out of Halloran. It was, to her reckoning, one of the most divine sounds she had ever heard. Certainly, it was the most seductive and it only inspired her to kiss Halloran harder, while revelling in the rough and smooth of his beard, which all this time had been concealing firm, hungry lips.

Pinned against the wall, the ferocity of the kiss intensified. There was nowhere for Kitt to go, and nowhere she wanted to go. The pair started pulling at each other's clothes, pressing their lips and bodies harder against one another. Halloran's was a kiss deep enough to drown in, one that left Kitt gasping for air. She hadn't felt this way since . . . since . . .

Kitt's eyes were open wide in an instant. Without warning, she pulled away and shoved Halloran backwards. He was strong, but the shove was unexpected and knocked him back a step. He stood there, panting but not speaking.

'I have to go,' Kitt said.

How could she be so stupid? She had resolved the fall-out from her last broken heart a mere ten minutes ago and here she was starting the cycle all over again.

'Is – is that what you really want?' Halloran asked.

Kitt frowned up at him. 'I – I—' a buzzing sounded from the front of her satchel. The pair looked at the bag and then back at each other. Kitt made an apologetic look as she reached in and pulled out her phone. It was a text from Evie. Kitt swiped to bring up the message. Her eyes widened as she read and her hands began to shake.

'What?' said Halloran. 'Kitt, what is it?'

Kitt frowned and shook her head at Halloran. 'It's Evie . . .'

'Is she all right?'

'She's . . . she says it's her.'

'What's her?' asked Halloran.

'She's the murderer.'

THIRTY-THREE

Halloran sighed as he sat next to Kitt at the table in Evie's kitchen. It was a rickety old rectangular thing that Evie had spotted in a local charity shop. Kitt ran her fingertips over the roses carved into the edge of the table.

'She said this table was love at first sight,' Kitt said. 'But she didn't have her car with her at the time to get it back. So we carried it all the way up Holgate Road. Rush-hour traffic gawking at us.'

Halloran closed his hand over Kitt's. She looked at their hands, resting together on the table for a moment and then, shaking herself free, stood up.

'There's got to be some clue in this place about what's really going on.'

Kitt left the kitchen for the living room where a sullen Banks was turning over the cushions on the settee, running a gloved hand along the crevices.

'Looks as though you've got things covered in here,' Kitt said, making for the door that led to the stairs. She could hear Halloran following close behind her, his steps heavier than hers on the wooden stairs that were covered with a thin floral carpet.

Kitt swung open the door to Evie's bedroom, turned on the light and scanned the room.

She had an oak dressing table – second-hand like everything else she owned – sitting near the window on the left of the room. On it stood a mannequin head with a red wig perched on top.

It looked like the same wig the killer had been wearing in the CCTV footage. It was one of the many incriminating items Halloran and Banks had found when they entered the property. They hadn't needed to break in. Kitt knew where Evie kept her spare key – underneath one of the gnomes in her backyard.

'Kitt . . .' Halloran began.

'It's not right. It's not,' Kitt said, pacing up and down next to Evie's bed. 'Look at this,' she said, grabbing a fistful of floral bedsheets. 'These sheets are the chintziest things ever to be manufactured. These are not the bedsheets of a murderer.'

'Kitt,' Halloran said. He took a step towards her, but she walked over to the opposite wall and leaned against it.

'The wig. The chemicals in the bathroom cupboard. The stationery set, complete with fountain pen. The cloak. It's an abundance of evidence. It's a set-up.'

'Or, it's the simplest explanation,' said Halloran.

'She was with me the night of Owen's murder.'

'She said in the text that Ritchie is her accomplice.'

'But he has an alibi for the first murder too. He was at work. You've seen the CCTV footage.'

'Maybe the footage had been tampered with. Or it wasn't showing the correct date – CCTV footage gets out of sequence. Especially in private businesses who only really keep it as insurance if something goes down on their property and someone threatens to sue them over it.'

'Mal,' she said, staring at Halloran. 'I know her. She wouldn't do this.'

The inspector walked over to Kitt. He ran a hand through the front of her hair. 'I don't want it to be Evie any more than you do. But, she did once hurt herself really badly, is it really such a stretch that she might hurt someone else?'

'Yes,' said Kitt. 'You don't know her, you don't understand.'

'Hey, don't shut me out here,' Halloran said, his voice stern. He put a hand against the wall, either side of Kitt's head, and fixed his eyes on her. 'I know you.'

'We met a week ago.'

'I know you,' the inspector repeated. 'I've read you. Every page. Every word. The spaces in-between.'

'Then trust me,' said Kitt, but she could already see from the way in which his eyes lowered to the floor that that wasn't going to happen.

A second later, the rusty sound of trumpets could be heard. Muffled, but still recognizable as the intro to 'Kiss Me, Honey Honey'.

'Evie's phone,' said Kitt, looking first around the room and then down at the floorboards. 'It's coming from underneath us.'

Halloran looked down at the polished wooden floor,

tracking the sound. Kneeling, he prised up a loose board to reveal Evie's phone. The caller ID said 'Mum'. Alongside it was an envelope. It was addressed to Kitt.

'Should we answer that?' Kitt asked.

'Let's call her mum back in a few minutes when we have a clearer picture,' said Halloran. He handed Kitt the envelope. Her hands shook as she accepted it and tore open the seal. She pulled out the heavy cream stationery. It was the same paper that had been used to write the notes pinned on the victims. Tears came to Kitt's eyes as she read.

Dear Kitt,

I know you'll be the first to defend me. I know you won't want to believe I could do a thing like this. But I am the reason Owen is no longer here. I'm the reason the others are dead too. The night I murdered Owen, I crept out of your cottage after you'd gone to sleep. I knew you'd had a lot to drink and wouldn't wake again until morning. I took a taxi to Owen's new place. Even though I'd planned it, I didn't know for sure I was going to kill him until I poured that glass of wine. But he shouldn't have done what he did to me, and the same goes for the others.

Working in a salon, you hear a lot of sob stories. That's where I found out about the break-ups. Until it happened to me I didn't think much of it. But I couldn't let it go, being humiliated like that. I don't see why anyone should have to. There are no penalties for breaking a heart. The culprits aren't locked away or even fined, and there should be a consequence, a punishment. The heartbroken are the true victims. That pain is worse than dying.

Of course, there's no life left for me now. I couldn't go on doing this for ever, and I never intended to. I would get caught eventually. So I decided I'd confess and at the first opportunity, fill my pockets with stones and walk into the river. That way the pain will finally be over.

I don't deserve to ask you for anything, but perhaps as my friend you'll grant me this anyway. When you think of me, please don't think of all this. Think of that day back in August when we walked the moors. That day when the whole world was a sea of purple. When you think of me, think of the heather.

All my love,

Evie

Halloran looked at the note. 'Is it Evie's handwriting?'

Kitt nodded. 'But just because she wrote it, it doesn't mean she . . .'

'Kitt . . .'

'She might have written it under duress, or someone might have tricked her.'

Halloran put his hands on Kitt's arms. 'We've got all available units out looking for her. Her car is still in the garage, and we've alerted the train and bus companies, so she's not going to get far. When we find her, we'll get to the truth, but you might have to at least be open to the idea that Evie is responsible.'

'How can you say that to me? Knowing what Evie means to me?'

'I take no pleasure in it. But listen. The letter says she sneaked out of your house that night. Ritchie has no alibi for the second murder. What about the third, does Evie have an alibi for that?'

'Yes, it was the day after the funeral. I went out for a drink with her,' Kitt said, her eyes widening.

'What time?'

'Between seven and nine-thirty.'

Halloran shook his head. 'The murders have all taken place between ten and midnight.'

'What about the other night? When the killer attacked Evie and Jazz and Heather?'

'Probably staged to help Evie look more innocent,' said Halloran. 'Ritchie had been released, and when we questioned him he was without an alibi again.'

'Why am I even talking about this? The logistics don't matter,' Kitt said, shaking her head.

'They do to me, it's my job to get them straight,' said Halloran.

'Yeah, and it's my job to look out for my friend.' Kitt shrugged Halloran's hands away and stepped around him.

'Kitt . . . I'm trying to help you. I've stood in exactly the same position as you are now. You need to look at the facts.'

Kitt shook her head at the inspector. She wanted to find out exactly how he'd been in the same scenario, but whatever that scenario was it wasn't this one at all. This situation was about Evie, and Kitt knew Evie could be trusted. She just wished Halloran would trust her enough to believe her.

'Whoever's really behind this, you're playing into their hands a second time. Evie didn't do this, and if you won't believe that, I'm going to prove it.'

With this, Kitt turned and ran towards the door. She heard Halloran call after her, but she wasn't listening. Ten seconds later, she was out the front door and walking briskly in the direction of Holgate Road. Evie had said she was going to walk into the river. If she had to walk the length of the Ouse and the nearby Foss all night to find her, that was what she'd do.

THIRTY-FOUR

Kitt wasn't sure if it was the light or the cold that first woke her. But she started when she found herself not in the cosy folds of her bed back at the cottage, but on a time-worn bench by the river. Once her tired eyes had taken a moment to look around, it registered that she was partway down North Street between Lendal Bridge and Skeldergate Bridge.

Her shoulders sank in remembrance of the fact that she had spent most of the night before wandering the banks of the river. In her note, Evie said that she was going to drown herself. Kitt thought the note a hoax, another elaborate trick by whoever was behind these murders, but despite this, she wasn't willing to take the risk. Either that note was the truth, or it was a clue about where Evie really was. Whatever the situation, Kitt knew she had to do all she could to bring Evie back to safety. Unfortunately, scouring the riverbanks had achieved nothing except invited a bitter chill into her bones and, eventually at five a.m., exhausted, she had paused on this bench. Just for a minute.

Kitt unzipped her satchel and rooted out her phone to

check the time, but the damn thing had run out of battery. She rubbed her eyes and sighed. The sun was coming up. Given the time of year that would make it some time after seven thirty. The library was about twenty minutes from here – it was probably best to go there than go back to the cottage. She was so tired that if she caught even a glimpse of her own bed she didn't trust herself not to fall into it and never be seen again. She couldn't afford to rest right now. Evie needed her.

At the library, she could pay a visit to the ladies' toilet and make herself look somewhere near respectable before trying to come at this situation from a new angle. There just had to be a more logical explanation than Evie being a secret criminal mastermind.

Standing up from the bench, Kitt pulled the strap of her satchel over her head and began walking against the flow of the river, towards Rowntree Park. Putting her hands in her pockets to keep them out of the cold, she felt something hard and rough. Pulling out the object, she looked down at the rock Ruby had given her, resting in her hand. The old woman had told her to hold onto it whenever she felt out of her depth. Now was definitely one of those times. She returned her hands to her pockets and let her fingers caress the rock's many faces as she walked.

Watching the currents twist and contort, Kitt thought again about the letter Evie had written. Why would Evie write that letter? Not voluntarily, that's for sure. All along, since the very beginning, the killer, or killers, had been doing all they could to pin these crimes on Evie. The break-up note. The wine. The diazepam. The chemicals. The fact that the killings only took place when she and her alleged accomplice were able to commit the acts. What about the red wig? Was it coincidence that the wig happened to be the same colour as Kitt's hair? The best friend of their preferred scapegoat. If the logistics had worked out a little differently, would the killers have tried to suggest Kitt was more involved in the killings than they already had? If the killers had intended all along to make the police believe Evie was the culprit, they could have gone so far as to kidnap her and tell her if she wanted to live she had to write a letter admitting her 'crimes'. There were no signs of forced entry to Evie's house, but that had been the pattern all the way through this case. The victims had all gone willingly.

At that thought, a shiver unrelated to the cold morning air skittered down Kitt's spine. Who was this mystery person in their midst manipulating this whole situation?

In the letter, Evie claimed to have overheard the other stories of heartbreak at the salon. It was plausible someone could do that. When Kitt went for beauty or hair appointments, she always asked the person serving her if they would mind if they didn't talk. Often, Kitt was met with a smile and a look of relief in the eyes of the therapist. It must be exhausting talking about holidays, boyfriends and girlfriends all day long. You were bound to hear the same thing over and over again. Except that once in a while, you'd probably hear something out of the ordinary. Some unexpected story of devastating woe, just like Evie claimed she had in the letter.

Just because the idea was plausible, however, didn't mean that it was true of Evie. Perhaps that was how the real killer had found their victims and if that were true it would mean the killer was . . . somebody who worked at the salon.

Kitt cast her mind back to the night she and Evie had been arrested at the Belle's Ball. Everyone from the salon had been sitting around that table, talking about the murder case.

One of them had been the killer, and one of them had had more to say than anyone else.

Jazz.

She had speculated that the murderer was still in town. How had Deniz described her bookshelf? Macabre. Filled with books on serial killers and crime novels. Not only that, but Jazz had pointed the media eye straight at her and Evie. She had claimed she had been ambushed, but what if that was misdirection? She had just as much access to poisonous chemicals as Evie did. If anyone at the salon was a suspect, it was Jazz.

Kitt was only a short hop from the library now and there she would be able to look into this further, and get Grace on the case.

As she approached the dark figure of Skeldergate Bridge, though, Kitt paused and the breath caught in the back of her throat. Slowly, she walked towards it, towards the spot where just the night before Halloran had pressed her against the cold stonework. She placed the palm of her hand flat against the bridge, and closed her eyes, as though if she concentrated hard enough she might still be able to feel the vibrations of that moment, the firmness of his lips, the tickle of his beard, the grip on her long hair that was at once gentle and rough.

'Kitt?'

She jumped and turned to see her assistant, presumably on her way to the library.

Kitt whipped her hand down from the stonework, and Grace frowned.

'Everything . . . all right?' said Grace, looking her boss up and down.

'Yes, I, er . . . thought I saw a loose stone in the brickwork here.'

'A loose stone?'

'Yes, can't be too careful given how much weathering this bridge gets from the river. You have to report that kind of thing to the council straight away.' Kitt put both her hands flat on the side of the bridge and made a show of pushing against it. 'Seems secure.'

'OK . . .' Grace said. 'Kitt . . .'

Kitt turned again to face her assistant.

'Is everything really all right?'

Kitt tried to come up with a breezy answer, but she couldn't get the words past her teeth. Her eyes filled with tears and she shook her head. 'Everything's gone wrong.'

Grace put her arm around Kitt. 'Come on, let's get you a cup of Lady Grey and you can tell me all about it.'

Shaking with the effort of holding back tears, Kitt nodded and managed something that resembled a smile. The pair walked towards the library in silence. Grace squeezed Kitt now and then for comfort, while Kitt looked over the rising river as one question streamed through her mind, over and over: Evie, where are you?

THIRTY-FIVE

'*Grrrrrrrr,*' said Grace, pushing away the mouse and slumping in the chair behind her desk.

'Regardless of what dead end we've hit now, there's no point wrinkling that beautiful material by slouching,' said Kitt, referring to the turquoise kurta that Kitt had always admired. Though Grace always undercut the formal lines of the garment with a pair of black jeggings underneath, it still had an almost majestic quality about it.

'Wait until you hear the dead end before you make that assumption,' said Grace, sitting up straighter.

'All right,' Kitt said. 'Hit me with it.'

'Jazz is not involved with these murders. Or at least, it's really unlikely.'

'You haven't found anything on her?'

Grace shook her head. 'It's more what I *have* found. She's quite the Facebook addict. She's tagged on nights out with friends most evenings. Including all three nights the murders took place.'

'Halloran did say she had alibis, though he didn't say how

solid they were. Don't forget, though, that all along the police thought this was the work of more than one person – maybe someone is doing it for her.'

'I just can't find anything, anywhere in her online presence, that even hints at motivation. She's a social butterfly, well-liked, absolutely all of her interactions are kind or funny or sweet. There's nothing there that hints at anger or pain . . . it's sort of sickening.'

'But whoever is behind this is deeply manipulative. It could be a charade,' said Kitt, not quite willing to let go of this theory yet.

'But, if you think about it, Jazz has actually been a victim of the killer in a way. He—'

'Or she . . .'

'Yeah, or she – they – attacked Evie, Jazz, and Heather the other night.'

Kitt sighed. 'Halloran thought Evie might have staged that to make herself look more innocent. The same logic could be applied to Jazz.'

'All right, how did Jazz seem after the incident the other night?'

'Shaken, she was really shaken and it seemed genuine enough . . . but . . .'

'What?'

'Heather . . . she didn't seem so afraid.'

'Wasn't she the one who got stabbed?'

'Cut . . . but yes, she was the one who got injured, and she was the one who risked going up to the killer even though it could have been anyone . . . oh God!' Kitt gasped, brought up short by a horrible realization.

'What?'

'Evie's letter. The last line . . .'

'What about it?'

'She was talking about a day out we had on the moors a while back and she told me she wanted me to remember that day when I remembered her. That when I thought of her, I should think about the heather.'

'You think it was a message from Evie? That she wanted to point you towards Heather?'

'Why didn't I see that sooner? It was the last line of the letter. The last line of any piece of writing is always really important.'

'I can't think that a night of no sleep has done much for your powers of deduction. But . . .' Kitt raised an eyebrow at her assistant. 'Wouldn't Heather have seen what she was trying to do? If she could orchestrate all this, then she's probably meticulous enough to spot something like that.'

'Yes, but Halloran also said killers like this play a sort of game, to see how close they can get to being caught without actually being caught. So maybe she saw it, but decided to let it play out.'

Grace shook her head. 'This is all beyond wild for this sleepy little city.'

'You'll hear no argument from me about that,' said Kitt. 'But I can't let it lie. Not while Evie is missing. I'll have to go and see Heather.'

Kitt's mobile hummed as it vibrated along the desk.

Thankfully someone on reception had a charger that fitted her phone, so she had been able to charge it back up. When she had turned it on, she had been praying for some message from Evie, but there had only been several concerned voicemails from Halloran. Picking up the phone, Kitt saw his name flashing across the caller ID.

'Halloran?'

'Kitt, God, it's such a relief to hear your voice.'

'I know, sorry. As soon as I got your messages, I texted you. I wasn't avoiding you or anything.' She was still annoyed with Halloran, and the temptation to delay her response to him had been there, she couldn't deny. But she knew too well the feeling of waiting, and couldn't inflict it on anyone else. Besides, game playing was exhausting and unnecessary.

'I went to your place a couple of times on my travels last night, and passed by the library. You weren't there. Where were you?'

'Out looking for Evie.'

'On your own?'

Kitt wondered if she should lie to Halloran, but on reflection, she didn't see why she should. He wasn't her keeper. 'Yes, but you needn't worry, I didn't get lonely. I'm very good company.'

'You shouldn't have done that. It was dangerous.' There was a faint hint of a growl in Halloran's voice that Kitt didn't much appreciate. What did he expect her to do when her friend was missing? Sit at home rereading *War and Peace*? Ordinarily, Kitt wouldn't have been averse to that, but this was something of an emergency.

'She's my best friend,' Kitt said, gritting her teeth in the hope that her voice sounded something like a growl too.

Kitt heard a sigh from the other end of the line. 'I'm not likely to forget that any time soon.'

'Has Ritchie confessed yet?' Kitt did all she could to make this sound like a genuine question rather than a snide remark. A whole cocktail of emotions were swishing inside her when it came to dealing with Halloran.

'Not yet. He's denying it all, but there's too much evidence to ignore now.'

'Except DNA or fingerprints or anything that categorically ties him and Evie to the murder scenes,' said Kitt.

'Murder investigations are seldom as perfect as they are on TV.'

'Look, it's pointless wasting time arguing. I've got to get on.'

'Kitt, we are still looking for Evie.'

'As a murder suspect?'

'That's the official line.'

'And . . . unofficially?'

'Unofficially, I'm hoping we find her alive and well with an explanation for all this.'

'I appreciate that.'

'Say we'll talk tonight.'

Kitt paused. She didn't want to sink any deeper into this infatuation with the police inspector who believed her best friend had committed triple homicide. But perhaps agreeing to talk to him was Kitt's opportunity to tell Halloran straight that it was best they kept their distance.

'We'll talk tonight.'

'All right, and in the meantime, don't do anything stupid.'

'I'm afraid that would be breaking a thirty-five-year habit, but I'll do my best.'

'I'll pick you up at the library if you text me with a time.' Kitt could hear the smile in the inspector's voice. She wished she didn't feel a fluttering inside at the prospect.

'Good enough.'

The librarian hung up the phone to find that Grace was eyeing her with a level of scrutiny she could have done without. 'Maybe you should text him back and tell him about Heather.'

'There've been so many twists with this case. I can't take anything else to him unless I'm sure that it's a genuine lead. We haven't got any more time to waste. Evie's life could be at stake.'

'So what's the plan?'

'You start looking into Heather, and text me if you find anything.'

'Where are you going?'

'I'm going to see Heather, see if I can find something concrete to tie her to all this. If Michelle asks, I'm not feeling well and have gone to the chemist for meds.'

'God, Kitt, be careful. You could be walking into the scorpion's nest here.'

'Don't worry about me,' said Kitt. 'Knowledge is power, and I'm a very well-read woman. I've got a plan.'

THIRTY-SIX

There was a sign on the glass doorway of Forever Young beauty salon that read 'No walk-ins. Appointment by online booking only'. Kitt had a feeling, however, that Heather would make an exception for her. After all, she had recently used her connections with the police to make sure Heather got home safe and sound after being wounded by an anonymous cloaked attacker . . .

Kitt pushed the door open and a bell rang as she stepped onto the plush, cream carpet. Despite the number of muddied shoes that must have walked over it since the season began to turn, it looked clean to almost clinical levels.

The whole room had been painted lilac and smelled, as most salons did, of acetone. To Kitt's right, there was a glass counter, with a telephone, notepad and fountain pen on it, but there was no sign that anyone was in the building. Kitt paused and looked at the glass counter again. A fountain pen . . . it was a Stanwyck. And the paper it was resting on was the same colour as the paper used in the notes in the killings. Was it exactly the same paper? Surely Evie would have remembered that if she had seen it when she came in for her manicure? But then, she had only been to this salon once, and attention to detail wasn't Evie's strong point. She reached out to touch the paper . . .

'Oh, Kitt, hello,' said a familiar, velvety voice.

Kitt brought her hand back to her side as casually as possible and tacked on a smile. Heather was standing in an inner doorway, which probably led to a treatment room at the rear. Another woman was with her, presumably a client, pulling on a dogtooth cardigan and heading towards the coat pegs near the door.

'Thanks, Heather,' the woman said. 'Perfect as always.'

'No problem, I've got you booked in for next time. I'll see you then,' Heather said, as the woman grabbed her coat off its hook, said an additional goodbye, and exited the salon.

Heather walked towards Kitt then, her white canvas trousers and a loose, navy top flowing in neat lines over what the librarian judged to be a well-toned body.

'Hi Heather, so sorry to bother you. I know you must be busy, but—'

'Wanting a sneaky eyebrow appointment, are we?' asked Heather, staring just above Kitt's eye level.

'Oh. No,' Kitt said, fighting the urge to bring a hand to her forehead and explore just how bad the situation up there had become in the last week. Funnily enough the state of her eyebrows hadn't been of paramount importance.

'Oh, sorry,' Heather said, the tightening of her jaw muscles betraying the fact she understood her misstep. 'Despite the sign on the door I tend to get a few people asking if I can squeeze them in for a quick re-shape on their lunch breaks.'

'Not to worry. I'm actually not here on beauty business—'

'Everything all right?'

OK, thought Kitt. She wasn't sure if she had any acting skills. But if she did, now was the time to employ them. She allowed every muscle in her face to droop.

'You haven't heard, then? Well, there's no reason why you should, the police are trying to keep a lid on it.'

'Keep a lid on what?'

'I'm not supposed to say anything, but I can trust you to be discreet, can't I?'

A thin smile spread across Heather's lips. 'Of course you can trust me.'

'Well, if anyone asks, you didn't hear it from me, but there's been another murder.'

The smile on Heather's face was fixed into place, but she swallowed, hard. 'What?'

Her voice was over-polite given the circumstances.

'Oh, I know, it's awful, isn't it? It's just like the other murders. Poison. A pen stabbed through the heart.'

'But, but – that can't be right. There can't have been another murder.'

Kitt frowned at Heather. 'What do you mean?'

Heather's eyes widened just a fraction. If Kitt had blinked she would have missed it. But she didn't miss it. She had what she came for: a reaction, even if it was minuscule.

'I mean,' Heather said, pausing, biding her time, 'it's too horrible. I can't bring myself to believe it.'

'I didn't want to believe it either,' said Kitt. 'And it gets worse. Evie's missing.'

Kitt had thought this ruse through with care, mingling facts the killer would know with a fact they would know couldn't be true to make the story sound more plausible, and as a consequence knocking the killer off-balance, putting them at a disadvantage for once.

'Missing? Oh no,' Heather said, but she didn't ask any questions. There was no query about when, how or why, which Kitt thought would have been natural questions to ask if Heather knew nothing about Evie's disappearance.

Kitt did all she could to look concerned before she spoke again, which, given how desperate she was to find her friend, wasn't difficult. 'You haven't seen her, have you?'

'Who?'

'Evie. You haven't seen her?'

'No, no, I haven't.' Heather rapped her long nails on the desk. 'So, was there anything else?'

Kitt smiled. Heather wanted to get rid of her. She no doubt wanted to be alone so she could check into the non-existent murder. The one murder she hadn't seen coming.

Time for phase two.

'Well, now that you mention it, I could use a friend to talk to right now.'

'A friend?'

'Yes, you don't mind, do you?'

'I—'

Kitt's phone buzzed in her pocket.

'Oh, excuse me,' said Kitt. 'That'll be my assistant at the library. They can't cope three seconds there without me.'

Aware that Heather's breathing had become somewhat irregular, a faint hint of panic showing, Kitt unlocked the keypad on her phone and sure enough there was a text message from Grace sitting in her inbox.

Scrolling to the screen, Kitt read:

Heather left by her fiancé on her wedding day two years ago according to FB. Angry block cap posts directed at her ex. Hopefully you're already out of there . . . but if not get out asap. Will try calling police station.

'Everything all right?' Heather asked, stepping closer than Kitt had expected and startling her enough that she dropped her phone. Heather reached for it, but Kitt managed to snatch it up herself just in time.

'I'm fine, sorry. I need to get out of the habit of being jumpy. I've been a little bit on edge at the thought of a serial killer roaming the streets.'

'I think we all have,' said Heather, that thin smile resurfacing.

Phase two had been to talk to Heather and try to weed out a motive, but Grace had done that now. She could report all of this to Halloran, and the police could take it from here.

'I'm so sorry, it turns out I'm going to have to get back to the library after all. There's been a filing emergency – such is the excitement of my life.'

Heather's face brightened at once, probably because she was going to get rid of Kitt quicker than she'd hoped. 'Oh, I understand,' she said. 'And I am so sorry to hear about Evie. I do hope she turns up all right.'

'Me too,' Kitt said, looking at Heather. 'I shouldn't like to say what I would do to anyone who might have hurt her.'

Heather's eyes narrowed just a touch, but Kitt wasn't going to hang around long enough for Heather to realize she was onto her. At least, that wasn't the plan, but as she turned back to the doorway she noticed something that hadn't been in her line of vision on the way in. The set of hooks by the door where several coats were hanging.

They looked to be men's coats, which struck Kitt as odd given that Heather appeared to run the salon single-handedly, and there was nobody else in the salon right now as far as she was aware. Then, on looking closer at the arrangement, she saw it. Hiding underneath one of the other coats was a hint of turquoise material patterned with blue raindrops. Kitt pushed the heavy brown coat on top of it to one side and gasped.

'This is Evie's coat.'

No sooner had the words left Kitt's mouth than Heather's hands were around her throat. Unexpected, tight, and unrelenting, Heather's grip from behind was suffocating as she tightened her fingers around Kitt's airway. Kitt hadn't had a second to take a breath, and already sensed the world around her blurring. She pulled at Heather's fingers, but they wouldn't budge, and her arms and legs were weakening from the lack of oxygen.

Then, a thought came to her.

She dug in her pockets for something sharp, anything

she might use as a weapon, but all she had in her pocket was her mobile and . . . something else. Something hard and rough.

Clutching it as tightly as she could, Kitt drew the rock Ruby had given her from her pocket and smashed it down hard on Heather's fingers. She repeated this again and again. Heather cried out, her fingers loosened, but didn't totally let go. Kitt continued to smash stone against bone until the fingers withdrew, just long enough for Kitt to make a dash for the door.

Heather, her hands bloody, lunged after Kitt as far as the threshold but no further. People, witnesses, were walking by. There was nothing more Heather could do without arousing suspicion. Clutching her throat, Kitt didn't take the time to look back, but instead ran as fast as she could up Bishopthorpe Road in the direction of town.

Hands shaking, she fumbled for her mobile and dialled.

'Halloran?' she gasped, but then groaned as his voice-mail clicked in. Hanging up the phone, Kitt dialled 111 for the police switchboard. 'Hello, I'm trying to get in touch with York Police Station. I've got vital information about a murder case they're working on,' Kitt told the operator as she power-walked across Skeldergate Bridge in the direction of the police station.

THIRTY-SEVEN

Fifteen minutes later when Kitt stepped through the entrance of York Police Station there was a commotion going on at the front desk and it didn't surprise Kitt in the least to see who was behind it.

Grace and Ruby were blabbering almost incomprehensibly at the man standing behind the counter who, Kitt had learned from her last visit to the station, was called Jasper. For some reason they had worked themselves up into a state where they were both speaking at once and consequently it was possible only to pick out the odd noun or verb. Words like 'salon', 'danger' and 'murder'.

You would think at least two of those words would arouse some concern, but Jasper's face was unmoved as he told them both in the most neutral voice Kitt had ever heard from a person to calm down.

Stepping towards the fray, Kitt placed a hand on each of her friends' shoulders.

'Kitt!' shouted Grace, throwing her arms around her boss.

'You're alive!' Ruby said, joining in the hug, which was,

to Kitt's mind, more like being caught in the coils of a boa constrictor than a comforting embrace.

'If you thought I was dead,' said Kitt, shrugging the pair off just enough that she could breathe, 'then why didn't you call 999?'

'Well, we weren't totally sure you were dead,' said Ruby.

'And we didn't want to misuse the number,' said Grace.

Kitt nodded, gently disentangled herself from the group hug, and then turned to the man at the counter.

'Jasper, I've been trying to get through via the switch-board for the last fifteen minutes,' said Kitt.

'I couldn't deal with the phones because I was trying to get to the bottom of what these two were talking about,' he said. 'Something about a psychic vision. Not Ms Barnett's first, it should be added.'

Kitt turned to Ruby and sighed. 'Couldn't you have dialled down your "psychic abilities" just this once?'

'It's not something you can just turn on or off, love,' said Ruby.

'Indeed,' said Kitt, before turning back to Jasper. 'Is Halloran here? This really is urgent.'

'Inspector Halloran is currently engaged with a suspect.'

'Not any more he's not, what's going on?' said Halloran's voice.

Kitt turned to see him and Banks standing just in front of the double doors that led back to the interrogation rooms.

As he looked at her, she remembered that she was still in yesterday's clothes, had had about two hours' sleep, and had just been unexpectedly choked. She had hoped to go home and freshen up before seeing Halloran that evening, but as there were so much bigger things to think about, Kitt couldn't bring herself to care. It seemed Halloran didn't much care either. Not just about how she looked, but about what anyone else might think.

Frowning, he marched towards Kitt, placed two fingers gently under the librarian's chin and tilted her head upwards. Kitt didn't know why she let him, maybe because she wanted a professional opinion on how bad the damage was after Heather's attack. Maybe because his skin against hers was the best thing she had felt in a long time. Or maybe, she just liked the idea that he cared what happened to her.

Halloran's face darkened as he studied her neck.

'What happened?'

'I got a lead on the murderer. It's Heather. I tried to call you, but you didn't pick up, I . . .' Kitt placed a hand against her throat. It was painful to speak. What she wouldn't give for a soothing cup of tea.

'She tried to choke you, didn't she?' said Halloran, his jaw setting.

Kitt nodded. 'I noticed Evie's coat – we've got to help her. God knows where she is, or even if she's still alive.' Kitt stopped short at that thought and shook her head. She mustn't think things like that. Evie had to be alive.

'Where did you see her coat?' asked Halloran.

'It was hanging on the pegs near the door in Heather's salon. She realized I had seen it. She nearly killed me, but I hit her with a rock.'

'A rock?' said Banks. 'You just carry rocks around with you, do you?'

'It was . . . a gift,' said Kitt, 'from Ruby. It has magical qualities . . . apparently.' From Kitt's expression it was obvious to all that the librarian didn't believe a word of what she was saying. That didn't stop Ruby from beaming a big smile and pointing her thumb at herself.

A glint appeared in Halloran's eye for just a moment before vanishing. He sighed, removed his hand from Kitt's chin and rested it against her cheek. 'I'm sorry.'

Kitt frowned. 'What are you sorry for?'

'If I'd had the right person in custody, this wouldn't have happened.'

'Mal—' The word was out of her mouth before she could stop it. The librarian shook her head. 'I should have come to you first, before checking it out. I just didn't want to bother you if it was a dead end.'

'This investigation was never your responsibility, it was mine.' Seemingly remembering himself again, the inspector folded his arms across his chest, looking around.

'Did you get her to talk? Say why she'd done it?'

'There was no time for that.'

'But we know why,' Grace interjected. 'She was left at the altar on her wedding day two years ago and, from what I can tell, never really got over it.'

'So she's taking revenge?' asked Halloran.

'Seems that way,' said Kitt. 'She's a real-life Miss Havisham. Granted, she's not sitting in a yellowing room with a rotten wedding cake, but from what Grace says about her Facebook profile, she didn't take the whole being jilted thing lightly.'

'There's something else,' said Grace. 'I've just found out how she hunted her victims down.'

'How?' Halloran and Kitt asked together and then exchanged a little smile.

'She was advertising on LoveMatch, offering a discount to any subscribers who booked an appointment with the salon.'

'What better way to hear about dating horror stories than through a dating website?' said Kitt.

'And people put so much online these days,' said Grace. 'Once she'd heard their break-up stories, it was just a matter of watching them for a while, getting a sense of their lives.'

'But she couldn't have done it alone,' said Banks. 'Assuming her accomplice isn't Ritchie, that he's been set up like Evie, who's in on it with her?'

'She mentioned a boyfriend,' said Kitt. 'At the Belle's Ball . . . right before you arrested me.'

'Just about to crack the case, were you?' Halloran said, with a gleam in his eye.

Kitt shrugged, raising her palms to the off-white ceiling. 'Now we'll never know.'

Halloran shook his head before turning to his partner. 'Banks, we need to bring Heather in before she makes a run for it.'

With that the pair turned their backs and began to strategize.

Ruby sidled closer to Kitt and nudged her elbow. 'Least you 'ad some help today, eh love?'

'How do you mean?' said Kitt.

'That rock I gave you didn't let you down.'

Kitt resisted the urge to roll her eyes, and instead smiled at the old lady. 'No . . . but it wasn't quite of use in the way you suggested it might be—'

'And let's not forget the coat.'

'The coat?'

Ruby shuffled in her seat. 'I told you that a blue coat would be important to this case.'

'You never told me any such thing.'

'Oh. Didn't I? I meant to mention it, must have slipped my mind.'

'Well, thanks for almost helping me out,' Kitt said. She almost chuckled but couldn't quite manage it. Not when Evie was still out there and in trouble.

'So . . .' said Grace.

Kitt looked at her assistant. Somewhere, off behind the double doors she had walked through more times than she would like, baritone voices echoed.

'Anything you want to share with the group?' Grace pushed.

'I've told you everything that happened.'

Grace eyed Halloran and then looked back at Kitt. 'Doesn't seem that way.'

'There's nothing to tell,' said Kitt, pressing her lips together.

'It's true lovey,' Ruby said, looking at Grace. 'The way he was with her just then said it all.'

'*Shhhh,*' said Kitt, noticing that Halloran was on his way back. She wasn't sure what, if anything, was really going on between her and Halloran, but she didn't need the interference of Grace and Ruby.

'Right, Banks is going to the salon to pick up Heather. I'm going to her home address in case she's shut up shop and to see what – or who – else I can find there. Jasper, alert the train station and the bus depot.'

'I'm already on it,' he said, picking up the phone.

'I'm coming with you,' Kitt said to Halloran.

'You can't. It's not safe.'

'If Evie is anywhere alive, she's there. She needs her best friend. I'm coming.'

THIRTY-EIGHT

Sitting in the passenger seat in Halloran's car, Kitt felt her eyes drift, not for the first time, to the inspector's hand, resting on the gear stick. She chided herself for focusing on that kind of detail. On how easy it would be for her to reach down and place her hand over his, as though they were two lovers on a road trip when in fact they were on their way to apprehend a serial killer and, with a bit of luck, rescue her best friend to boot.

'You thinking about Evie?' asked Halloran.

'Yes,' Kitt said, because that was what she should have been thinking about. In fairness she had thought about nothing else for the past twelve hours; perhaps it was OK to give herself a break. 'I really hope she's at Heather's. I don't know where else she could be.'

'I hope she's there too,' said Halloran. 'If she's not . . .'

'What?'

Halloran remained silent.

'If she's not there, what?' Kitt pushed.

'It's not a good sign.'

Kitt's lips trembled. 'You mean ... it's more likely that she's ... dead?'

'That's a worst-case scenario.'

'What's the best-case scenario?'

Kitt looked at the inspector. She couldn't tell if he needed to pay as much attention to the road or whether he, for the first time since they'd met, was avoiding her eye. Like Kitt he had had either very little or no sleep last night. The circles around his eyes looked even darker than they had a couple of days before. But something else that Kitt couldn't quite put her finger on made him look older than he had even ten minutes ago.

'Mal ...'

'Under those circumstances, the best-case scenario is that she was working with Heather.'

Kitt's mouth hung half open. 'You don't still suspect ...'

'It's my job to suspect,' came the returning growl.

'You know ...' Kitt glared at him and her breath huffed out through her nose. 'Some things in this world are more important than your job.'

'Oh, really? Like what?'

'Like friendship, and love and faith in people.'

'When I'm on the job I don't have the luxury of having faith in people.'

Kitt looked out of the windscreen at a homeless man drifting up the street, asking passers-by for change. 'Not even me?'

'This isn't about my faith in you.'

'Yes, it is.' Kitt couldn't tell if her voice had raised in

volume or if it just sounded louder than she'd like in the enclosed space of Halloran's car. 'Evie has been my friend for eight years. I know her. I've told you that over and over again, but you won't believe it, you won't believe me.'

'We're not always the best judge of character,' said Halloran, his hands clenched around the steering wheel.

'Speak for yourself.'

'I am . . .' he said. He tried hard to mask it, but there was a waver in his voice.

Kitt stared at him. 'What is this about?'

The car stopped at a traffic light. Halloran hit the steering wheel with his right hand in what looked like defeat and glanced over at Kitt.

'My wife, she was killed by a friend. A police officer.'

Now it was Kitt who felt she couldn't look directly at him. She stared into the red of the traffic light ahead. 'So, that was what you meant. When you said you'd been in my shoes . . . I'm sorry.'

'You didn't know.'

'I don't know what to say, except that nobody should have to go through that,' said Kitt.

'Nothing to say. I failed her, and I can never let anything like that happen again.'

'You didn't "let" it happen,' Kitt said, but Halloran wasn't listening.

'I can never . . .'

'What?'

'Trust.'

'You did not fail her,' said Kitt. 'Your friend failed you.'

The traffic light turned green and Halloran's attentions were on the road again as the car shunted forward.

'I know what you're saying is true,' he said. 'I would say the same thing to someone in my position. But . . .'

'I know,' said Kitt. 'I know how damaging it is to have your trust broken.'

'I wish you didn't.'

'And I wish I could be of more help, but any advice I offer on this score would be pretty hypocritical.'

'How so?'

'I'm sure you didn't miss the fact I haven't had a relationship since Theo.'

'Maybe not a romantic one, but you did let Evie in.'

'Yeah,' said Kitt. 'That's true. She, almost right away, made me feel safe around her, you know?'

'Feeling safe is more important than almost anyone realizes. Something you learn day one of police training.'

'I imagine police officers also need people they can feel safe with,' said Kitt.

Halloran smiled at her. 'We do.'

Halloran slowed the car and turned into White Rose Street, which, according to the police computer system, was where Heather Young lived.

The inspector pulled the car in to the side of the road.

Suddenly, Kitt pointed ahead. 'Halloran. That's her! That's Heather.'

'Getting into that car? Who is that with her?' asked Halloran.

'He looks familiar,' said Kitt. She stared at the stout young man with a shaven head bundling somebody into the back of the car. A woman, bound at the wrists . . .

Kitt gasped. 'I can't place him. But I won't even give you three guesses as to who he's pushing into the back of that car.'

'Evie,' said Halloran.

Kitt unbuckled her seat belt.

'Where are you going?'

'To get my Evie back.'

'You're not going to manage that on foot, look.'

Heather was already in the driver's seat as her accomplice slammed the back door before taking his place next to Heather in the front. The engine revved. Kitt caught a fleeting image of a familiar face staring out of the back window before the car sped off to the end of the street.

'Evie!'

'Don't worry, we're going to get her back. Hold tight,' said Halloran, as he too revved the engine before flicking a switch on the dashboard and the sound of sirens filled Kitt's ears.

THIRTY-NINE

Halloran pressed a button on the gear stick. 'This is officer number 9969 calling for back-up, driving south on Crichton Avenue, over.'

'Officer 9969, DI Halloran, receiving, over,' a woman's voice crackled over the radio.

'We are in pursuit of suspect driving a red Ford. Licence plate Alpha, Juliet, five, three, Lima, Victor, Sierra. Suspect has a missing person in their vehicle and may be armed, over.' As he spoke, Halloran swerved around a slow-moving Volvo and, as per the inspector's earlier instructions, Kitt held onto the sides of the seat to steady herself.

'Received, dispatching all available units in that area,' the woman said. Halloran pressed the same button on the gear stick as he had before and looked hard at the road in front of him. Even in the most serious moments of their investigation, Kitt had never seen him look so stern. His blue eyes narrowed as they focused on the target up front. The red Ford, now a few cars ahead, veered in and out of this lane and that in an attempt to put as many obstacles as possible between it and the police car in pursuit.

Beyond the inspector's chiselled profile, the neat, red-brick houses of suburbia flashed by. A moment later, Kitt sensed a yellow light blazing in her peripheral vision. Tearing her eyes away from the inspector, a smile formed on her lips as she saw two more police cars waiting at the end of Crichton Avenue. Kitt's smile soon faded, however, when the Ford made a sharp right. It was so quick, Halloran had to slam on the brakes and pull the handbrake hard just to make the turn. The rear end of the car skidded with a force that made Kitt's stomach turn over, but Halloran stepped on the accelerator and the vehicle soon righted itself. Digging her fingernails deep into the edges of her seat, Kitt glanced out of the back window to see the other police cars tailing them, sirens wailing.

Turning to face forwards again, Kitt squealed as pedestrians leaped out of the way of Heather's car, and then, deciding that her squeals were probably somewhat distracting to the inspector, covered her mouth with her hand.

'Sorry,' she said, having recovered herself. 'Rather new to this car chase business.'

'Not to alarm you, but it's been a few years since I've been in one myself.'

'Very comforting,' said Kitt, wishing she could shut her eyes, but desperate to keep them open to see what would happen next.

Heather's car made another hard right down Grosvenor Road. It was a narrower street than the others. Kitt watched as Heather's car scraped a line of vehicles parked on the left, leaving some with scratches, others with dents, and taking the wing mirror off a small van.

'What is she thinking?' asked Kitt. 'Does she really expect to outrun you on these narrow residential streets? Hardly likely to result in a clean getaway.'

'She wasn't expecting us to get to her on time,' said Halloran, following the car down yet another right turn. 'She's panicking, which means sooner or later she's going to make a mistake.'

'The other cars aren't following us any more,' said Kitt, glancing out of the back window again.

'No, protocol is to split and try to cut the vehicle off so we can surround it.'

'Makes sense,' said Kitt. 'Unlike Heather's driving,' she added as she saw the red Ford make a left onto Bootham.

'Oh God, she's heading towards town,' said Halloran, gripping the steering wheel tighter.

'During the lunchtime rush in York?' said Kitt. 'She really must be mad. Why would she do that?'

Halloran shook his head. 'If she'd gone the other way she'd have wound up on the A19, which is a single carriageway road with nowhere to turn or hide. She's not exactly driving a Ferrari so she can't outrun us. Maybe she's planning to lose us in the backstreets and ditch the car.'

'Here's hoping there aren't too many people hanging out of the pub doorways having a liquid lunch today,' said Kitt. 'From what we've seen, Heather's not the type to let anyone get in her way.'

Completely ignoring the red traffic light at Bootham Bar, Heather's car turned in the direction of the Theatre Royal to a chorus of hooting horns. Halloran followed close behind, but even disgruntled rush-hour drivers knew better than to give a police officer with his sirens blaring that kind of fanfare.

A second later, Heather pulled the same trick at the lights on Museum Street and a deep green Mercedes knocked into her. It was hard enough to make her pause, but not enough to stop her completely. She reversed an inch or two and then swerved around the Mercedes. Too quick for Halloran to cut her off. Too quick for the driver to get out of the car and confront her. But that didn't stop him from rolling his window down and shouting after her. The windows in the police car were up so Kitt couldn't hear what the man was shouting, but they weren't complicated words to lip-read.

Halloran swerved around the Mercedes and chased after Heather's car. Heading over Lendal Bridge, Kitt watched the red Ford weave in and out of the queueing traffic, missing a second collision with a black Citroën by fractions of an inch. It was so close, this time she really couldn't bear to watch. She took a deep breath instead, pressed the button to open her window, and tried to focus on the view of the river below.

'You all right?' Halloran asked.

'Don't worry about me, just focus on the road,' said Kitt, really regretting that egg mayo sandwich she had shared with Grace just before she'd left to face Heather. She hadn't felt this queasy since one of her school friends dared her to brave the Terrorizor ride on a school trip to Flamingo Land. That must have been twenty years ago now, but she still felt the churn in her stomach when she thought about it.

Kitt's insides turned over again as the car veered to the left. She closed her eyes, just for a moment.

'Yes, we've got her,' said Halloran.

Kitt's eyes sprang open again and she realized they were on Skeldergate, a road that ran parallel to the river. Up ahead, some distance beyond Heather's red Ford but approaching fast were the police cars that had been trailing them earlier. Heather's car lurched to a stop, but only for a second before veering left down a side street.

'That street leads to the wharf,' said Kitt. 'They'll be cut off by the river.'

Halloran smiled. He had already made this calculation. The chase was over. Heather had nowhere to go.

The inspector made the same hard left Heather's car had made a few seconds before, just in time to see Heather Young drive full throttle off the edge of the cobbled wharf, splashing into the murky waters of the Ouse.

Halloran slammed on the brakes. The wheels screeched as the car jerked to a halt. The librarian and the inspector watched, wide-eyed, as the red Ford began to sink nose-first into the river.

'Oh my God, Evie!' said Kitt, grabbing Halloran's arm. 'She was tied up.'

Without a word, Halloran whipped off his seat belt and swung open his door, leaving an open-mouthed Kitt behind.

FORTY

Swinging open her car door, Kitt chased after Halloran. By the time she had bustled around to the front of the vehicle, he had yanked off his shoes and thrown off his jacket.

Kitt watched him, her jaw still hanging loose in disbelief. 'You're not . . . Halloran, you can't go in there, the current is too strong,' she said, glancing at the dark grey waters. The undertow was inching the sinking car downstream. All Kitt could think about was the number of drownings she'd read about in the newspaper. Every year more souls were lost to that river. She was merciless, and everyone who lived near her knew it.

'I have to,' Halloran replied, 'I don't have time to argue about it.'

Kitt could hear the sirens of the other police cars approaching. 'Mal, please, don't go in there alone. Wait for back-up.'

Halloran pointed at a life preserver hanging in a metal stand, painted orange, by the water's edge. 'Throw that life ring to me when I signal. Under no circumstances are you to follow me into the river. I mean it. If I die, it's an acceptable loss, but if you die, the department has a lawsuit on its hands.'

'There is nothing acceptable about you dying.' Kitt raised her voice in the hope it would get through to him.

'It doesn't matter what happens to me, it's Evie who matters now.'

'It does matter what happens to you,' said Kitt, and then, realizing the truth, spoke it out loud. 'It matters to me.'

'I told you, I don't have time to argue,' Halloran said, his voice soft. A second later he turned and ran towards the sinking car. Kitt watched as he got as close as he could on land. When he was level with the car, he pulled his baton from his belt, held his breath, and jumped in with an almighty splash.

'Mal!' Kitt shrieked after him as the approaching sirens got louder and louder. The other police cars pulled up on the wharf. Banks got out of one and Wilkinson got out of another.

As instructed, Kitt scurried over to the life preserver and unhooked it from the stand. She saw Halloran swimming towards the rear of the sinking car, his dark hair slicked to the back of his head, his white shirt clinging to his body. He must have been freezing. The waters of North Yorkshire weren't that clement in the summer months. In October they were deathly cold. Still, the one consolation was that Halloran seemed to be a strong swimmer. His strokes were long and broad enough to overcome the current. But his strength couldn't last for ever. He would tire. Kitt could only pray he would be back safely on dry land before that happened.

Even from ten feet away, Kitt could make out Evie's muffled screams, frantic and shrill. It was the worst sound she had ever heard in her life. Tears streamed down her cheeks as she watched Halloran pulling with all his might on the car door handle, trying to open the rear door. It was locked. He shouted at Evie to move back, away from the window and, using his baton, he dashed the safety glass in the rear passenger side with three swift blows. Using his baton to clear what remained of the window, Halloran reached with both hands into the sinking car. A moment later, Banks's voice was in Kitt's ear. 'Oh my God, you let him go in there?'

'"Let" is a bit strong,' said Kitt, glancing at Banks. 'Heather and her accomplice are still in the car.'

The pair watched as Halloran heaved a limp, saturated body out through the window.

'Oh my God,' said Banks again, her voice full of fear. 'Is that Evie?'

'I'm afraid so,' said Kitt, glancing up and down the river to see if any of the tourist boats were about to help. No such luck. And as the summer season was over, there weren't any tourists milling about in self-drive boats either.

Evie couldn't have weighed that much, but due to the fact that he was immersed in cold water, the strain of pulling her out of the car made Halloran growl loud enough to be heard from land.

'Now, throw it now,' Halloran shouted at Kitt, as he started a one-armed paddle back in their direction. Not wasting another second, she threw the life preserver with every ounce of strength she had in the direction of Halloran and Evie. It didn't quite reach them and Halloran had to swim a few more strokes to catch hold of it. He then lifted the ring over Evie's arms and head and made sure she was secure.

'Pull her into land,' Halloran called. Kitt did as she was asked, and, with help from Banks, reeled in the shivering Evie. Her hair was twisted into unruly clumps and her eyes wide with the chilling shock of the water. More alarming than any of that however, was the amount of blood pouring from her face. She seemed to have two gashes. One on her right temple and another on the left-hand side of her jaw. The cuts looked deep, but Kitt could only hope they seemed worse than they really were.

In less than a minute, Evie was in reach and between them Banks and Kitt hoisted her out of the water. Wilkinson lent a hand, and Kitt was surprised by how difficult it was to pull her upwards onto the wharf. Kneeling at the edge of the river, hands still bound, Evie coughed and spluttered and began to cry.

Kitt squatted so she could put her arms around her friend.

'You'll be all right now,' Banks said, untying the ropes around Evie's hands.

Turning back to the river, Kitt picked up the life preserver again, ready to throw it to the inspector. But when she looked back at the water all she could see was the roof of the almost completely submerged Ford, and no sign of Halloran.

FORTY-ONE

'Mal!' Kitt screamed and then said to Banks: 'Oh God, he's got too tired. The current has sucked him under.'

Tearing her eyes away from Evie, Banks looked over at where Kitt was pointing.

Without a word she started taking off her shoes and jacket just as Halloran had done.

'Wilkinson,' she shouted at her colleague. 'Get some bandages out of the first aid kit for these cuts. I've got to go after Halloran.'

'Banks, no, you mustn't,' Kitt said.

'I have to,' said Banks.

'No, Halloran wouldn't want you to,' she said.

'Well then, he shouldn't have bloody well jumped in himself,' said Banks. 'Be ready with that life ring,' she said, before striding to the edge of the wharf, taking a deep breath and diving into the river. She came up for air a few seconds later, gasping with the shock of the cold but heading, undeterred, in the direction of the car in the hopes of finding Halloran.

Free of her bonds, Evie rolled onto her back and lay on the hard stone cobbles of the wharf, moaning and bleeding.

'Oh, Evie, my God,' Kitt said.

Wilkinson brought over some bandages and a blanket. He wrapped the blanket around Evie's shoulders and then started trimming and taping bandage along the cuts, whilst keeping half an eye on the progress of Banks.

'This is just temporary until you get to hospital,' said Wilkinson. 'You're probably going to need a few stitches.'

Looking at the deep gouging on her friend's face, it seemed to Kitt that Wilkinson was understating the matter slightly, but better that than alarm Evie.

Kitt divided her attentions then between rubbing the circulation back into Evie's arms, and scanning the river for any sign of Halloran, or in case Banks signalled for help.

'I thought I was going to die,' said Evie. She seemed to be crying, but she was so saturated from her ordeal it was difficult to work out the exact source of all the water.

'I know, love. It must have been terrifying. How did they get hold of you?' Kitt asked, trying to ignore the fact that the bandages on her friend's face were turning red quicker than she'd like.

'They tricked me.' Evie closed her eyes as she spoke. 'They invited me out for a drink, but said they had to stop off at their place on the way.'

'And they held you hostage there instead?' asked Wilkinson, his attention split between Evie and Banks, who, Kitt could see, had reached the car and was swimming around it, looking for signs of life.

'They tied me up. Gagged me,' said Evie.

'Kinky,' said Kitt, willing to attempt anything to distract herself from how frightening those cuts across Evie's face looked. Evie's eyes flashed at Kitt. She was fighting a smile, and winning. 'Too soon?'

'Maybe wait till I'm at least in dry clothes?'

'Noted.'

Wilkinson smirked, while looking out once more at the river. But all too soon the smirk was replaced by an anxious stare as he searched the river for his colleagues.

'Did you find that letter?' Evie asked through chattering teeth. 'It wasn't true, any of it. They said they'd kill me if I didn't write it, like they had the others.'

'I didn't believe that letter for a second,' said Kitt.

'I knew you wouldn't. They tried to make me believe you would though. They said all my friends and family would think I was a murderer, and that I might as well kill myself like the letter said. I refused and they said they would do it for me and make it look like a suicide. I've been tied up at Heather's house since last night. Earlier this afternoon they . . . held a knife against my throat and made me swallow six diazepam tablets.'

'Oh my God, Evie, I'm so, so sorry this happened to you,' Kitt said, shaking her head and trying to digest everything her friend was telling her whilst keeping one eye on the river.

'Given what had happened to their other victims I thought that was going to be the end of me. I can't remember much because I was in and out of consciousness. I didn't know where I was, or what they were going to do with me.' Evie covered her face with her now-free right hand and then winced as she accidentally knocked one of her wounds.

Kitt leaned forward to comfort the poor soul, but the sound of more glass smashing drew her attention. Banks was using her baton to smash at what little of the windscreen was still above water. After a few hard swipes, the windscreen started to give and shortly after a large plate of the glass floated upwards and was carried off by the river, narrowly missing Banks. Banks took a deep breath and submerged her body again, leaning forward into the front of the car.

'Is she really trying to save Heather?' said Kitt.

'She wants her to face the charges for what she's done,' said Wilkinson.

'Oh God, why isn't she coming up?' said Kitt, her eyes fixed on the last visible part of the car roof.

Wilkinson and Evie, like Kitt, could do nothing but stare at the water. It probably wasn't more than a minute but it felt like a lifetime, and then Banks's face sprang out of the water. Her mouth wide, gasping for air. She had a limp-looking but vaguely conscious Heather in her arms. Trying not to think about the fact that the person Banks had pulled out of the water wasn't Halloran, Kitt threw the life preserver out to the sergeant. She reached for it and, with the help of Kitt and Wilkinson, the pair were guided back to shore.

Heather had enough strength to frown at Kitt as she was hoisted over the edge of the wharf. Her long blonde hair was matted and her skin was almost blue. She lay face down, breathing hard, and spat out a stream of river water. Next, Kitt pulled Banks up over the ledge. She was gasping and wincing. From the look on her face it seemed even breathing was painful for her.

'I've got to go back for Halloran,' said Banks.

'No,' Kitt said. 'You can't. You're exhausted. You'll drown.'

'We can't just leave him to die,' Banks said.

'I know,' said Kitt. She looked out at the water. Halloran had told her she wasn't permitted to follow him into the river, but when he spoke those words he probably thought he had a good chance of coming out alive. She couldn't just leave him. She couldn't just let him die.

Kicking off her suede boots, she edged close to the water and looked into the river below, readying herself for the cold.

'No way,' said Wilkinson. 'If anyone else is going in there, it's me.'

'Are you a strong swimmer?' Kitt said, tilting her head at him. He looked as though he'd snap like a twig at the slightest pressure.

'I'm all right,' he said.

Kitt shook her head and started to remove her coat.

Slowly, she stepped towards the edge of the river and took a deep breath. 'Courage, girl. Strength, metal,' she said, but as she looked again into the watery depths, something made her pause. There was a dark shape just visible in the water. A face. A man's face. The eyes a dark, unearthly grey. The head splashed out of the water, Kitt shrieked and jumped back in surprise. It was Heather's accomplice. Or perhaps her boyfriend? Either way, seeing him at close range, she knew where she recognized him from. He'd been working behind the bar at Ashes to Ashes the night that Kitt had interrogated Ritchie. His job there would have made planting evidence in Ritchie's locker a cinch. A moment later, Halloran's head also splashed out of the water. He took a deep breath, spluttering from the water he'd swallowed.

Kitt helped the officers pull first the suspect and then Halloran out of the river. The second Halloran's hand was in Kitt's she breathed a sigh of relief. For his safety, and for the fact that she wasn't going to have to jump in the river after him – that really wasn't on her list of preferred activities.

Halloran, soaking and scratched from shards of glass, was panting hard enough to split his lungs. Glaring at Heather, he used what must have been the last of his strength to manoeuvre himself into a kneeling position. He looked at Heather who, courtesy of Wilkinson, had already been hand-cuffed. 'Heather Young, you are under arrest for perverting the course of justice, the kidnapping of Evelyn Bowes, and for the suspected murder of Owen Hall, Adam Kaminski, and Tim Diallo.'

'Whatever,' Heather said, glowering at Halloran. 'None of it matters anyway.'

'I suspect you'll feel differently when you see the inside of a prison cell,' said Halloran. 'Or maybe if you have any capacity for understanding what your ex-fiancé will feel when he sees you on the news.'

Heather gritted her teeth. 'You don't know what you're

talking about. Lloyd will understand. He will see then, how much I love him.'

'I wouldn't count on that,' said Halloran.

'Shut up!' Heather screeched, before fixing her eyes on Evie. 'Owen got over you so quickly, you know. All the others needed persuasion. But he invited me into his own home with barely any prompting. Just the promise of a good time.'

Evie's eyes widened and more tears followed those that had already fallen. Kitt gripped her friend's shoulder.

'All right,' said Wilkinson. 'That's enough out of you, you can put the rest in your confession.'

'My pleasure,' said Heather, as Wilkson pulled her to her feet. 'I won't spare one detail. How easy it was to seduce them into a situation they weren't coming out of alive. How they looked, right before they died.'

'Come on,' said Wilkinson, pushing the ranting Heather off towards his car.

Banks, somewhat recovered from her untimely swim, cuffed the bartender from Ashes to Ashes, who was still struggling for breath.

Halloran looked at Kitt and smiled; she smiled back, but the triumph written across his face was swiftly erased. The officer's brow crumpled in agony. He clutched a hand to his side. Kitt could see blood gushing from around his hand.

'What the—' Kitt moved his hand for a moment and found a deep wound in Halloran's side. She pressed both their hands against the cut, applying pressure. 'What happened?'

'H-Heather's boyfriend,' he stuttered, 'had a knife.'

Kitt lay him back on the ground. 'We need an ambulance,' she shrieked at Banks.

'They're already on their way, or should be. I called them when I saw the car in the river,' said Banks.

'Bloody government cuts, you'd die before an ambulance reached you,' said Kitt.

'Comforting,' Halloran groaned.

'Sorry.' Kitt winced, stroking his hair.

'I'll go and check on their status,' said Banks. Wilkinson helped Banks back on her feet and she straggled back towards her car to use the radio.

Kitt took off her crimson winter coat, folded it under Halloran's head, and brushed his hair out of his face. He coughed and his eyes didn't seem able to focus on one thing. His white shirt had been ripped to shreds during his ordeal and was covered with blood. The tearing had revealed the tattoo on his right arm. It was a woman's name. 'Kamala'.

Halloran had his wife's name inked on his skin. Kitt's stomach tightened and her throat felt as if it was closing up. There was something unbearable about looking at it, about knowing he had loved someone else so much that he had committed her name to his body.

'I'm sorry about all this,' Halloran moaned.

Remembering where she was, Kitt shook her head and smiled down into Halloran's face. 'I should think so that you're sorry. What a pain you are, getting injured. Most inconvenient.'

He managed a weak smile. 'Don't pretend that the wounded soldier look doesn't work for me,' he stammered, his teeth beginning to chatter.

'Mmm, all right. I'll give it to you. You're about eight per cent more attractive with a bloody slash across your stomach. But you're not to tell anyone I said so,' Kitt said, taking Halloran's free hand and squeezing it.

Halloran squeezed Kitt's hand in return. 'I thought girls from the Middlesbrough area were supposed to be tough. Surely this is no more than a scratch to you?'

'Oh, it is only a scratch, but it's impolite to make a person feel like they're over-dramatizing at a time like this,' Kitt said. Halloran's eyes had a momentary glint in them, a suggestion that if he could have smiled just then he would have. In the same instant Kitt heard his breathing starting to slow.

'I don't want to be here.' The words drifted out of Halloran's lips.

'Funny, I was just thinking the same thing,' said Kitt. 'Where do you want to be?'

As Kitt spoke she watched Halloran's face contort into a smile, but just as before, his smile faded far too soon. His eyes began to close.

'Mal,' she said, and then again, 'Mal!' Kitt had read somewhere that the most comforting sound a person could ever hear was their own name. She understood that paramedics were told this when they were training. It could help people feel safe, and sometimes keep them conscious. In this case, however, the cold had eaten away at Halloran for too long and Kitt had no choice but to watch as his face lost all expression, while the ambulance sirens lamented somewhere in the distance.

FORTY-TWO

'I look like the Bride of Frankenstein,' said Evie, sitting up in her hospital bed and for the first time daring to look into a mirror at the wounds that had been carefully stitched along her right temple and left jaw. 'This is the giddy limit.'

Kitt shook her head at her friend's phrasing. Even in extreme circumstances, it seemed, Evie had the energy to insert some antiquated saying or other into the conversation. 'I always thought Elsa Lanchester rather alluring in that role.'

Evie let the mirror fall into her lap and scrunched her lips up at Kitt.

'It's your peculiar expressions, not the stitches, that make your face a funny one to look at,' Kitt added with a twinkle in her eye.

Evie turned the mirror to her face again. 'Oh God, I do look a bit funny when I pull that face, don't I?' She let out a short giggle, but in an instant she was running her fingertips along the side of her stitches, assessing the damage. Kitt only hoped her friend would heal from all that had befallen her in the last few weeks. Not just physically, but emotionally.

'Hello you two,' said a familiar voice.

'DS Banks . . .' Kitt's eyes widened as she turned to see the sergeant wearing a pair of black slacks and an over-sized grey hoodie. Her brown hair hung limp and damp around her shoulders. Given her past exchanges with Banks, it wasn't a shock to Kitt that it took something as dramatic as a near-fatal car accident to get the officer to let her hair down. She was standing just inside the cubicle Evie had been assigned, bordered with a thin blue curtain.

'I think now that you've dragged me out of a river, we can shift to a first-name basis,' Banks said.

'Charlotte, then,' said Kitt.

'Charley,' Banks corrected.

'Charley,' Evie repeated. 'I like that.'

Kitt watched her friend studying the officer. Banks certainly did look a lot different out of a suit and with her hair down. Everything about her seemed softer. Even more surprising was how coy Banks looked on hearing Evie compliment her name.

'How are you feeling?' Banks asked, taking a couple of steps further into the cubicle.

'Fair to middling, all things considered.' Evie shrugged. 'The doctors said there's likely to be some scarring. So I'll either have to have some kind of treatment for them or take up a new career.'

Kitt turned to her friend and frowned. 'Why? You love being a massage therapist.'

'I know, but not many salon owners are going to employ someone with facial scarring. Not exactly the picture perfect image the beauty industry thrives on.'

'Nonsense,' said Kitt.

'I don't really agree with Kitt on much,' said Banks. 'But I'm siding with her on this. People won't disregard your vocational skills because of a couple of scars.'

'You don't think?'

'If they try, you can refer them to me,' said Banks. 'Besides . . . scars can be beautiful, you know.'

'You really think so?'

'I do,' Banks said with a smile, but then she glared across at Kitt, who was beginning to feel a little bit like a third wheel. 'Halloran's asking for you, Kitt. Walk out of here, down the corridor and take a left. His room is three doors down on the right-hand side, if I remember correctly.'

'Oh, all right,' she said, wondering if he really had asked for her or if this was just a way of Banks securing some alone time with Evie. 'I'll go and check in with him.'

Kitt squeezed Evie's hand and the patient gave her a grin to let her know it was OK to leave her. She then turned and walked out of the curtained cubicle, towards the door and followed Banks's instructions.

The door was open and Halloran was sitting on the edge of his bed. A male nurse was trying to coax him back into a lying position.

'Please, Inspector,' said the nurse, who was dressed in blue scrubs. 'The doctor says you can't get up yet.'

'I'm perfectly fine,' said Halloran, wincing even at the effort it took for him to push a hand through his dark hair, which was dishevelled from his impromptu swim. It had looked similar last night, after Halloran had kissed her, after she had run her fingers through it.

'Is this patient giving you trouble?' Kitt asked.

Both men turned. Halloran's frown morphed into a slow smile.

'I'll take it from here, don't worry,' Kitt assured the nurse.

He looked between Kitt and Halloran, and with a nod left them alone.

'You need to do as you're told and rest,' Kitt said, pressing Halloran's shoulders back and signalling with her hand that he should prop his feet up again.

'Well, maybe I don't mind being helped into bed so much by you,' Halloran said, placing a hand on hers.

She stared down at their hands resting together on the mint green hospital blanket. She followed the line of his left arm up to the sleeve of the T-shirt he was wearing. His tattoo was all but covered again now, but Kitt knew it was still there underneath. That if this went any further she'd have to accept the fact she was living in the shadow of another woman.

'Kitt?' Halloran said, looking from her face to the spot on his arm where her eyes were fixed.

She raised her eyes to meet his, and smiled. 'Banks said you wanted to see me?'

'Of course I wanted to see you,' he said, his brow dipping as he studied her face.

'Any news on the Heather front?' Kitt asked in an attempt to steer the conversation onto more professional lines.

'Yes . . .' Halloran said.

Kitt raised both her eyebrows, waiting.

'According to Wilkinson, her boyfriend shared his whole life story. How Heather had spent months planning this, moving from Manchester to York to set up a new business, placing the advertisements on LoveMatch. She even got him to use his apparently top-notch IT skills to hack into social media accounts, financial and medical records, in the hopes they'd find something they could use in their deception. They had a few stories to work with, a few people they could pin the blame on, but Evie's diazepam prescription was listed in her medical notes, as was the overdose. According to him, that's why Heather chose Evie as the scapegoat. She knew she'd be able to exploit those things. Added to that was the incriminating message chain on her Facebook account. They knew it would throw the investigation in a particular direction and that if it was clear the killer wasn't working alone, alibis wouldn't hold quite the same weight.'

'What I can't understand is why the ex-partners of the other two victims didn't list Heather as one of the people who knew about their sob stories. If she'd turned up on two of those lists, we would have known she was involved sooner.'

'Well that's where they were a bit clever, and goes some way to answering the question about why they didn't strike sooner. Would you really remember a conversation you'd had with a beautician four months or six months after the fact?'

'No, I suppose I wouldn't,' said Kitt. 'I suppose I'd focus on the people who were a bigger part of my life.'

'And that's exactly what Zoe and Francis did. The boy-friend said they toyed with framing Zoe Gray for the murders, hoping the police would think her theatrical tendencies had got the better of her. But they knew they had to bide their time. That acting on the information right away would increase the likelihood of them being caught. But when they looked into Evie's background and found so much to exploit, they decided that was the time to strike.'

'If they were that concerned about getting caught then arguably Heather shouldn't have left a Stanwyck fountain pen resting on her desk.'

Halloran nodded. 'That goes to show how over-confident they'd got about getting away with it. There was nothing like that on display when Banks and I paid Heather a visit at the start of this case.'

Kitt shuddered. 'And what about those fountain pens? Did either of them let slip what that was about?'

'Yes, one of the creepier elements of the boyfriend's con-fession. Heather told him that when her fiancé left her, he wrote a note with a Stanwyck fountain pen that once belonged to her deceased mother.'

'I bet he wrote it on the same paper as she used to write notes on the victims too,' said Kitt.

'I expect you're right,' said Halloran. 'She bought those

pens over a period of two years, in cash, from charity shops. That's why we couldn't trace them.'

'The boyfriend must have been properly under her thrall to do all this with her,' said Kitt.

'Unfortunately, I rather get the impression that he just enjoyed it.'

Kitt sighed. 'All this mess, just to get back at her ex-fiancé?'

'She's unhinged, remember that,' said Halloran. 'When things like this happen to some people, they want to lash out at the person who's hurt them, but they love them too much. So they hurt other people instead, channel their feelings that way.'

Kitt shook her head. She didn't want to relate to Heather's plight in any way, but if she was honest with herself, she understood. Not what Heather had done, but the feelings behind her actions. What had Evie written in that letter at Heather's request? That those who break hearts aren't ever punished for the pain they cause. Kitt would never have administered the punishment herself, but for a long time she had believed that Theo deserved to suffer for what he had done to her. The irony was, he had been suffering, and would always suffer for that fatal decision. He would be loved by others, Kitt was sure of that. But nobody had a love quite like hers, and Theo had lost that. For good.

'Kitt,' said Halloran.

She started out of her thoughts.

'About that kiss . . .'

She smiled at him and gently placed her fingers over his lips, enjoying the tickle of his beard against her skin. 'Not now, love. You've got to get your strength back. You've no doubt got to get down to the station and tie up all kinds of loose ends, and just like me, you need a good night's sleep. Let's talk tomorrow, eh?'

Halloran kissed the three fingers Kitt was holding over his lips. She closed her eyes, savouring the tender touch of his skin against hers. Right then, it would have been the easiest thing in the world to wrap her arms around him. To tell him how desperate she had been when she thought he wasn't coming out of the water. To admit that in spite of the fact he had arrested both Kitt and her best friend for murder, she still wanted him. It would have been the easiest thing in the world for anyone else, except Kitt – a woman who had practised keeping her distance for many years, and right now was still under the illusion she needed thinking time.

'I hear you're giving our nurses grief, Inspector Halloran,' a woman's voice said.

Kitt looked over her shoulder to see a doctor writing a quick note on the clipboard she was carrying.

'I hope you're writing down that he's being a difficult customer,' Kitt said, withdrawing her hand from Halloran's lips and joining the doctor at the end of the bed.

'Oh yes,' she said, her voice mock-stern for effect. 'I'll make sure to use red ink as well. So the rest of the staff have fair warning.'

The doctor turned to Halloran. 'Time to take a closer look at this wound.'

Despite the seriousness of Halloran's injury, Kitt wanted to chuckle at the doctor's manner. Halloran had spent the last week being, for the most part, stern and serious. It was sort of comforting to know even he couldn't escape being spoken to like a baby by medical professionals.

'I'll leave you to it,' Kitt said, reaching up to draw the curtain.

'Shall I come by the library tomorrow?' Halloran asked; his tone conveyed that he really wasn't sure what her answer would be.

Kitt paused. As she looked back at him, a slow smile formed on her lips. 'Around midday suits me, and if you could see your way to getting my coat dry-cleaned, having used it as a pillow, I'd be grateful. Walking around smelling like the river wasn't on my to-do list this week.'

Halloran laughed, and then winced at the pain that caused him. Slowly, Kitt closed the curtain.

On her walk back to Evie's cubicle, Kitt fiddled with the *Jane Eyre* pendant that hung around her neck and put the palm of her free hand flat against her chest. There was a heat, somewhere inside. Not the painful searing she was used to, but the homely warmth of an open fire on the coldest of winter days. It was comforting, enveloping, safe. It was new.

FORTY-THREE

The next day was painfully ordinary in comparison to the deathly riverside drama of the day before. After all that had happened, however, Kitt was almost pleased to be heading off to a finance meeting, an experience she would usually dread. When she returned to the enquiry desk, she discovered Grace sitting in her seat. Kitt's trilby was perched on her head, and she was speaking to someone on the telephone.

'Yes, well, as I say,' she said in the over-the-top accent she used whenever she was impersonating her boss, 'I had very little to do with the resolution of this case. It was really down to the talent of my very hard-working assistant, Grace Edwards. Such a charming, well-rounded, saintly figure around the office really. She photographs very well too, in case you were wondering. Do you need me to spell her name for you again?'

Kitt crossed her arms. Grace glanced in the direction of where Kitt was standing and her eyes widened. 'Yes, well,' she let out a flustered little chuckle. 'I must dash now. Just had a Dewey decimal-related emergency, you know how it is, this librarian lark. Toodle pip.'

Grace slammed down the phone. 'Hello boss,' she said, removing Kitt's trilby and placing it on the desk.

'When have I ever said "toodle pip"?'

'Y-you always say toodle pip . . . don't you?' Grace tucked a dark curl behind her ear and flashed a sweet smile.

Kitt put a hand on her hip. 'No, I do not. I give you a fair bit of slack, but let it be known that impersonating me and using the words "toodle pip" is a hard red line.'

'I was just handling media enquiries about the investigation, like we agreed.'

'Yes, well I think it's best I field those from now on,' said Kitt, and as Grace was raising two fingers to the side of her head, she added, 'and there's no need for that cheeky salute of yours either.'

Grace lowered her hand and pressed her lips together. 'Maybe I'll take a look at the student enquiry box.'

'I think that's a good idea,' said Kitt.

''Ello love,' said a familiar voice. Kitt turned to see Ruby hobbling towards her, accompanied by Evie.

Kitt narrowed her eyes. 'Hello you two . . . is this a synchronized visit?'

'No lass,' said Ruby. 'Complete coincidence, we met on the way in. Just happened to come and see you at the same time.'

'You don't believe in coincidences,' Kitt said, tilting her head. She looked at her watch. 11.55. Halloran would be here soon. Today, Kitt didn't believe in coincidences either.

'So Evie's obviously here because I let slip that Halloran was coming to see me around the midday mark,' Kitt said, while Evie giggled and slumped down in the seat nearest Kitt's desk. She was wearing heavier eye make-up than usual, and had brushed her hair forward in a manner that part-covered the stitches along her temple. Kitt didn't have the heart to dig at Evie for wanting a distraction from her war wounds. She still wasn't sure exactly how her friend was coping with the new contours of her face. It was a situation she would have to monitor closely in the next few weeks to make sure Evie was really as OK as she was pretending to be.

Ruby, however, was another matter.

'So, you obviously somehow know that Halloran's on his way here,' Kitt said to the old woman.

'I 'ad a vision,' Ruby said, nudging Kitt's arm.

'Try again.'

'Oh all right, one of the women who travels on the 59 with me is a nurse at the 'ospital. She heard off someone who heard off someone else that a police inspector was having a romantic moment with a librarian in one of the cubicles. She knew all the details.'

Kitt sighed and brought a hand to her forehead. She had no idea why she had let herself get so ruffled by the intrusive media presence over the past week. No piece of information was private or sacred in a small city.

'Having a party, are we?' said Michelle as she approached Kitt's desk and eyed everyone in attendance. Kitt smothered a smirk as she noticed Evie's eyes dart to the floor. She had told Evie about Michelle's gorgon glare on more than one occasion, and she was now a bit wary about looking straight at her.

A week ago, Michelle's negativity, not to mention insensitivity after all they had been through lately, would have riled her, but not any more. After all the drama of the last ten days, Michelle's petty attitude seemed small fry. 'Couldn't have a party without you, Michelle,' Kitt said with a short chuckle.

'Wouldn't have thought you'd have time anyway,' said Michelle, 'with all the swanning off you've been doing.'

'Swanning off?'

'I have it on good authority you left half an hour before your shift ended on Monday evening.'

Dear God, this woman had spies everywhere.

'And don't think your absence yesterday afternoon went unnoticed either.'

Kitt insisted on keeping the smile on her face, despite the less than cordial tone in Michelle's voice. 'You can chalk it up as time off the ten days of annual leave I didn't get around to taking last year.' She kept her tone very level and very calm, which meant her boss didn't really have scope to come back in a heavy-handed fashion. Instead, Michelle sighed and looked pained.

'Don't worry,' said Kitt. 'The murder case is over. There won't be any more swanning off ...' but then, on seeing Halloran's face at the top of the staircase, she added, 'except for right now ...'

Michelle glared as Kitt strode towards the inspector, and

she wasn't the only one watching after her. Kitt smiled as she drew closer to Halloran. He was back in his suit, and Kitt's coat was draped over his right arm, wrapped in dry-cleaning plastic.

He opened his mouth to speak, but Kitt put a finger to her own lips. '*Sssssh*. It's not safe to talk here,' she said, and then looked back at Grace, Evie, Ruby, and Michelle, who were all staring at them. Halloran tracked her line of sight and then let out a short laugh.

Beckoning him, like the brave, carefree women in the books she read might do, Kitt started down the staircase, walking at a brisk pace through the reception area and out of the front doors towards the river. It was a bright day for October. The waters sparkled, and the spires of the Minster glinted beneath the autumnal sun.

'Everything sorted out with the case? Heather locked up without any trouble?' asked Kitt. She had other things on her mind, but she would feel a lot safer knowing the arrest had been a success.

'She's written a full confession,' said Halloran. 'It makes for shocking reading. She's showing no remorse.'

'She let that one rejection destroy her,' Kitt said, folding her arms across her chest.

'And the lives of many others,' said Halloran, with a despondent note in his voice.

'Makes you think,' said Kitt, 'about the importance of letting go of things.'

'Yeah,' said Halloran. 'Hanging onto the past does lead to dangerous places . . . Kitt—'

'I know you like to be in control,' Kitt said, glancing at Halloran, 'but I want to take the lead on this one.'

The familiar gleam shimmered in Halloran's eyes. 'As you wish.'

The sound of those words leaving his mouth sent an excitable shiver down Kitt's spine, but she ignored it and turned to face Halloran square on. 'So, it's fairly obvious you're into me.'

Halloran burst out laughing, and Kitt joined in for a moment before he composed himself again.

'Really, and what makes you think that?'

'Oh, let me count the ways,' said Kitt. She looked at Halloran. He was smiling, but he hadn't got the reference. 'That was a little nod to Elizabeth Barrett Browning there.'

'I'll take your word for it.'

'Oh dear.' She brought her hand to the side of her face. 'There is so much to teach you. I've got my work cut out.'

Halloran took a step towards Kitt, brushed her hair away from her ear, and murmured, 'I've got plenty of things I can teach you.'

Kitt's breath caught in her throat as she imagined what those things might be. She pulled her head back a fraction so she could look up at him. 'The thing is, I'm all for letting the past go, but . . . you have a tattoo of your wife's name on your arm.'

Halloran lowered his eyes. 'You noticed.'

'Hard to miss,' said Kitt. 'It's a beautiful name though.'

It didn't feel right to say it out loud, but Kitt meant it. It sounded exotic. She imagined Kamala to be very beautiful.

'I loved her, Kitt, just as you loved Theo. Neither of us is sixteen.'

Kitt pressed her lips together and ran a hand over his beard. The softness was so inviting.

'You're definitely not,' Kitt said.

'We've both got a past.'

'We have, nothing can change that,' said Kitt. 'But I still want you.'

A slow smile spread across Halloran's mouth. 'I want you too.'

'Glad we got that settled, now if we could just iron out a couple of particulars . . .'

Halloran's smile widened. 'Like . . . ?'

'I just want you to be upfront about what it is you do want. If it's just sex, that's fine . . .'

'Is it now?' Halloran raised an eyebrow, and Kitt gave him a playful tap on the shoulder.

'If it's more, that's fine too. I just want to know. I just want honesty. We've . . . we've got trust to build.'

Halloran studied Kitt's face. Slowly, he gathered her hair in his hand and wrapped the copper strands around and around his fist until he reached the base of her hairline. With each turn of his hand, Kitt's breathing deepened. She knew that people must be watching them, and she didn't care. All she could focus on right now was the way he gently pulled her head back so she was looking up into his eyes. 'It's more,' he whispered, before leaning forward and delivering a deep, hard kiss. The heat of it spread far beyond Kitt's lips, down to her toes, out to her fingertips, and straight through her heart.

ACKNOWLEDGEMENTS

This book benefits greatly from the expert input of Sarah Urwin, Hazel Nicholson, Dan Freedman, Matthew Tyson, and Amanda Lawson. These people have offered guidance on numerous elements of the story including the methods of journalists, police procedure, medical matters, librarian life and exactly what might happen to a car if it was driven into a river. I'm very grateful to all of you for helping my librarian sleuth on her journey to the page.

In addition, I'd like to thank people who have read my work and offered encouragement and feedback when I needed it most. People like Claudine Mussuto, Ann Leander and Graham Lawson. A special thank you also to my long-term writing partner Dean Cummings who has so far done an impressive job of preventing me from scurrying completely down the rabbit hole – no easy task.

Thank you to Irene Georgiou, Aneta Mitchell and Androulla Georgiou from Highgate Library. You have fed me cake. You have kept a smile on my face. You are proof that librarians and library-loving folk deserve a lot more credit for what they offer communities than they ever get. This book is dedicated to people like you.

Gratitude to all the friends, family and colleagues who cheerlead for me on a weekly basis: Mam, Dad, Sheena, Elaine, Barbara, Ray, Steven, Phil, Christine, John, Tom, Gigi, Katie, Katell, Jackson, Maria, Louisa, Mags, Karl, Eloise, Ian, Nigel, James, Matt and Paul. Your positivity helps me stay on the path when the ground gets uneven.

Heartfelt thanks to my Guardian Agent Joanna Swainson who about three years ago asked that fateful question: 'why don't you write a mystery set in York?' She then nurtured me through many rejections whilst working tirelessly to find a suitable publisher. You are a gem.

Deep appreciation is also due to my editor Therese Keating. Thank you for taking a chance on my rabble cast of characters, and me. Thank you for making the editorial process a joy. I have been humbled by your professionalism and sensitivity from the very beginning and consider myself a very fortunate person to be working with you and the Quercus Fiction team on this series.

And finally, thank you as always to my husband Jo Pugh who is very understanding about the amount of time I spend in my pyjamas come deadline time.